The Plutocrat

Rory Harden

THE PLUTOCRAT

Black Spike Books

www.plutocratbook.com
www.roryharden.com

Published by Black Spike Books

US First Edition

Version 1.00

Copyright © Rory Harden, 2015

ISBN 978-1-910665-27-5

Cover photo of ringtail lemur in Madagascar by Nancy Crockett.

For John Cameron

"Fuck my victims."

- A famous financier.

CHAPTER 1

I t was a quiet house, dug in on a quiet street, low down in the quietest neighborhood of a quiescent and sequestered town, on a spoiled and subdued frontier, buried in the interior of a vast and under-populated continent that determinedly meant to go on about its business — until the Earth gave out or its luck did — with unquiet satisfaction.

But it hummed with electricity, this house. And it held all the world's secrets within it.

Or it would, if Ricky Ponton had his way. And if he didn't, he was prepared to destroy it. Today might even be the day.

The house lay on the far side of town, but he could see it remotely, on the thin device he held between his trembling thumb and his delicate forefinger. Every room, every corner, every window, every door. The view from all four sides. The front yard, with its deliberately-neglected foliage. The weedy drive, with its undriven car. The side passageway, with its carefully-positioned rubbish bins and over-spec air-conditioners. The never-used barbecue deck at the rear, its planks prickling in the heat.

If he wanted to, he could observe, from the vantage point of a shaggy eucalyptus across the road — named for a happily-unpronounceable mineral — whether or not there were intruders on the buckling roof.

But Ricky, a mischievous elf in a broad-shouldered country, would already have known that. The sensors would have alerted him. And the house, a shonky fibro bungalow you weren't supposed to look twice at, would have known what to do without even asking him.

He slipped his state-of-the-art control surface into the breast pocket of his specially-tailored, mud-colored safari shirt, sat back on the bonnet of the bashed-up Holden VX Commodore he'd purchased for three hundred dollars the day before, raised his military-grade binoculars, aimed beyond the railway tracks, and squinted down at the town from the monumental pile of rubbish that gave it its name.

What was he looking for? A car. A white Toyota rental with a distinctive mascot nodding on its rear shelf: A blue crow, but no beady eye. The eye would be missing. The car would drive slowly north-east along the Silver City Highway, then turn right on Iodide Street and ascend, in plain view and via a crumbling switchback track, to where Ricky waited, high up on the remnant of the Line of Lode, with the miners' memorial and the restaurant (not yet open) to his right.

And if he were to ask himself what was he feeling, at this moment, as the Corolla of destiny presumably approached — which he wouldn't, because all sentimental solipsism had long been purged from his system, like corrupted data — it would be this: Desperation tunneling through his innards like a suffocating miner grasping for a chink of light. It was ninety-four days since they'd taken her. You could do a lot in ninety-four days; it was all online to read, if you could bear it. It sank to the bottom of his servers, and pooled there. If he were to get her back, he needed something to bargain with.

Something big.

Come on, little Toyota. I'm waiting for you. I'm dying here.

But then, today might really be the day. It was the stupidest — noblest? — risk he'd taken so far. You *never* met a provider in person. You wanted safety? It lay in the realm of machines; in data wrapped and re-wrapped, passed along, encrypted and re-encrypted, until it turned into fossilized gibberish whose sedimentary layers only Ricky could strip away and interpret. After that, data turned into information and information became — what? Hadn't someone once told Ricky that information wanted to be free? What the hell did *that* mean? Ricky didn't know and didn't care. What mattered was that secrets got out. People hated when that happened — some people. Yet Ricky loved it, and he knew it was right.

But standing up here, alone, on this mountain of spoil wasn't right at all. Okay, you couldn't lock up data. And all that freedom-loving information couldn't be un-liberated. Plastic restraints and sensory deprivation meant nothing to bit streams or databases. They didn't fear the earth beneath their water-cooled cabinets. Such terrors were for people. Just ask Kerri.

He would have to leave Broken Hill soon; he knew that. Australia, too, in all probability. You could feel when the whole match started to go that little bit extra-legal: The crowd went quiet.

So, bye-bye too-generous homeland, hello foreign lawyers.

Once more through the binoculars: No person of interest on the Silver City Highway. And again with the remote vision: No special ops on the veranda, no hazmats checking out the bone-dry hot tub.

Instead, the surprise came from directly behind him. He turned around. Sloughing across the scrappy parking lot towards him was some bloody crate of a vehicle — a pumped-up, jacked-up Land Rover? Where had it come from? There was only one road up to the top of the Line of Lode — and he'd been watching it. That was the *whole point*, after all.

He stood his ground; whatever the hell this thing was, it didn't look *official*. As it got closer, he saw the splatter across its radiator grille and lights. No fly wire, no bug screen — had it driven up from Mildura? It was another big year for locusts. What kind of idiot braved the swarms without protection?

The Land Rover pulled up behind the Commodore. As far as Ricky could tell, it contained a single occupant. This occupant didn't dismount immediately. He

— but a slight, feline figure, so maybe *she?* — cut its engine, and waited. Ricky shrugged, provocatively, then made a *so-what-then* gesture with his cupped hands.

The driver's door opened — it seemed to take a kick from the inside. And what then emerged, Ricky thought, was something that didn't belong in the outback — not even the *near-outback*. A thin, sinuous man, with sticking-up blond hair, designer wrap-around shades, immaculate drainpipe jeans and shiny, black, wing-tip shoes. He rubbed the tops of these shoes, in turn, against the back of his turn-ups. Then he spoke.

"Now, you must be Ricky Ponton. Am I right? The bad guy with all that wicked data?"

American, Ricky thought. Where were the others? They never came singly.

But the American was ahead of him.

"Hey, relax. It's just me. For now."

Just him. Just some crazy Yank — but which variety? Not a *journalist* — look at that fancy leather jacket; journos wore suede or what they liked to call *sport coats*. And this bloke wasn't over-weight. Not *private security*; they didn't customize their vehicles. And they didn't smile. Random whistle-blower? Shocked at what was really going on at that big new special-ops base up in Darwin? No. Didn't look terrified. Some kind of post-modern spy? Again, no: Totally unarmed, as far as Ricky could tell.

What, then?

"Look down there," the American said.

On the Silver City Highway — a small white car.

"He's not in it."

"What?"

"Check out the car. Go ahead. See the big blue bird up back? That's the car, as advertised — okay? But your guy's not in it. Go ahead, zoom in."

Through the binoculars: White Corolla, blind crow, driver in shades with collar up and hat pulled down despite the mounting heat of the morning.

"I don't know who that is," the American said. "But it sure ain't your Mr. Lin."

Ricky, Ricky! You don't need to be in control all the time. You understand that now, don't you, love? Shut up, he thought, shut up and let me breathe. Take charge, Ricky, you young bludger. Stop whinging. Don't buckle under.

"Who the hell are you anyway?"

"Well, Ricky, you can call me Jay. We'll do the get-to-know-you later. Take another look."

He felt his head turn, almost against his will.

"See there?" Jay said. "Far side of Iodide?"

A big, black SUV with darkened windows. Not a model common in Australia.

"And back here — see? Corner of Chloride?"

A second.

"And then, way back on Silver City?"

The third. Three would be enough, wouldn't it? One for Ricky, one for Mr. Lin, one spare with all the hardware.

"Your people?"

"No, Ricky. Not my people."

"No? Fuck you."

He stepped towards the Commodore, but Jay grabbed him by the wrist with a grip that belied his fussy-neat, middle-aged cool.

"No, that's not gonna work. Allow me."

The American threw Ricky aside and dropped into the Commodore's wasted leather seat.

"Follow me in the Jeep." He indicated the Land Rover. "Keys are in it. Just up to the edge of the lot, okay?"

"What is this? What are you doing?"

"You really wanted to meet with Mr. Lin, isn't that right?"

Ricky stared at him. Mr. Lin was already history on Iodide Street.

"Isn't that right?" Jay repeated.

"Yeah, but —"

"Well then you need to come with me."

"Why?"

"Because I got him."

"You —"

The Commodore's creaky door slammed and its window squeaked down.

"Get in the Jeep, you hear? And don't worry about me, I'm used to driving on dirt."

Jay snapped on his seat belt and yanked it tight — way tight. Then the Commodore tore a trench across the spoil of the parking lot in the direction of the access ramp. Ricky watched. Then he turned to the Land Rover. What choice was there? Stay here and be buried? Suffocate while the lawyers tried to dig him out with a spoon? Or bust out for the outback and the red dirt of freedom with this lunatic Yank?

And what might he have done with the real Mr. Lin?

The Commodore had vanished. Ricky scraped his way up into the Land Rover, then had to shuffle himself across the gearbox because the steering wheel was on the wrong side. Had Jay *imported* this piece of crunky British crap from the States?

Ricky got the thing rolling and juddering and pulled it around at the top of the ramp. And there was Jay, some fierce kind of grin on his face, pumping up the slope towards him. Oh and yeah — there was the Commodore: Upside-down, smoking, blocking the ramp at its narrowest point, just after the final hairpin.

Jay jumped into the Land Rover.

"So how much d'you pay for that? Two-fifty?"

"Three hundred."

"Aussie?"

"Aussie."

"Well worth it, in my opinion. You want to drive?"

Ricky began to think, but gave up in disgust.

"No."

They switched seats. The Commodore belched into flames.

Jay stuck the Land Rover into low-range.

"Aren't you forgetting something?" he said, tapping Ricky on the breast pocket.

"Shit!"

4

He took out the controller and checked all the cameras. Nothing happening. Everything normal. No SUVs.

"They know about your little data center," Jay said. "So…"

Ricky winced. Whether or not this cocksure, clothes-horse cowboy was truly poor little Ricky's friend-in-need, he had no idea. But the bloke seemed to know the game.

The Land Rover jerked forward. Jay pointed it towards the rear edge of the parking lot, on the opposite side to the empty restaurant, the unvisited memorial and the exhausted boomtown that still tantalized itself with dreams of a new life to be achieved, any day now, through civic partnership and specialty tourism. And there, at the edge, were Jay's tire tracks. Somehow, he'd driven this dirt-bucket up the bare, industrial scree left behind by Australia's original wave of dedicated diggers. (If you cared to see how the present wave chose to memorialize itself, you could contemplate all that real estate wedged around the rim of Sydney Harbor — and a lot of secrets there, too, Ricky thought.)

"You better do it," Jay said, as they took the plunge.

Ricky scrolled to the extreme right and tapped at the red icon. Next, he entered the passkey, and confirmed his intentions, twice. Then he switched to the view from the eucalyptus. There would, of course, be nothing to see — not unless entry were forced. In which case, there would be a firework display. But he could almost feel in his bones the chattering and skittering of the drive heads as they zeroed out each and every one of his secrets — again and again and again.

"You got backups, I presume?" Jay said, spinning the Land Rover past a concrete culvert.

Ricky couldn't help it; he began to laugh.

"I guess you're a pretty smart guy," Jay said.

He was, wasn't he? Cool, smart — and in control. The bastards hadn't got him yet — and they never would. But that didn't mean they didn't still have a heap of shit to make amends for. Of course he was smart. Look at that: A flip of the thumb told him that his servers in Brazil and Norway had already taken up the strain. More secrets for everyone! Courtesy of Ricky P., the pint-sized Aussie battler-brat, now the scourge of the secret classes, keeping them awake at night, proving once and for all that it wasn't *who* you knew, but what you knew.

"This evil, subversive, troop-endangering conspiracy of yours?" Jay said, as they hit the bottom of the slope and the Land Rover battered its way across waste ground towards the highway. "What do you call it, again?"

"What?"

"Big something."

"Oh. Big Data Underground."

"Yeah, that's it." Jay made a clucking sound with his tongue. "Kinda pretentious. I woulda called it something different."

"Oh? Like what?"

"Uh, something like, say, Leaks-R-Us. You know, user-friendly."

They bumped up on to the highway. Ricky closed his eyes.

"So where are we going?"

"To see Mr. Lin."

"And where is Mr. Lin?"

"He's on my ranch."

"Ranch? What ranch? You've got a ranch?"

"No, what do you guys call it? It's a sheep station."

Ricky opened his eyes again and stared at side of the American's face. He was concentrating on the road — the Land Rover drifted at speed — and he wasn't grinning any more.

"You have a sheep station?"

"Sure. Just bought it."

"You..."

"Don't believe me? You'll see. Sheep and everything. Not sure what I'm gonna do with them. Maybe you can advise me."

"You want sheep advice from me?"

"I feel responsible. Okay, we turn off here."

Jay flung the Land Rover off the highway into an industrial zone. They bumped past loading bays and refrigerated warehouses and entered a road train marshaling yard. Jay aimed the Land Rover at a double-trailer livestock carrier and accelerated.

Ricky felt himself tense up. Why more crazy driving, he wanted to know; was it really necessary?

"Hold tight," Jay said.

They hit the trailer ramp, barreled up inside the trailer, skidded the length of it and came to rest against two tractor tires that someone — Jay? — had fixed to the end.

"Have to take kind of a run at it," Jay said.

"What are we doing in this thing?"

"Don't you have drones in Australia?"

"Well, I —"

"I know you have planes."

A lot of laughs, this bloke.

"Now, you can stay here," Jay said. "If you prefer. Or you can ride up front with me. It's a long way."

Ricky took a deep breath. A long ride. Maybe put the control thing aside for a little time-out?

"We can talk. There's a refrigerator in the cab."

Ricky looked at his new friend. The man was enjoying himself again.

"There's beer in it."

"All right," Ricky said. "All right. We'll talk. I've got a couple of things I want to know about you."

"Cool. Let's get this rig rolling. You ever driven one?"

"No. You?"

"No. Came with the ranch. I mean, *station*."

Between them they hitched up the rear ramp. Then they stood and looked at their new ride.

"Hey, how hard can it be?" Jay asked.

Who was this bloke? Had he really snatched Mr. Lin out from under the clampdown and penned him up with his hapless sheep? What chance now for Kerri?

Ten minutes of blood-pumping maneuvers, and they were back on the highway. Burning up inside the road train's monstrous cab, Ricky flicked the sweat from his unlined forehead and checked the outlook from the eucalyptus.

The bungalow was on fire.

CHAPTER 2

S andy Quayle shivered in the cold. Winter had come early, sweeping in with a brutality that seemed vengeful, and almost personal. She could take it, now. At first, it had been hard — so hard that survival had seemed impossible. And so it would have been, she felt sure, had she not found her way to the village.

Here, the physical dependence of one person upon another was made manifest. And the kind of debts that you incurred served only to anchor you in solidarity against misfortune, rather than isolating you in misery.

Sure, technically, she was homeless. But she had found a home.

It lay in an unregarded and barely visible crevice, a sloping, wooded gully in an angle between the interstate and the state highway. As she surveyed it now, with its tents, tepees, improvised shacks, log fires and washing lines, she remembered that she had once believed herself to be rich and self-sufficient. She had been wrong on both counts.

A woman very much like herself — but four years younger, at forty-eight, and going by what now seemed the more formal and pretentious name of *Sandra*, rather than Sandy — had truly thought that she had achieved *success*: The beautiful home; the secure and rewarding career; bullet-proof good health; the go-getting businessman husband with *plans* for the future. That whole *Dream* thing, in other words.

Wrong on all counts.

Another one of those *financial* things had blown in, like a moral tornado, picking its victims. Such events weren't any more predictable or preventable than real tornados — so respectable opinion held — but they sure did punish the guilty. Or some of them, at least, Sandy thought.

And as the wind whipped around her well-wrapped ankles and shook the pine trees above her head, Sandy Quayle reminded herself that she *was* to blame, somehow. She knew this, and believed that it was only right that she should suffer the consequences. Well, at least for a time.

So had her adult life been one big mistake?

Young Sandra — home-schooled in math, motherhood and modesty, and brimming over with what she sincerely believed, at the time, to be Christian charity — would have said so. But then along had come Johnny-boy, and young Sandra's eyes had been opened to what might just be possible, if you only got wise to the ways of money. You know, like those folk on Wall Street, or on cable TV.

Now, she felt as though she'd been suckered into a cult. Money was dangerous. The *idea* of money was seductive, and corrupting. And, sometimes, it might just be evil. Thus she was ready to give the faith of her youth another try. Could you do that? Was it allowed? God welcomed sinners back, didn't he? Sure, unless there was something in the small print.

So, anyway, she felt that she could atone. Perhaps, once she'd atoned enough, grace would follow. It was worth a try.

And you could never kill a dream, right? Forget the sex and the violence and the Hollywood politics — *that* was the one thing the movies got right. Some things you never surrendered, however defeated you were.

The village was good. Despite the privations, and the personal problems of some of its residents, it was a place of peace and even — if you were prepared to look at things in a certain way — of dignity and equality.

But the village felt under threat. The land it stood on, though useless for any other purpose, belonged to the Country Club. Rumor said that *something* was going to happen.

And, despite her feelings for the village, Sandy Quayle had resolved to leave. There was still some fight left in her; she felt healthy again and there was a renewed clarity in her mind. This was still America. Things were still possible. Dreams did not have to die. They could be put on hold. She just had to find a way. Any way. And she needed to think.

She would have to wait a while yet for her turn in the "kitchen", and there was little else to do. So she arranged her insulating layers for maximum warmth, stooped to scoop up the shopping bag in which she stowed her special possessions and made her move.

For privacy, she parked herself on a thick, dry root under cover of one of the pine trees that common opinion held too big and dangerous to fell for fuel. The pine-needle thatch above her cut out some of the fall chill, and blocked the accusatory glare of the full moon.

Luck, she thought. She needed luck. So much depended on luck. If she saw the merest hint of it, she would grasp at it, and not let go.

But before she could conjure any, an intervention came. It wasn't providence, or the kind of petty good fortune she seemed to remember but which ran at a premium these days, like a five-dollar bill on the sidewalk, and it certainly wasn't grace.

It was Hunter Bill, with a sack over his shoulder, looking older, mangier and yet more enthusiastic than ever. His offerings were better than road-kill, but they turned her stomach and she always politely declined.

"Oh, Bill," she said. "You know what I'm going to say."

"Rabbit? Squirrel?"

"No thanks, Bill. Appreciate it and all, but..."

"You sure? Got raccoon tonight!"

"Raccoon? How'd you catch a raccoon, Bill? No, don't answer that."

"What's a matter, Sandy? You a vegetarian now?"

"Maybe I am, Bill. I don't know."

Technically, she was. Her dinner would consist of pasta from the pantry on Mellon Street. If she got lucky, someone would spice it up for her with some vegetables.

"It's fresh and it's organic," Bill insisted, with that pitiful sincerity of his.

"I believe you."

Actually, if he caught his racoons or his other critters up on the golf course out back of the Country Club, or anywhere nearby, then they were most likely laced with Emerald Lawn and Verminator Supreme. That stuff couldn't be healthy. The mainstream media were probably right about that.

"Listen," Bill said. "You want to come by later to my, uh..." Bill didn't really have a tent. "To my place..." He rounded off his invitation with a nod and a jiggle of his sack.

"Bear it in mind, Bill. See ya."

Bill stood his ground for a moment and pursed his lips. Then he looked up at the moon.

"You know what's happening, right?"

"No, Bill. What?"

"China."

"What about China?"

"Damn moon-shot. They're up there now. Think I can see 'em."

She waited. Bill's shoulders slumped.

"Know what worries me?"

Sandy shrugged. Bill pointed at the moon with his free hand.

"We left our flag up there. You follow me?"

"I follow you, Bill."

Hunter Bill rubbed his bony brow, then shook his head and waddled off in search of potential new markets. He might well find them, she thought.

So how had Bill ended up in the village? There was something about him, hidden behind that folksy-woodsman style of his, that made Sandy think that he'd fallen further than she had. No doubt bad luck was involved. It always was. But had there been *pride*, too?

Sandy knew about pride.

On the far side of the interstate, down a twisty, landscaped private road, just off the state highway that led into Stimsonville (remember all those car dealerships?) you could still see it: Her beautiful, prideful home. So artfully built! All those extraneous gables; double pillars by the front door; windows so narrow that you had four to a room, but with classy sashes that used actual weights instead of friction; more bathrooms than bedrooms! And so on.

You deserve this mini-mansion! Or so said the broker's brochure.

Look, Sandra, I watch the market, okay? It takes a tumble, we flip out. No-brainer, sweetie.

Well, they flipped out all right. And then Johnny-boy flipped out permanently, in due course — but that really came under Anger.

Hunter Bill claimed he'd *scouted* the area recently. The house might be *bank-owned*, he'd told her, but the rabbits in the front yard sure weren't.

Sandy suspected — no, to be truthful, she was pretty certain — that there had been something fishy about the paperwork. But wasn't it better to be punished too much than too little?

So much for Pride.

There had also been Sloth.

When you watched TV, as Sandra did before she became Sandy, you learned that exercise, in large amounts and with the right clothing, kit and attitude, made you a better person. From this it followed that you would be a healthier person. Virtue conquered disease.

Sandy had to conclude that, despite all those power-walks with Candace and Melanie, she had fallen short. Sure, she had recovered, but insurance was a thing of the past, and these things came back, didn't they? And sometimes she felt dizzy and too tired to move. Maybe it was just hunger; but could it be diabetes? Next time they had one of those open-air clinics at the mall, she would walk over and get in line.

She paused. This stuff was too depressing. *Fight back, Sandy!*

And look — life went on: Over by the "kitchen" people were eating hot food and enjoying it; on the far side of the encampment, Hunter Bill was sharing a joke, at least, if not his catch of the day, with those two girls who slept in the old Mercury. (The car was some kind of *violation*, it seemed. Nothing had happened yet, but its loss would be a blow to the community.) And tomorrow, Thursday, she would get to have her weekly shower.

Thursday was Ladies Night, and quite a scene. The shower had been rigged by Gary, who said he used to be a contractor, and claimed to have installed the "waterfall" shower that Johnny-boy had thought so essential. Where the water came from was a little mysterious. The rumor was that Gary had found a way to tap into the automatic irrigation system up on the golf course.

And human progress continued. The Chinese were going to land on the moon!

Wow, and, if that wasn't enough, it was dinner-time! Her slot in the "kitchen" had opened up. She headed for the warmth of the fire. Someone had moved her dried pasta, but it looked like it was all still there. Gary, useful as ever, offered her a pot of water.

While she was waiting for it to boil, she noticed a commotion at the side of the camp nearest to the road, a little-used country lane that came off the state highway and functioned mainly as service access to the Country Club. Bright vehicle lights shone between the pine trees, generating a confusion of shadows.

The Stimsonville tent city was really more of a tent village. The population varied, but was currently about a hundred. And since it hid amongst the pines and was cut off on two sides by the interstate and the state highway, it didn't attract much attention. Unlike the much larger, more famous encampments in California and Tennessee, it didn't get visits from New York feature-writers or west coast independent documentary film-makers. Sandy thought this was a pity, because small towns really were the soul of the nation.

Anyway, the only regular visitor was the local sheriff, a lugubrious and generally sympathetic fellow — excepting the issue of the Mercury — whose

12

rationale for stopping by was always simply that he was "monitoring the situation". He came by on his own. Sometimes he brought canned food. But tonight there seemed to be multiple vehicles.

She glanced at the pot. Still not boiling; what she needed was some more dry wood for the fire. But before she could begin to search, she heard raised voices from the direction of the road. It was the two girls. They were yelling at their car, which looked to be moving under its own volition. But no, there was some kind of a tow-truck. The Mercury was being hauled up on to it. Well, we had *that* coming, she thought. You couldn't get away with breaking the rules forever.

Then came more lights; and the slamming of doors; and an angry voice yelling something though a bullhorn. To her left, she glimpsed Gary slip away into the darkness, his most prized possession — his toolbox — under his arm. To her right, over on the road, she saw three black vans. Each bore the same logo on its side — a stylized sun beaming down upon green fields. There was a name: *Fairmeadow* something. Behind the vans was a heavy dumpster truck. And beyond that, almost out of sight, was the sheriff's patrol car, with its lights out. A still shadow in the driver's seat.

Something buffeted against her shoulder and a camera flashed in her face. When her sight returned she saw that her cooking fire had been kicked over and her dinner lay in the dirt. The camp had been invaded by men in black uniforms and ski masks. They carried long sticks — those things that people used to call billy clubs. What couldn't be smashed — the nylon tents, for example — got thrown into the dumpster.

She wondered if the sheriff could see what was happening, because surely... But something caught her attention. It was Hunter Bill, teetering out from behind a tree at the back of the camp. His frantic gestures could only mean *follow me*. She decided this would be a smart thing to do, even if it should turn out later that he really just wanted her to help him catch more critters or foil the Chinese moon mission.

So she grabbed her shopping bag and ran.

The woods were full of fugitive shapes, stabbing beams and heavy breaths. Nobody spoke. It was a silent scramble for sanctuary — though where that might be, Sandy had no idea. The Country Club? How would that work? Wouldn't it be a little — what was the word? — impertinent? Her fellow villagers, who mostly kept out of the woods, seemed to have little sense of direction. Most of them would end up down on the service road. Hunter Bill, by contrast, was taking the high road in his long stride and she struggled to keep up with him. As for the Mercury girls? They were not to be seen.

On she went, straining her eyes as her manic woodsman flitted this way and that through the trees. The shopping bag slapped against her chapped shins.

Eventually, Bill must have realized that he'd gotten too far ahead of her and had stopped to let her catch up. By now, they were in the bushes that skirted the golf course. Amazingly, the whole thing was lit up. Somebody was playing golf at night.

Bill looked like he was lit up, too.

"You know what this is?"

Did Bill have a conspiracy theory? He often did.

"You know, it makes sense."

Right then, very little made sense to her — except for one, simple, obvious fact: That her term in purgatory still had some time to run.

Bill gestured to her to sit. She plumped down on a patch of dry grass, taking care not to spill the contents of her shopping bag.

"Shh!" Bill said, as if she had any breath left with which to speak. He withdrew a child's toy telescope from the cavernous interior of his coat and aimed it at a gap in the bushes. Was this what he used to track his prey?

"Look!" he said, passing her the telescope.

"Oh, no — I don't think —"

"You gotta look!" he said, forcing the instrument into her hands. Sometimes you just had to humor him, so she wiped the eyepiece with her sleeve and peered through the thing.

She saw two men standing at the edge of a beautifully-trimmed circle of grass. In the center of the circle was a flag. About five or six feet short of the flag were two neon-yellow golf balls — vital accessories for playing at night? — but the men appeared to have suspended their game in order to conduct a spirited conversation.

Perhaps ten years apart in age but neither younger than sixty, they dressed similarly, in warm slacks and wind-proof bomber jackets. The older, shorter man's jacket bore some kind of military insignia; the other's made Sandy think *Ivy League*. Their faces and hairstyles might have been purchased from the same catalog, she thought: Strong brows, square chins, perfect noses, fulsome hair — gray-streaked and swept back. The older man used grease on his; the younger's shivered in the breeze like cotton candy. And while the younger man's face retained some softness, the other's looked tough and creased. This aggressive cast was accentuated by his steel-rimmed glasses, shoulders that seemed too wide for his body, and the way he flicked at the grass with his putter.

"Recognize 'em?" Bill said. He sounded excited.

"No, Bill. Should I?"

"Hear what they're saying?"

"No, they're too far away." She lowered the telescope. "Perhaps we should —"

"We gotta get closer."

"No, I really think we should —"

But Bill had produced a cell phone from that junk-filled coat of his. And it looked *very familiar*, in its sparkly pink case!

"Bill! That's Donna-Marie's phone! Did you steal it?"

Bill looked taken aback. His mouth fell open.

"Now, you *know* that's wrong!"

Donna-Marie ran what she called her *cell phone stand* in the village. Whenever she managed to get enough credit on her account and sufficient juice in her battery she would put out her shingle and wait for business. If you had fifty cents you could make a domestic call. International calls were available by special arrangement and prices were negotiable. Cell phone reception was iffy in the camp, and Donna-Marie didn't do refunds, so customers were routinely advised to seek higher ground.

"I was making a call!" Bill said. "But then all hell —"

"You know I don't like that word. Did you pay for it?"

"Sure! Fifty damn cents!"

She gave him the kind of reproachful frown she used to give Johnny-boy's wild-girl nieces when they were all living together in the trailer.

But really — a call? Who could Bill possibly be calling? She felt a pang of sadness; Bill lived in a fantasy world.

"Looks like a conspiracy to me," Bill said, brandishing the cell phone like a Bowie knife. "There's an app on here. I'm gonna bug 'em."

Well, that just proved her point for her, didn't it?

Bill got down on his hands and knees and, like some demented attack-rabbit, bobbed off into the bushes. She decided to wait for him. You didn't want to be alone in the woods; terrible stories circulated in the village. Even if only some of them were true, well...

With a quick, mumbled prayer — the first in a while — and a supreme effort of will, eyes closed, she erased them from her mind. There followed a long moment of floating in the void, and then it hit her: She was *truly* homeless.

Not homeless in the sense of losing the mini-mansion; not homeless in the manner of a person living in someone else's trailer; not homeless as in sleeping in your car. She had no money. Should the temperature drop even further, the clothes she wore might not be enough to keep her alive through the night.

Her friends and associates — all but one of them — had been dispersed. Where would they all go? The shelter in Stimsonville had been closed since the last elections.

She believed that her behavior in the camp had been exemplary. That she had been a good neighbor, a friend in need, a shoulder to cry on — none of this could be in doubt. Then again, she lacked the skills and resources of people like Gary and Donna-Marie and Hunter Bill. And this meant that her contribution had inevitably been... Well, she didn't quite know how to think about it.

Those hateful words that had become so common these days — *moocher, freeloader, deadbeat, subprime* — well, they didn't apply to *her*, surely. They couldn't. And yet she felt a debt, a nagging guilt. What did it mean? Ah, but if you really thought about it, there was some small solace to be had: Out there somewhere, walking about, heads held high for all she knew, were people who were guilty as you-know-what — but whose guilt *didn't nag*. She, Sandra Quayle, was superior to such people.

Then came the merest rustle in the bushes: Hunter Bill was back. She felt glad that she was a person, not a critter. Bill's face looked flushed — with triumph?

"Just as I thought," he said.

"Aha! And what conclusion did you come to, Bill?"

"It looks bad, all right. The old guy with the nine-iron? I know him. I don't trust him, Sandy."

It occurred to her again that Bill must have had a former life quite different to hers and, for a fleeting moment, she wondered what it had been like.

"No, I mean, did you figure out the conspiracy?"

"Maybe. Need to do some research."

Research? Even before tonight's events the camp had lacked Internet access. And the public library in Stimsonville had shut down years ago, about the time they were turning off the street lights. If you bought a cup of coffee you could have Wi-Fi. But the coffee cost three dollars.

"Well, you do that. Then we can all sleep safe in our beds!"

Bill gave her that sour smile of his. Really, he did lack for the personal graces sometimes.

"Let me ask you something," he said.

"Okay."

"You really don't recognize those two guys?"

"No."

"Not even the old guy?"

Had there been *something* about him? Did it matter? She shook her head.

"You keep up with the news, Sandy?"

"No. Why on Earth would I want to do that?"

The news was always terrible. It was mayhem, vileness, pornography. Why did the mainstream media need to say all those horrible things about America?

"So you didn't catch the *Journal* this morning?"

That sour smile again. She really ought to tell him to stop it.

"No. I did not."

And where, for that matter, did Hunter Bill get his newspapers delivered?

"Then I guess this'll come as a surprise to you."

"What?"

"There's a Committee to Save America."

Now if he was going to get all political, or disrespectful, then she might just have to consider taking her chances on her own in the woods.

"Is there now? Bill, do you really think America needs a committee to save it?"

Bill looked at her as if she'd said something truly weird. Which was weird in itself, she thought, because *he* was the weird one.

"They're here to confirm their nominee. Their candidate."

"Candidate? For what?"

"For President."

"Oh, Bill. You're so full... So full of crap! There. You made me say it."

Bill sighed.

"As a matter of fact, I do need to..."

"Oh, no! Well you take yourself off over there, you hear? I don't need to see that."

Who was she kidding? She'd seen plenty in the camp.

Bill got to his feet.

"All righty. But you stay here, Sandy, okay? Don't you move."

With barely the snap of a twig, Bill shimmied off into the murk of the pine woods. She let out a long sigh and her breath hung on the still air like clean linen on a washing line.

It was still hanging there when something hard nudged the flappy toe of her right sneaker.

It was a fluorescent orange golf ball.

16

CHAPTER 3

Sandy Quayle knew nothing about golf, except that it came with a price tag. Johnny-boy used to fantasize about joining the Stimsonville Country Club, Resort & Spa, and *trading up* from fishing on the lake to *networking* on the green. But that was never going to happen. The fees had been almost as much as their mortgage payments were by the end.

How much did a golf ball cost? She picked it up and inspected it. Printed on the ball was some kind of heraldic shield, which contained the letters "W" and "P". Someone's initials?

What should she do? Leave it where she found it? Hurl it back on to the course? Oh, but no — she might hit someone, and then what? Wait for Bill to return and get his opinion? No, Bill would just take it and sell it.

And right now, poor old Mr. WP was up there, hunting for his ball, searching this way and that. Would he be pleased, or even thankful, if some generous-spirited person were to return his property to him and spare him his fruitless efforts? Well, maybe. Sandy had learned that gratitude was an unreliable quality. But she really needed that *luck*.

She hauled herself to her feet, collected the shopping bag, carefully, in her right hand and wrapped her left around the ball. Then she pushed her way uphill through the bushes.

Almost at once she came upon a six-foot-tall chain-link fence. It ran through the midst of the bushes and was painted green — presumably so as not to offend the sight of the club's members, while still providing them with the security they expected. For a moment she thought she would have to abandon her plan. Then she saw the hole: Someone had removed a square section of the fence, at ground level. Bill? First theft and now vandalism? Really, you had to fret for the man's soul.

The hole, she calculated, was just big enough. Should she? Mr. WP would laugh when she told him, wouldn't he? Sandy the raccoon, fences can't keep her out! Down she went. On the way through, she felt the back of her coat rip. But she had so many layers underneath; it wouldn't make much difference. On the far side of the fence, she stood up again, checked her shopping bag to make sure that nothing had fallen out, and advanced into the light.

It was brighter than she'd expected. Amid the blur she immediately made out the shape of a golf buggy, with driver. Just to the right were three men. One held a golf bag, the second some kind of briefcase, and the third, the shortest, a club. That had to be Mr. WP.

"Drop the bag!"

The voice came from her left. Her eyes focused on two men dressed in black jackets and hats. They looked almost identical to the men from *Fairmeadow* — but they had guns, and one of them had a German Shepherd on a chain.

"Down on the ground! Drop the bag!"

This time from the right — two more men, rifles raised.

"Drop the bag! Last warning!"

She let her shopping bag fall to the ground.

"Get down!"

She lay down on her stomach. Out here the grass was wet — was it Gary's irrigation system? For a few moments there was silence. Then a radio crackled. Some words were spoken, but she couldn't make them out. Nobody moved.

Then the radio blared again and one of the armed men began to approach her shopping bag, one step at a time — she could see it out of the corner of her eye. He knelt down on the grass. First he leaned slowly to one side, and then the other, as if the bag were a rare animal that might take fright and vanish. Then he lowered himself to the ground, pulled down a visor in front of his face and, holding his rifle at arm's length, poked its barrel gently into the opening of the bag. Next he levered up the barrel, so as to expose the bag's contents to view.

Humiliation. But *her own fault!* Why hadn't she listened to Bill?

This inspection seemed to last much longer than necessary. But then all at once it was over, the man was on his feet, her bag was upside-down in his hands, its precious cargo cast on the ground, the dog all over it.

She felt the pressure of a boot between her shoulder blades, and the travel of gloved hands over her exposed portions. Presently this stopped, and she was left alone.

When she dared to look up, she saw that Mr. WP was in conference with his security detail and the man with the briefcase. The dog was enjoying a drink to the rear of the buggy, while the caddy organized his clubs. Nobody looked her way.

For a moment she wondered who Mr. WP might be. Was he especially important or did every club member enjoy such protection? Might Bill's ravings about *Committees* and *Presidents* be less than completely mad?

Well, you know, she really didn't mind. Let them organize their *Committees*. Let Bill fuss over his *Journal*. Let the Chinese colonize the galaxy. She, Sandra Quayle, now that her moment of terror had passed, was going to do what she'd d—n well set out to do.

She struggled to her feet. Then she raised her left hand, uncurled her fingers and, gripping it firmly between thumb and forefinger, presented the orange golf ball on high for all the world to see.

The caddy saw it first. He touched his boss on the elbow. One by one, heads turned.

Mr. WP, she was now able to observe, was a fine, sleek, mature specimen. Beneath his navy-blue wind-cheater, he wore a crisp white shirt, open at the neck, under a pale-blue sweater. Though a little generous about the waist and somewhat jowly around the face, with his clear eyes, plum-fresh cheeks, brilliant teeth, elegant, raked-back hair and rich, smooth forehead, he was the picture of prosperous health. His lips appeared set in a tolerant smile, like those of an indulgent uncle who'd done well on the stock exchange. Sandy had never had such a relative, of course, but she'd occasionally imagined one, during the trials of early adolescence, when the family's resources had always seemed so inadequate — and he'd looked quite a lot like this.

Mr. WP looked her way — and registered the ball. His expression became one of delight and surprise, as if an old friend had unexpectedly dropped by for tea. He took a step forward, but then changed his mind and tapped the caddy. Sandy waited. When the caddy got close enough, she simply handed him the ball. He nodded but said nothing. Then he retreated and offered up the ball for his boss to inspect. More nodding. The caddy unzipped a pocket on his golf bag, dropped Sandy's ball into it and took out a fresh one.

Then everyone looked at her and waited. *Well*, she thought, *that's it — I've done what I came to do.* Guardedly, and with an eye out for the dog, she collected her shopping bag, picked up her possessions and stowed them. Still they watched her. She backed away, towards the bushes and the hole in the fence.

Then, by purest accident, her gaze met with that of Mr. WP. The tolerant smile morphed into something more decisive. He turned to the man with the briefcase — some kind of personal assistant? — and spoke into his ear. The assistant frowned and seemed to protest. But Mr. WP was firm. The assistant shrugged and began to march towards Sandy, reaching inside his padded jacket as he did so.

By the time he stood in front of her he'd removed his wallet. It was stuffed with money. He selected a bill and offered it to Sandy. She took it and thrust it into her pocket without looking at it. Then she turned to the bushes.

"Wait."

She turned back. The assistant was in a crouch, the briefcase on his knees. He removed a piece of paper from the briefcase, scrawled something on the bottom of it with a fountain pen, and stood up again.

"Here."

Sandy took the piece of paper, folded it and slipped it into her shopping bag.

"Good night."

The assistant turned and trudged back to his boss with a gait that seemed to say *happy now?* Sandy took one last look at that peaceful, indulgent, almost *kind* smile, and dived back into the bushes.

Bill was waiting for her, his hair standing on end — but it did that quite often anyway.

"*Sandy!* What did I *tell* you!"

Oh, and what a telling-off he gave her, indeed. But she deserved it, didn't she?

When he was done, she showed him the piece of paper. He flapped his arms with comic despair.

"BREAK THE DEADLOCK!" she read. "The Man to Save America."

"That's the guy," Bill said. "Just like I told you!"

She read on. Concerned citizens were urged to vote against partisanship and return America to its democratic roots. Only one man could defeat the special interests and restore the Republic. There followed a picture of this man. He stood behind a lectern labeled with the letters "NACF". Behind him were two American flags, angled jauntily.

It was Mr. WP. His name was Willard G. R. Prince, which Sandy thought sounded pretty fancy. After that came a web site address and an exhortation to volunteer at your local campaign headquarters — and here Mr. Willard G. R. Prince's assistant had jotted down an address on Mellon Street.

"What's NACF?" she asked.

Bill sniffed.

"New American Century Fund. Guy's an investor. Makes a ton of money. But you need an invite."

"An invite?"

"Yeah. He give you anything else?"

"Yes."

She reached into her pocket and pulled out a five dollar bill.

CHAPTER 4

M r. Lin's material was comprehensive, convincing, urgent, important, shocking, occasionally devastating — and an utter disappointment. Comprising video, official documents, and secret internal Party reports and communications from the Organization and Propaganda departments, it detailed villagers displaced and dispossessed by politically-connected developers; tainted products; the covering-up of environmental scandals; the rigging of pollution statistics; the non-enforcement of building codes in earthquake zones; atrocious working conditions in factory towns; the ever-popular corruption of local party bosses; the fabled mistreatment of officials detained under the Central Discipline Inspection Commission's *shuanggui* procedure; the never-ending self-enrichment of *princelings*; the time-honored repression of religious minorities; and, that grand old tradition, the theatrical harassment of dissidents.

Nothing new, in other words. Almost all of it could go online immediately, Ricky thought. It might do some good. He'd forward it to Norway for the identity-protection work.

There *was* a memorandum from the Central Leading Group on Foreign Affairs that complained vaguely — at least as translated by Mr. Lin — about *inappropriate relations* between unnamed Chinese and American business interests. It was unusual and mildly intriguing, depending on the nature of the *relations*.

But there was nothing he could bargain with; Kerri was out of luck. Egregious, rampant and breath-taking as they were, none of Mr. Lin's corruptions appeared to implicate anyone higher than Provincial Committee level. The Americans would laugh at him. Speaking of which...

Mr. Jay Percival hadn't yet got around to explaining what he was doing in Australia, and why it involved Ricky. He claimed to be a former employee of the Central Intelligence Agency. Ricky's database of American secrets backed this up — but did he quit or was he fired? Predictably, perhaps intentionally, this was unclear. These days, Jay said, he was a self-employed consultant, specializing in Africa. The database had nothing to say about that. And when Ricky noted that Jay's work must pay pretty well if he could afford to go about buying sheep stations, the American had cracked up at him. All right then, Ricky thought, we'll wait.

And so now he sat on the front deck of Jay's *ranch house*, tinny in hand, watching Jay's jackaroos instruct their new boss, and Mr. Lin, in the art of herding sheep with motorcycles. They all seemed to be enjoying themselves. Personally, Ricky sympathized with the sheep.

So what did this smart-arse Yank, who, by the way, seemed to be absolutely bloody *loaded*, to judge by the fancy computer gear he kept in his kitchen, want with Australia and poor, persecuted little Ricky? How about we ponder the geopolitics for a bit and then spot the connection?

What did Americans think about when they thought of Australia? Sydney Opera House, kangaroos, Crocodile bloody Dundee. Yes, but what about your strategic types? They thought, *dirty great aircraft carrier* in the western Pacific. Hence the attraction of Darwin for the special ops crowd.

So far so good. Now, what's the connection between our can-do *consultant* who loves Africa and the US military posture in the Northern Territory? Who's stirring things up in these two regions? Answer: China. Easy enough, isn't it? China's cutting up rough in the South China Sea, which, for some reason that the Pentagon's top analysts can't put their laser pointers on, China seems to regard as its *back yard*. And China's all over southern and central Africa, digging up treasure, putting down infrastructure, discomfiting some of the locals, sure, yet not actually enslaving them like the bloody Europeans did.

But the Yanks don't care if the Chinese are putting Tanzanian chicken farmers out of business, so there must be something else going on.

Who's been specializing lately in Chinese secrets? Ricky. And who blew the whistle on that super-secret, revised version of the China-containing Air-Sea Battle scenario that had to be publicly rubbished — junior officers gone rogue and so on — because no one in the Australian government had been informed about the use of Aussie territory, supposedly? Kerri.

Almost there. But not quite.

Ricky had to wait until after dinner, which Jay insisted on cooking himself, whilst monitoring all those busy devices in his kitchen.

"How'd you like to see where they shear the sheep?"

"Why not?" Ricky said.

It was a dark, sun-baked wooden shed that reeked of lanolin, sweat, oil, and warm electrics. Fear, too, Ricky thought — but was it the animals' or his? The electric shears hung on metal hooks attached to the barn's uprights, their coiled black cables looped up into the eaves.

"Tried it yourself, yet?" Ricky asked.

"No. Get kind of squeamish around animals."

Right, Ricky thought; might mess up those shoes, too.

"How's the financial situation?" Jay asked.

"Difficult."

The major credit card and Internet payment companies had been arm-twisted into black-listing Big Data Underground. Who said the US Congress never got anything done? Ricky had to rely on smaller operators that weren't always trusted by his right-thinking but timorous supporters.

"Yeah, figures."

Jay removed one of the shears from its hook, inspected it, wrinkled his nose at it, and replaced it.

"How's the situation with Kerri Law?"

Ricky kicked at one of the uprights.

"Difficult."

"She really an Elvis fan?"

"Yes, she is."

Kerri had been a contract cleaner at the US embassy in Canberra. She'd found the Elvis CD in a waste-paper bin. It wouldn't play on her stereo, so she put it in her computer. She'd been hoping for "Love Me Tender", but what she got was Air-Sea Battle, the bootleg version. She'd shown it to her dad, a retired and defeated union official, who'd recommended Ricky.

"You paying for her lawyer?"

"Yes."

"That's got to be expensive."

"It is."

"They really want to send her to Virginia?"

"Apparently, they do. Or somewhere."

"Why'd you let her go to London?"

"She has friends there. She thought she'd be safe."

"That's a little naïve."

"I would have stopped her. She was on a plane before I knew."

Jay let out a long, noisy breath, as if Ricky's troubles were almost more than he could bear.

"Plus," Jay said, "you've got Mr. Lin to worry about. *He's* not going back to China. I guess he's kind of your responsibility, too."

Thanks, Ricky thought. Spell out the obvious for me. *Never* meet providers in person.

"And you've lost one of your server farms, and the Australian government is getting ready to whisper a formal complaint out of the side of its mouth once our guys in the black SUVs catch up with you and ship you out."

"Your guys?"

"You know what I mean."

That was enough, Ricky thought. Why not cut straight to the proposition?

"Stop fucking with me, Jay."

"Ready to talk?"

"Ready."

"All righty."

Jay cast his gaze around the shed. There was a short wooden pole, propped up in a corner. He retrieved it.

"Come over here."

In the center of the floor, Jay drew a ragged circle in the dirt.

"Here," he said, marking a cross at one point on the circle. "That's Khaukphyu in Myanmar."

He made another cross.

"That's Chittagong in Bangladesh."

Two more crosses.

"Hambantota in Sri Lanka. And Gwadar in Pakistan. That's your *string of pearls*, right there."

He looked up at Ricky as if he felt that Ricky ought to be impressed.

"Well, I'm impressed," Ricky said. "What is it?"

"Some people look at this and what they see is strategic encirclement."

"Of the Indian Ocean?"

"Yeah. Obviously."

"So those are bases?"

Jay shook his head.

"No, no, no! Ports. Purely commercial. Built and operated by China."

"But they *could* be naval bases? One day?"

"You betcha."

Ricky wondered if Jay expected him to deliver up computer blueprints for secret underwater Chinese submarine pens. If he did, he was going to be as disappointed as Ricky had been with Mr. Lin. Chinese military secrets were far, far harder to get hold of than American ones. For good reason.

Jay leaned on his stick.

"Let me tell you about my boss."

Jay had a *boss?* No, the bloke answered to himself, didn't he?

"Go ahead."

"His name is Walter Gabo. He's one of these ANC elder-statesmen guys who —"

"I know who he is."

"Sure. Political guy like you. You would."

"So what's his problem?"

"His problem is, he remembers the Cold War."

"So tell him to get over it."

Jay pointed at the eastern coast of Africa with his pole.

"What if, Walter says to himself, they decide to add another pearl or two?"

"Thought they loved Chinese investment over there. Just like we do here."

"They do. This whole *peaceful rise* thing? They're totally into that. It's the *strategic rivalry* that gives them pause."

"With you guys."

"Yeah, with us. Their — Walter's — feeling is, they've done that once, don't want to do it again."

"Another Cold War — fought out on their patch?"

"That kind of thing."

All very fascinating, Ricky thought. Jay could dress it up a bit and stick it in an op-ed in the New York Times.

"Isn't he being a bit alarmist, old Walter?"

"He's heard rumors."

"Tell him to relax. What's it all got to do with me?"

Jay propped his pole up against a pillar and rubbed his hands together slowly.

"Now, I don't want you to over-react. No offense, but you're obviously one of those jumpy, intense guys. I can understand it. I get it. But I don't want you to freak out, okay?"

Ricky began to get that tunneling feeling again.

"Why would I freak out?"

Jay paused. Then he stroked the bridge of his nose.

"Some people in my old office have gotten in touch."

The ripe, animalistic fug in the shed seemed to condense on Ricky's skin. This bastard had almost seduced him. He'd turned the Commodore into a flaming barricade, plucked Ricky from the jaws of the rendition mill, spirited him off to the outback, cooked him dinner, hinted at some kind of bloody bailout, flattered him with geopolitics, and it was all a wind-up! His chums from the bloody *office* were about to jump out! Where were they, then? Had they disguised themselves as fucking sheep?

"I *said*, don't freak out, Ricky."

"Where are they?"

"Back home behind their desks."

"What *the fuck* do you want?"

"Calm down and I'll tell you."

"I want to get out of this bloody shed."

"Yeah, why don't we?"

Outside, the air had cooled, the light had gone, and the southern sky was out on parade. Its sudden, implacable beauty — such a contrast to the murky northern skies of Ricky's early career — brought down a sullen peace upon him. And those were real sheep, for fuck's sake. *Don't freak out, Ricky. Stay in control.*

They began to walk slowly back toward the house.

"I want you to go to Hong Kong," Jay said. "And meet a guy there."

Ricky let this modest suggestion hang in the dry air. Another *in-person?* No way. It was impossible in any case.

"I can't go there. China's off-limits. Even Hong Kong."

"We'll come back to that."

"Who's this *guy?*"

"Well, he's kind of special, Okay, they tell me he is. Got some hot shit direct from the bowels of the PLA."

"Sounds enticing."

Actually, military secrets from the inner sanctums of the People's Liberation Army would almost certainly qualify as *hot shit*. It was the sort of stuff he'd been hoping for from Mr. Lin.

"There's a problem, though."

"And what's that?"

"This guy. It was all set up. The *office* sent out a team. It's all systems go, everybody's expecting to get a citation from the director. Then the guy turns around, and you know what he says?"

"No. What?"

"He's only going to deal with *you*."

"Me?"

"You."

"Why?"

"Well, that's a good question. Far as I can tell, nobody knows. Or, if they do, they're not telling me."

Ricky looked up at the sky. It was as obvious, he thought, as the Southern Cross.

"It's a setup."

"Could well be."

"So I'm not going. Can't, anyway."

Jay stopped.

"Whatever this guy's got, I want it."

"Good luck."

Ricky kept walking. Jay caught up to him.

"Isn't this right up your alley?"

"Normally, yes."

"Could be the entire Chinese military posture in Africa. Plus how they plan to counteract a US response."

"Big stuff."

"No kidding."

Ricky stopped.

"Look, why are you even doing this? I don't get it. You've got all that money — from somewhere — why don't you just retire?"

"And do what? Play golf?"

Jay prodded Ricky on the chest with his forefinger.

"I'm like you. I'm on a mission. This is my life. I'm out on my own."

"What about your *friends* in the *office?*"

"You need to understand that they're not my friends. They hate me almost as much as they hate you. I bailed out when fire-power became more important than brain-power. They don't forgive. But a few of them are amenable to a deal."

"There's a deal?"

"Yeah. Ask me what's in it for you."

"Tell me."

Jay took a deep breath and stretched out his arms.

"Look at that sky. Amazing. But look — you got to understand the context here. People are going crazy back home. It's Sino-phobia. Our bat-shit politicians are going nuts. They're on Freedom News talking about manifest destiny. This moon-shot thing doesn't help. We got some dumb plutocrat, says he'll deal with China if the people make him President in November. And they damn well might! It's a volatile situation. And it needs to be handled carefully."

"By you?"

"You, me and Walter."

"And your *frenemies* back home?"

Jay let his arms flop to his sides. And was that a snort or a chuckle?

"Well, that's where it gets interesting. What we have to do — well, I guess this is really *your* job — is *detoxify* the material before we give it to 'em. We got Mr. Lin here to help you."

"You mean fake it up?"

"Broadly speaking."

"Why couldn't we cut them out altogether?"

"They know who the guy is. We don't."

"Why doesn't he contact me directly?"

"Don't know. Maybe they've got him holed up somewhere. Maybe he thought it was too risky."

"Sounds risky all right. Anyway, I told you. I can't do it."

"That's crap. Here you go."

Jay pulled something out from the rear pocket of his skinny jeans and handed it to Ricky. It was a British passport. Ricky flipped it open. There was his picture: Semi-long, dirt-brown hair, straggling across his curved forehead; round, too-small ears sticking out either side; pinched mouth; bottle-top chin; florid cheeks and an expression at once grumpy and mordant. There were prettier pictures, he thought, but perhaps none so accurate. He looked like an IT guy with a secret sorrow. Which, of course, he was. And his name was David Thatcher.

Jay looked happily inscrutable, like a bad poker player with a winning hand.

"That's right. You get to be a spy. You get to have your *own* secrets! Man, are you gonna be thrilled."

"You've got to be bloody joking, mate."

"You can do the accent, I guess. You lived there long enough. Radicalized in jolly old England!"

Long enough was right. Here came the slideshow: Ricky, the little Aussie kid who was useless at rugby and cricket; Ricky the truculent teenager with no proper respect for authority; Ricky suffering under depressive skies as everyone else got on their bikes and made a mint; Ricky the promising student who couldn't see past the moldering bureaucracy or block the stench, as it then smelled to him, of a culture in terminal decay; Ricky the trouble-making foreigner, always on the radar; Ricky, faking identities and raking through the dustbins of the powerful, because the Internet isn't up to speed yet; Ricky, the fucking idiot, radiating self-pity after his beautiful blonde girlfriend, two inches taller than him and two social classes out of reach, turns out to be an on-duty employee of the Special Branch (or was it MI5?); Ricky, on a plane back to Australia, and good riddance.

But Jay was saying something.

"I said, the deal is, you get Kerri back. No strings. What do you say?"

CHAPTER 5

The food pantry on Mellon Street had closed down. Did this mean that times were getting better, and its services were no longer needed? Sandy Quayle hoped so, but there was no explanation posted, and the appearance of the rest of the town, she feared, did not support this hypothesis.

She had spent the night in the woods with Hunter Bill and, in a way, it was lucky that the village had gone, because imagine having to explain *that!* Of course nothing *untoward* had transpired. But people like Donna-Marie certainly liked to talk, didn't they? Bill, it turned out, had been industrious. He'd constructed a chain of hides. And one of these had afforded them shelter. To Bill's chagrin, though, it had not been a fruitful night, hunting-wise. Maybe all that commotion had scared the critters away.

In the morning they'd descended to the camp site. It was deserted. What a mess! And such a shame, too. For all its privations, the village had worked somehow. It'd had *spirit*. But perhaps this upset was just what she needed — what they all needed. A wake-up call. To get up, and get out there, and start making things happen. She'd outlined these thoughts to Hunter Bill, but he didn't seem to think much of them.

They'd scavenged enough for breakfast — no *wild meat* for Sandy, just some damp cookies — and then Bill had announced his intention to *move on*. He was going to head south, or maybe southwest. The weather was better down there and that's where the future was. If there was one. Sandy could come with him if she wanted, but she'd better understand that he set quite a pace, and he wasn't about to let her slow him down. He explained this in an offhand, brusque sort of way, but she wondered whether he secretly yearned for her presence at his side. Had he once had a family?

She'd let him down gently. And he seemed to accept it. But then, when she explained her plan, he got all out of sorts. Well, she couldn't help that. When you were handed an opportunity, you had to take it. What if it were the last chance you were ever to get?

Unlike some people, Sandy didn't care to go on about God all the time. But when you were given a gift, what were you supposed to do? No, she didn't mean the five dollars. That was just, like, a kind of tip for returning the golf ball. What she meant was the invitation, from Mr. Willard G. R. Prince personally, to join his campaign for President.

Bill's response to this had been very vulgar indeed. But she forgave him. She was convinced — almost entirely convinced — that something significant had passed between them, when her gaze had met with his — Mr. Prince's, not Bill's. All right, there was a tiny bit of doubt. But surely, she ought to have faith? How could you live if you questioned every last drop of providence? You'd rationalize yourself to death, like those sad scientists over in Europe. So did she have enough faith? Well, if not, she'd just have to get herself some more.

She looked at her reflection in the food pantry's dusty window. Looking good in the camp had been a challenge. Looking *clean* had been a challenge. But she was proud — no, make that satisfied — with the way she looked this morning. It was certainly the best she could have done.

Okay, she had resorted to subterfuge. But she felt confident that the good works to come would cancel that out. At a gas station on the state highway, she'd loitered outside the restroom until a suitable victim — a smart, elderly lady with a sagging Cadillac — emerged. Then she'd staged a little song-and-dance and cadged the key. Once inside, she'd set to work. And how fortunate she was that she'd managed to hang on to her shopping bag!

She'd trimmed her hair, washed it and dried it under the electric hand-dryer. Then she'd pulled it back in a scrunchie. Though there was barely enough space in the restroom, she'd disrobed, rinsed herself down and dried off with toilet paper. Then she'd slipped into her alternate set of underclothes and climbed back into her mom jeans and polo shirt. The rip in her coat was much worse than she'd thought and she'd made the tough decision to discard it. She couldn't show up looking like *that*.

Her extra layers went into the shopping bag. It bulged, but that couldn't be helped. By now someone was banging on the door, so she finished up by applying a thin layer of the foundation that Donna-Marie had given her. It was too light for her skin — not surprising, given Sandy's long sojourn in the outdoors — and made her look a little ghostly, but it was better than nothing.

Then she'd exited the restroom and handed the key to an attendant, who said some rude things about who was and who wasn't allowed to use the facilities — but that was really *his* problem.

Fortunately, it was a sunny day, so the walk into town had not been unpleasant. She'd done it in just over three hours.

According to the *invitation*, Mr. Prince's local campaign headquarters was located about four blocks east of the food pantry. If Sandy squinted she could see, far off, beyond the boarded-up storefronts, the weedy parking lots, and the empty intersections, a tiny effusion of red, white and blue. That had to be it — flags! Fluttering in the breeze! It lifted her heart.

She was about to set off when she heard a *whoop-whoop* behind her. It was the sheriff in his patrol car. He rolled up to her and buzzed down his window.

"Hey, Sandy. How're ya doin' today?"

He seemed a little uncomfortable. Was there something on his mind?

"Oh, I'm just fine!"

"You happen to see old Bill anywhere?"

"Uh, not lately."

"When d'ya last see him?"

"Last night."

"Last night, huh?"

She couldn't see his eyes, because of his reflective shades. But she registered that lascivious twist he gave his lips.

"Know which way he went?"

"No."

Okay, Bill had said he was heading south or south-west. But Bill said a lot of things.

"Thing is, we got a complaint. From the Country Club. Vandalism. You know anything about that, Sandy?"

She shook her head.

"No? You're not holdin' back on me, are ya?"

"Oh, no. I wouldn't... I mean..."

The sheriff lifted his glasses and rubbed his eyes.

"You know what *obstruction of justice* is, Sandy?"

She froze.

"Was it Bill that done it?"

This was horrible! What could she say? She was sure that it *was* Bill, but she had no proof...

"I —"

"Nah, I'm just fuckin' with ya. You take care, Sandy, ya hear?"

He buzzed his window up and rolled his car lazily down Mellon Street.

She felt her mood sag. He'd been so casual with her. Disrespectful. He hadn't even mentioned the eviction. Well, things in Mr. Prince's world would be different. Of course they would. Sandy needed to get herself into that world. And stay there. She took a deep breath and resumed her march.

Plus, Bill had been so cynical. And wasn't it *exactly* that kind of attitude that had caused so many of today's problems? He hadn't been present when Sandy and Mr. Prince met, had he? No, so he wasn't entitled to say those things. There *was* something special about Mr. Prince. Bill might not *get it*, but then he hadn't seen the way that Mr. Prince had overruled his snooty assistant in Sandy's favor. It might seem a small thing, but... Well, *she knew*.

The campaign office occupied a former hardware store. It was crammed full of desks. On each desk were two computer screens. The people behind them looked very young. What if she were rejected for being too old? This moment of panic dissolved when she spotted a mature woman in a navy-blue skirt suit and pearls. The woman looked up and caught Sandy's gaze. Then she put down the tablet computer she'd been studying, strode briskly to the front of the store and cracked the door open. Sandy saw that she was wearing an ID tag. Her name was Barbara van Dornen and she was a *Campaign Supervisor*.

"Can I assist you with anything?"

It seemed more like a challenge than a solicitation. The voice was velvety, a commanding drawl, off-putting. But Sandy wasn't about to be put off.

"I came to help."

"Okay."

Spoken with the word stretched out and then a pause.

"May I ask what with?"

"The campaign. Mr. Prince's campaign."

Another pause. Barbara's left hand rose to her lips as if it expected to find a cigarette there and then, having failed to do so, tucked Barbara's hair behind her ear.

"Oh my dear, you had me on the wrong track there. Come along in. Everyone's welcome. Of course they are. We need all the help we can get."

Sandy found herself guided — quite firmly, she thought — to a conference table in an office at the back of the store. In the course of this excursion, she felt Barbara sizing up her mom jeans, her faded polo shirt and her flappy sneaker.

"Been toiling in the yard this morning, working up a sweat? I mean, if you have as many leaves to rake as we do — my *God!* All right, you sit there."

Sandy sat. Barbara saw the bag.

"Been shopping? I thought that store had closed."

"Oh, it did."

"You're not one of these *environment* people, are you?"

"No, I —"

"I'm joking. It's been a little crazy around here lately. I'm sure you're setting a good example. Okay. We'll get some details and then we'll put you to work. So, start by filling this out."

Barbara pushed a sheet of paper across the table at Sandy.

"I'll be right back."

Barbara made a decisive exit from the office. Sandy heard her tell *Charlie* that the *demographics* were *looking up*.

She took a pen from her bag and wrote her name on the form — Sandra Quayle. Very nice. But where did Sandra Quayle live? What was her cell phone number? Her email address? Her web site (if any)? She wrote down the address of the mini-mansion, permitting herself a transgressive smile at the thought of Barbara driving by and recoiling at the state of the lawn. For cell phone number, she wrote down the last number she'd had. The phone had gone in the yard sale. Someone might get a surprise call. She made up an email address, calling herself *sandyquayle1963*, and using Johnny-boy's defunct domain.

After the personal details came a list of *policy issues*. Sandy was requested to check those that she had any knowledge of, or interest in, and which she believed she was competent to talk about in a confident and authoritative manner. She scanned the list.

Uncontrolled deficit spending.

She thought about that for a moment. Everybody knew it was a problem. All the experts on Freedom News used to say so, back when she watched TV. It was a moral issue. Sandy could talk about moral issues. No problem there.

Check.

Unaffordable entitlements.

Well, if they were unaffordable, they were unaffordable, weren't they? What else was there to say?

Check. This was fun, wasn't it?

Reducing the burden on America's entrepreneurs and small businesses.

Wow, this one hit close to home! To hear Johnny-boy tell it, it was d—n near impossible to make an honest living any more. And the reason was, all the *burdens* that the government put on people. Now, Sandy wasn't so naïve as to think that Johnny-boy always knew what he was doing, but all those failed enterprises and lost jobs — well, she could talk forever about *burdens*.

Check.

She pressed on through the list, gaining confidence as she did so, checking most of the entries. She skipped *Bold action to stabilize the international monetary base*, even though it sounded good, because she had no idea what it meant; and she gave *Harmonization of foreign asset accounting* a miss because it sounded way too technical, however wonderful it might be.

She checked *Dealing with Chinese aggression* because, even though *Dealing with* sounded a bit mealy-mouthed, and despite her shaky knowledge of international politics, she'd had a lot of experience with aggression. In the last year or two, especially.

The last item was *Reconfiguring American exceptionalism for a new century*. That sounded a bit weird. What did it mean? Everyone knew what was exceptional about America — freedom, basically. Why would that need to be *reconfigured?* Perhaps it meant that freedom was under greater threat than ever. It certainly felt like it, sometimes.

Check.

At the bottom of the form was a space where you could pledge a donation. She left that blank.

Setting her pen down with a satisfied sigh, she glanced up at the back wall of the office. There was Mr. Prince himself, pictured in a poster, arms folded, the lights of Manhattan behind him, that kindly smile on his lips and a twinkle — for real or computer-enhanced? — in his eye. The caption underneath read *You Can Count On Me.*

Yes, and *you* can count on *me*, Sandy thought. Although not for a donation, alas. But that face — smooth and solicitous, with its indulgent eyebrows and its beneficently-receding hairline — how could it fail? He looked like America's rich uncle, with a heart of gold.

On a table below the poster was a clear, plastic display case containing some kind of architectural model. Sandy got up and went to inspect it. *Willard G. R. Prince Center for the Performing Arts (proposed), Stimsonville*, she read. Mr. Prince was a philanthropist! Well, of course he was; how small-minded of her to be at all surprised.

"We're waiting for matching funds from the state."

Barbara was back.

"They're pleading poverty, would you believe?"

She picked up Sandy's form and scanned it.

"My! You *are* going to be useful!"

To Sandy's relief, she didn't mention the missing donation.

"Follow me. We'll get you set up with Megan."

Megan was blonde, energetic, thirty-ish and generally spiky. She was the *Phone Bank Manager.*

33

"So it's *Sandy?* Okay. I need ten minutes to set you up on the system. You want to make a coffee run? It's at the end of the block. Get me a skinny latte, Columbian, grande, yeah? Just put your bag under the desk here. Oh, and get me an extra shot in that."

Well, she could hardly refuse, could she? At the coffee shop she handed over her five dollar bill. Megan's coffee cost three dollars, plus another fifty cents for the extra shot.

"Thanks," Megan said, when Sandy handed over the drink. "Where's yours?"

"Oh, I didn't want one."

A white lie, yes — but still a lie.

"I live on coffee. How're your IT skills?"

All those hours in front of the screen with Johnny-boy! Trying to get the numbers to work. And Johnny-boy cursing the machine out.

"Oh, not bad."

"Great. So here's your profile," Megan said, as Sandy settled in behind her desk. "Update it as necessary. The system selects the target, dials the number, tells you if they've answered. You read from the script, *here...*" Megan tapped the screen. "...and, based on how they answer, you click on the nearest matching response *here*. Then the system pops up the next thing you say, and so on. Got it? We'll put it in test mode and see how you do, okay? I'm the voter. Put your headset on."

It was exhilarating!

Megan played one character after another. Sandy read out her questions. Megan replied. Sandy clicked. On they went. Megan — what a smart young woman she seemed to be — got ever more tricky — more vague, more ornery, more combative, more contradictory, and even a little aggressive. Sandy read and clicked, and clicked and read. Eventually, as she seemed to achieve a kind of *flow*, she began to improvise. She didn't understand everything she was reading, but she quickly realized that that wasn't the point: It was all about engaging with the emotions of the target — or the *voter*, rather. And she was *so good* at that!

"Not bad," Megan said, when it was over. "You'll do okay. We'll start you with *leaners*. See what the system says. Then maybe move you up to *switchers*. Have fun!"

And she did.

The hours absolutely flew by in a way that they hadn't for years. The *targets* mostly seemed to respond to her voice. Like Megan's impersonations, they were mixed-up, confused, angry or disheartened. But what really struck Sandy was that — unlike Megan — they *complained*. About their jobs, their incomes, their debts; their mistreatment by boss or bureaucracy; their healthcare, or lack of it; the decline of their neighborhoods or towns. And then something else. It was inchoate and almost unspoken: An overwhelming sense of loss. The loss of *America*.

She did what she could. Absolutely, she understood their concerns, and so did Mr. Prince. But the true communication went on in the modulation of her voice, in its rise and fall, in the pauses and the punctuations; in her living breath itself, it almost felt. She was *feeling their pain*, and they could tell. Yes, and not like you-know-who with some greedy girl under his desk!

A lot of people wanted to talk about China, but, weirdly, the system never gave her anything to say about that. Even though she'd offered to *deal with the aggression*. Maybe it was a bug.

At six o'clock, with a chilly night looming, Megan said it was time to stop. A fresh shift would take over — and drag people away from their dinners, ha-ha!

"So, Sandy. Where're you parked? Want to walk with me?"

"Oh, I didn't drive."

"No? How the hell did you get here? You want a lift?"

"No, I think I'll just —"

"You know it's not safe to walk around here at night, right? I mean, we got that pan-handler deli place shut down, but even so..."

Think, Sandy, think!

"Are you okay?"

But before Sandy could answer, Barbara's oaky-smoky voice rang out from the front of the store.

"Megan! Sandy! You're needed. Follow me."

A sudden emergency had arisen, Barbara explained. The company hired to cater the Pioneers' Reception had fallen down on the job. Extra hands were required, pronto.

Yes, and Mr. Prince would be there in person.

CHAPTER 6

They drove to the Pioneers' Reception in Barbara's Escalade. It was much nicer than Johnny-boy's Malaysian SUV, Sandy thought, though probably not available for no money down and zero per cent interest for the first two years.

The Reception had been organized at the private home of one of Mr. Prince's local backers. It was some home, she thought. If you took ten or twelve of the mini-mansions and stuck them together, and then erased all of the other houses from the subdivision, you might have ended up with something on this scale. It was located to the north of the city, close to the Country Club. Barbara called it the *Danthrope Estate*. Happily for Sandy, their drive did not take them past her erstwhile estate.

Barbara dropped Megan and Sandy off at the rear of the house.

"I guess we're *working* for our suppers tonight," Megan said. "You don't mind, do you?"

"Oh, no."

At the mention of *supper*, she noticed how hungry she was.

"When you get to know Barbara, you'll understand that you just don't say no."

Sandy reckoned she'd got that figured out already. They entered an industrial-scale kitchen. How many people could you feed from a place like this? Probably the whole village, Sandy estimated.

Their job, they were told, was simply to fill in for a couple of *wetbacks* who hadn't shown up. Megan didn't seem to flinch at the word, but it brought a little warmth to Sandy's cheeks. Once, Sandy had been bold enough to venture out loud, in front of Hunter Bill, her take on Donna-Marie's immigration status. Bill, quite rightly, had slapped Sandy down. She remembered his words: *It don't matter a damn, Sandy! She's the phone lady. We need her!*

Anyway, all they had to do was clear tables. And, at the end of the night, Mr. Prince himself would express his appreciation.

"Actually, this could be fun," Megan said. "New experience! D'you think there'll be tips? Hey, with *this* crowd we could clean up!"

Sandy wondered how Megan had put herself through college. Most of Sandy's year had waited tables at some point. And one thing that everyone knew, and Megan apparently didn't, was that the correlation between the wealth of the diner and size of the tip was small.

"Well, let's hope so," she said, adding, "else we'll be stuck down with the low-income people."

Megan laughed. Sandy realised that she'd said something funny. But no, it wasn't funny.

Then the kitchen erupted into hissing, clanging, steamy life and the work began. Sandy showed Megan a few tricks — just enough to save her blushes but not enough to expose Sandy's professionalism. But the waiters and cooks could tell, she thought.

The Pioneers themselves were seated around a table in the shape of a hollow square, outside on a covered, heated terrace. Beyond the terrace were formal gardens, tennis courts and a swimming pool. There were about twenty-five Pioneers — all but two of them men, all of them white, the youngest aged about forty. Mr. Prince was not to be seen; there was a single empty chair.

"What's a Pioneer?" Sandy asked, during a lull.

"Someone who contributes ten million."

"*Ten million?*"

"Not to the campaign, obviously. That's still illegal. To the super-PAC. Oh, and what we're seeing here tonight? That's not *coordination*, okay? In case you're worried."

Well, Sandy *hadn't* been worried — should she be? *Ten million?* It was hard to keep her sense of reality the right way up in this place. She felt almost as if she were floating an inch or two above the marble floors and the forbidding rugs; was it the sheer otherworldliness of the *Danthrope Estate*, or was it just an empty stomach? Perhaps she would wake up in a moment and find that it had rained during the night and her feet were soaked; or, in a better dream, that Johnny-boy was back, and he really had gotten the message this time.

"Barbara's a Pioneer," Megan said. "She took over when her husband died."

"But she's not having dinner?"

"No. Looking after Mrs. P. Poor Willard. I guess everybody has their problems."

"I expect they do."

But what was Mrs. Prince's? Sandy didn't dare ask.

The dinner dragged on, the courses kept coming, the dishes piled up in the kitchen and still Mr. Prince did not appear.

"Where is he?" Sandy asked.

"Oh, he'll just come out and say his thing when they're all done," Megan said. "He's really private, you know? Not a big socializer. It's all one-to-one relationships, so they say."

That might make sense, Sandy thought, recalling her night on the golf course. If Mr. Prince wanted to be President — if he was serious about *saving* the country — he'd want to pick his confidants and advisors carefully. He'd keep his counsel. And he'd need people he could trust, people he really knew. People who got it.

"Want one of these?" Megan asked, offering Sandy an untouched plate of stuffed pastry parcels.

"Oh, do you think we should?"

"It's just going in the garbage. What are they gonna do, fire us?"

"Okay."

She took one. It tasted of... Well, she wasn't sure, but it was rich, creamy, salty and vaguely nutty. She couldn't help herself. She took two more. And then another.

"Well, look at you!" Megan said. "How'd you keep that figure?"

"What's this — slacking on the job?"

That hickory voice — Barbara was back.

"All right, people. It's speech time. Megan — I want you to collect everything. And I *mean*, everything. Sandy, you help. Bring it all to me."

Off she strode, the silky snap of her suit ringing in Sandy's ears.

"What does she mean?"

"Recording equipment," Megan said. "Phones, cameras, any kind of audio or video gear. *Everybody*, especially the staff, okay? Nobody takes chances any more. Not after what happened. Now, what we need is a big plastic sack..."

They started with the kitchen, collecting every device they could find. Then they took to the terrace. The Pioneers knew the game, it seemed. They all found it quite a hoot. Sandy noticed that a very large TV screen had been installed on one side of the terrace, in front of the hot tub.

"What's that for?"

"Hmm. Don't know."

They delivered their bag of contraband tech to Barbara in the garden lounge, then retreated to the kitchen, where they relaxed and ate some more.

"Jesus! I want *your* metabolism," Megan said.

Then, as the kitchen staff labored over the clean-up, Megan lapsed into small talk. Her boyfriend had gotten a job on Wall Street — not with the New American Century Fund like Milly van Dornen, more's the pity, but never mind — and they were planning to move to the city as soon as Hartley found them an apartment. The problem was, you couldn't find anything decent for under one-point-five, so they might just have to start out in Brooklyn. Yes, Hartley *was* a funny name, wasn't it? That was because Hartley was English, and they always had funny names, didn't they? And, besides, his family was very grand, and his father was actually a lord! He'd been so *embarrassed* when he'd told her. And Megan's jaw had practically hit the floor, and so, obviously, Sandy could imagine how jealous Megan's friends were.

Sandy said yes, she could.

And Megan herself hadn't decided yet what she was going to do. After the campaign, she meant. If Mr. Prince won, which Megan felt he was *basically bound to*, given the state of things, perhaps she would offer to work in his private New York office. Though if she wanted to do *that*, she'd have to stay off Barbara's shit list, wouldn't she?

Sandy said yes, she supposed so.

And what plans did Sandy have for life under the new Prince administration — Megan was assuming that Sandy was now with them for the *duration?*

Sandy said that she, too, hadn't decided yet. But, like Megan, she was considering a move.

"You two! Come and see this!"

Barbara's whiskey-dry voice commanded them outside and on to the terrace.

The Pioneers had rearranged their chairs to face the enormous TV screen. Sandy noticed that the table had been cleared but for a single, half-empty wine glass by Mr. Prince's seat. Mr. Prince had been and gone.

At the top of the screen, she saw the words *Inner Mongolia* superimposed over Chinese characters. Below that stood a towering rocket with a red and yellow nose cone. It was the Chinese moon launch! Well, that just went to show how much Hunter Bill *really* knew. He thought he could see the Chinese *up there*, and they hadn't even blasted off yet!

The bottom half of the screen filled with smoke and fire. After a moment of roaring, crackling hesitation, the rocket began its ascent. The Pioneers broke into jeers and ironic applause. A chant of *U-S-A* rose up above the receding grumble of Chinese rocket motors.

Well, it was all very fine landing on the moon, if they wanted to, Sandy thought. But really, didn't the Chinese have bigger priorities back down on Earth? Someone in the camp — not Bill, who seemed to be in awe of China for some reason — had told her that they had to import baby formula, because the local supply was full of poison. Well, they needed to get *that* fixed, didn't they?

While everyone else watched the Chinese rocket vanish into the sky, she went to collect Mr. Prince's wine glass. To reach it, she had to push his chair in. As she did so, something fell from the chair to the floor. She picked it up. It was a hundred dollar bill.

Rule One of waiting tables was that *all tips must be shared*. But was this a tip? It had been on the chair, not the table. Ah, but it might have fallen off the table on to the chair...

She slipped it into her pocket before anyone could register her predicament, and took the wine glass back to the kitchen. It probably was a tip — from Mr. Prince himself. He had *expressed* his *appreciation*. So ought she to share it with the waiters? With Megan? Well, Megan obviously didn't need it, but it went against the principle of the thing to...

But no. No, there was a more convincing explanation. The money was intended for Sandy alone. Mr. Prince had left it on the chair with the specific expectation that she would find it. *He knew.*

So Sandy asked Barbara to drop her off in front of the Stimsonville Bellvue Grand Hotel, whence she would take a taxi home. She bade goodnight to her new colleagues, and promised to be at the campaign HQ on Mellon Street bright and early tomorrow morning, at eight o'clock. She watched the Escalade plough its way through the traffic, and waved until it had disappeared.

Then she walked ten blocks west and checked in at a motel that offered rooms for thirty dollars a night.

She unlocked her room, stepped inside and let her gaze wander. The huge, king-sized bed. Its fresh, white linen. The bathroom, with its shower and hot water. The windows, with their drapes. The door itself, with its lock and its key.

She flung herself on to the bed and cried tears of joy and relief.

Then she remembered that she'd left her shopping bag at the office.

CHAPTER 7

T he eviction began at dawn. And, because Teresa Wolfe happened to be working the daybreak shift, she got to witness it. Teri, as she was known to everyone except the disappointed grandmother in Poughkeepsie for whom she was named, had warmed up the machines, topped up the grinders, and loaded the pastry display cabinet — and this all done with the attentively ironic care due to such matters when the guiding intelligence behind them belonged to a once-soaring, now totally-grounded, thoroughly under-employed and impossibly over-indebted modern-languages graduate of the University of Pennsylvania — when it started.

The TV screens behind the counter were, by management ordinance, supposed to remain tuned to financial channels, so that clients of Bean Village Coffee could pump themselves up on the S&P 500 or the DAX while they waited for their caffeine. But Teri liked to flip one of the screens to Freedom News — for the entertainment value, obviously, but also because the Wall-Streeters — and not just the guys — liked to look at FNN's mega-primped anchors. And Teri thought it was pretty funny, too — watching those money-horny lame-brains ogling the cheese.

The sound was off but the pictures told the story: City authorities had exhausted their patience; the threat to public health could no longer be ignored; business leaders feared for the impact on the local economy; the Mayor had spoken, and now the Robin Hood Party encampment in Battery Park was outta here. Or it would be very shortly, once the requisite muscle and machinery had been marshaled. Not forgetting the legal logistics, of course — although that could be straightened out afterwards, if necessary.

ROBIN HOOD IS HISTORY, she read. And this morning's perky anchor looked pretty pumped about it, too.

Since Pearl Street, where this particular branch of Bean Village was strategically situated, lay but a short jog downhill to the Battery, and as Pedro and Aliyah had shown up on the dot — they had a better attendance record than Teri, but so what? — Teri decided that this particular scene would be *way too good to miss*. So, offering up the convincing cover-story that she just needed to *run a quick errand*, she left her post, slipped on her old Penn jacket, took to her heels and headed south.

Thanks to FNN, she made it to the park before the cops had finished putting up their barricades. But wait, wait, wait — *were* they cops? A lot of them wore black uniforms with a weird logo. Fairmeadow Solutions? What the hell was that? Well, whatever. The word had gotten out and the camp — look at the size of it now! — was in a ferment.

Teri dodged her way through the mêlée and secured a position at the eastern edge of the park, close to the ferry terminal. This, she figured, offered her the best chance of slipping away if — when — things got nasty. Dressed in her Bean Village chinos and Ivy League sweats, she didn't look much like a Robin-Hooder, and, if challenged, she would say that she was on her way to Staten Island to help her disabled grandmother. She jumped on to the seat of a park bench — the type that had multiple arm-rests to pre-empt sleepers — took out her phone and flipped it into video mode.

Start with a slow, cool, tracking shot across the site, she thought. Get all the tents, the banners, the stoves, the musical performers, the mime artists, the hippies, the dreads, the anti-capitalists, the anarchists... Were they really anarchists? They seemed awfully well behaved. Now also get the anticipation, the mounting excitement, the little panic attacks — people stashing their valuables — and all the natural, automatic defense mechanisms of an organism sensing imminent attack. She ought to get some neat footage, she thought, if the phone had enough memory left. The global clampdown reaches Manhattan, and Teri Wolfe captures it live!

On the far side of the encampment, a line of police vehicles drew up. Out got the cops, in no particular hurry it seemed, adjusting their helmets and visors. Then, to her right, in front of the ferry terminal, she saw a phalanx of black vans. That logo again — the jaunty sun and the luscious grass. She panned and zoomed. Out of the vans came black-clad men — and honestly, there was nothing wrong with calling them *goons*. God, she thought, these Fairmeadow crowd-busters were even better kitted out than the cops; they looked like movie extras.

She zoomed in further: No ID on them at all, how about that? Unlike the cops, they got straight down to it. Their mission was pretty obvious: Grab the ring-leaders. They knew who they wanted: Their leader had pictures, and he knew how to point. In they went, in groups of five — what did you call that, was it *snatch squad?*

Teri zoomed and focused. On the far side of the park the cops were lined up, still waiting. Waiting for Fairmeadow to complete their surgical extraction?

But the Robin-Hooders were on to the game now. The noise went up — yelling, crying, shrieking, desperately reasonable exasperation, breaking voices — and the fighting started. Still the cops waited. Maybe this was the time to slip away? While being an innocent bystander was still just about plausible? No, she couldn't: This was too big; this was Teri Wolfe living in history, not Teri Wolfe forgetting to sprinkle the chocolate or breaking another twenty.

The Fairmeadow goons looked like they'd gotten what they came for. They were dragging their prey back to where the vans stood, engines running. A Chinese girl, with shoulder-length hair. A young black guy, trying to help her, pushed to the ground. This whole ring-leader thing, though, was bogus. Everybody knew that — except for Freedom News, to whom it was obvious, as usual, that foreign instigators had ginned the entire thing up and taken in a whole generation of lazy, gullible, slacker air-heads. As something of a slacker herself — yes, she admitted it, what else was she supposed to be five years out of college and three years out of hope? — Teri knew that the Robin-Hooders disdained leadership or hierarchy the way they reviled Wall Street, Washington, the Pentagon and, yes, Bean Village itself. That was why they all wore those shirts: *I Am Robin Hood.*

Okay, now there were small explosions going off. Was that smoke or gas? And junk and garbage were being thrown. The cops looked like they were readying themselves. A few more frames of video, she thought, then down off the bench and into the ferry terminal and safety.

She finished her video and slipped the phone into her jacket, but then changed her mind and stuffed it into the rear, button-down pocket of her chinos. Then she jumped.

But she went nowhere. There was an instant of *huh?* Then she went up, and backwards off the bench. There were three of them, and they had her, all hundred-and-nineteen pounds of her, by the arms and legs. They were heading for the black vans. She started to kick.

"Get the phone!"

She felt hands on her butt. Gloved hands that couldn't undo the button. *Stupid!* She kicked some more. Her feet came free and hit the ground. Then she unzipped her jacket, shimmied out, and left them holding it.

And, being small, light, agile, shit-scared and incredibly pissed, she was sliding through the mob before they could lift their visors.

She ran all the way back to Pearl Street, which at least prevented her from freezing. But the atmosphere in the coffee shop turned out to be, well, *chilly.* According to Pedro, the regional office in Trenton had been calling for her — and calling, and calling — and wanted to hear back from her about this errand she'd been running for the last hour and a half. *Shit!* The last thing she wanted was another lecture from frigging *Trenton.* Let them do their worst. Pedro and Aliyah shook their heads with the kind of knowing sadness, Teri thought, that only legal aliens could really get away with.

The TV screens had been flipped back to financial news, and Teri didn't feel like pushing her luck any further, so she went into the store room, shutting the door behind her, and replaced the memory card in her phone with a new one. She hid the old one under a ten pound can of French Roast. Nobody liked French Roast, so Teri never put it on the menu. After that she put her apron on, breathed deeply until her heart-rate returned to normal, and then wandered back out into the store to see if anyone wanted to order a coffee.

And the day dragged on like it always did, until...

"Teresa Wolfe! Oh my God!"

Shi—it! It was Teri's least-favorite former college room-mate, last seen at graduation chugging Krug in a Jaguar with some dunce from Yale, Milly van frigging Dornen. It had to be some cosmic joke. But it wasn't a very funny one.

"Hi, Milly. Long time. How are you?"

"I'm great! Everything's going really *well*. Life's really *wonderful*, and all that. So! Wow! I, ah... Are you..."

All right, come on, let's get it over with, Teri thought.

Milly frowned, ever so slightly, but her smile remained intact.

"Are you... Are you, like, *working* here? Or something?"

Or something — meaning Milly could not compute.

Teri glanced down at her Bean Village apron, wrinkled her nose, then looked up again at her wide-eyed, open-mouthed varsity pal.

"Yup. Looks like it."

Milly seemed mystified, but also pepped-up and eager, as if someone had proposed a surprise visit to Bergdorf Goodman.

"Oh! Uh, cool. But why? What's the thinking?"

The thinking?

"It's just a job, Milly. I do it for the money. Everybody needs a job."

No, she shouldn't have said that. It was slightly bitchy. It had never been a secret that Milly van Dornen would never need to work.

"Well, sure. Even me — hah, hah!"

"You have a job?"

"Oh, absolutely. You better believe it! I'm slaving away nine-to-five, just like... Just like everybody else."

Nine-to-five? Who did she think she was? Dolly Parton?

"So what are you doing?"

"PR."

"Who for?"

"New American."

"I don't know what you mean."

"Oh, the New American Century Fund. You know, Willard Prince?"

All right, that made sense. Milly's ma had some longstanding and close connection to the famous plutocrat. It had been the source of a lot of scabrous humor at Penn, which Milly hadn't appreciated.

"That's really impressive! Well done!"

Oh, the snarkiness! What a total witch she was sometimes. But Milly didn't seem to notice; she still hadn't solved the mystery du jour.

"But why a coffee shop?"

Teri sighed and wiped her hands on her apron.

"It's tough out there, Milly."

Milly's face creased with sympathy.

"Yeah, I *heard* that."

There was a pause. Teri couldn't stop herself drumming her fingers on the counter.

"So what you're saying... So this is, like, *all* you could get?"

"Uh-huh."

The smile, at last, had gone. Teri instantly wished it would come back. But Milly was thinking. Her eyes glazed over and her brain seemed to take a short vacation.

"Oh my God! You know what?"

"What?"

Milly lowered her voice and leaned forward across the counter. The smile came back. Teri stopped tapping.

"I heard them talking in the office yesterday. I think there might be an opening..."

"What do you mean, an *opening?*"

"A job. A *proper* job! Oh my God, Teri! You'd be perfect!"

"Milly —"

"No, listen to me, Teri, listen. We were always, like, the best of friends, and I don't really know how we got separated? Okay? I mean, I searched for you online, but... But this is great! We can make a new start. You know, the adventure continues and all that?"

The adventure?

Milly took out her phone. It resided in a bejeweled emerald case.

"So. Give me your number."

Oh, what the hell...

Teri recited it and Milly tapped it in.

"And your social —"

"I'm not online much, these days."

"No problem. Cool. So I'll get back to you on that."

"That's fabulous. Thanks, Milly."

There was a long pause, during which they looked at each other and Milly smiled and Teri didn't.

"Okay, then!" Milly said, at length. "Um, I'm just gonna have an espresso? Do you have French Roast?"

"No. Sorry. Kenya or Columbian."

"Kenya?"

"Coming up. Anything to eat?"

Milly shook her head.

"Not really."

So then Milly handed over a twenty and Teri handed back the change. She got Milly's espresso, which Milly chugged in one, still smiling.

"Okay, gotta go! This is so great!"

A skip to the door, a wave, a flounce of her designer top-coat and she was gone.

Later that afternoon Trenton called to announce that Teri was fired.

And, shortly after that, a text message arrived, inviting Teri to an interview the next morning at an address on Park Avenue.

Park Avenue?

CHAPTER 8

Ricky Ponton winced at his reflection in a pristine expanse of glass as he strode through Chek Lap Kok airport. In order to pass as the respectable British banker "David Thatcher" he'd had to smarten himself up. Amongst other things, this meant wearing a suit — something he hadn't done for twenty years. He didn't find all this fakery too convincing himself, but Jay Percival, the freelance American pot-stirrer and Ricky's new accomplice, had judged it *fine and dandy*.

He passed without effort and with supreme efficiency through a perfectly air-conditioned immigration hall.

Then came the long ride though the smog that seeped down from the factories of the Pearl river delta. In a retro-plasticky, red Toyota taxi, Ricky sped between aggressive outgrowths of gargantuan residential towers, past monstrous container ports, over dizzying suspension bridges, across Lantau to the swarming Kowloon traffic and the Majestic Harbor Hotel. To pass the time, he fretted about what Jay had openly admitted to be the *possibility of a set-up*.

But how likely was it that Jay's *frenemies* at his former *office* would attempt to grab an Australian citizen, albeit one masquerading as a Brit fat-cat, on Chinese territory? If you were talking Italy or Germany, say, Ricky would have said *too bloody risky, mate*, right from the outset. But China? If you thought the US was touchy about sovereignty, try the Chinese — yet another sphere in which the Yanks were being out-done. If it were ever to emerge that a rendition team had operated on Chinese soil — even, perhaps especially, in Hong Kong — the diplomatic consequences, to say the least, would be ugly. And Jay had promised that, in extremis, there would be ugliness aplenty. The relevant parties, he said, had already had their cages rattled.

Then again, shipping Ricky out, were he to be nabbed, would be a cinch: He'd just driven past one of the biggest container ports in the world.

So the question was, how much did they hate him? Well, it wasn't just Kerri's Air-Sea Battle blow-up and subsequent trip to Heartbreak Hotel. Consider the highlights from the charge sheet...

Video from the War Zones, showing helicopters shooting up an unarmed crowd, and drones bombing the wrong house.

Classified military medical reports, with related internal investigations attached, pertaining to deceased detainees.

Whistle-blower complaints, documented in full, describing high-level knowledge of, and complicity in, host country abuses.

The hypocritical accommodations of European governments to said abuses, plus records of suspicious aircraft movements.

Incriminating money trails that flowed like the Amazon into Latin American politics.

Suitcase cash, disbursed to handy warlords and convenient tyrants.

Illegal surveillance of ethnic, religious and political groups; infiltration, provocation and entrapment.

Internal State Department communications in which America's top diplomats said what they really thought about the clowns and crooks who ran the rest of the world.

Sometimes Ricky thought that it was the last of these that really got to them. As for the first three, didn't bad things always happen in war? Yes. And that was one more reason why you didn't want to start the bloody wars in the first place.

People had a right to know. They might not *want* to know, they might not *listen*, and they might still vote for the *same bastards*, but truth had a value all its own. Think back through the catalog of horrors that comprised the last three centuries. Then think about pretending it never happened.

Or, alternatively, try to get a grip, Ricky; it's espionage today, not agit-prop essays for crummy student mags.

The Majestic Harbor Hotel swung into view. Ricky hopped out of the taxi and took in the fuzzy panorama that spread across the water before him to the rampant verticality of Hong Kong island. Why did he suddenly feel lifted — almost intoxicated — with notions of freedom and progress? Paradoxical, eh?

And when he reappraised the same outlook from his hotel room, those feelings morphed into shock and — yes, why not? — awe. He'd been to Hong Kong a few times, under his own flag, before he'd been warned off. The city seemed to rebuild itself between visits. They were even filling in the harbor to make more land.

Jay, the cashed-up Yank, clearly hadn't attempted to save money on the room. It was spectacular, full of gadgets and equipment, all of which, Ricky found, could be controlled from a tablet computer. This same device now welcomed Mr. David Thatcher to the Majestic Harbor Hotel and recommended that he sample the authentic Cantonese delights to be obtained at the Heavenly Garden rooftop restaurant — and *touch here, please*, for the menu. Ricky touched. The menu impressed as much as the room. *Ganchao Niu He* for three hundred Hong Kong dollars. What was that in Aussie? Forty-five? Or about fifty US. Not bad for a plate of beef and noodles. Good thing Jay was paying. And where *had* the bastard got all that money from anyway? Was it true that the CIA had its own printing press? That was one secret he'd love to possess.

He selected a Tsingtao from among the fake English beers in the mini-bar, and wondered what happened next. His only instruction from Jay, or anyone, had been to show up and *see what happened*. Then he noticed the envelope on the bed.

Aha! This would be it. He was a *spy* now, according to Jay, so he was fully prepared to chuck on a dinner suit and bow tie, take a chauffeured Rolls Royce limo to the waterfront, jump in a speedboat — piloted by either a nifty bird in a bikini, or else some stiff-necked Royal Navy type — and permit himself to be piped on board an upside-down, submerged ocean liner, now refurbed as your ultimate spy HQ, where he would be served either a G&T or a cup of tea, plus all the secrets he could eat.

He ripped open the envelope. It appeared to contain a bus ticket. How disappointing. But all was not lost — it was a ticket for one of those hop-on, hop-off, open-top red tourist buses. On the accompanying map, one of the stops had been circled, and a date and time had been written alongside: Four o'clock that afternoon. Fair enough; he didn't mind a free bus ride. It was a perfectly pleasant thing to do on a lazy Sunday, even if the smog did knock a couple of hours off his life. But would the *guy* be among his fellow riders, or would it be the gang from the *office?*

He took a stroll through the lingering haze, amid swarms of excited, prosperous-looking visitors from the mainland, reacquainting himself with Kowloon, and noting all the new restaurants, hotels, shopping malls and office towers that had managed to wedge themselves in around the teeming — and now pricey — tenements of the old town. Look what the Brits had given up! Not that they'd had any choice, and quite right too. Wasn't there an old Chinese saying? Something about the boot being on the other foot?

He wandered through the park in Tsim Sha Tsui, the site of a fort grabbed by the British in 1861, when Kowloon had been occupied. The fort had overlooked Victoria Harbor and was thus a strategic asset. Not much use now, Ricky thought — all those towers in the way.

Then he slogged through the shopping crowds up and down Nathan Road, and wondered if he'd ever seen such a rip-roaring display of full-on capitalism. It made Sydney look like a sleepy, provincial town. What was the name of that Brit politico who liked to go on about the *global race?* Dream on, mate.

Finally, having checked the time on the special phone that Jay had given him, he made his way down to the Star Ferry Pier, took his place on the upper deck to avoid the worst of the diesel fumes, and made the fifteen-minute crossing to *Central*. Once there, he followed a short but complicated route along elevated walkways to the Bus Stop of Destiny.

Ricky Ponton, *international spy*, waiting for a bus! Hilarious, right? Had James Bond ever taken public transport? And what, if anything, did our Ricky have in common with that great avatar of post-imperial denial? Nothing — not the height, the hair or the teeth; not the looks, the clothes, the sex-appeal or the sexism; not the class — not by a long chalk; not the self-confidence or the violence; no establishment to dress him down, but then pick up the bills and pay his pension; low, dirty politics in place of diamond-class patriotism; no deniability, gadgets or backup; and he couldn't really do the accent anyway, whatever Jay thought.

Oh, but wait, there was one thing, wasn't there — a relentless bloody-mindedness, not to be confused with Ricky's visceral anti-authoritarianism (which was a feature, not a bug). Now consider Ricky's global network of powerful, truth-telling computers, which, respectable opinion said, threatened to undermine democracy and bring down the established order — and maybe he really was the villain, after all? He even liked cats.

All right, calm down, he thought; here it comes — just get on the bloody bus and *see what happens*. He climbed on board, collected his headphones, ascended to the upper deck, finding that he had it to himself, and took a seat at the rear. Perhaps the bus would fill up en route. He plugged his headphones in and selected *GB-English*.

A loop around the International Financial Centre, a building so generous that, were it to fall over, it might almost have filled in the harbor and created a land bridge to Kowloon, and the bus headed east. Alongside the PLA building — a construction from the latter days of the colonial period that resembled a rotating air-purifier (if only!) on a pedestal — the bus paused. According to Ricky's map, this wasn't an official stop, and the Sunday traffic was light. Perhaps he was supposed to admire the architecture? The commentary informed him that this was the Hong Kong headquarters of the Chinese People's Liberation Army, and left it at that.

The bus moved on. A small, gray-haired man in a beige wind-cheater appeared at the top of the stairs, avoided looking at Ricky, and took a seat at the covered front end of the bus. Ricky watched. Was this the *guy?* Really? He's our mind-blowing, epoch-making whistle-blower from the PLA, and he gets on the bus outside the PLA HQ? What was the Chinese for chutzpah? But this guy, whoever he might be, wasn't a member of the *nomenklatura* — they liked their hair glossy black.

The bus rolled on. Assertive and declarative, the commentary made up for what it lacked in historical perspective with twangy music. But the *guy* wasn't listening. He sat still, looking neither left nor right. Could he see Ricky's reflection in the bus's window? And was that a hearing aid, or what?

The bus progressed. But it did not fill up. As far as Ricky could tell, most stops were moderately peopled with eager tourists, but they weren't getting on. At the harbor-dominating convention center in Wan Chai, a young Chinese man in a bulky jacket made a point of ignoring Ricky before parking himself six rows from the front on the right. No girlfriend? Mum not trekking down from Sichuan after all, and the ticket too good to waste?

At Victoria Park, a second young man boarded and sat on the left, three rows behind the first. Well, we know there's a shortage of girls on the mainland, Ricky thought; no need to go into the reasons why. And these loners had a similar taste in fashion, too.

When the third got on at Gloucester Road, and sat three rows in front of him, Ricky decided that he had a problem. When the bus got to the Peak Tram stop, assuming nothing had happened by that point, he would make a break for it. Everyone who came to Hong Kong wanted to see the view from the Peak — from which, these days, you could practically see the edge of the American empire receding — and there was almost certain to be a big crowd.

But when it got there, the bus pulled up short of the stop, disconcerting its expectant crowd by pausing long enough only to admit a tall, sallow westerner in a gray raincoat, who elected to remain downstairs. Ricky sank back into his seat. That knocked it on the head, didn't it? The tunneling works in his stomach, suspended since Broken Hill, powered up again.

The bus moved on, edging past the landmark tower of a world-power bank. The dingy plaza under the skirts of the building teemed with people, almost all of them young women. Of course — it was Sunday. The city's three hundred thousand Filipina maids received one day off a week; they got chucked out of the house and the international financial elite sourced their own lunches. Enjoy your freedom, ladies, he thought.

He was about to rip off his headphones when the twanging music stopped and a different kind of twang took over.

"This is a message for Mr. Ricky Ponton, if he happens to be a passenger with us on this bus. Your tour will be ending early today. We apologize for the inconvenience."

The gray-haired man at the front of the bus had turned around. He talked into his wrist and gave Ricky a glare of informed disapproval. *Shit!* What now? Jay's final recommendation had been to *ditch the phone* if he got into trouble. So he looked down over the side of the bus, and what he saw there surprised him.

He saw a heavy, yellow dump truck — the kind of machine that belonged on a construction site. The really surprising thing, though, was what it carried in the back: A small girl in pink jeans and a Hello Kitty hoody. And a mattress. The girl caught his gaze and pulled open her hoody. She wore a T-shirt decorated with the Big Data Underground logo — a stylized baby hyena operating a computer (it wasn't Ricky's idea, but people liked it).

No, no, he thought; *that's* not going to happen.

The truck growled and sputtered three meters behind the bus, in the right-hand lane. They were on Des Voeux Road, in the gridlock zone. The bus edged forward. Looking up again, Ricky saw that the two young men were on their feet, and the American with the twang now stood at the head of the stairs.

There came a grinding, splintering sound from below; the dump truck had shunted a silver BMW out of its path and now stood parallel — just about — to the bus.

"Jump now!" the girl yelled. "Or forget it."

He ripped off his headphones and jumped.

What happened next passed in an agonizing blur, because several different portions of him impacted the truck in a way that wasn't optimal. But it felt as if the truck had reversed away, scattering the traffic behind it, and then barreled, horn blaring, the wrong way down a one-way side street. He lay back and tried to flex his right leg.

But he didn't get to enjoy the mattress for long.

"Get out, get out!"

The Hello Kitty girl was yanking on his arm. He hauled himself to his knees, shuffled forward, and allowed her to shove him off the back. And did he imagine it, or did the driver actually *tip* him out, too? Either way, he was on his arse in the middle of the road without much more effort on his part.

But not for long; she had him on the move again, dragging him by the wrist. They went into an office building, up a short escalator and then on to a much longer one that seemed as though it might ascend all the way up into some Heavenly Garden in the sky.

"Stand up!"

Was he not standing? Ah, no — *get up, Ricky!*

All right, now he got it: This was the mid-levels escalator. It went all the way from Des Voeux up to Conduit Road. Under cover, too. It was supposed to cut down on traffic. But the bankers who lived on the mid-levels had stayed in their cars.

They didn't go all the way up. Hello Kitty Girl dragged him off about half way. They stumbled through walkways, passageways, shopping arcades, designer malls; over covered bridges; past multi-story car parks; up and down escalators — and everywhere, everywhere... The maids. They sat together in their multitudes, talking, cooking, eating, drinking, singing, sewing, playing games, waiting to be let back into the house.

Then, just as Ricky began to think he would prefer to flop down with the maids and take his chances, they entered an office tower and ascended to the fortieth floor.

In a smart and spacious suite with views over the harbor, Ricky was offered a cup of *Iron Goddess* tea; was instructed that Hello Kitty Girl's name was Xin Jiao; and was further informed that Xin Jiao was a senior counter-intelligence specialist with the People's Liberation Army.

And when Ricky had finished his tea, Jiao said, there would be an opportunity for him to answer some questions.

CHAPTER 9

No, Xin Jiao said, flicking her lustrous fringe and looking to Ricky more like the lead singer in a Chinese punk-pop girl-band than a big cheese in military counter-intelligence, there was no *guy*. There had never been a *guy*.

Ricky had been more or less straight about his mission — a too-tasty, too-good-to-miss and now too-good-to-be-true mega-leak opportunity for Big Data Underground — neither mentioning Jay Percival, nor admitting that the flavor of the day had been specifically military. There didn't seem to be anything to be gained by holding back; Jiao knew who he was — she was even wearing his T-shirt. And even though they were in an office suite and not a military prison, Ricky couldn't scoot — Jiao had a couple of young guys in jeans and leather jackets loitering by the door. They looked like her backup musicians.

This girl, who could have been his daughter's school-friend — if he'd had a daughter, or, indeed, a wife or a family or any kind of social life that couldn't be encrypted for safe-keeping at his disaster recovery site in Iceland — made him feel, all at once, happy to be alive and depressed about the future. Happy, because the Chinese had got him and not the Americans — there was no question as to which interest he'd offended most, so far, and Jiao had given him tea, not a freezing shower — and also because, if he were now finished, then at least he'd gone out in decent spy style. But then depressed, because this girl, with her super-smartness and her super-competence, wore his T-shirt, he felt sure, with an extreme and very modern irony. And her hair, her blushing cheeks, and her cartoon-cute nose might just be, he thought, the pretty face of some global authoritarianism to come.

"So you wanted some secrets?" she said.

Her gave her a wan smile and nodded.

"But it was a set-up."

Yes, of course it was a set-up. Thanks, Jay.

"And we snatch you from the jaws of the Americans!"

"Mm. Thanks for that."

"You didn't finish your bus tour."

"No. What was the point of the bus, anyway?"

Jiao swiveled in her chair.

"They thought you might have other contacts in Hong Kong. So they used the bus like a..." She consulted one of her helpers. "Yes, it's in their emails. They call it a *roach motel*. We researched this. It means —"

"I get it," Ricky said. Ricky *the cockroach*.

"And they can't grab you on the street. Too many people notice."

"Someone probably noticed that truck of yours."

A stern flick of the fringe.

"We can deal with that."

Ricky leaned back in his chair, took a deep breath and exhaled slowly, relishing the lingering perfume of the tea.

"So what now?"

Jiao didn't reply, but the corners of her mouth puckered. What was so amusing?

"Didn't we just have, you know, an *international incident?*"

"No," she said, serious now. "Not at all. They don't want one. We don't want one. Very bad for everyone. *Nationalism*, you understand? We don't want to have to control our people. And they can't control their politicians. So nothing happened."

"Nothing?"

Jiao shook her head.

"Well, what about me?"

How likely was it that Jiao had plucked Ricky from the righteous fire and plied him with exquisite tea just for the hell of it? And even though she would, no doubt, uphold Chinese sovereignty until Yangtze ran dry, didn't she, just like Jay, want something?

"You wanted some secrets," she said.

He stared at her. The fringe had settled in place, as if it had made its mind up.

No, no, he thought. That's not how it works. *You* don't give me tea and secrets. *I* get them from sources, and *I* expose corruption, abuse and hypocrisy, and *I'm* a bloody hero. Not a stooge. Not a propaganda mouthpiece. Not another willing bloody helper for the clampdown, and lock me up if you don't like it. He almost said that last bit out loud.

But if Jiao had spotted the indignation in his soul, she didn't let on.

"We do a lot of hacking here," she said. "It's very patriotic. Good fun. Nice job for a girl who used to work on a farm. You think so, too? Yes, we like it here."

Work on a farm? Well, why not? This was China, the land of opportunity and social mobility, where you could rise to the top with nothing but a dream and an uncle with a red telephone.

"We don't hack *you*, of course. Well, we try — but you are too clever."

Reassuring? Not really. This girl was beginning to terrify him.

"So. We have some secrets for you. We think you will really like them. Now we will show you."

Jiao must have flipped some secret switch under her desk, because the office's floor-to-ceiling windows now became opaque and an opulent screen attached to the wall activated itself. Jiao got up and began to tap and swipe at it. Ricky turned

54

his chair to the left and watched. As he did so, a chill — or was it a thrill? — ran down his indignant spine. This farm girl had harvested some of the finest IP addresses on the market — even some that were masked, proxied and buggered about with so much that you practically needed a supercomputer just to get in.

"You know *this* one, I think?"

He certainly did.

A teasing brush of the fringe.

"Yes. But too good for you, I think. For now. Such a greedy man! We find something else."

More swiping and tapping.

"Ah, look here!"

Jiao had opened up a trove of corporate emails. They belonged to a big, state-owned Chinese telecoms and computer hardware company.

"You know this company, Weihan?"

"Yeah, I've heard of it."

If you searched Ricky's database for *Weihan*, you noticed that it was a popular target for the patriotic ire of those members of the US congress who thought that Chinese tech companies wanted to bug the shit out of the US, and should therefore be shut out of the US market — which was most of them.

Jiao had stuck her thumbs in the pockets of her pink jeans, and was twisting on her heel, as if she were on a first date but trying to act cool.

"Do you like this?"

Could be interesting, he thought. But wasn't there a slight problem here?

"Um, Jiao — why exactly would you want to give *me* insider dirt on one of your biggest state-owned —"

The thumbs came out of their pockets so that Jiao could hold up her hands to *stop him right there*. She gave him a scowl that obscured her faux-innocence for a long moment.

"Not state-owned! Not any more. Now we have your..."

She really didn't want to say the word, did she?

"...your *privatization* in China."

"Is that right?"

"We don't call it that."

"Okay."

"Weihan wants to work in America. They want to cooperate with American companies."

"Cooperate? Or take over?"

Jiao shrugged.

"So they cannot be state-owned. If Weihan is *private*, the Americans are happy."

"Should they be?"

Jiao turned back to her screen and resumed her tapping and swiping.

Why would the PLA want to dish the dirt on a top Chinese tech company? What would Ricky be getting into if he went along with this? Or if he didn't?

Jiao's presentation proceeded through a collection of Chinese tech firms, industrial conglomerates and banks. All, Ricky was given to understand, had filthy secrets that ought to be shown the light of day. Jiao said that it was necessary to *discipline* those who failed to acknowledge the Party's new, tougher strictures on corruption, even if it had to be done in unconventional ways.

Ricky found it hard to believe that the Party was afraid of its own capitalists — but perhaps the times were changing? He noted that all of these supposedly wayward enterprises were private; and he recalled Mr. Lin's puzzling discovery that Party chiefs were worried about *inappropriate relations* between Chinese and American business interests.

"Mind if I make a call?" he asked, when Jiao had finished and was preparing fresh tea.

"Go ahead."

Ricky installed himself in a private corner of the office and called Jay. He described his bus ride, and Jay laughed. Then he explained his new predicament, and Jay fell silent.

"Well?"

"I'm thinking," Jay said.

"You see, what I think," Ricky said, "is, if I *don't* do it, they'll —"

"You better do it. Besides, I need you back here."

"All right."

"Yeah. So get back, soon as you can. I gotta send you to Madagascar. Take care."

He hung up before Ricky could respond. *Madagascar?* Did Jay say *Madagascar?* Should Ricky call back? No, deal with it later. Drink some more tea. Promise to love and obey Jiao, and be careful not to dis the Party.

Then get the hell out of here and spend some more of Jay's hot cash.

He sipped his tea. Jiao pushed a memory stick across the table.

"Put this on your web site."

He slipped the memory stick into his shirt pocket.

"I'll have to run it by some people first."

"Of course. This is all true. No forgeries. No fakes."

"Sure. Leave it to me."

Jiao leaned forward and parted her fringe so that Ricky wouldn't have any trouble seeing her eyes.

"You have seen what we can do here."

"Yes. Very impressive."

"You have a very nice web site. It is shameful if something happens to it."

"*A* shame."

She blushed.

"Excuse me?"

Kids, he thought.

"It would be *a* shame."

"That is what I am saying."

"Right. No worries, then. Got the message."

He finished his tea.

"Any chance of a lift back to the hotel?"

"Of course."

And so, later that evening, ensconced in his very own, very private nook in the Heavenly Garden, Ricky Ponton rewarded himself with a plate of *Ganchao*

Niu He for fifty American dollars, and a bottle of Hardy's Special Reserve to go with it.

Then he sat back, looked up into the swirling, illuminated murk of the night sky, soothed his raw throat with a slug of wine, and asked himself what could possibly be going on in Madagascar. Not that it mattered; whatever crackpot proposal Jay had in mind now, it wasn't going to happen. No bloody lemurs for Ricky. Perhaps a holiday in Norway?

But *Madagascar?* What was in Ricky's database? A military-backed coup, to be followed by delayed elections that never quite happened. And then, when they *did*, and the long-suffering Malagasy people got themselves a shiny new President, disputed results meant that the wrangling went on — two camps, equally corrupt and venal, in a proxy fight, with the *international community* posing as referee but mostly distracted by more violent events elsewhere. Pretty much what you'd expect. So what, then?

And thus at length, with shameful reluctance, when he'd exhausted all possible theories and contingencies, he put down his glass, pushed his plate away, and thought about what Kerri Law would be doing for dinner tonight.

CHAPTER 10

Sandy Quayle slept the sleep of the weary striver — something she had once been, and was determined to be again. But only until three in the morning, according to the clock-radio combo that was bolted to the night stand by her motel bed.

Awake with a vengeance, the final frames of her dream fading fast — Johnny-boy signing his way through a stack of loan documents while Hunter Bill and the sheriff built a hideous bonfire in their front yard — she felt her stomach cramp with hunger. She really hadn't been able to eat that much at the Pioneers' Reception; the opportunities had been limited, and, towards the end of the evening, Megan had begun to look at her funny.

But she felt seized with the knowledge that, were she to walk two blocks west, she would find herself standing before an all-night waffle house.

How much money did she have left? After all, she was back in the world of money now, and it was time to get serious.

Well, she'd started the day with five dollars. Then she'd spent three dollars and fifty cents on Megan's coffee from Bean Village. That left a dollar fifty. But then had come Mr. Prince's hundred dollar bill — the one that had so impressed the motel clerk. The room had cost thirty. Thus her total net worth, excluding the clothes she'd worn all day and the contents of her shopping bag — left behind at the office, worryingly — was seventy-one dollars and fifty cents. If she spent two more nights at the motel, her net worth would shrink to eleven fifty. Or perhaps zero, if Megan drank as much coffee as she claimed. And that left nothing for food.

The conclusion was inexorable: She could only afford one more night of luxury.

That being so, she offered up a silent, preventative prayer against gluttony, and yielded.

At the waffle house the order she gave to her server — Maria, according to her name tag — comprised eggs over-easy, hash browns, Colonel Jack's sausage, and bacon, for nine dollars and twenty-five cents; root beer for a dollar thirty; and cinnamon apple pie with whipped cream on the side, for four dollars ninety-five. Total cost of meal: Fifteen dollars and fifty cents. This would collapse her net worth to fifty-six dollars exactly. But it would be worth it. She hadn't eaten like this for — how long now? — it must have been more than two years. And it would be at least twenty-four hours before she got this hungry again.

Maria, though she looked exhausted, delivered Sandy's food with a friendliness and solicitude that Sandy felt she didn't deserve, and that didn't even seem like management policy. There were food stains on Maria's skirt. Had she noticed? Sandy considered a tactful aside, but decided against it.

After she'd finished her meal and declined coffee or tea — never mind gluttony, she felt nauseous from the cream — Sandy lingered in the restaurant, watching the other diners and reflecting on her changed circumstances. Maria kept an eye on her, but didn't seem to mind.

After a decent interval, she brought the check and left it on the table.

Sandy's first day as part of Mr. Prince's campaign for President had been a success, had it not? Barbara's initial aloofness and skepticism had been overcome. Megan, a young woman with big-city aspirations, who might have disdained a small-town volunteer twenty years her senior, and who refused to be intimidated by the lower end of the Manhattan real estate market, had, nonetheless and perhaps despite herself, been captivated by Sandy's performance as a telephone canvasser. The *system*, after all, had spoken. And everyone knew that computers now ruled the world.

Mr. Prince certainly knew that. Sandy had gathered, from the chatter in the office, that the astonishing and *consistent* success of Mr. Prince's New American Century Fund depended largely on its deployment of computer technology. Whatever software it was that Mr. Prince had developed, it was miles ahead of the competition and a source of immense bafflement to them. So valuable was Mr. Prince's chief Software Architect, in fact, that his contract was said to be the most enviable pair of *golden handcuffs* in the business. Of course, the machines could only do so much on their own; they worked their alchemy under the guidance of Mr. Prince's *bespoke strategy*. The general parameters of this strategy were known, Sandy was told, but not the details. And of course, the Devil — Sandy knew this for sure, didn't she? — was right there, in the details. No other investment shop could replicate Mr. Prince's strategy, and so it was this dual advantage — the *algorithms* combined with that unique brain — that made the New American Century Fund more exclusive than any country club in America.

Observing her fellow diners in the waffle house, Sandy figured that she probably stood a better chance of getting into the NACF than any of them. Mostly solitary, preoccupied and hunched over their food, they were surely as price-sensitive as any of Mr. Prince's computers, albeit in a different way.

Beyond the enticing, neon-rimmed windows of the restaurant, traffic on the main route west out of town was light: Mostly eighteen-wheelers and sagging pickups that, Sandy guessed, needed to be somewhere by dawn.

Sandy felt herself balanced between invisibility and this twilight world of work. Which way would she fall? The diners in the waffle house were simply refueling, with as little joy as the eighteen-wheelers felt when they filled their tanks, before submitting again to the grind. They were America's sinews, but you could see that they had atrophied. All power, all vigor, had been appropriated.

The *system* preferred to talk to voters about renewal and reinvigoration, but sometimes, for a certain kind of target, it would assert the need to *take back our country*. Though she was wary of populism and recoiled from anger, Sandy felt in her soul that there was something in this. From precisely whom or what America needed to be retrieved was a little beyond her understanding, she had to concede. But it was a task that demanded selflessness and devotion, and a gentle spirit of supreme intelligence. Was Mr. Prince to be this paragon? Well, if anybody had any other ideas, Sandy was ready to listen. Failing that, she'd made her choice.

But if she were not to become invisible again, Sandy would need yet more *luck*. Plus, right now, she needed to address some practicalities.

First came the issue of clothing. Later that morning she would show up at the Stimsonville HQ of the Prince Campaign wearing — having slept in! — the same clothes she wore the day before. Barbara would not be impressed. Megan would look askance. Sandy's other clothes were in the shopping bag, which, she prayed, remained untouched under her desk. If she got to the office early, could she sneak in, grab the bag and make it to the restroom before anyone noticed? Perhaps. The permanent solution to this problem was to request a campaign sweatshirt, and wear it every day with her black sweatpants.

Second, it was inevitable that at some point she would be asked, and have to divulge, details of her personal circumstances and home life. Until she became firmly established with the campaign, she felt, the truth would have to be deferred. But messing with the truth was such a terrible sin — and hadn't it gotten the country in such a mess, too? — that this could only be justified as a short-term tactic.

Third, money. She could have one more night at the motel. Then what?

Actually, how would it be if she didn't worry about money? What if she just had faith? Mr. Prince presumably had enormous faith in his bespoke strategy. And it had worked out pretty darned well for him. Sandy would have faith in Mr. Prince. He *knew*, obviously. And he hadn't told Barbara or Megan, and probably not the Pioneers, either. First five dollars, and then a hundred. He was looking down on her, if you like, and looking after her. Discreetly, of course. He had to think of his position. You probably needed all the discretion you could muster when you dealt in *algorithms* and *golden handcuffs*. If Sandy continued to shine, then... Well, perhaps things would happen.

Faith was the answer. Backed up with hard work and, perhaps, with a little honest cunning.

She counted out fifteen dollars and fifty cents, placed the money neatly on top of the check, and left the restaurant in high spirits. Then she negotiated her way back to the motel along the darkened highway. When she glanced back over her shoulder she saw Maria, silhouetted in black, immobile in the waffle house window, encircled by neon.

S andy's second day at the office was a roaring success. She timed her arrival perfectly, reuniting herself with her shopping bag, and then making her dash. Thus she was able to present herself to Barbara — chestnut pants suit, cream blouse, silk scarf — and Megan — pale, tight jeans and lime cashmere polo — in her trusty black sweatpants and pink acrylic sweater. Fashion goddess? Come on, get real, people — it's our very own Sandy we're talking about here! Hey, let's send her to New York with Megan, she deserves a makeover!

Sandy spent the morning working again with *leaners*. But the system was so impressed with her that, by lunchtime, she'd been upgraded to *switchers*, a more challenging category. Megan remembered that it was her turn to do the coffee run, and brought Sandy back a grande latte, plus a blueberry muffin. Things were going so well!

And then one of Mr. Prince's local backers — he owned one of the remaining car dealerships on the state highway, it seemed — stopped by to deliver the proceeds of the previous day's fund-raiser golf tournament up at the Country Club (and get himself photographed and uploaded doing so). And he brought free pizza for all the volunteers! Donald was such a great guy, according to Megan; and a fine brute of a man, in Barbara's opinion.

Donald handed the cash — it was loose in a tote bag that bore the golf club logo, untouched since the golfers had tossed in their contributions — to Megan and asked her to count it. They'd raised fifty-two thousand exactly, Donald said. Megan, eager not to miss an opportunity to network, it seemed, or let her pizza get cold, delegated the task to Sandy.

Sandy took the cash to the back office and counted it, dividing it into thousands, and securing each bundle with a rubber band. Fifty-two exactly. She was about to exit the office to collect her share of the pizza when Donald blocked the doorway, holding a brown paper bag.

"Got a little extra for ya!" he said, with a car-dealer's wink, handing her the bag. "Just a little side-deal, you know. Willard's idea. Keep up the good work — I hear you're doing great!"

Then he was gone. She looked inside the bag — more cash, already sorted and secured. When she counted it she found that there was exactly a thousand dollars.

A thousand dollars! No, it was impossible. She counted again. But it was true. Mr. Prince had given her a thousand dollars. *Just a little side-deal. Keep up the good work.* She had kept her end of their unspoken bargain and, once again, he had delivered.

And yet she hesitated. A hundred dollars was a plausible tip from a man as wealthy as Mr. Prince. But a thousand? That wasn't a tip; it was something else. At the very least it betokened the entering into of some kind of conspiracy, even if a benign one. A *side-deal?* Could Donald have meant anything other than that Mr. Prince entertained a special concern for Sandy, and wanted to encourage her? It was for the sake of the campaign, to be sure, but could there be some further purpose?

Or had she simply misconstrued Donald's meaning entirely? Sandy concluded that, somehow, she would have to test this thesis on Megan before she took the money for herself.

The afternoon's work went even better than the morning's. Sandy began to anticipate, and improve on, the system's arguments. Her targets — angry, bitter, despairing, or simply depleted — responded to her voice; it was the note of quiet faith with which she augmented her tone that did it, she thought.

Then, about half an hour before Sandy's shift was to end, Megan over-rode the system and let Sandy talk to some ninety-per-centers. These were voters who, the system calculated, could be prevailed upon to change their customary voting allegiance only ten per cent of the time. Sandy needed to detach them from one or other of the major parties, in favor of Mr. Prince.

For one set, the system asserted that Mr. Prince would instigate a return to the economic rigor that their preferred party had abandoned. For the other, the system promised that Mr. Prince would restore the avenues of opportunity that their habitual party had neglected. But Sandy over-rode the system herself, telling both groups that Mr. Prince wasn't a politician at all, and couldn't ever be, because he had integrity, heart and faith — and that she, personally, had been touched by all three of these qualities. It was a testament that she offered sincerely, although she did not go into specifics, and her targets, she felt, were mostly disarmed by it, if not entirely swayed.

Megan, sitting alongside and monitoring the system's analytics page, seemed disarmed, too.

"Hey, you're really good. You know that?"

Then the shift was over, and Barbara declared a timeout. Some exciting news had arrived. Firstly, the latest batch of polls now showed, for the first time, that Mr. Prince had a statistically-significant lead over both of the main-party candidates.

Second, the campaign had decided that now was the time to shift its main operating base. Stimsonville, long the Prince family's sentimental home, or *country seat*, as Barbara put it, had served its purpose. Mr. Prince's heartland credentials had been established. The campaign now needed to ramp up its engagement with the media, and press home its economic and financial message. This meant a move to New York.

"And I'm sure you're all as surprised as I am!" Barbara said, speaking up to cut through the cheers and hollering. And it was safe to go there now, she added, given that the *Robin Hood rabble* had been swept off the streets.

There was a looseness in Barbara's tinctured voice, Sandy thought, and she looked a little unsteady in her heels. Had she been drinking?

It then emerged that Megan had been selected to transfer to the New York campaign HQ — which was pretty convenient for *her*, Sandy thought, but never mind. And then it was announced that Megan, in turn, had selected Sandy to accompany her! If, that was, Sandy's family didn't have a problem, and Sandy herself could manage to take time out from all her other activities?

"Oh, no problem at all!" Sandy said, wondering as she spoke how many nights you could afford in New York for a thousand dollars.

"Sandy will hook up — I mean *shack up* — with Megan," Barbara declared. "Okay with you, Megan?"

"Sure," Megan said. "And we'll see about that makeover."

"All right. Well, let's get organized here, we got a new shift coming. I'll be at the Longhorn if anyone wants to join me."

The Longhorn, Sandy knew, was the bar-restaurant at the Bellvue Grand. It was the smartest place in town.

"And Megan? Take care of the golf money, okay honey? Hah! Money honey. That's funny. So long, people."

Barbara sashayed out into the street.

Megan turned to Sandy.

"Did you count it?"

"Yes, but —"

"Fifty-two thousand exactly, right?"

"Yes, fifty-two. But there's a bit more in —"

"A bit more?" Megan sighed. "Donald said *exactly*. What kind of businessman is he? I guess you don't have to *count* to sell cars. Look, we've done the paperwork, and it's already in the system. Give me the fifty-two and just hold on to the change for now, okay?"

Megan's tone of voice told Sandy that "the change" was something she'd prefer not to be bothered with ever again. Unlike Barbara, Megan was into the big picture, not the details.

But it wasn't "change", it was a thousand dollars. And Sandy's experiences with businessmen, banks, brokers, loan-sharks, debt-collectors and money-changers in general had taught her that they never under-counted. Donald had said *fifty-two*. Not *fifty-three*, or *fifty-two and change*.

So the money had to be hers. What other conclusion could she come to, given Donald's behavior? She and Mr. Prince were co-conspirators. But in the best cause.

And she was going to New York, a place she'd only ever been to once before, on a college trip. She'd be staying with smart, street-wise Megan — although exactly *where* was a mystery, because Megan hadn't bought her million-dollar apartment yet, had she?

All the same, it was exciting! Look what happened if you only had faith!

Then she remembered that she had failed to leave a tip for Maria, and felt so shamed and upset that she had to run to the restroom.

CHAPTER 11

Teresa Wolfe — known to all the world as Teri, except for one irreconcilable grandmother and a single former room-mate, the ineffable Milly van Dornen — woke to find that the heat in her building had gone off again. The building, a four-story brick slab with ugly, antique fire escapes and even uglier factory-style windows, was owned by a retired realtor who had cashed in just before the last crash, and now lived in Florida. She was hard to get hold of. So was her building maintenance contractor. The unreliability of the twenty-five-year-old HVAC system was, according to popular suspicion, a deliberate cost-saving measure. Outages were rumored to correspond to spikes in the price of heating oil.

The building crouched in deepest Bayonne, just off Kennedy Boulevard. Teri shared a one-bedroom apartment with two fellow food-service industry employees. In theory, this was against the rules. But, so long as the rent got paid, nobody seemed to care. Teri's two room-mates, Alicia and Burgandy, worked for a catering company that serviced retirement care homes. Because they worked different shifts, they could multi-task in the bedroom. Teri got the couch. Between them, they could just about afford the rent of eleven hundred dollars a month.

But it was tight. There was no slack in the budget. They each had college loans to pay off; Teri's amounted to ninety-four thousand dollars.

Teri rolled off the couch, wrapped herself in a blanket, and tried to decide which was worse: The shock of a cold shower, or the humiliation of Pedro and Aliyah's furtive glances. Since she was already late, she selected the latter and began to hunt for her clothes. She would need to wrap up warm today.

Teri's commute comprised four phases. First, she walked the four long blocks to the Light Rail stop at 45th Street. When the wind blew in from the Hudson, it could be a freezing slog. Then she rode the train to the fancy towers at Exchange Place, that little bit of Jersey City that longed to detach itself from Hudson County and glob on to lower Manhattan. Here she boarded a PATH train and burrowed beneath the Hudson River, leaving one world for another. Once on the other side, at the World Trade Center terminus, all that remained was the ten-minute march to Pearl Street and Bean Village.

Oh, wait a moment. Trenton — *shit!*

She'd been fired for checking out the Robin-Hooders down in Battery Park. Okay, there might have been more to it than that; it probably wasn't *totally* political. But it was a fuck-up, all the same. And it was happening at a bad time. Alicia had had some back problems; her co-payments meant that she wouldn't be able to make her share of the rent this month, and Teri had promised to cover it. What was she going to do?

The more jobs you lost, the harder it was to get another. And Teri feared the approach of that unofficial threshold beyond which simply being out of work made you unemployable. She couldn't go back home again; Dad's union contract had been voided by the state legislature, and he knew what was coming. Mom thought they could rent out Teri's old room.

But the mere thought of some desperate stranger lying awake in the very bed where Teri had dreamed of finding that special partner who would be more practical than she was; of fixer-upper makeovers in upcoming neighborhoods; of smart new suits for the office; and of short stories in magazines — well, she didn't need to make herself feel any more morose or washed-up than she already did.

She sat down on the couch, still clasping the blanket around her waist. Was there anybody she could call? How about her old, go-to college professor — the amateur ornithologist whose room it was always safe to go to after dark? Maybe he could set her up with another gig tutoring the SAT-challenged offspring of the ruling class. The conditions were unspeakable; the parents, unreasonable; and the kids, uneducable. And it paid less than Bean Village. But it was *something*.

She groped under the couch for her phone. And when she looked at the screen she saw the message from Milly van Dornen.

Now she remembered. Should she cut back on the cheap wine in the evening? Well, maybe.

Milly, whose nickname amongst her college pals, cruelly but not without cause, had once been *Princess Mildred van Porno*, had found Teri an opening. Or a potential opening, at least.

She was expected to present herself on *Park Avenue* at eleven that morning. So it would have to be the cold shower after all. *Shit!*

*

I t was one of the best apartment buildings — perhaps *the* best — on the Avenue, according to Gloria, Mr. Willard G. R. Prince's Personal Secretary. Many believed it to be the master-work of the great architect, Candela, the Mozart of the pre-war triplex. Even though it opened to shareholders — it was a *cooperative*, of course — in 1933, in the depths of the Depression, it had never ceased to be a beacon of aspiration for America's original aristocracy; for her giants of industry; or, more recently, her wizards of finance. Even now, when some claimed that America had fallen into a new kind of depression — Gloria didn't accept that, nor did Mr. Prince, and a young Ivy League grad like Teri surely had no truck with such pessimism — the building went from strength to strength: Mr. Prince had maintained a residence here for the last twelve years.

Well, eleven years, to be precise; during the first year the apartment had been remodeled.

They sat in the *library*, having entered by private elevator and having traversed an entrance hall more spacious, Teri calculated, than the entirety of the Bayonne one-bed *plus* the apartment next door. And, sure, the walls were lined with books. But they looked like they'd been ordered by the yard; you didn't get to own a pad like this by *reading*, right? The furniture and décor might have been transplanted from an English stately home — or, rather, the TV representation of one. Nothing looked *old*. The fireplace looked like it had never been used. What had it all been like before it was remodeled?

Well, Gloria said, if Teri got the job, then she would be seeing a lot more of Mr. Prince's superb New York home. A *lot* — in fact, she would be living here.

Living here? What had frigging Milly done — sold Teri into servitude?

But Gloria was talking. She, Gloria Steynhuis, was purely Mr. Prince's personal secretary. His business, financial, and — of course — political affairs were handled by others. Nonetheless, at this particular moment, it was a case of, well, *all hands on deck*.

Thus the campaign had asked Gloria to recruit an assistant, in order to document the *human* side of Mr. Prince's unprecedented and, undoubtedly, historic run for the top office. Now, obviously, a team of professional film-makers had already been hired to produce the official record of the campaign. What we were talking about here was, instead, something more informal — the lighter moments; the candidate relaxing with his family, unbuttoned or *unplugged*, as the campaign liked to put it.

The idea was to reinforce the campaign's political message, but in an accessible, soft-focus way. An entire section of the electorate did not respond to argument, apparently, or to facts and figures; they responded to emotion — so long as it was organized and presented appropriately. The campaign wanted video snippets, a blog, a social-media feed, and such-like. Authenticity was key. They wanted it produced by a *hip* and *credible* twenty-something, preferably a female college graduate with artistic leanings, who would herself look, well, *appealing* on camera. While technical assistance would be available, the whole production, Gloria had been given to understand, needed to look *amateur* — but in the slickest and most professional way possible.

And that was where Teri came in. Milly had said that Teri was a whizz with a video camera, and knew how to put a sentence together. And now that Gloria had seen Teri in person, it was clear that, with a little work, Teri could be made to look presentable, too.

Well, *thanks*, she thought. Jesus! What had Milly gotten her into here? You know, really!

"Milly says you're reliable and discreet — and very loyal."

Well, Milly was a dope; that was the truth. And desperate for friendship, as opposed to what appeared to pass for human contact within the status-freighted, transactional matrix she'd been born into. Okay, she was a sometime-sweet, funny, naïve dope — if that helped. No doubt she felt she was doing a very sweet, helpful thing for Teri. Perhaps even now she was hugging herself with pious joy. But if she'd really known Teri at all…

"That's really sweet of her."

"And *are* you?"

"Oh, I would say so."

Don't fuck with *me*, Ms. Personal Secretary!

"It's very important. Normally, we'd run a standard background check. But there isn't time, and the campaign wants this to look like a spontaneous, family thing. And since you're such good friends with Milly, we can stretch a point and call you *family*. So..."

"I'm sure Milly would vouch for me."

She would, too.

Gloria slid her glasses down her nose and looked at Teri over the top of them. Skepticism? Yeah, okay — but was there any need to be so obvious?

"And I'm sure you wouldn't let her down."

"Never."

A pause. Gloria slid her glasses back up her nose. Teri pretended to admire the fireplace.

Did she really want this so-called job? Did it actually pay any money? And if she had to live in this Masterpiece Theater apartment — like where, under the stairs? — then what about Bayonne? And did the job end when Prince won — or, preferably, lost — the election?

"Obviously, it's a temporary position," Gloria said. But you will have a *golden* opportunity to network."

Yay! Teri Wolfe networks her way to personal success and lifetime achievement. Take that, Trenton!

"And the new administration will have a number of entry-level appointments to fill..."

Great! Teri gets to work for the new plutocracy. The money would be good, right?

"...subject to a full background check."

Ah.

"So, how much do you want this job, Ms. Wolfe?"

Yeah, that was the question. Suppose she said *a lot* — even if it seemed like the last thing in the world she ought to be doing?

"Oh, well this is, like, an incredible opportunity for me. I really, really want to do it."

"You'll have to live here. In the staff wing."

Staff wing? In an apartment? Of course — the old servants' quarters from 1933.

"Not a problem."

"Starting immediately."

"That's okay. I'm available."

"There won't be much time off."

"I'm fine with that."

I'm in, Gloria! It's too crazy to miss. Thank you, Milly! But what about the money?

"I believe there's a salary," Gloria said. "I don't know what was decided, but it'll be adequate."

Adequate. Ok—ay...

"No health benefits, obviously."

"Not an issue."

Teri was healthy. She knew she was.

Gloria stood up and smiled. But was it an *authentic* smile, or just part of the campaign?

"Then welcome aboard. I'll show you your room, and then we'll talk about the meeting, and how you need to conduct yourself in his presence."

Wow, she thought. This was sure as hell going to beat selling coffee to bonus babies.

*

A nd thus began Teri Wolfe's translation from humble food-service worker to modern-day indentured scribe.

In her staff bedroom, tiny even by Bayonne standards, Teri paid attention to Gloria's strictures on etiquette. The *family* always took precedence and Teri should defer to them; Mr. Prince was a family-first man and a great believer in the American family as an institution. This, of course, went a considerable way in explaining his enormous appeal. Mr. Prince was always to be addressed as *Mr. Prince*, and not *Willard* or, indeed, using any other soubriquet that Teri might have heard. (Meaning, Teri construed, don't call him *Fat Willy*, or *Prince Regent* — apparently coined by some wags at Yale who discovered that the middle initial "R" in the man's name derived from some ancient Anglo aristo called John Dexter Regent — or by his most demotic nickname, *that rich guy*.)

Then, in Bergdorf Goodman, Teri dressed and undressed while Gloria and Gloria's personal shopper fitted her out in preppy outfits that might almost have come from Gap but were just that little bit better — for those who could tell the difference. The difference, Teri figured, amounted to about six months' rent for the dump in Bayonne, but hey — now she *really* felt Ivy League, as she had never done before, and in a very meaningful way.

Back in the library on Park Avenue, in the presence of Mr. Prince's personal lawyer, a pin-striped owl with a face as stony as any of the library's mock-Roman busts, Teri signed a non-disclosure agreement that ran to twenty-six pages, as well as receipts for a laptop computer, a super-spec tablet, an HD camcorder, and all associated cables, bags, accessories, manuals and consumables.

In the *scullery*, Gloria told Teri that she ought to be able to find enough room amid the crockery to do her work; for reasons of security, the apartment did not use Wi-Fi, but a cabled connection was available here. Teri should be aware that a private security company had been hired to monitor all electronic communications in and around the apartment; and also that Mr. Prince's tableware collections were very valuable.

In her own, compact, private office, adjacent — and, it seemed, directly connected — to Mr. Prince's own chamber of solitude, Gloria gave Teri the executive summary of Mr. Prince's historical pedigree as an American patriot. She began with the sturdy merchants who stood firm against wicked British taxes, moving on to the fearless pioneers who financed expansion to the west and fostered the growth of agriculture in the south; the brave, can-do traders who held the nation together by providing the union army with whatever it needed; the far-sighted entrepreneurs who taught the country to embrace the railroads; the tireless industrialists who sacrificed so much to make America the richest nation in history; the real-estate geniuses who had *literally* built the shining city on the hill; the Wall Street giants who had given the man in the street a share in American prosperity; and now, in the present, the culmination of all this struggle — Mr. Willard G. R. Prince himself, and his brothers and sons, who had bestowed upon the entire world a weightless, frictionless form of pure finance whose benefits were almost beyond imagining. There was more to it, of course; Teri would be expected to do her homework.

Wow, Teri thought: From smugglers to banksters, a criminal full-circle. She also noted that Gloria had no personal effects in her office — stuffed toys, comical cartoons, family photos, World's Best Mom mug; stuff like that. Weird, huh? Put that together with Gloria's ultra-conservative, gray, buttoned-up suit and her aggressively bouffant blonde hair, in some retro sixties' style (which Teri thought was kind of pushing it for someone who'd probably been forty-nine for quite a few years now) and what did you get? Right, exactly. A tad on the scary side. But when did Teri get to meet *that rich guy?*

Tonight, Gloria said, Mr. Prince was to host a private dinner for the Committee to Save America — yes, the name *was* somewhat hyperbolic, but there'd been foolish public talk of *malaise*, and this was politics, after all — and Teri would be expected to attend, although strictly without her recording equipment. On this occasion, it being her first outing, Teri would be chaperoned by her great friend, Milly van Dornen, whose mother, Barbara, would also be in attendance.

Jeez, it just got better didn't it? Though Barbara was kind of a concern. Milly's mom was a smart cookie and might just know a few things about Teri that her sugar-biscuit daughter didn't.

"So," Gloria said. "You've just got time to clean yourself up and get changed. I'll see you in the library at seven."

She gave Teri a nod that seemed to mean *now get out of my office*. Teri got the message and retired to her cubby-hole in the servants' quarters.

Whereupon, she decided, she would ask herself this question: *What the fuck?* What the fuck had she gotten herself into? Could she actually go through with it? Wait, wait, wait — through with *what*, exactly?

Oh no, Teri. No, no, no. *You* can't be the one to pull the plug on Mr. Restore Our Democracy. *You've* got enough problems. Let somebody else do it. Would Fat Willy really be any worse than the other two guys? Yeah, probably, a little. But so what? Think of the entertainment value. Just don't do anything really stupid, okay? Go along for the ride. Have some LOLs on the side. Take the money — it's going to be adequate, they say. Sure, but what's adequate these days? How about the ninety-four thousand dollars in outstanding loans that don't even go away if you're bankrupt?

No bailouts for over-educated deadbeats like Teri.

Anyway, it wasn't up to Teri to decide whether America got to have its first *Prince Regent*, right? Damn right. Let the voters decide, even if *you*, Teri, are helping to manipulate their emotions. Oh, big deal. Just go along, get along with the plutocracy. It's already happening anyway, yeah? Don't even *think* of a post-election exposé. No, no — *stop* thinking about it! *Now!*

Okay. Now let Teri have her shower in the staff bathroom, change into the new clothes that somebody else bought her, and prepare to meet the people who were going to save America.

Oh, yeah — and Milly and her mom.

CHAPTER 12

Teresa Wolfe, the slacker radical turned indentured scribe and (so it had been said) adequately-paid handmaiden of plutocracy, figured that if you could have morph-mapped the aggregate wealth of this top-shelf library crowd on your top-of-the-range tablet (which you couldn't because all such devices had been sequestered in the vestibule by an imperious blonde and her shrunken, fifty-something assistant) then, just as Africa would shrink to the size of Belgium while Westchester ballooned, the library might have aced it over the outer boroughs to become visible from space. From which vantage point, she imagined, the Chinese astronauts presently assembling the components of their monstrous moon-exploration vehicle might also have observed a temporary deformation in the Earth's pluto-magnetic field — enough, perhaps, to precipitate above Park Avenue an effulgent display of the *aurora financialis*.

Was it really so fanciful? The single square foot of library floor currently tenanted by her petite frame was worth, she calculated, more than twice her entire year's salary before tax and deductions at Bean Village. These people gave off a staticky, monetizing force field; it was almost as if they were aliens, invaders from some advanced planet possessed of superior financial technology, alighting on Earth to plunder its resources and enslave, or harvest, its people. Yet they didn't look like master-race marauders, she thought; nor, at least superficially, the ravening brutes of science fiction. No, far from it — they were delicate creatures, never mind the loud voices and the over-stuffed confidence. Look at those silky hands, those dewy, frost-free cheeks — and all that bone-china décolletage. These were fragile beings; they needed protection. And so they had lawyers, private bankers, personal assistants, limos and drivers, servants like Teri. And, most of all, each other.

Like stars falling together under the pull of one other's gravity, they circulated in the library, drinks in hand, trinkets shining, pulsating with dark energy, but shielded from the body-disrupting radiation of the low-income belt by the library's tight-packed stacks of unread and irrelevant wisdom.

But the heavenly body around which they all desired to orbit — Chinese designs on the moon notwithstanding — was Mr. Willard Gaffney Regent Prince, the next President of the United States. Or *Fat Willy*, if you will. The guy on whose watch America lost the moon, or was about to.

Jesus, Teri — stop thinking this shit! You blurt it out once and the gig's over. And you haven't had any fun yet. And you won't be able to pay the rent. And you'll never get another job. And... *Okay, got it.*

Fat Willy hadn't shown up yet. But he was the talk of the town, and town was all here. The word was that Willy, alerted by wearable technology running bespoke software, had taken to his in-apartment trading room to execute yet another audacious play on behalf of the New American Century Fund. The library, Teri could see, was all in favor of *that*. However, she believed she had discerned an interesting class divide — yes, even at *this* exalted level! Milly had said that most of tonight's attendees were long-time investors. But a minority — debutantes, suppliants, suck-ups, social-climbers, greedsters and lickspittles, Teri surmised — were not. Milly had called them *aspirants*.

"So what exactly are they aspiring to, Milly?"

"Well, it's the returns."

"What about the returns?"

"I guess they're consistent?"

"How can that be?"

"They just always are. It's the, you know, the bespoke —"

"That's bullshit, Milly."

"You know you can't use your language around here, right?"

"Oops. Beg your pardon."

Anyway, the slightly creepy Gloria, Teri's new boss and Fat Willy's personal secretary, had given the two varsity pals their mission for the evening. Since it was Teri's first time out, in this *milieu*, Milly would be *babysitting* (Gloria seemed to get this inadvertent joke but it went over Milly's head). Because recording equipment — now and forever at gatherings of this nature — was strictly forbidden, Milly and Teri's assignment was to seek out the younger members of the Movement to Save America (as distinct from the *Committee*, which comprised an older and very select bunch), and to get a handle on their thoughts and feelings. It was widely appreciated, Gloria said, that young libertarians — and there were more of them by the day — favored Mr. Prince. The campaign wasn't surprised, but wanted to understand exactly where the kids were coming from, so to speak. To this end, Milly and Teri had been issued with paper notepads and pencils and released into the library.

And it was as they began their search for high-value targets that Milly said something disturbing.

"Hey, my mom's looking for you!"

"What? Where is she? What about?"

"Oh, she just wants to catch up with you."

Shit. Barbara van Dornen, Milly's mom, was one of those search-and-destroy mothers, who'd run her daughter's life like a military campaign, keeping intelligence on all Milly's friends, contacts and acquaintances — boyfriends most particularly, of course, which was probably why Milly had gotten through so many — and mostly didn't care to take prisoners. If Barbara had been tracking Teri's glittering career — that crazy ride she'd taken between graduating from Penn and landing on her aching feet at Bean Village — then Teri could be busted. Did Barbara ever close a file? Wasn't she a one-woman FBI? Did she know about the performance art thing? The punk rock group? The environmental provocations? That *embarrassing* video blog? (She couldn't delete it because she'd lost the password; it remained a lurking peril, like an untethered sea-mine — but as close as a tap or a click!)

So Barbara had to be avoided. Just in case.

"Where's your mom now?"

"I guess she's with Megan and that woman they found in Stimsonville. D'you want me to —"

"Wait, backup. Who's Megan?"

"Oh, she's the one taking everybody's phone. She's with the campaign? Kind of pushy, but I guess she's okay. You know, with the hair and all. You are *not* going to believe this. Her boyfriend —"

"And who's this woman from Stimsonville?"

Milly seemed put out that Teri didn't care about Megan's boyfriend. Milly missed the point an awful lot — unlike her mom.

"Well, it's kind of weird. She just walks in off the street, and they put her on the phones — you know, hassling people to vote — and it's like she's some kind of genius. But then she also comes across like she's basically dumb? That's what Megan says."

"An *idiot savant*, you mean?"

"A what?"

"Never mind. Let's go over here."

Teri led Milly to the far end of library, away from the vestibule, its confiscated phones and its human zoo.

They fastened on to a gang of thrusting young libertarians who said they were in private equity. So what did they think about, you know, stuff? It turned out that they were eager to unload. Teri and Milly got their pencils out.

The conservative project, they thought, had gone off the rails. Sure, the Southern Strategy had worked for a long time, plus cultural issues and all that shit, but it was fucked, played out. Teri noted that Milly didn't object to their language — but then, these were boys talking.

And, sure, the old parties, they were fucked, too. They sucked up money, but they never delivered, not really, on deregulation and getting government the fuck out of the way. It was time for a realignment. Prince was The Man. Oh, and bring on the NPP.

They also thought that Reagan Pruett, the country cross-over singer who'd scandalized the Superbowl half-time millions, was shit-hot and darned cool. *Boys*, Teri thought. Yuck. But what was the NPP?

She scribbled her notes, taking care to make them illegible. Then she scanned the horizon. Now, where was Barbara? *There* — over by the fireplace on her own, ignoring the complete works of Anthony Trollope, looking like she was on the hunt. Shi—it!

Most people were nursing flutes of Champagne. Barbara lugged a bottle of red wine.

"Let's go over there."

Teri led Milly to an alcove — a large bay, in fact, that let out on to a terrace with views across to Central Park. Here they found some junior investment bankers. What was their take on, you know, crap in general?

They were heavily into the NPP. It was essential for American competitiveness. Weihan was a great example. It was going to be a new era. There were things we always thought we knew — that China would forever be a competitor, for example. But the new paradigm was almost here. Forget about global imbalances. Level playing fields! Transnational jurisdiction! Freedom enshrined forever by treaty and check out those torts!

Yeah, and how about that Reagan Pruett? She just did it again, did you see? Cool!

Teri pulled Milly aside.

"Did you understand any of that?"

"No. You?"

"Just the bit about friggin' Pruett. I *can* say friggin', right?"

"I guess. If you must. What do we write?"

"We'll just say they're optimistic about the future, and they like this NPP thing."

"What is that?"

"Got me. Let's not worry about it."

Barbara had disappeared from view. Was she sneaking up out of sight, or had she gone for another bottle?

"Let's go outside."

"Teresa — it's cold out there!"

"Just for a moment."

They stepped out on to the terrace. The night music of the city echoed up from its urban canyons. But somehow, up here, it sounded muffled, like a movie with the sound turned down. Milly hugged herself to keep warm — or perhaps to protect herself against radiation from the low-income belt. Teri, of course, was immune. She had been exposed.

Then Milly shrieked. Teri turned.

"Whoa! What happened?"

Milly stood frozen, mouth agape.

"*Milly?*"

"I don't know — something... Something hit me!"

"Huh? Like what?"

"It flew into me."

"You mean a bird?"

"No, I don't know. It was hard."

"Where'd it go?"

They looked. Milly grabbed Teri's arm.

"Can you see anything?"

"No," Teri said, after a pause. "Maybe a chunk fell off the building. It's pretty old."

"But —"

"Let's go back inside. You're right. It's really cold."

In they went.

But oh, what a friggin' liar she was! She'd seen it all right — small, shiny-black, kind of octagonal, hovering in the shadows. Some kind of toy friggin' drone! Someone was trying to spy on Fat Willy! The nerve! But who could it be? Who could possibly afford three hundred bucks for a thing like that?

While Milly recovered from her ordeal, Teri conducted her own half-assed reconnaissance. Barbara was back — this time in the middle of the room, talking to a bullet-headed man in a tux who looked sixty but tough. Time to move on.

"Uh, Milly? Do you know *those* guys? Over in the corner?"

"Oh no, Teri, they're just —"

"Let's talk to them."

They were IT types from Silicon Valley. Whizz kids. Nerds. Brats. Billionaires.

They were into Big Data, scalability, the network effect, IPOs, campuses, cool innovation, reforming society and libertarianism. Especially libertarianism. And, inevitably, the NPP.

They had no opinion regarding Reagan Pruett, but had a lot of harsh things to say about outdated intellectual property laws (software patents excepted).

Teri and Milly listened, smiled, doodled with their pencils and moved on.

"I *tried* to tell you," Milly said.

It was true. She had tried. Poor Milly — always trying to steer Teri straight.

They voyaged on again, Teri ever careful not to fall within Barbara's gravitational field, to discover youthful real estate investors, hedge fund strategists, venture capitalists, bond traders and stock brokers. It was quite the cross-section of vibrant, young American society, Teri thought. And she began to imagine her first campaign blog post:

> As I discovered at the coolest party in town, a glittering fund-raiser for the Movement to Save America, young people today just aren't buying into their parents' government. They're doing it for themselves. Their role models aren't the kind of people to sit back and wait for stuff to come to them — they're start-ups and entrepreneurs, people like country cross-over star Reagan Pruett, who...

Teri felt a firm hand on her shoulder.

"Teresa!"

But it wasn't Barbara, luckily; it was Gloria.

"Teresa. Go fetch your video camera and go down to the lobby. There's something going on in the street. I want pictures. Go!"

Well, this sounded exciting! Could there be a video snippet in it for the blog? Teri abandoned Milly to a chapter of emerging-market players and made for the servants' quarters to retrieve her camcorder. Crossing the vestibule, she encountered the Sage of Stimsonville. The woman sat alone, still, on a straight-backed chair, with nothing to do, it seemed, but guard a stash of phones, tablets and other contraband tech. Had anyone even offered her a drink?

"Hi," Teri said. "I'm Teri."

"Oh, I'm Sandy. I..."

"Nice to meet you, Sandy. Cool." Teri made an expansive gesture, indicating the vestibule's Bayonne-dwarfing vastness.

"Quite a place, huh?"

Sandy shifted in her seat; she didn't seem comfortable in her clothes, a smooth gray suit that looked brand-new and contrasted with her blotched and sand-papery skin.

"Yes. It certainly is."

"So you work with Megan?"

"Yes. That's right. I do. Do you know her?"

"Nope. Not yet. Apparently she's pushy but okay. That right?"

"Oh, no, no. I wouldn't — I mean..."

"Look, I gotta run. There's something going down in the street, apparently. Catch you later."

She retrieved her camera and took the stairs, not wanting to wait for the sluggish elevator. On the way down, she pondered the mystery that was evidently *Sandy*. The woman had walked into the local campaign office in Hicktown, aka Stimsonville, and had blown them all away with her telephonic talent. Truly weird, but good luck to her. Where, though, had she walked in from? That shrunken, weather-beaten look — Teri knew she'd been looking at someone who'd spent way too much time in the radiation belts.

In the lobby, she saw that the head doorman and his assistants had barricaded the main door with antique furniture.

"What's happening?"

"Bunch of yahoos out there, yelling about something."

"Demonstrators?"

"Assholes. Where're the cops?"

Teri waved her camera.

"Um, look — I'm supposed to get pictures, so —"

"Use the service entrance."

One of the assistant doormen escorted Teri to the rear of the building and released her into the street via a steel door.

"I'll wait. Knock three times. Take care..."

He gave her a protective smile. Wasting his time.

"Thanks!"

She ran around the block to the front of the building and activated her camera. And there they were: Those banners, those chants, those jaunty but sinister masks. It was a Robin Hood Party demo. Somehow they'd found out about Fat Willy's little soirée. How rude of them to intrude. What gave them the right? Ah, but perhaps they were all young libertarians?

She zoomed in to get her pictures, but then hesitated. The cops weren't here yet; they would bring their own cameras. These flash demos tended to disperse like sea mist just before the cops arrived. So Teri's footage might be used to identify... But no — look, they were all wearing masks. So no problem.

She advanced, employing what she fancied to be a cat-like tread, zooming and panning. It was a small demo — only about forty of them — but they were making a decent noise. Zooming in again, she spotted someone — a girl to judge by the shape — operating a device that hung from a strap around her neck. Twin joysticks! So the mystery object that had biffed Milly in the midriff was a Robin Hood drone! Talk about fighting fire with fire. Well, except that the Robin

Hooders' drone probably wasn't armed. And what did they expect to see, apart from a bunch of rich people getting sozzled?

Then, for the second time that evening, she felt a hand on her shoulder.

"You again!"

She spun around — and whoa, those masks were way scary up close!

"You were in Battery Park!"

"Uh, yeah? So?"

"Who are you working for? And turn that thing off."

She lowered her camera but let it run.

"Working for?"

"Is it Fairmeadow?"

"Who?"

"Have you been, like, *following* me?"

"Uh, no..."

"Do you know where I live?"

"Don't think so."

"But you do recognize me, don't you?"

"Not with that stupid mask on."

"Oh. Right."

The mask came off. And now she recognized him. The black guy whose partner — girlfriend? — had been snatched by... Oh, right, *Fairmeadow Solutions*, the rent-a-goon mob. The very same outfit employed to oversee electronic security in and around the apartment.

"Okay, gotcha now," she said.

"So who are you and why are you always filming us?"

This, she thought, was going to be tricky to explain.

"I'm Teri," she said. "And you are..."

"You better call me Robin."

"*Robin*. Okay. Well, here's what happened, see. I was working on Pearl Street, at Bean Village, and I heard —"

"That shit coffee place? How could you work *there?* Do you have any idea how they treat —"

"It was a job, dickhead! Do *you* have a job?"

No answer. No job? Maybe he really was a libertarian.

"Okay. Sorry. Go on."

"Anyway, I lost the job. Happy?"

"I said sorry."

"Sure. Anyway, I was just bored, and you guys were down there in the park, and I like to shoot video, so..."

"Yeah, well, you realize what you shot, okay? You got them taking my friend. We don't know where she is. We can't find out. They won't tell us."

There was a pause. It was only, what — a day and a half ago? But he sounded serious.

"They say it didn't happen."

"But it did."

"You saw it. You videoed it."

She nodded.

"I would like to have a copy."

"Okay."

"I'm assuming you have the original somewhere safe?"

"Absolutely."

"And where might that be?"

Ah. She'd hidden the memory card under a can of French Roast in the storeroom at Bean Village. Problem. But it was definitely safe there — nobody ever asked for French Roast. Well, except Milly, obviously. Which just proved the point.

"I think," she said, judiciously, "that it's better if you don't know."

"So who are you, all of a sudden — little Miss M from freaking James Bond?"

"Do you want it or not?"

"Yeah, okay, sorry. I'm feeling a little *stressed*, okay?"

Diddums.

Another pause.

"Fine," he said, with a decisive shuffling of the feet. "Here's what we'll do. Tomorrow. Lunchtime. Get yourself a sandwich or something. In a paper bag. Go into the park. Sit on a bench somewhere. Let's say by the rink. The memory thing is in the bag. You eat, you get up and go. And you leave the bag."

"And you collect it?"

"Uh-huh."

"Kind of old-school, isn't it?"

"We can't do anything digital or electronic. They see everything."

"Freakin' James Bond shit, then."

"Has to be."

She thought for a moment.

"Not sure if I can do tomorrow."

"We'll be there every day. Between twelve and two."

"Might still be tricky."

"Why? And why are you here anyway? I almost forgot about that."

Teri permitted herself a long sigh.

"You really want to know? I'm not sure you're going to like it..."

"Tell me anyway."

So she did. And he seemed impressed. There was a very long pause. He was thinking.

"You could be our mole," he said at length.

"Mole? What is that? Some other kind of spy shit?"

"What information do you have access to?"

"Information? I told you, I'm just a friggin' servant."

"You could poke around. Eavesdrop. Hack into their systems."

"*Hack into their systems?*"

"Sure. Whose side are you on, anyway?"

What a bastard! But that *was* the question, wasn't it?

"You don't want this idiot to win, do you?"

"No. But..."

"You know what'll happen. It'll be the end of everything. No way back. A total fucking plutocracy."

"You're making it sound kind of bad..."

"And then there's the NPP. We'll get that, too. On steroids."

Teri held up her free hand.

"Can I ask you something?"

"Sure."

"What's the NPP?"

He sighed with what sounded like the weariest frustration ever.

"See, this is our problem. Nobody's heard of it. It's all been done in secret. It's a complete new layer of international law. Written by corporations. Superior to US law. There's going to be a treaty — the New Pacific Partnership. Sounds harmless, right? There's a shitload to it, but here's a taster, okay? You, as a citizen, will never be allowed to sue any of these corporations ever again. For any reason. They, on the other hand, will have the right to sue your ass if you do anything — anything at all — to damage their profits or their interests, which they define any way they like. They call it *free trade*, or *transparency*, or *harmonization* or whatever. It's the rule of corporations. Forever. No national government can challenge them, because they can sue. In their own international court. Are you following all this?"

She was going to say that it sounded just a tad conspiracy-theory, but he hadn't finished.

"And this guy Prince — we think he wants China in too. Think about it."

"But isn't he all for standing up to China?"

"You buy that?"

Did she? She wasn't sure. She needed to think. But she couldn't think now because some new commotion had erupted. Black vans had blocked the Avenue. The Robin Hooders were on the run.

"Gotta go," Robin said. "Tomorrow. In the park."

He pulled his mask down and was gone. Teri raised her camera, still recording, and backed away towards the rear of the building and the service entrance.

Three knocks and she was in.

Then a breathless dash upstairs and she was on her narrow bed in her cubby hole, any idea of *fun* abandoned, sweating, panting and wondering whether she could possibly be cut out for all this freaking serious James Bond shit.

CHAPTER 13

Sandra Quayle — as she was before *The Fall* — had never doubted the power of prayer. For a time it had seemed to pay off reliably, like the blue-chip health insurance she used to have. But Sandy Quayle felt a little different: She had to wonder why its benefits kicked in so capriciously, so bizarrely and, in Sandy's case, after such a long delay. Perhaps you weren't meant to understand. If you could, you'd be able to work the system. And that would make God look bad.

But what worried Sandy most pressingly was the thought that her new state of grace might be only temporary. How much, exactly, had she put in the spiritual meter? It must have been more than she'd ever realized, to bring her the gifts she'd received. Really? And how, exactly, did *luck* translate into grace? Did it all depend on her attitude? Was it contingent on faith?

It had started with a five dollar bill up on the golf course at the Stimsonville Country Club and Spa — and an invitation. She had known at once that this was an invitation she could not refuse; she had to assume that was generally how it worked with grace. You knew it when you saw it. Or else you blew it. And, although some of the less modest conceits of some of Christ's least modest followers didn't always sit right with her, she wondered if — never mind the incongruous venue — *this* might be what it felt like to be *reborn*.

After the five dollars, there had been the hundred dollar bill that Mr. Prince had left for her at the Pioneers' Reception. This had paid for her stay at the motel, but it had also led to temptation. You could see how these things worked. And, of course, she'd forgotten Maria's tip. That, in turn, had led to an orgy of penance. But, learning as she went, she'd put things right: In the middle of her second and final night at the motel, having set the alarm on the clock bolted to the night stand, she had revisited the waffle house. And there — praise be, really! — she'd found Maria topping up the all-night breakfast bar. Lamenting her unwonted forgetfulness, Sandy had begged Maria's forgiveness, which came instantly and all but wordlessly. When she had said all that she could think to say, Sandy had pressed a twenty into Maria's greasy and prematurely wrinkled hand.

The scene had occasioned a whole lot of tearfulness on Sandy's part and, she had to admit, no little embarrassment on Maria's, but a wrong had been righted and Sandy had put herself back on track. She slept soundly for the rest for the night.

The twenty, of course, had come from the thousand dollars that Mr. Prince had sent to Sandy via Donald, the car dealer. The motel clerk wouldn't break a hundred a second time, so, not wanting to ask Maria to do it, Sandy had tried every gas station, bar and restaurant along the highway until she'd gotten lucky.

And today had been a long day, too. So now, as she sat in the vestibule of Mr. Prince's beautiful city home, waiting for Megan, she felt tired, drained, her body a little off-kilter. Well, it wasn't surprising. The long drive from Stimsonville in Barbara's Escalade had worn Sandy out, but not so much that she couldn't admire Barbara's unflinching assault on the Manhattan traffic. Megan had offered her a glass of Champagne — the real thing, too, and not sparkling wine or the oily, yellowish stuff that Hunter Bill used to suck on. Sandy had felt tempted, but she had declined. She would feel better tomorrow.

And the mystery of where Sandy and Megan were to stay had been solved. Barbara had brought them to a new apartment building a few blocks south of Central Park. The building thrust itself high above those to its north, so that the triple-height duplex apartments at the very pinnacle could enjoy views across the tops of their neighbors' spires to the entirety of the park. The apartment had been purchased, and furnished, by one of Mr. Prince's backers, a *bumptious* and *hyperactive* computer genius, Barbara had said — a little disrespectfully, Sandy had thought — from the Valley. This restless guru, alas, had not yet had time to move into, or even inspect, his new property, so Megan and Sandy had the use of it until further notice. They merely had to register their fingerprints — and passports, had they been aliens, as many of the residents were — with Security.

From the upper level of her bedroom, Sandy could see joggers, a boating lake, baseball diamonds — and was that a skating rink? And trees, of course. Lots of trees. It was almost like living outdoors. But she'd had enough of that.

Megan had gone to fetch someone who wanted to meet with Sandy. She now returned, accompanied by a tall, tense-shouldered bald man in a tuxedo. He looked about sixty years old, but moved with a vigor and energy that Sandy found shocking. People of his age in the village, Hunter Bill excepted, hardly moved at all.

"Sandy, this is Ray Krall. He's our Campaign Director. The big boss. He's very interested in you."

Krall, Sandy instantly thought, a flutter of panic in her stomach, could never have been a store-keeper, or an engineer, or a desk-worker, or a church-goer, or a good neighbor or even faintly classy. He looked like a prize-fighter who'd won a lot of money and had gone into business, yet still worked out every day in his garage. This was Mr. Prince's Campaign Director?

"So you're the one they're all tellin' me about?"

Sandy didn't know what to say.

"That's her," Megan said.

"One for the record books. I ain't seen figures like that nowhere else. Maybe I'll write a thesis."

He held out his hand.

"Ray. Pleased to meet you."

Sandy stood and shook. His hand felt warm and clammy. He was overheating in his tux.

"I'm Sandy. Very nice to —"

"Okay then," Krall said, addressing Megan. "We'll be in Willard's private study if anybody wants us."

Megan looked as if Krall had just disinvited her from a party.

"But don't you need me to —"

"Nah, we'll do just fine. Besides, somebody gotta keep an eye on *that*."

He smirked down at the box of confiscated phones and tablets.

"I reckon there's some wild shit in there, hey Sandy? What do you think?"

"I —"

"These people. I tell you truly. They never delete nothing. Maybe they tell someone to do it for them. Then they act all surprised and hurt, you know?"

He laughed and shook his head.

"Come on."

Krall launched himself across the vestibule towards the corridor that led to Mr. Prince's private quarters, acting like he owned the place — which he never could because he was *not* Mr. Prince, and never would be. Not even close. She struggled to keep up. The suit she wore was hard to move about in. Megan had bought it for her and there had been no time for a fitting. Sandy had never worn clothes like these and they were too tight.

"Guess you're a risin' star all right," Krall said. "I tell you this, Sandy. You keep it up, you'll get to meet ol' Willie Boy hisself."

Willie Boy? And she *had* met Mr. Prince!

"You'll be able to say you knew him *before* he was President."

But I do, she thought. *And I know him better than you.*

Krall showed her into a small, paneled office and offered her a seat in front of the largest antique desk she thought she'd ever seen. On the walls were pictures of well-dressed, prosperous men, often seated behind a desk such as the one before her. This private exhibition reached back into time: The older photographs were black and white, and before that there were drawings and paintings — Mr. Prince's ancestors?

Krall seated himself in Mr. Prince's chair and swiveled from side to side. For a moment, Sandy thought he was going to put his feet up on the desk, but he was simply pulling up his socks. He took a small device from his pocket and positioned it on the desk, pointed towards Sandy.

"You don't mind if I record this? It's purely for research purposes."

"I guess not."

"Thankin' you."

Krall took a deep breath and grasped the arms of his chair.

"Sandy, do you know what this election's about?"

Given her hours on the telephone, and how well everyone had said she'd done, this seemed like a strange, and perhaps insulting, question.

"Oh, I think I do, yes."

"And what would you say it's about?"

She thought for a moment. How could you sum up such a complicated bundle of feelings, longings, hurts — and fears?

"It's about America."

Krall picked up a pen from Mr. Prince's desk and rolled it between his fingers.

"I give you that."

He seemed to be waiting for her to say more.

"It's about who we are as a..."

What was she trying to say? Her words had all dried up.

Krall waggled his pen, holding it delicately by the base.

"See, that's about what I figured. That's what's special about you."

"I just meant —"

"The magic don't work when you talk to me. It's only when to talk to *real people.*"

Well, she certainly *preferred* to talk to real people.

"Don't you worry though, Sandy, it's all fine. We are just going to let you do what you do, and we are rightly grateful to you. Are we good?"

"Well, I suppose we are, yes."

More importantly, Sandy and Mr. Prince were *good.* Perhaps it was necessary for Mr. Prince to employ a man like this. There were people out there who would pull Mr. Prince down, if they could. People driven by greed or envy or lust. People without faith. Cynics, like Hunter Bill.

"That's what I want to hear. So let's just try a few more questions, okay?"

"Okay."

Krall gazed up at Mr. Prince's molded ceiling, as if seeking inspiration.

"Sandy, do you worry that America's in decline?"

What a question! It felt like a trick — no matter if you said *yes* or *no*, the answer seemed to come out wrong.

"It's okay," Krall said. "It's just one of these mean questions, you know? Can get people riled up, or all tied up inside or discombobulated. But we're fighting an election here, so we need to deal with it. You with me?"

"People think they've been betrayed. Like something's been taken from them."

Krall nodded and twiddled his pen.

"Uh-huh. Now, say you see Willard Prince out there, and he's sayin' our best days are still ahead. Do you believe him?"

"Yes, I believe him! Why would he lie?"

More pen-twiddling.

"Why indeed?"

She waited.

"And are you at all concerned, Sandy, that China is going to... To surpass the United States?"

Surpass? What did he mean by that?

"I know they're up there with their *moon mission.* I don't care about that. If they really want to take our flag, well, I'm sorry, but I'm just going to have to say that I don't particularly appreciate that."

Krall leaned forward across the desk.

"You're frettin' about that flag up there, Sandy?"

"I am not *fretting* about it."

"Okay. That's interesting."

Krall tapped a button on his recording gadget.

"Do you worry about economic figures and shit that like, Sandy? You know, your GDP..."

"Ray, please don't use that language in front of me."

Krall smiled and put his pen down.

"You gotta excuse me, Sandy. It's where I come from. My apologies."

So where did he think *she* came from? It couldn't have been so different.

"I do not worry or *care* about economic figures," she said. "They can mean anything."

"Sure. Okay. Good."

He tapped his recorder again.

"You know what? I think that's enough. Let me give you this..."

He reached into his pocket and took out a small, red object.

"This here's a memory stick. It's like a security thing. When you use the system, you have to plug this in before you can log on. Here."

He handed it to her.

"Don't lose it. Assuming you're agreeable, Sandy, we want you to come downtown and work with us. At the campaign HQ. We got a whole floor. Right above where the New American Century Fund is. Got a deal on the rent."

"Downtown?"

"We'll get you a car service. You'll be doing what you were doing before. Only on the big system."

"I just talk to people. That's all I do."

"And that's all we ask. I guess there'll be a bonus of some kind. At least if we win, which we will. And who knows — maybe the guys downstairs'll give us some tips."

"Tips?"

"You're not already invested, I take it? In the NACF?"

She let that insult lie where it fell.

"Nope, me neither."

Sandy's suit had no pockets. So she simply closed her fist around her memory stick.

Krall eased himself up out of Mr. Prince's chair and gave it a gentle spin, leaving it facing the wrong way. Then he stepped past Sandy to open the study door.

It was immediately apparent that something unwelcome had happened. Krall leaned out into the corridor and yelled.

"What the hell?"

A barrage of replies came; Sandy couldn't make them out.

"Robin Hood?" Krall said. "Fuckin' *Robin Hood?* Jesus!"

He ran out into the corridor leaving Sandy alone in Mr. Prince's private study. She didn't know what to do. So she waited.

After about five minutes, nobody having come for her, she got up and began to wander.

From the far end of the corridor came a hubbub of voices. She walked towards it, swinging her hips awkwardly in her tight suit and treading softly in her stiff new shoes. The noise came from an enormous room full of people. They were all dressed up, like Ray Krall, but none of them looked to be sweating. The walls of the room were lined with books: This had to be Mr. Prince's private library. Sandy imagined him there, alone, a book open on his lap, sunk in contemplation. Had he actually read all of these books? Well, even if he'd only read half, imagine what he must have learned.

Something impelled her to step into the room, even though she felt she didn't belong there. Almost immediately, a waiter materialized beside her and presented her with a tray of drinks. She felt a little bruised from her encounter with Krall — he had been uncouth and disrespectful — and she felt a little rebellious. So she took a flute of Champagne. Heck, it wasn't temptation; she deserved it.

And then a second waiter offered her a kind of pastry nest with something dark and glossy in it. Well, she couldn't drink on an empty stomach, so she took it. But this was awkward; she had to hold her glass and her memory stick in the same hand. Over by the large bay window, there were was an empty couch. Perhaps it would be better if she sat.

As she navigated to her seat, easing herself between knots of guests — variously garrulous, chatty or raucous — she picked up on a smell in the library. It was something rich, fusty and sweet. Could it be the books? The people? Or was it just the smell of money?

And she caught snatches of conversation.

Another crash? Well, I don't know. But the last one wasn't so bad now, was it?

No, Costa Rica's a bust. Somebody screwed up. They're looking at Belize.

Consistent? Nobody really buys that. We're talking about an edge.

You think so? But what if they really are better capitalists than us?

Weihan is the model. It's the way forward.

Will you please stop worrying about the working-class conservatives. That's why they hired Krall.

So if we put this guy in, what's he gonna do about the Fed? That's what I want to know.

"Hey, you dropped something!"

In the tricky process of seating herself, Sandy had lost her grip on the memory stick. And now here was the spiky, brown-haired girl from the vestibule picking it up for her. She looked a little frazzled, but perhaps that was normal for her.

"Here. Can I sit with you? Teri, remember?"

"Of course. Thank you, Teri."

"So what is that?"

Sandy hesitated.

"Oh, is it, like, secret?"

"Are you with the campaign, Teri?"

"I sure am."

"Only, you don't look like..."

"No kidding. I'm not a donor, or anything. I do blogs and videos for the kids. The young voters."

"Not for the working-class conservatives?"

"Uh, no. Not really."

She was quite petite, this girl, Sandy thought. Seemed smart, too. Trustworthy?

"How long have you been with the campaign?"

"Just started, basically. Finding my feet, you know."

"So am I. Perhaps we can help each other."

"Sure!"

"This…" She held up the memory stick. "Is what I have to use to access the big system. Ray Krall gave it to me."

"Oh, the big boss."

"Well, he's a big something-or-other."

Sandy took a slurp of her Champagne.

"Haven't met him. Heard stuff, though."

"He just left me sitting there. Teri, what is *Robin Hood?*"

The girl seemed to sit up in her seat.

"That? Just a bunch of protestors. Crazy people. They were outside. They've gone now. You haven't heard of them?"

"No."

Teri lowered her voice.

"They want to *share the wealth around.*"

"Really?"

The girl flapped her hand beside her ear.

"Totally nuts."

"Are you working downtown, too?"

"Me? No, I work here. My office is the scullery. I actually live here."

"In this apartment?"

"Servants' quarters."

"Seriously?"

"It's like that show on TV."

This girl was kind of funny. It felt like you could relax with her. She made you feel… *Happy?* Sandy took another slurp.

"So what's in this big system of yours?" Teri said.

"Everything, I guess."

"Wow. I didn't get one of those things."

"Well that," Sandy said, putting on a fake frown, "must be because you're just an uppity servant girl, and you're living under the stairs. While I… Well, I'm a rising star, and I'm living with Megan in Josh Merriweather's apartment in the Aspire Building."

Teri put on an exaggerated grimace — open mouth, wide eyes.

"No!"

"Yes. Ask Barbara."

"Barbara? No, I take your word."

Sandy realized that she'd finished her drink.

"I'll get you another one," Teri said.

"Oh, no, I —"

But then there it was in her hand. There was a pause while they sipped their drinks together. Then Teri asked a question.

"So, uh, what do you think of our candidate?"

"Mr. Prince?"

"Yeah. Mr. Prince."

Sandy looked at the girl. She didn't seem lost, adrift or hopeless, like so many other young people. Was she a cynic? Surely not, or she wouldn't be here. Did she have faith? That seemed questionable. But Sandy felt she was a good person — honest and not disrespectful.

"Well, Teri, I've been thinking that God sent him to do this. I truly believe that."

There was an awkward pause. But it didn't last as long as Sandy had feared.

"Do you really think so?"

"I do, Teri. Maybe you're too —"

"No, no, I get it. So he — Mr. Prince, I mean... He's on a mission?"

"Yes."

"To save America?"

"Yes."

"And... I guess what I'm wondering is, how did you..."

"How did I come to that conclusion?"

"Yes."

"I had a certain experience."

"What, like a... Like a revelation?"

"Something like that."

"You want to tell me about it?"

Sandy looked at the girl again. Too quick off the mark, she thought. Too eager. Needed to be taught patience.

"Not now, Teri, no. Perhaps once we get to know each other better."

"Okay. That's cool. No problem. D'you want another —"

"No thanks."

"Sure. Uh, this penthouse of yours? Is Barbara staying there?"

"No. She has her own townhouse."

"Oh, that's right. Milly told me."

"Milly?"

"Barbara's daughter. So, anyway — maybe I can call by? You know, after work?"

"I thought you servant girls didn't get time off."

"I'll sneak out."

"All right, then."

It was okay to encourage the girl, Sandy thought. Probably, nothing would happen.

But just then something else did happen. The library spun into a ferment because the news had broken that another naval crisis had blown up in the South China Sea; and that, as a matter of urgency, Mr. Prince was about to make a ground-breaking announcement that, for once, would force China to sit up and take notice.

CHAPTER 14

Ricky Ponton was no stranger to Struggle Street. The problem was, Struggle Street had gone global. No bloody lemurs for Ricky! Right? Wrong.

He didn't hear about the naval crisis until he got off the plane in Antananarivo, having traveled — still burdened by his *alter ego*, the go-anywhere British banker David Thatcher — via Nairobi, given his recollection that, despite its being one of the shittiest airports in the world and still reeking of smoke on account of having half burnt down within recent memory, it was much less spied-on than Paris. He wasn't so sure now: New Chinese-built terminal buildings gave the appearance of being just as fully bugged and surveilled as everywhere else.

He'd been all set to stroll back to Sydney, in defiance of Jay's instruction to report to Lemurland, when word had come through — via Big Data Underground, confirmed with glee by Jay — that the Australian government was having second thoughts about Ricky's citizenship. The Foreign Office in London had announced, gratuitously, that what remained of the United Kingdom was no longer in the mood to entertain his presence. And the US — surprise! — had put him on one of their lists. What this meant in practice was that Ricky was running out of planet. He could have South America, possibly, or one of the dodgy bits of Africa, or Russia.

Or Madagascar.

He found himself a taxi — some kind of relic that used to be a Renault 4 in the 70's — and braced himself for the long ride into *Tana*. It looked like no one had built, or even repaired, any roads here between the departure of the French and the arrival of the Chinese. The road into town was not a highway. It was an endless street market, continuous but for a swampy gap where the US embassy, a Texas-sized fortified warehouse, glowered. Why so big? In such a poor and unregarded country? Well, Ricky figured, the rent was probably cheap. And just across the Mozambique channel you had the badlands of East Africa — Tanzania, Kenya, and Somalia. Why not play it safe-ish in Lemurland?

The street food looked incredible, and Ricky was starving. But he knew better. Stick to cooked food in the hotel. This was a country where half a village could die of bubonic plague.

But why, apart from not having anywhere else to go, was he here anyway? Did it have something to do with the naval crisis? And what was Jay Percival, the CIA apostate and amateur sheep farmer, holding back? It seemed to Ricky that the unexpected recent happenings in Hong Kong — his recruitment by Xin Jiao, the leader of the punk-pop wing of the People's Liberation Army, for example — had not been such a surprise to the subtle, shiny-shoed American. When he got to Tana, Ricky would go shopping for a phone and give the guy a bell.

His hilltop hotel turned out to be a pleasant surprise: Spotless, airy, built largely out of local rare hardwoods that would have been worth an illegal fortune in a Chinese furniture warehouse or an American guitar factory, and staffed by beautiful, friendly people who just happened, statistically, to be the ninth poorest in the world. From the window of his room, Ricky could look way down to a large covered market; a wide, teeming boulevard; and an elegant but defunct railway terminus. Or he could gaze way up to his left at the historic old city, the *Haute Ville*, with its palaces (not all of them burnt-out shells), mansions, cathedrals and contested presidential residence. On the hill opposite was a jumble of commercial buildings, most of which appeared to date from the 50's or the 60's.

What he really needed, though, was lunch. And then, a bank. Plus a backpack and two bodyguards.

He didn't have any problem recruiting minders; the hotel staff were used to this kind of thing. Jay had told Ricky that he was wiring money, and that you got a lot of *ariary* for your dollar. And Madagascar was — let's be honest — what you call a *cash economy*. But it turned out that Jay's arithmetic had been flawed; Ricky had to send out for a second backpack. It seemed like an awful lot of money, but never mind; Jay's ex-Agency pockets were bottomless. Having witnessed his stash squashed into the hotel's safe, and with a decent wad secured about his person, he set off alone to find a phone, making every effort to look like a gun-toting drug dealer, rare species smuggler or timber trafficker, and not a clueless tourist.

It didn't take him long to find a mobile phone stand. But it did take him a while to negotiate with its proprietor the price of a call to Namibia, whence Jay had retreated, leaving his sheep — and Mr. Lin? — in the lurch.

"I bought you a house," Jay said.

"You what?"

"It's up in the north west, on the coast. Beautiful location. You'll love it. Kind of a *distress sale*."

"What are you talking about?"

"Well, the guy's some kind of French auteur film director. Got sued by a fifteen-year-old actress, know what I'm saying? I had to outbid some Russian guy. Got you a good deal, though. Eighteen million dollars."

Eighteen million dollars. In the ninth-poorest country on Earth.

"No, Jay. I mean, why are you buying me houses?"

"Couple of reasons. Can you hear me?"

It was difficult. The noise from the market and the forever-backed up traffic filled the boulevard with an aural fug almost as thick as the smoke that had blown in from the southern plateau, where subsistence farmers were busy burning a third of the country's land area to refresh their exhausted soil.

"Just about. Go on."

"All these problems you've been having. I've been giving them some thought."

"Thanks."

"Sure not getting any better, is it?"

"No."

"I mean, even if you do what they're demanding — you know, shut down Big Data, hand over all your files... They're not going to let you walk away, are they?"

"No."

"And then you've got the people who trusted you, who depended on you. What about them?"

"Right."

"They're even worse off than you. Like Kerri."

"Yes."

"You're running out of places to go."

"I know."

"Nobody wants to live in Russia."

"No."

"You need a sanctuary."

"Too bloody right, mate."

"This house can be your sanctuary. Think about it. A refuge. Calming ocean views. Gentle breezes. A demi-paradise for all your leakers, your whistle-blowers, and your disgruntled government employees. You must have dreamed about it."

Did it make any sense? Here was a guy who'd bought a sheep station on a whim. Had all that dirty money gone to his head?

"It's remote and inaccessible," Jay said. "You have to fly in. If you know the coastal waters, you can get there by boat, but it's risky. Got its own well. Own beach. Runs off solar power. Satellite Internet. The locals are very, uh, *autonomous*. So as long as you're nice to them..."

"What about the politics?"

"Well," Jay said, sounding increasingly pleased with himself, "the great thing about being dirt-poor is, there's no economic leverage. Not gonna get your ass kicked out of the WTO. Plus no land borders. A big old slice of nowhere with no roads, in the middle of an ocean. You *will* have to pay off the politicos, but you've got two factions who are both basically pro-Chinese, that being where the money is, so you just play 'em off against each other."

"I don't have any money."

"Yes, you do. You got a bag full."

"Two bags."

"Whatever. More where that came from."

So, *sanctuary* then, but at a price and on Jay's terms. There was something almost mediaeval about it. But there was more, wasn't there?

"You said there were a *couple* of reasons."

"I did."

93

"So what's the other?"

"I'll tell you. But no freaking out, okay?"

Not again...

"You still there, Ricky?"

"Yeah. So tell me."

"All righty. Now, you remember *the guy?*"

"What guy?"

"The guy you didn't meet in Hong Kong?"

Despite the heat, Ricky felt the sweat condense all down his spine.

"He doesn't exist."

"Oh, sure he does! He just got a tad scared. Had a panic attack, if you like. Heard what your little friend Jiao was up to. So he backed off. Guess where he is now? He's right there with you in Antan — , uh, Antana —"

"*Tana.*"

"There you go. He's an engineer. A *military* engineer. I want you to go meet with him, bring him up to the sanctuary, treat him nice and find out what he's got. Find out why there are Chinese military engineers in Madagascar. Okay?"

Ricky noticed that the phone stand owner was agitating for a top-up. He pulled a bunch of ariary out of his pocket and handed them over without counting them.

"Ricky?"

"Are you sure about this, Jay? If I go and get this guy, and your pals from *the office* show up again..."

"They won't. Trust me. It's a beautiful house. Corsican marble. Tropical garden. Fuckin' lemurs everywhere."

Well, what choice was there? Is was the lemurs or *Russia.*

"Never mind the lemurs. Where's the guy?"

"Well, he didn't want to come into the city. Says there are too many Chinese people there."

This was plausible. Tana was full of Chinese-run stores selling anything cheap that could possibly be manufactured or assembled in Shenzhen or the Pearl river delta.

"Get yourself a four-wheel-drive," Jay said. "And head out towards the north east. There's kind of a ring road, takes you to route 2, which goes east. Look out for the brickworks. The guy's waiting at the brickworks."

"Does this place have a name?"

"Yeah, but it starts with "A" and it's twenty syllables long. Forget about it. Just look for the bricks."

"What about the guy?"

"Mr. Yu."

"And where's the *sanctuary?*"

"It's called La Cachette Lémurienne."

"Cute."

"Got its own strip. Just tell them when you hire the plane. They'll know it. Call me when you get there."

"Fine. Is that it?"

"Yeah. Don't get bitten by any animals."

Jay hung up. Ricky handed the phone back to its owner, who gave Ricky a skeptical frown and plugged the phone back into its solar charger.

And then Ricky realized that Jay's whole *sanctuary* pitch had so bedazzled him that he'd forgotten to ask about the naval crisis. It seemed weird that Jay hadn't mentioned it, given the fuss he'd made about Chinese *strategic encirclement* of the Indian Ocean; the Chinese had just complained, after all, that the Americans were threatening their trade routes to India and East Africa. Just as suspicious was the idea that two warships, equipped with the best navigation kit available, would both accidentally steer off course towards each other at the same time. Who wanted a confrontation? Jiao worried about nationalism. That rich guy who wanted to be President stood to have his China-bashing bluff called. Military chiefs knew that *accidents* got you fired. Well, Ricky wasn't going to call Jay back now; the guy was only tolerable in small doses. He'd bring it up next time.

Renting a car turned out to be problematic. So Ricky fetched one of his backpacks from the hotel, paid his bill, and purchased a second-hand Nissan from a lot cluttered with scooters and clapped-out Citroëns. The Nissan was far too old to have satnav, so Ricky bought a map. Luckily, the traffic moved so slowly that he had plenty of time to study it.

After fifty minutes of bumper-to-bumper, he made it on to the ring road. And that was when he began to wonder if Jay Percival hadn't been chucked out of the CIA for sheer bloody incompetence.

He pulled the Nissan over on the side of the road. And he looked.

Up the road, down the road, kilometer after kilometer, across a great, open, brown expanse — the panorama was the same. It looked like a scene from ancient Egypt. He'd been expecting a plant, or a factory, or maybe just a big shed. But there were no buildings.

Bricks, sure. Bricks everywhere. As far as you could see. Stacked up in tottering piles, pyramids and ziggurats, some of them with fires lit underneath and lazy wisps of smoke wafting from the top. And hundreds of people, making the bloody things *by hand*, ankle-deep in mud, the men and boys stripped to the waist.

Just look for the bricks. Nice one, Jay.

Ricky got out of the car and began to trudge along the raised shoulder of the road. Perhaps Mr. Yu lay in wait, sweltering, hunkered down amid the toiling multitude. (Though why he couldn't just have hung out at the Snack Bar at the airport seemed like a good question to Ricky.) Would Mr. Yu spot an irate Australian marching up and down the highway? Would he proceed to leap out from behind one of these baking, Pharaonic piles, clutching his military secrets, a glow of muddy elation on his face?

As it happened, he didn't. Ricky got back in the car.

Now what? He had no phone, the agreed procedure having been to rely on the hard-to-trace services of Madagascar's independent telecoms entrepreneurs. And he didn't want to hang about in the capital, with its everyday hazards, its choking smoke, its traffic, its supersized US embassy and its political risk. Besides, he could practically hear the lemurs of La Cachette calling out to him. *Did* lemurs call out? He'd be answering that question soon enough.

He started the car and put it in gear. And then he noticed something. This stretch of road wasn't the busiest — but now there was nothing. No traffic at all.

He peered into the distance. Just about visible in the haze was the junction where the RN2 took off east to Andasibe and the main port of Toamasina. Stationary trucks. Flashing lights. He pulled the Nissan around to face south. About a kilometer away, a road-block and more flashing lights.

He felt his foot tremble on the brake pedal. What a beautiful set-up. No way out. No Jiao and no truck to the rescue this time. No fearsome Party to protect him. Bloody Jay. *They won't, trust me.* But they never gave up, these bastards; they had their own, special, *exceptional*, shit-eating pride. And they'd wired the whole bloody world, so they would always find you. Even here. And these poor sods, trying to dig themselves out of poverty, brick by brick, didn't realize that you escaped one prison just to find yourself in another. Did they have camera-phones to record and blazon to the world what was about to happen? Probably not.

For five minutes nothing happened. The brick workers didn't stop. The lights at the road-block continued to flash. Then there was movement. A single vehicle emerged. Ricky waited. It crept forward, a black smudge in the shimmering smog. A little closer, and he could make out a large, new SUV. Closer still, and he could see its antennas, and two occupants — bulkier than your average Malagasy. A little more and — why not? — Maryland license plates.

Ricky put the Nissan into four-wheel-drive and low-range. *Fuck it* — why not make them work for their prize? Then he pumped the accelerator and the car bucked across the broken edge of the road and slid down a shallow embankment. He put his foot down again. The car clattered down a blocky staircase from which bricks had recently been cut. He sped up across a slick flat, fishtailing and scraping the corner off one of the ziggurats. In his mirror, he saw the SUV inch off the road fifty meters back from where he'd made his exit. Did these guys know how to drive? Maybe he had a chance.

He bumped down into some ruts made by the donkey-carts that hauled the bricks and then barreled along, thumping on the horn with his fist. The brick-makers got out of his way, but barely gave him a glance. Behind, the SUV had fallen back.

Now, he thought, there really was a chance. But which way? If he could get to the RN2, which he knew to be a good road, by local standards, he could blast out of town and find somewhere to hole up in the first settlement he came to. He yanked the wheel to the left, scraped the car out of the ruts, skittered up a crunchy slope of broken bricks and then slithered down the other side into a trench of heavy mud.

Ricky put the car into reverse and eased on the accelerator. The car jerked backwards, then slid forward again. He pressed harder. The wheels spun. He tried to rock forward and back again. It didn't work. He tried reverse again, and full power. Smoke, steam, burning rubber. *Shit!* And the worst thing? He *knew* how to drive, and these bastards didn't. But no, that wasn't the worst thing at all. Erase that thought, *idiot*.

He got out of the car and crawled to the top of the brick scree. There was the SUV, its doors open, occupants outside, propped up against the bonnet, arms folded. What was wrong with this picture?

CHAPTER 15

eri Wolfe had been forced to rise early, squeeze herself out of her cubby hole, shower for all of half a minute in the staff bathroom, chug a cup of coffee in the staff kitchen, and then trot over on foot to a hired meeting room at the Plaza Hotel. Gloria had rapped on her door at six in the morning.

Teri had to do this because Fat Willy had elected — no, let's be accurate, had been forced — to convene a press conference to explain exactly what he had meant the previous evening by *taking the tough choice to be China's critical best friend.*

Presumably, he'd had time to think that particular bombshell through overnight. Or his people, at least, had been given an opportunity to defuse it. Either way, it promised to be good entertainment.

And it had to be in the hotel because, for reasons held to be obvious and yet unmentionable, journalists were forbidden entry to the apartment. Well, the *mainstream media* were, at least. According to Milly, access was granted only to a very reliable coterie of *Friends of Willard*, or FOW's. These inky eminences operated at what Teri liked to think of as the *bow-tie* end of the market.

The room was packed and giddy with anticipation by the time she got there. Teri took a seat in the back row and cranked up her camcorder. On stage were a row of chairs; a lectern bearing the logo — not too classy, Teri felt — of the New American Century Fund; two of those glass projection screens that everybody always pretended not to see; and, at the back, a row of immaculately furled flags — all stars 'n' stripes, and no red-and-yellow ones either, as far as Teri could tell. So much for *best friend*. Let's get critical!

At the back of the room and half-way down the sides were the professional camera crews and the TV journalists. She immediately spotted one of her favorites: Flint Gunner of the Freedom News Network. You couldn't miss him; he was seven feet tall, about half as wide, had shoulders that would have done for a line-backer or a rocket launcher, and had a head in the shape of a mallet. In idle moments at Bean Village, Teri would occasionally flip to *Flint Gunner's National Security Bunker Hour*, which went out at three in the afternoon and was said to be popular with seniors. Right now, Flint was studying his notes. He looked engrossed. By his side, and rising only slightly above Flint's elbow, was a shabby fellow in a raincoat, who had a round, screwed-up face and nasty raked-back ringlets. The look on his mug was superior, satirical, menacing. Teri had no idea who this creature was, but she shuddered anyway.

And now the show began. The seats on stage started to fill. First up, the glossy blonde girl called Megan, Stimsonville Sandy's room-mate in the coveted Aspire Building. Why would they put *her* on stage? To soften the visuals? *Get me a woman up there, dammit!* This theory gained strength when, next up, Ray Krall took his seat. He looked as though he'd spent the night chewing one of Fat Willy's Persian rugs, and had just been presented with the bill. But then Barbara stepped up, and the theory began to look weak. Teri scrunched down in her chair and held her camera higher to obscure her face. Two smooth-cheeked young nerds completed the team; these were the policy wonks who could find China on a map and knew the name of the Prime Minister. Or President, as the case might be.

There was a pause in which reverential adjustments were made to the lectern and the microphone was tested. Then Mr. Willard G. R. Prince, the next President of the United States, strode into the room, mounted the podium, and gripped the lectern like it was a rogue trader who'd just lost the Fund a packet.

"The United States has a long and proud tradition," he began, and right there, Teri thought, he'd already made at least two dubious assertions, "of standing firm against all foreign aggression..."

It was a history lecture. She felt the audience give up a silent, collective sigh. Prince just went on and on. Was that *Lexington and the shot heard 'round the world?* Did he just mention *Little Big Horn? Appomattox? Pearl Harbor?* On he went. You could feel the life-force seep out of the crowd. Was this a shrewd and deliberate tactic? Krall's face was a blank. *Omaha Beach!* Then a judicious fast-forward, skipping the sixties and the seventies, to *Mr. Gorbachov!* And then another nifty advance to the present day and the War Zones and *honoring our troops.* Basically, the answer was, she decided, that President Prince would uphold all of the nation's finest traditions, were the people of a mind to confer upon him the hallowed office of Commander-in-Chief. Uh, what was the question again, Teri?

Prince looked as if he were glad to have cleared all that up.

Okay, so any questions?

How about Mr. Gunner from FNN? Wait, get him a microphone. Oh, he doesn't need one? Okay...

"Uh, I guess what people want to know is, are we best friends with China?"

Prince drummed his fingers on his lectern and made a face that put Teri in mind of someone sucking on a particularly sour cherry. Then he sniffed and stepped back from the lectern.

"Ray?"

Krall got up and took his boss's place at the microphone.

"Flint, you know as well as I do that that ain't the right question. You want us to show our hand? You want us to put our cards on the table? That's no way to act tough, and you know it."

Teri glanced at Gunner. He looked confused, as if Krall had just whacked him in the nuts with his own clipboard. And before he could figure out what had just happened to him, Krall moved on.

"You there. Mr..? Who? Give him the mic!"

"Nigel Weese. London Globe."

It was Gunner's pal.

"Ask your question."

"Well, isn't it a bit funny that these two ships should just happen to bump into each other —"

"My understanding is, they did not bump — uh, we have no evidence of a collision."

"Well, all right, if you say so. Came awfully close, though, didn't they? Did someone put the wrong post code in the satnav, or what? I mean, it's pretty convenient, isn't it? If, for the sake of argument, you had someone who wanted to *torpedo*, as it were, this trade pact thing —"

"A full investigation is under way. At present, we are not at liberty to speculate as to —"

"Only it would have to be someone on each side, though, wouldn't it, because otherwise —"

Krall was giving Weese the evil eye.

"Thank you, sir. That's *one* question each — okay, people?"

Teri stole a glance at Weese and angled her camera with maximum sneakiness. And wow! If a weasel could smirk, that's *exactly* what it would look like. Weese elbowed his larger partner and beckoned. Gunner lowered his massive head so that Weese could whisper into his ear. The big guy's expression morphed from low-lidded bafflement to slit-eyed suspicion. Teri decided she knew who wore the pants in *that* relationship.

Krall batted away another dozen or so meandering, lackluster queries, relaxing into his preferred folksy style once it was clear that the gathering had accepted, reluctantly, that Prince was not going to confess on camera to being a secret China-lover. Then it was all over.

And now, Teri thought, steeling herself, it was time for some *James Bond shit.* Before Megan, or Milly, or Gloria, or Krall, or — God forbid! — Barbara got a hold of her, she would jump the number 4 train at 59th Street and head downtown to Pearl Street and Bean Village, to retrieve the secret microfilm. Or SD card, or whatever.

But she didn't get far. Weese was in the way.

"Look, Flint — it's the new girl! Nice camera!"

"Uh, excuse me —"

"*Teresa*, isn't it?"

"Teri. Um, look, I've got to —"

"Get some nice pictures of us, did you?"

"Well, I..."

"It's all right. We don't mind, do we Flint?"

"Hell, no. *No problemo*, Nige. No way."

"He's used to it anyway, you see, Flint is. Camera loves him. Bit of a pin-up. With Reagan voters, at least."

"Mm-hm."

"Settling in all right, are we? Nice to have connections, isn't it?"

Fuck this, Teri thought. She had to get out of here. But the two of them were, in their very different ways, quite an intimidating presence for a hundred-and-nineteen-pound slacker with authority issues.

"She a journalist?" Gunner asked.

"No, Flint. She's a *blogger*."

Gunner snorted.

"Oh yeah? *Blogger!* How about the blonde?"

He seemed to mean Megan.

"Never mind about her, Flint."

Weese leaned forward, violating Teri's personal exclusion zone like a fake Taiwanese trawler scouting some disputed island. His breath was like a fine wine, Teri thought — fruity, with hints of tobacco and a long aftertaste.

"Listen, love. Here's my card."

He thrust a scrap of cardboard into her hand.

"If you've got anything interesting from the bunker, if you know what I mean, you just give me a tinkle. All right?"

"Sure. Whatever. But they made me sign this —"

"Got a lot to learn about journalism, hasn't she, Flint?"

"Sure does."

"We'll have to help her along."

Teri plucked up courage, pushed past them, and then legged it for the exit. *Jesus!* The James Bond shit couldn't be any worse than that, could it? Well, definitely not any creepier. That guy Gunner was funny to watch on TV, but in person... And that pal of his? Yuck.

Teri hit the subway and rattled all the way down to Broadway, where she hopped off and bowled down Wall Street, dodging bonus babies and back-office drones, hanging a left at Pearl Street and barging her way into Bean Village. It was busy, as was customary for nine in the morning. Pedro and Aliyah were at full pelt, loyal and hard-working members of the Bean Village family. Unlike some, eh? And look — a new employee! Teri's replacement! Jeez, Trenton could really move when they wanted to. Teri studied her successor: Female, check; mid-twenties, check; depressed-looking, check; arts grad, check. She wouldn't last long. But never mind. Teri needed a quiet word with Aliyah. She loitered at the back of the line, pretending to study a flyer offering night classes in structured debt.

When her chance came, and Aliyah was alone at the counter, Teri pounced.

"Aliyah!"

"Teri! How are you doing?"

"Pretty good. Not bad. Um, Aliyah, I kind of left something in the back. Could I..."

"Teri! Staff only in the back! You know that."

"Yeah. Yeah, I know. But, it'll only take —"

"So what did you leave?"

"Erm, it's just a little, you know, one of those memory card things."

"Okay, I tell you what. I get it for you. Where is it?"

Well, okay, it made her look like an idiot, but so what?

"It's under that big can of French Roast."

"Ooh! I get it. Nobody ever look there!"

"Yeah. Exactly."

"Wait here."

Aliyah vanished into the store room. Teri kept an eye out for Pedro and Teri two-point-oh. They were clearing tables at the far end of the shop. Aliyah didn't come right back. Teri glanced at the TV monitors: There was Krall sandbagging Gunner over the China thing. Where was Aliyah? Come on!

But Aliyah returned empty-handed.

"You know what, Teri? Julianne, I think she reorganize. No French Roast. All gone."

"Gone?"

"Sure."

"Well, maybe it fell on the floor?"

"No, I look. Plus I sweep last night."

"Shit."

"Okay, so what you got on there, anyway?"

"Oh, just pictures."

Aliyah folded her arms.

"Ah, pictures. Hey, you download some more, huh? I know what you like."

"No, Aliyah! It's not... Never mind. Thanks anyway. You take care, okay? See you later..."

"Sure, you be careful, too."

Teri stepped out into Pearl Street. What now? Do a no-show in the Park? Blow Robin off? She trudged back to Wall Street.

Then she had an idea. Only a block away, on Water Street, was Prince's New American Century Fund. And, right above that, was the campaign HQ. And in the HQ was Sandy, God's phone-bank messenger to humankind. Teri could check out the HQ, hang out with Sandy, and avoid both Barbara and Gloria for a while. But maybe an offering would be appropriate. Teri checked the cash in her purse; there was just enough. She marched up the street to the Coffee Truck and bought two large slugs of rocket fuel. It did occur to Teri that Sandy's out-of-towner stomach lining might not be up to the job, but hey — it'd be a real New York experience for her.

In the lobby on Water Street, she flashed her campaign ID and hit the elevators. The campaign was on floor ten. Just for the hell of it, she pressed the button for nine as well. But it wouldn't light up. Weird, huh?

Up on the tenth floor, Teri surveyed the Prince Campaign headquarters: One big, open-plan floor; lots of cubicles with low walls; a couple of conference tables; a wall of glass offices, with blinds on the inside. Lots of little pennants on the desks: Half and half Old Glory and the NACF logo. Posters of Prince looking as if he'd gotten up that morning and launched a battleship and endowed an orphanage, before taking the train to work. A lot of clean-looking kids with computers. Security cameras.

Sandy was in one of the cubicles. On seeing Teri, she removed her headset.

"Hey, Sandy! I brought you something!"

"Oh, thank you, Teri. You're so kind! Let me get you a chair."

Teri sat and removed the safety cap from her coffee.

"So how's it going? Have you clinched the thing for us already?

Sandy blushed.

"They've put me on disaffected former home-owners."

"Sounds tough."

Sandy took a moment to ease the top off her coffee.

"Yes."

Teri pointed at Sandy's screen.

"And this is the big system, huh?"

"That's it."

"Cool."

Sandy took a gulp of her coffee. There was a short delay, then...

"Oh my! Oh my goodness, Teri!"

"Good stuff, right?"

"Oh my!"

"Yeah, it's real. Mind if I browse?"

"Where did you get this?"

"Coffee Truck."

While Sandy recovered from her caffeinated sensory overload, Teri flipped through the windows on Sandy's screen. It looked like some serious IT shit: Sandy's script, with its prompts and answers and search facility; pages of metrics; 3D graphs; trending subjects; news feeds; intra-campaign email; a logon screen...

She paused at the logon screen. There was Sandy's user name, *SandyQ*, and her password, asterisked out. And a nice picture of her, presumably for security purposes. But the rest didn't look quite right. There were five menu options: *Prince for President* was the first. So far so good. But how about *NACF (Private)*? Or *London (Private)*? Or *Cayman (Private)*? Or *Family (Private)*?

Sandy was coughing into a paper napkin.

"You okay there, Sandy?"

More coughing.

Teri clicked on *NACF (Private)*. A new window opened. *Fund Snapshot*, she read. Underneath was a list of numbers, some of which were on the humongous side:

Total Invested: $249,378,772,250.00

Total Redeemed: $51,875,900,000.00

Certain other fields, such as NPV, VAR and Total Income, were blank. But *shit!* This looked like the real thing. There was *no way* that Sandy was supposed to see this stuff.

"Teri?"

Teri clicked the window shut.

"Can you fetch me a glass of water? It's at the back."

"Sure."

While she fetched Sandy's water, Teri homed in on the crucial issue: Sandy's red security key. Someone had not configured it correctly. Or maybe Sandy had been given the wrong one. Either way, someone had screwed up. Big time. But what to do?

Now, obviously, the correct and proper thing to do was to bring the matter to the attention of Technical Support. Was Teri going to do that? *Hell no*, as Flint Gunner might have said. What was that guff that Robin had spouted? Teri could be a *mole* on the inside? She could *hack into their systems?* Well, what do you know! So she'd lost the memory card; big deal. Maybe she had something better. She would keep the rendezvous in the Park after all.

But what about Sandy? Suppose somebody else spotted this almighty screw-up? Would Sandy get in trouble? Nah, she was obviously clueless. She was the most innocent person Teri thought she'd ever met.

"I don't think I can drink any more of that."

"Maybe next time I'll go to Bean Village."

"Yes, they have nice coffee."

"So, what time d'you get off, Sandy?"

"I'm on until six."

"Is it the former home-owners all day?"

"I think so."

"Guess there's a lot of them. Okay, I'd better let you get on."

Sandy picked up her headset.

"So, do I get to check out the penthouse tonight?" Teri asked, noting the way Sandy's shoulders sagged at this.

"You're welcome any time, Teri."

"Okay! So we're cool! Bye!"

Teri made for the elevator bank, slurping her rocket fuel as she went. Bean Village coffee was just about okay — but only if you paid the fifty cents for the extra shot, which almost nobody did.

But she didn't take the elevator; instead, she snuck down the stairs. The tenth floor had your standard, glass, fire-safety doors. But the ninth floor had what looked to be reinforced steel doors. No glass, no handles, no buzzer, no nothing. It looked like you could get out this way, but not in. She didn't loiter, because there were two security cameras above the doors, one for each direction. So how did you actually penetrate the NACF — without an invite or Sandy's dumb luck?

Teri bumped and clattered back to 59th Street, after which she located an ATM and withdrew fifty dollars, noting that her checking account balance now stood at $282.15 and her savings account balance at $0.39, and wondering when her adequate salary might begin to kick in. Then she bought a sandwich and headed into the Park. It was a little after noon.

When she got to the rink, she paused and squinted up into glare of the declining sun. And there it was, head and shoulders above the rest, looking like it was about to shove them out of the way and annex the Park for its own purposes — the Aspire Building. How strange to think of poor, bewildered Sandy wandering about up there, at however many thousand dollars per square foot, worried about scratching the marble or dinging the gold leaf, a prisoner in a plutocrat's playpen. And there was still something mysterious about Sandy; Teri would definitely have to dig deeper.

She sat on an empty bench and ate her sandwich. Upon finishing, she parked her paper bag prominently in the middle of the bench, and adjourned to the next bench along, crossing her legs and leaning back, hands clasped behind her head, in order to catch a few, final, pale rays before winter.

She held this position for quite some time. It began to hurt. Then...

"You're *supposed* to go away!"

She sat up. It was *Robin*.

"Hi," she said. "Nice day!"

"Why are you still here?"

"It's a free park."

"You were just supposed to... Oh, forget it."

He grabbed the sandwich bag and rummaged inside it.

"Erm, here's the thing..." she said.

"Where is it?"

"Well, I kind of..."

"What?"

"Kind of lost it."

He seemed to struggle for words.

"But then why... What is the point of..."

"Let me explain."

It didn't really look like he was in the market for explaining, so she thought she'd better pop his anger bubble before things went any further.

"You do realize that Robin Hood wasn't black, don't you? It's like Santa Claus. Everybody knows they're white. They just are."

He stared at her for a long moment. Then he capitulated and flopped down on to the bench beside her.

"Sorry about your friend," she said.

"That's okay. We'll find her."

"Sure you will."

"All right. Talk to me."

So she did.

"Wow," he said, when she'd finished. "Do you think we really could?"

"But it was *you*, with all the moles, and the hacking and all that."

"Yeah, but... That was just bullshit. Crazy talk."

"Uh-huh. So. Do you want to or not?"

CHAPTER 16

S andy Quayle thought that Teri Wolfe was a decent, thoughtful, bright young woman, if a little on the pushy side. But then, everyone she'd met recently, with the exception of Mr. Prince, seemed pushy: Ambitious Megan, imperious Barbara, Barbara's assertive daughter Milly, and Ray Krall, who might even be a bit of a bully.

Perhaps Sandy had simply lost touch with the modern world, during her years of exile. Had things gotten even tougher, even harsher? She recalled her encounter with the gas station attendant. Sometimes it seemed that America was just so darned cross with herself and had lost all patience. Sandy found it hard to say why, as did her targets. The former home-owners mostly blamed themselves, and yet they were full of anger at so many different things.

Or was there something *wrong* with Sandy? Well, as of now, all her past failures stood to be erased by a moment of grace. Yes, that was correct — it wasn't just *luck*. So no, she didn't believe so. And Mr. Prince apparently didn't think so either.

Anyway, Sandy's private opinion was that Teri seemed the nicest of the bunch. And what a life she had before her. For all the servant-girl jokes, Teri was obviously on the way up. What a chance she'd been given! After the campaign she would, no doubt, move on to even better things. She probably had a boyfriend. He would be a reliable young man, calm and sensible to balance out Teri's impetuosity. Perhaps they were already planning their first home together. They wouldn't be able to afford anything on Megan's budget — never mind Josh Merriweather's — but it would be their special place. They'd furnish it. Decorate it. Make it their own. Settle down. And then...

"Sandy! How're you doing with your home-owners?"

Former home-owners, she thought.

"Oh, Megan, hi. I'm doing real good."

"The figures look great. We didn't think we'd get any of these people. Most of them are deadbeats. You're a genius!"

"Not really."

"You're finished in ten minutes, right? Want to do something fun?"

105

"Well, I don't know —"

"Oh, come on! Please? Hartley and me, we're looking at apartments? Ray's driving us. He says he knows how to nail a deal. You know, if we like something. But I need a girl friend with me. Otherwise, these boys..." Megan rolled her eyes. "They think a kitchen's where you store your beer. They think *one* bathroom is enough!"

Sandy felt tired, and her stomach had yet to recover from Teri's coffee, but she couldn't bring herself to say no.

"Well, okay. Yes, it does sound like fun."

"We'll be in the lobby in fifteen."

Sandy worked for another ten minutes. She spoke to a fifty-nine-year-old woman in Allentown, PA, who had re-mortgaged the house she'd lived in for thirty years in order to pay for her husband's drugs. Her husband had died anyway, and she'd lost the house. Then there was a forty-five-year-old man in Greenville, SC, who said his job in wind turbine manufacturing had been outsourced to China. Neither believed that Mr. Prince would do much to help them, they said, but they might vote for him anyway because he stood up for America.

She was glad to get off the phone.

"This is going to be *such fun!*" Megan said, as Sandy emerged from the elevator. "And this is Hartley. He just flew in."

Megan's boyfriend was tall but not particularly slim. He had light brown hair that had already started to recede, and he wore a dark gray suit and blue-and-white striped shirt. His tie bore an elaborate design that, Sandy guessed, probably had some special meaning.

"Hi," Sandy said.

"Hello! Lovely to meet you!"

Oh, that's right, Sandy thought — Megan had said that her boyfriend was English, and his father was something grand.

Ray Krall was there too, dressed down in denim and a leather bomber jacket.

"Hey Sandy," he said. "I love your work. You remember to unplug your..."

He meant the red security key.

"Yes, I remembered."

"Then let's hit the road."

Krall's car was in a parking garage at the end of the block. It was a large, black BMW. Mr. Prince, Sandy recalled, had gotten into trouble, unfairly, for admitting that his family owned a *bunch of Cadillacs.* Well, at least they were American.

To Sandy's surprise, Krall turned out to be a careful driver. And, despite what Megan had said about not being able to afford Manhattan, it seemed that they were headed uptown.

"So what's the budget, guys?" Krall said.

Megan, seated next to Sandy in the back, leaned forward.

"Four million."

Then she turned to Sandy.

"It was just impossible. So Hartley talked to his father."

Sandy nodded.

"His father runs the Fund office in London."

"Oh," Sandy said, "so that's —"

"But somehow *Pa* can't give Hartley a job!"

A theatrical shrug from Hartley in the front passenger seat.

"He says they don't need any structured debt guys."

"But they need Milly!"

"Just for PR. They wouldn't let her near the trading floor."

Krall continued to coax his car north. Eventually they parked outside an apartment building close to the East River.

The first viewing went quickly. Hartley seemed impressed, but Megan rejected the kitchen and all three bathrooms. Krall was quiet.

They moved on a couple of blocks to a second building, where there were three *possibles*. Hartley loved the views. Megan disliked the floors, ceilings and walls, respectively. Krall seemed to take it all in his stride. Sandy began to wonder how there could be so many people who could afford such apartments; these were huge buildings. And also why you would worry about the floor when you could just put a rug down.

Then, five blocks to the south and only two blocks from the Park, they found it. Megan was ecstatic. There was just one problem, according to the broker: The price had gone up. By three hundred thousand dollars. Sandy and Krall left the prospective home-makers alone in the kitchen — which was about the same size as Sandy's had been in the mini-mansion — to talk through the issue together. The broker stepped out of the apartment to call the sellers.

But it wasn't long before the volume in the kitchen went up and Sandy began to feel uncomfortable. Krall quietly closed the kitchen door and ushered Sandy down the hall. They entered a bright, sparsely-decorated living room which had been professionally enlivened with flowers and bowls of fruit.

"You thinkin' what I'm thinkin', Sandy?"

"I might be."

"Why don't we make ourselves comfortable? This could take a while."

Krall sprawled across a sofa. Sandy settled herself carefully into a leather-and-chrome armchair. Krall took a minute to check his messages on two separate phones and a tablet. Then he sat up and leaned forward towards Sandy.

"Know what I'm going to do when the campaign is over?"

Sandy said nothing; how could she possibly know?

"I got this... I guess you'd call it a cabin. Up in the Adirondacks. No heating or nothing. You have to build a fire. My plan is to head on up there. All on my own, you know? Gonna do some hiking. Chill out. Maybe I'll write my memoirs. Or make a start, anyhow. Maybe I'll put you in there, Sandy. You okay with that?"

No, she didn't think she was okay with that, whatever he really meant, but she simply said, "If you want."

"Because the fact is," Krall said, "I'm finished with politics after this. Maybe we'll all be finished. How about you?"

"Me?"

"What are *you* gonna do?"

"Well, I haven't..."

She'd told Megan that she hadn't decided what she was going to do. But something in Krall's voice deterred her from using that answer now. For years, up until her encounter with Mr. Prince, she'd thought no farther ahead than the next day or the day after. This habit had refashioned her soul, which had been forcibly slimmed down, just like her body.

She could imagine Teri's future life, and perhaps even Megan's, kind of. But not her own. All she had was Mr. Prince — for today, and tomorrow, and a little bit more. And that was that. If she couldn't find anything else to cling on to, in her new world of money, then afterwards, and much more so than Krall, she would be *finished*. And there would be no memoirs.

"Goin' home?"

"Home?"

"Stimsonville."

"I..."

"You know, to that big old house of yours."

"House?"

"The one with the little pond in the front yard, and the white fence and the red mailbox?"

The pond had dried out and filled with litter, according to Hunter Bill. And the fence had gone, probably to be used as fuel. For all she knew, the mailbox continued to collect threatening letters. What cruelty did Krall intend to inflict on her?

"What I want to say to you, Sandy, is this," he said. "You and me, we ought to stick together."

"I just wanted to help. I wanted to help Mr. Prince. It doesn't matter if..."

"No, it don't matter, Sandy. You're right. But listen. You can help that guy all you want. That's great. They all love you, because you've truly got something, and that's real. But I got to tell you a couple of things. Like I said, this is my last campaign. And I do believe I am going to win. Why? Because people are afraid and they're angry — I mean, Jesus, you know that better than I do. Then they look at the other two guys, and they feel worse. They want a savior, Sandy — and that's what we're giving them, ain't that right? I don't mean it's like a religious thing, exactly. But we got a guy who already has *the power*. Nobody tells him what to do. He doesn't need anybody else's money. And *that alone*, by the way — it just makes the donors even hotter for him. He's already achieved what they see as *greatness* — and that's what we're selling, ultimately. Most folk, they cannot begin to figure out how the world works. So they are going to settle for a story, if you tell it right."

"But it's not a story. It's true."

Krall rubbed his eyes.

"I'm gonna be making some money out of this, Sandy. I want to be honest about that. I got a pretty good deal out of them, and I am going to deliver, and I'm worth it. To *them*."

"Ray, it doesn't matter to me how much they pay you."

"I get that, Sandy. But I see you, and what you do, and I listen to you on the phone. And I do a little research, and... And I just cannot go out like this. Do you understand?"

If he had a problem with his conscience, so what? It was nothing to do with her. He was a mercenary. What he had said about Mr. Prince was cynical. You couldn't really understand Mr. Prince and what he stood for, or what he offered America, unless you had *heart*. And Krall was heartless.

The broker had appeared in the doorway to the living room. She held up her phone, grimaced, and shook her head. Krall got up.

"Sellers?"

"Yuh. They won't budge."

"Let me talk to them."

Krall took the phone and pushed out into the hall. The broker shrugged.

"Seller's market," she told Sandy. "What're you gonna do?"

Krall was gone for about two minutes. When he returned, he looked unhappy.

"Four million."

He gave the broker her phone back.

"Oh, but that's wonderful. But how did you —"

"Just told them who they were messin' with. Why don't you go and..."

"Yes, I'll tell them. This is so amazing."

She headed for the kitchen to break the happy news. Sandy looked at Krall. What threat had he employed? And why had he done it?

"Still don't get it, Sandy? I tell you, we are sticking together. Whether you like it or not."

And then the atmosphere in the living room lit up as the apartment's joyful new owners entered, hand in hand, teary but triumphant, and the broker called in to her office. Sandy thought Megan looked like the happiest girl in America.

"There's still the co-op board, but..."

"They're gonna love you," Krall said. "Trust me."

And so then it was determined that Megan and Hartley just *had* to go out to dinner to celebrate, and Megan further decided that it made sense for her to stay at Hartley's hotel, as he had to fly back to London the next day.

"Come on then, Sandy," Krall said. "Let me drive you home."

That was neither possible nor desirable, Sandy thought. She would merely go back to the Aspire Building.

As before, Krall drove smoothly and carefully. He didn't speak until he'd patiently docked his car in the building's half-empty underground parking garage.

"Mind if I come up? I'd kind of like to see the place."

"Okay."

Once inside the apartment, Sandy sat on the huge, white, U-shaped couch in the main living area and looked down into the Park. It was dark now, but she could still make out the shape of the rink, picked out in twinkling lights.

Krall wandered the apartment on his own, hands in his pockets, pushing doors open with his feet. He looked like a bored tourist in a museum, she thought.

"Well, I guess I like the view," he said when he'd finished. "Have a good night. Hope you sleep well."

"Thank you."

He left, clicking the door shut quietly behind him.

She lay down on the couch and breathed deeply. What did this man want from her? Why couldn't he just leave her alone? And he knew about the house; what would he torment her with next? All she desired was to carry out the task for which she'd been chosen. She might have expected to be tested — but like this?

She considered praying, but then she looked around at where she was and decided to go and change into her sweats instead.

As she returned from her bedroom, Reception called. A Ms. Teri Wolfe had come visiting.

And, of course, the first thing the girl did — after the obligatory tour, and to Sandy's consternation — was play with the apartment's many high-tech gadgets. The remotely-controlled smart-glass skylights. The 3D sound system. The remotely-controlled video telescope. The voice-controlled kitchen. The smart lighting. The smart bathroom. All the other smart things. And the ultra-fast Wi-Fi.

And it was when Teri connected to what she said had to be some kind of movie server, that they discovered that Josh Merriweather's apartment was fully wired for sound and video. Yes, *every* room. Yes, *even* the bathrooms.

"Weird," Teri said. "This guy is *some* friggin' libertarian."

CHAPTER 17

Teri Wolfe had always suspected that when religious people freaked out, they *really* freaked out. That proved to be the case with Sandy. Maybe she'd had a bad day, or something.

It took Teri several minutes to calm Sandy down and reassure her that, despite appearances, it was highly unlikely that Josh Merriweather, or any of his people, had been monitoring Sandy's every, uh, movement about the apartment. These tech billionaires were eccentric. They were either born that way, or else they quickly became so after the IPO. They spent money on crazy stuff. Just because they could. Josh Merriweather might be a weirdo — Teri privately favored this view — but not a creep. He hadn't been watching Sandy; he'd probably been planning a mission to Mars, or designing an underwater city, or else figuring out a way to sell everybody Wi-Fi sandals.

All the same, at Sandy's urging, Teri searched the apartment until she found the server closet, and pulled the power cable out from the offending hub. Then she fetched Sandy a cup of green tea and sat her down on the U-shaped couch.

Encouraged to talk, Sandy told Teri about her evening hunting for the perfect starter-home on the Upper East Side. *Four million dollars*, Teri thought. Did Megan have any idea what she could get in Bayonne for that? And didn't she know that downtown was where the cool kids lived these days? The cool *rich* kids, that was. Yet Sandy seemed most exercised by Ray Krall. He'd done something to upset her, but she refused get specific.

In return, and to further the calming process, Teri told Sandy about her afternoon in the scullery, blogging, at Gloria's insistence, on how exciting it was to open a brokerage account in your twenties and — who could say? — why you might just turn out to be the next Willard Prince. All you needed, apparently, was to believe in America. Mr. Prince, Teri was to remind her readers, only invested in America.

"But there's an office in London," Sandy said.

"I guess that's so foreigners can invest."

"Foreigners? What sort of foreigners?"

"Don't know. Rich ones?"

111

"So they would own…"

"Part of the fund, yes."

"Oh."

Teri studied Sandy's face. When she let go of that tight-lipped expression she usually wore, it sagged.

"*Cayman*. Those are islands, aren't they?"

"In the Caribbean."

"Why would…"

"It's a finance thing," Teri said. "They all do it. *Offshore banking*, it's called. I guess it's about privacy." *And tax evasion*, she thought.

"I don't really understand."

"Join the club. Don't worry about it."

They sat together in silence for a long moment.

"It's a great view," Teri said. "You can see, like, the whole of the Park."

"Million dollar view," Sandy said.

Teri figured it was more like eighty, but said nothing.

"Would you mind if I went to bed?" Sandy said. "I'm so tired."

"No, of course not. Do you want me to —"

"No, Teri. You can stay as long as you like. Stay all night. I don't mind. Actually, I think I would like it. And I hate to think of you all scrunched up in your cubby hole."

Sandy got up and walked slowly to the stairs that curved up to the mezzanine.

"See you tomorrow."

"Sleep well."

When she had gone, Teri turned on the video telescope. You controlled it using a tablet computer and, she discovered, you could direct its output to the billionaire-sized TV screen in the living area. And you could record stuff. She zoomed in on the skating rink. Where was Robin now? What was he doing? Perhaps he was filling in his merry men on his amazing new scheme to undermine capitalism from the inside — i.e., Teri.

It would probably come to nothing, Teri thought. But it sure beat putzing around with toy drones. The possibility that something embarrassing to Prince could be found in London or the Caymans, or in the Fund itself, was surely high. Nothing had changed since the last crash. The same con-games and rackets went on. It seemed that the number of stones you had to turn over before you found something nasty was precisely one.

Robin claimed that the Robin Hood Party had sufficient *in house* expertise to spot financial wrong-doing or anything ethically or politically foul. All Teri had to do was get hold of the raw data.

Well, that was one challenge. There were two others. The first was the question of Sandy's password. And the second was the little matter of *betrayal*.

But Teri had made a vow to herself, barely two days ago, to resist any and all temptation to fuck with Fat Willy's campaign, no matter what opportunity arose, and however odious, hypocritical or corrupt he and his gang of thieves turned out to be. Now okay, thus far, she had no more evidence of malfeasance than when she'd started this job. That wasn't the point. Here she was, about to jump into the *spy shit*, right up to the fake pearls that Gloria insisted she wear.

112

Was this really a good idea? Could she betray Sandy by stealing her red security key under the cover of friendship? It didn't help that Sandy appeared to worship Prince, as if he were the amalgamated second coming of King Solomon, St. Francis of Assisi, and Ronald Reagan. Now, if you wanted someone to stick it to the self-deceiving and the superstitious — to creationists, climate-deniers, trickle-downers, faith-based whatevers and other flat-Earthers — and to do it with agreeable savagery, then Teri was normally your girl. But maybe not in Sandy's case.

And yet it was Sandy herself who swayed the jury. She clinched the verdict. The woman had a story. There could be little doubt that it was a sad one. She didn't want to tell — yet. But these people — Krall for one, by the sound of it — simply wanted to exploit her. When they were done, they would sling her out with the garbage.

Whatever happened, she was going to get hurt. But Teri would be around. And she'd make Robin help, too. That was for sure.

Sandy's bag lay on the opposite wing of the couch. Teri crossed over and sat next to it. She unzipped the top. Then she sat and looked at the bag. There couldn't be much in it. She listened. No sound of anybody — Sandy — moving about. Teri pulled the bag open and looked inside. There was so little. No purse, but some change — and nine hundred-dollar bills? No cosmetics, just a comb. A few pieces of campaign literature. The electronic key to the apartment. And the red security key. She removed it from the bag. Stuck to it was one of those yellow sticky tabs. Sandy had written her user name and password on it.

Teri bit her lip. She almost hadn't wanted it to be this easy, had she?

She took the key into Josh Merriweather's study and closed the door behind her. Then she turned on his computer. Robin had said that the key might not work remotely, outside of the campaign HQ. If that were so, this whole thing got a lot more difficult — maybe impossible. She plugged the key in. There was a pause as the computer decided whether or not to go along with this nonsense. Then up came the menu, just as before, except that all the options were disabled. Teri entered Sandy's user name and password. The options turned from gray to blue.

Then there was a loud *whoop*, like a police siren. Teri almost fell off Merriweather's architect-designed chair. But it was merely an email notification; Sandy had new mail from Barbara. Teri turned off the computer's sound and, without thinking, clicked open Barbara's message. It was mostly campaign cheer-leading — Prince had polled top in the *best candidate for fiscal responsi-bility* category — but, at the end, Barbara asked if anyone at campaign HQ had come across a girl called Teresa, who had been hired by the family at the request of the campaign. And, if so, whether they had any *comments. Shit!*

Teri clicked the email shut and then spent a panicky minute figuring out how to mark it as "unread". So Barbara *was* on her case. Oh well, so what? Teri might just have to work faster.

She took some long, slow breaths to try to slow her heartbeat. Then she looked at the screen. Where first? *NACF, London, Cayman, Family?*

Robin had said that, with a sufficient sample of the NACF's trading records, it should be possible for the RHP's resident reformed financier — codenamed

Friar Tuck, ha, ha — to figure out the essence of Prince's *bespoke strategy*. The assumption, among the financial *cognoscenti*, was that Prince had an *edge*. It certainly wasn't as dumb and nefarious as front-running or insider info. Was it legal? Well, the done thing was not to express an opinion. Not out loud, anyway. And certainly not in writing to the SEC.

Teri selected *NACF*. Now, what did trading records look like, and where did you find them? She started clicking and scrolling. She'd expected to be overwhelmed with data, but it wasn't like that at all. There were plenty of spreadsheet-type screens and graphs, but often they appeared empty or blank. Perhaps she needed more system privileges than she had?

Eventually, under the *maintenance* function, she found something called *trading book backup*. Well, that sounded promising. She clicked, and was prompted to *select media*. Media? She ransacked Merriweather's study looking for *media*. In a desk drawer, she found a new pack of memory sticks and busted one out. One point five terabytes. That sounded like a lot. Would it be enough? Prince's strategy had to involve a hell of a lot of trading, right? She plugged the stick into the computer and clicked OK. Nothing happened. She waited. Another click on OK. Nothing. Then she realized that the backup had completed. She checked the memory drive and, sure enough, there was the file — *tradback.dat*. Wow! Merriweather's computer was one fast motherfucker. Well, it would be, wouldn't it?

She unplugged her backup and Sandy's key and shut down the computer. Then she tiptoed back into the living area and slipped Sandy's key back into her bag, remembering to zip it up afterwards.

Mission accomplished! She felt a guilty elation. And also a righteous thrill, that kind of canceled out the guilt. Would Robin be impressed? You betcha! Teri Wolfe — Queen of Spies! No, that didn't sound right. Princess? Even worse. Forget it.

She took out her phone — her crappy personal phone, not the fancy one issued by the campaign — and sent Robin a text message. *Lunch in park tmw?*

Two minutes later, a reply came: *OK, bring sndwch.* The romance of espionage, she thought. Yeah, you could kind of get it.

But what now? Go back to the cubby hole or raid Merriweather's concierge-replenished refrigerator?

And maybe his bar, too...

No contest.

CHAPTER 18

Ricky Ponton told Mr. Yu that he could pick any room he liked. There appeared to be plenty of them. Then he gave Mr. Yu *the tour*. Not that he'd ever been here before, of course, but La Cachette was *his* house now, and he felt proprietorial.

This corner of the fourth largest island in the world was undeniably beautiful, he thought. It was what you saw in TV documentaries. But it wasn't what you called the *whole picture*.

On the flight up, in a four-seater Piper Arrow that Ricky had selected over cheaper options in recognition of Jay's munificence, they had gazed down together at the raw, eroded redness of the Madagascan landscape. It looked like a scalded corpse. Mr. Yu's view was that a tipping point had been passed — the burning of grass and forest; the washing away of the soil; monoculture in the south, such as sisal; illegal logging in the diminishing forests of the north-east; vast mining projects — nickel, cobalt, gold, platinum; and now oil sands, and rare earths and heavy minerals, some of which had hitherto only been mined in China — ilmenite, leucoxene, rutile, zircon, monazite, garnet, sillimanite and spinel. And whatever the profits, and no matter how large the Chinese investment, Mr. Yu had said, the country's twenty-two million citizens were only going to get poorer — unless they made it to the top in politics.

"Shall we see the garden first?" Ricky asked.

Mr. Yu nodded.

He was a pretty cool customer, Ricky thought, a shrewd-looking, fit, fifty-something in an REM T-shirt, who'd probably seen a few things in his career as a military engineer. He'd sat out the scene at the brick works, and, from a safe distance, he'd more or less correctly interpreted its outcome. After which he'd had the resourcefulness to cadge a scooter ride back to the airport and waylay Ricky in the Snack Bar where he should bloody well have been in the first place. Mr. Yu had blamed Jay and, considering what had happened at the brick works, Ricky was happy to concur.

"Most impressive lawns," Mr. Yu said. "Do you employ a gardener?"

"I guess so."

Ricky had naturally assumed that the ambush at the brick works was another whack at the prize by Jay's former pals from *the office*. After all, despite Jay's earnest assurances, it had already happened once before. But the two guys hadn't shaped up to him. And something about them — was it their laid-back attitude or their total lack of paramilitary might? — had clued him in as soon as he saw their faces.

They'd introduced themselves as *Captain Kirk* and *Admiral Spock*, and had towed his Nissan out of the swamp. Then they'd announced that they had something for him.

Ricky and Mr. Yu strolled by an ornamental pool which had been carved out of a rocky outcrop.

"This is called *tsingy*," Mr. Yu said. "Limestone. There are some excellent formations in this area. You will see later."

"Sure. If you say so."

Kirk and Spock's gift to Ricky turned out to be a another memory stick. He was instructed to *listen up*. He and his partner, Spock had explained, represented the US military. Ricky said he'd figured as much. According to Spock, a senior stratum within the military felt burdened with certain legitimate concerns that could not be expressed through the regular military hierarchy, and especially not through the Pentagon.

Then Kirk had butted in to stress that their *interaction* with Ricky did not constitute any kind of approval or endorsement of Ricky's activities or of Ricky personally. In fact, they thought he was a sniveling little shit who endangered America's men and women on the front line, and did the terrorists' work for them. However, as military men, they were nothing if not pragmatic. *My enemy's enemy*, and all that. Ricky could have pointed out the historic flaws in this doctrine, but it didn't seem like the right time.

Anyway, the bottom line was that Kirk and Spock found themselves forced to use *unconventional avenues* to achieve their objective. The memory stick contained evidence — damning, according to Kirk — of the dangerous, un-American, unconstitutional, and downright traitorous activities of certain US global corporations. Kirk and Spock expected Ricky to disseminate these revelations immediately, all across his criminal, terror-loving network. Also included was a tranche of financial, ethical and personal transgressions, of the type all too common in top corporate circles. Such material was of no concern to the military. But Ricky should publicize it anyway.

Ricky had promised to give this patriotic data dump due consideration. (He would, of course, ignore any tacky scandal; he wasn't a tabloid newspaper.) *Consideration?* He was abruptly reminded that he'd just been given an order. After that, they'd hustled him past the police roadblocks, paid off the cops, and released Ricky into the wild.

And it was only when he was relaxing on the plane with Mr. Yu that Ricky realized he'd been through this deal before — with Jiao in Hong Kong. The only difference was that Jiao had given him tea. Both the Chinese and the US militaries had got it in for big business — their *own* big business. Why?

Mr. Yu had paused at a row of flowering bushes.

"Endemic," he said, in a tone of approval.

"Can't beat it."

The moment Ricky had arrived at La Cachette, he'd cranked up the satellite Internet system and forwarded Kirk and Spock's data to Norway, via the usual convoluted, multiply-encrypted, randomly-reconfigured server maze. Big Data Underground was still functioning. But the global corporations it was about to attack probably had more power to destroy it than any politician, spy or general.

"Let's go down to the beach," Ricky said.

"Why not?"

They followed a boardwalk to a wide terrace by a swimming pool, then descended balustraded steps to a pale beach that fringed a small horseshoe bay. At either end of the bay the land rose up into tree-topped limestone cliffs. The sun was sinking into the Mozambique Channel. Mr. Yu seemed impressed.

"This is all yours?"

"Think so."

Mr. Yu jogged down to the water's edge. Ricky followed.

"From here, it is about three hundred and fifty kilometers," Mr. Yu said.

"Across the channel?"

"Yes. To the south, it narrows to two hundred. Then it widens again."

"Uh-huh."

"And, of course, it also widens to the north."

"Mm."

"The depth varies from two hundred to four hundred meters."

"When you get out a little from —"

"Yes. The Madagascar plateau extends underwater to the north. This contributes to the eddies and gyres that are only found in this channel."

"Eddies and gyres?"

"Yes. But this is no problem for a large vessel. There is a warm current that flows south. It joins the Agulhas."

"Okay."

"I think your beach is very beautiful. Look up there!"

Mr. Yu pointed to the cliff top.

"Sifakas!"

"What?"

Ricky looked. Six or seven large brown-and-white shapes, swinging through the trees. The lemurs.

"Coquerel's sifaka is endangered. But I am not sure about these. Too far away."

"Shall we go in the house?" Ricky said. "And you can tell me what you've got."

"Oh, yes."

They walked back to the house. It was built from the local limestone in a style that Ricky took to be a mix of Hollywood and French colonial. Its former owner had left behind all of the furniture; it was chrome and leather and unsuited to a tropical climate. There were framed movie stills on the walls.

They found Ricky's cook in the kitchen. Introductions were made and menu items selected.

"The local people are *Sakalava*," Mr. Yu said as they sat on a veranda with their aperitifs. "Very nice people. Very ancient culture. But you must know their customs. Don't worry, I will tell you."

"Thank you."

"Do you have a boat?"

"A boat? I don't know."

"You have a boat house. I saw it."

"Really?"

"We can look tomorrow. No hurry."

Ricky sipped his beer.

"No. No hurry. But I'm kind of curious..."

Mr. Yu gave Ricky an indulgent smile.

"We will get into details tomorrow. But I will give you one thing now."

Ricky waited.

"What is the annual Chinese military budget?"

"How much? Er..."

"Last year it was one hundred and forty billion dollars."

"Quite a lot."

"That figure was announced at the National People's Congress. In America, they think the true figure may be forty per cent higher. But it is not."

"No?"

"No. The true figure is four hundred and ten billion."

"Ah."

"It is still less than half of what the Americans spend."

"Right, but..."

"But in China, prices are much lower."

"Toilet seats and such-like."

"What?"

"Nothing. Got any documentation?"

"Of course."

"What are they spending the money on?"

"Many things."

"Such as?"

Mr. Yu finished his Sancerre.

"Such as the anti-ship ballistic missile system. One thousand kilometer range. There is more. Let's leave it for tomorrow. I am ready for dinner."

"Sure. Until tomorrow."

So, Ricky thought, how about *that* for a starter. Four hundred and ten billion. More than twice what the Yanks thought. What the hell did they pay all those spies for? How would it play on the Freedom News Network? And how would *that rich guy* handle it?

"Where is your dining room?" Mr. Yu asked.

"I don't know."

They went to the kitchen and got directions.

*

Ricky awoke to a commotion outside his window. Hardened instinct kicked in before his conscious brain did. Emergency plan! But where was he?

He was in the squat in Camberwell. The Special Patrol Group were kicking over his dustbins and smashing his windows — the ones that weren't already plugged with plywood.

No...

He was in the bedsit on the Cowley Road, there'd been a riot, and the Anti-Nazi League wanted to use his phone, which he didn't have.

No, not there...

He was in the tent in Trafalgar Square, outside the South African embassy, and some Young Conservatives were peeing through the flaps.

No, no...

The boarding house in Kings Cross in Sydney?

The bungalow in Broken Hill?

Jay's sheep station?

He jumped out of bed. The tree outside his window swayed and shook. The lemurs — what had Mr. Yu called them? — were breakfasting on fruit.

Ricky got dressed and went down to the kitchen. Mr. Yu was already there.

"Good morning! And good news — you *do* have a boat. A *power boat*. Very impressive."

"Great."

"But I think we must have some help. These waters... We need a pilot."

Ricky helped himself to coffee and fruit — much of which he could not identify.

"We're going out on the water?"

"We must."

"That's where the, uh, military secrets are?"

"In a sense."

Ricky wasn't in the mood to push things; the impulse to control had faded, for some reason that he couldn't explain. Perhaps it was simply all *this*: His house, his garden, his beach, his sanctuary. He had never known much in the way of *security* — except, of course, for the type that shaped up to you in a uniform.

"Are military secrets all that interest you?" Mr. Yu asked.

"What do you mean?"

"Or is it just any kind of secret?"

Was it too early in the morning for this? Ricky thought it was. He gave the lazy answer.

"People have a right to know."

"Know what?"

"Anything that isn't going to hurt anyone else. Anyone innocent, I mean."

"Who is innocent?"

Ricky sipped his coffee. Was Mr. Yu going to get philosophical? Couldn't he just shut up and enjoy his boat ride?

"Most of us, I suppose."

"You?"

"Well... Look mate, I'm an activist. You can't help getting a bit... Compromised."

"No?"

"Look what I'm up against."

Mr. Yu nodded gravely, as if Ricky had just admitted to a debilitating condition.

"But you're getting some help."

"Yes..."

"Do you wonder why?"

Ricky refilled his coffee.

"Well, yes I do. Sort of."

Jay's ostensible worries about southern African sovereignty and neutrality were fine, he thought. The guy claimed to work for some South African elder statesman. There might be something in that. But what about this Sino-American joint military freak-out over corporate shenanigans?

"But you," Mr. Yu said, "are not so active. Not now. You are passive. You get the secrets and you publish them."

Not *now?* Did Mr. Yu know Ricky's history?

"I wouldn't put it like that. Look, I've been on the street. I've tried that. Didn't really work. Now there's another way."

"Technology."

"Yeah. Secrets are about power. When we expose them, power is... Redistributed. It's very *democratic.*"

"You are a fan of democracy?"

A jaunt on the ocean seemed ever more appealing. With luck, the roar of Ricky's power boat would drown out Mr. Yu's meanderings.

"Oh, big fan. Huge."

"How about in China?"

"Sure. Why not?"

"I am glad you think so."

"You're welcome. Ready to head out?"

Mr. Yu was ready, but still not in a hurry. They made another tour around the garden, and Mr. Yu took time out to photograph the lemurs — *Sifakas!* — with a camera he'd found in Ricky's library.

And Mr. Yu was right about the boat; Ricky was impressed. About ten meters long, it could accommodate a dozen people, he reckoned. It had two massive outboard engines on the back, and it was called *Madeleine.* The wife, or the fifteen-year-old, Ricky wondered.

They spent half an hour studying the manual and figuring out how to top up the fuel. Then they realized that the tide was out, and the boathouse stood high and dry above the mangrove-fringed creek that served as its private access. Fortunately, Mr. Yu discovered that it was possible to winch the boat by hand down its slipway.

Ricky started the engines, and felt encouraged by the throaty growl they made. But he let Mr. Yu drive; he was an engineer, after all. And he seemed to know a lot about the Mozambique Channel.

They chugged out of the creek into the ocean, navigating around some sandy shallows and bouncing on the colliding waves at the mouth of the creek. Then Mr. Yu opened up the throttle and they cruised north along the coast. Towering cliffs, caves, impossible white beaches, craggy pillars, miniature islands erupting from the blue-green water like prehistoric mushrooms — Mr. Yu had been bang-on about his *excellent formations.*

"Look," he said.

Teetering on top of the cliffs — thick, pale humanoid trees.

"Baobabs."

"Cool."

Presently, another creek opened up. As they drew closer, Ricky could make out a cluster of thatched wooden huts.

"Fishing village," Mr. Yu said. "I shall find a pilot. You meet your neighbors."

Some of the neighbors spoke a little French, so conversation was possible. Ricky thought he'd made a good impression. He invited the entire village to visit La Cachette whenever the mood descended, and offered to lend out his boat, free of charge, to careful drivers. Mr. Yu found his pilot: A wiry young man who asked to be called *Andri*.

The boat safari resumed.

"There is a bay," Mr. Yu said. "About twenty kilometers to the north. That is where we are going. It is very beautiful. Do you snorkel?"

"Uh, no."

Ricky had tried it once, out on the Barrier Reef. That was when he discovered that he had an incurable fish phobia.

"You must try!"

"Maybe not today."

He sat back in his seat and held on to a handrail as Andri took the boat out into the ocean and accelerated it to what was — surely? — its maximum speed.

Forty minutes later, they entered the bay.

And Ricky could immediately see why they needed a pilot. The bay was a world all to itself: Vast, intricate, a waterscape of channels, sandbanks, caves, cliffs — and those tree-covered mushroom islands, dozens of them. Andri brought the boat down to a putter, and they began to edge their way in.

Mr. Yu tapped Ricky on the shoulder.

"This is a sacred bay. We must pay our respects."

"Sure. Okay."

So long as it didn't involve fish...

Andri slid the boat up on to a sandy isthmus. They removed their shoes and jumped down into the water. Ricky noticed that Andri carried a bag. What was in it? Ritual and mumbo-jumbo made Ricky nervous.

They advanced into the forest, Andri leading the way, Mr. Yu following, Ricky bringing up the rear and watching, in official Australian fashion, where he put his bare feet. They wound their way along a narrow footpath; this was a remote spot, but people obviously came here regularly.

Then they stopped. Mr. Yu pointed.

"There."

"What? All I can see is trees."

"The big one."

"Oh. *That*."

It was the biggest tree Ricky thought he'd ever seen. Or the widest, at least. A giant baobab. Andri was pointing at Ricky's jeans. He took something from his bag and handed it to Mr. Yu.

"Here," Mr. Yu said to Ricky. "Put this on. It's a *kitamby*. Just wrap it around your waist like a skirt."

Ricky did as he was told. Then, in procession, the three of them made a slow, silent circuit around the tree.

"Okay," Mr. Yu said. "Take that off now."

"Finished?"

"Yes. We honored the ancestors. Now we talk military stuff. Back to the boat."

Andri took the boat on a painstaking circumnavigation of the bay. Mr. Yu pointed out fish eagles, and baby baobabs that sprouted from cliff faces. Ricky wondered if any human had ever stood atop one of these mushroom islands, with their monstrous overhangs, and had wondered how the hell they were getting down again. But for the water lapping against the side of the boat, and the subdued mumble of the engines, there was silence. The blue-green water rippled. The sun warmed his face. Ricky thought for a moment — just an instant, really — that if he could make a deal with the world he might just take it: Give me my house, my garden, my lemurs and my boat, and leave me alone, and I'll stop causing trouble. But it was only an instant.

"I don't see anything military," he said.

"You don't?"

Mr. Yu feigned surprise.

"Then prepare to use your imagination."

He picked up a tablet computer.

"Where'd you get that?" Ricky said.

"I found it in your gym."

"I've got a gym?"

"Yes. I have loaded some of my data. Look here."

Ricky squinted at the screen.

"This is a map of the bay, you see?"

"Uh-huh."

"That's before, okay? This is after."

Mr. Yu flipped to his next slide.

"Wow. What is all that?"

Superimposed on the map of the bay were a mass of interconnected gray rectangles. They obscured about a third of the area.

"See this?" Mr. Yu said.

"Mm-hm."

"That is a four kilometer runway."

"It's in the forest. Isn't that a national park, or something?"

Mr. Yu shrugged.

"And this?"

"It's in the ocean."

"On it. That is a floating dock."

"What's this thing that connects the dock and the runway?"

"A four-lane highway."

"Over the ocean?"

"Yes."

"What the hell is this thing, then?"

"It's for the Chinese navy. The largest naval base in the world."

CHAPTER 19

Sandy Quayle's day had gone well. Her new working life was only temporary, she knew. And Ray Krall was still out there. But that just meant she ought to take consolation in, and celebrate, every moment.

Megan had switched Sandy from *disaffected former home-owners* to *worried retirees with grandkids in college*. This was more encouraging. Although she and Johnny-boy had no children — would it have made any difference, or would they have fallen even sooner? — let alone *grandkids*, Sandy was able to reassure her targets that Mr. Prince was a family man like no other, and nothing was more important to him than providing for his sons (no daughters, alas!) and for their sons and daughters in turn. Well, except National Security, naturally! And Sandy knew this had to be true because Mr. Prince had a special *Family (Private)* area in his big system. The targets didn't need to know *that*, of course.

And although Sandy hadn't met any of Mr. Prince's family members yet — there had been no sightings of Mrs. Prince, and nobody talked about her — that was about to change. Because Barbara had told Sandy that the weekend was here, and that meant that the campaign's top brass were to relocate to the Prince family compound out in the Hamptons. There would be a strategy session, led by Ray Krall. Now, Sandy wasn't quite top brass — not yet! — but she and Megan had made such an impression on the campaign that Ray Krall had decreed that the two of them be available, should the strategy session require their input. It would mean another long ride in Barbara's Escalade. Sandy said she'd be delighted to attend.

The city had been exciting — but also exhausting. Something similar could be said, perhaps, for Teri Wolfe. And so Sandy felt sure that she would enjoy a break in the country.

As for Teri, well... Sandy had some concerns there. She'd left the Aspire building — in her black limo! — at eight fifteen. And she wasn't at all sure that Teri wasn't still there. There had been an empty wine bottle on Josh Merriweather's smart coffee table. Sandy had dropped it, noisily, into the recycling bin, and then strained her ears for suspicious sounds. Such as a hung-over girl falling out of bed, for example. But she'd heard nothing. Could be some work there for the boyfriend!

Anyway, Megan was making her own way out to the Hamptons, having scheduled appointments with decorators. So it was just Sandy, Barbara, and Barbara's daughter Milly in the Escalade.

Thanks to Barbara's driving skills, they made good progress out of the city. But then they got bogged down on the Long Island Expressway. This was normal, Sandy learned.

"You have to go through Hell to get to Paradise," Barbara said, as they crawled past Brentwood.

Gradually, the traffic eased and the sprawl began to thin out. Barbara cut down to Route 27. Just past a golf course, she turned right and exited the highway. They drove slowly through a small town of tree-lined streets, brick sidewalks, clapboard houses and smart stores with American flags out front.

Barbara glanced over her shoulder to Sandy in the back seat.

"Quaint, don't you think? This is Southampton."

"Oh," Sandy said. "I think I've heard of it."

Milly, up front, laughed.

"Yeah, really."

They drove out the other side of town and followed a two-lane road with hedges either side. Then Barbara took a left on to a private drive that wound lazily across what seemed to Sandy like a dozen acres, at least, of mowed parkland and mature trees. They passed a row of tennis courts; and then a greenhouse with two wings and a Victorian-style dome; and then ornamental gardens with fountains; and then a swimming pool with a pool-house that Sandy thought was only just smaller than the mini-mansion. Then they rounded a turn, and Sandy caught a glimpse of the ocean. Another turn, and they were in a courtyard at the rear of an enormous house. It had steep, pitched roofs; tall red-brick chimneys; dark-timbered gables.

"This is it," Barbara said. "Breedon Manor. Fake Tudor. Beautiful. Shame about the beach."

Sandy wondered what was wrong with the beach. It looked like, well, *paradise*.

As they got out of the car, Sandy saw that Ray Krall's BMW was already there, parked next to a very ostentatious red sports car. She also saw that the house was well-guarded.

"Secret Service," Barbara said. "Keeping an eye on us. Better mind what we get up to."

Sandy was surprised to find that the house looked exactly like the apartment — except on a larger scale and with vaulted ceilings. Even the books in the library looked identical. On Barbara's instruction, Milly showed Sandy to her room in the *north wing*.

"This room has some history." Milly said. "Kind of dark."

"Oh..."

"Don't worry, it's not haunted or anything. It's just like, there was a suicide? Way back in, like, nineteen-thirty."

"Really? Oh, my... In the Prince family?"

"No, they didn't own it then. There was this Wall Street guy? I guess he was a banker. Everybody thought he was rich, but he'd lost it all in the crash. So then he kind of faked it for a while, but people found out. And his family were like, how could you do this to us? And he couldn't stand the shame, they say, so..."

"That's horrible."

"Yeah, pretty gross. So, you're not freaked out or anything, are you?"

"Well..."

"If you are, you can swap with Megan. She's next door."

"I think I'll be fine."

"Okay. Dinner at seven. Us peons are in the kitchen. The bigwigs are having a quote, *banquet*, unquote. Like in honor of the generals, or something."

"Generals?"

"Uh-huh. Those two who are always on TV? They used to be in the military. Mom calls them *society generals*. See you later."

After Milly had gone, Sandy went to the window and looked down at the beach. It was deserted; the wind had picked up and there were whitecaps, and foam where the waves hit the shore. She thought it was the most beautiful beach she'd ever seen. There was nothing wrong with it at all.

Then she sat in the window seat and thought about Milly's story. Imagine that poor man. How terrible it must have been to have felt so sad, so bereft, that you would take God's gift in your own hands and... In fact, she couldn't imagine it. At times her own life had felt like a slow march through a landscape of suffering — and wasn't that true for so many people? — but this man had chosen to enter a darkened valley never warmed by God's love. Or perhaps anyone's. And Sandy felt so sorry for him because she knew that, though she had herself ventured at times into the shadows, she would forever have the strength to stay out of the dark. Perhaps she would say a prayer for him later. She would tell him there was no shame in not being rich.

But dwelling on such things was wrong when there was useful work to be done. She unpacked the few items she'd brought with her, collected up the notes she'd made at Megan's request, and made her way down to the library.

She set her notes down on the long, antique oak reading table. Then she noticed that a vase of flowers had gotten untidy and set about rearranging it. While she was doing so, two men entered the library. They looked to be in their mid-thirties, were dressed for business, and were engaged in animated conversation. Seeming not to notice Sandy, they sat together at the opposite end of the reading table. Yes, she thought — those high, sloping brows; the wide jaw with the small mouth; the perfectly triangular nose — these were Mr. Prince's sons. They looked pretty smart, didn't they? How proud their father must be.

She was wondering how to introduce herself, when one of the brothers looked directly at her.

"Would you bring us some tea?"

He turned to his brother.

"English breakfast?"

The brother shrugged.

"English breakfast. For two."

Sandy hesitated. What to do? *Someone* was going to be embarrassed, either now or later. Then she thought of that poor man alone in his bedroom and decided that this particular social calculus was not only beyond her but absurd. If they wanted tea they could have it. She picked up her notes.

"For two," she said.

Then she strode smartly out of the library in search of the kitchen.

Barbara was there, sitting at a table with a stack of newspapers. She was reading the Washington Post and sipping something amber from a glass tumbler. There was a faint smell of cigarette smoke in the air.

"Well, it's Sandy! How'd you like the house?"

"Oh, it's very grand."

Actually, she was beginning to find it cold and oppressive.

"I was impressed. First time I was here. Take a seat."

"Oh, but I have to..."

"What?"

Sandy explained the tea situation.

Barbara threw her newspaper down and mopped her brow with an imaginary towel.

"Oh, those boys! Something will *have* to be done. Sit down. I'll take care of it."

Sandy sat.

"Let me guess," Barbara said. "English breakfast?"

"Yes. For two."

"*For two.*"

Barbara set about her task. She knew her way around the kitchen, Sandy noted.

"They get this stuff shipped specially. I don't know where *from*. I think it tastes like bark."

Barbara made the tea in a large silver pot. She slammed this down on a tray along with a jug of milk and a bowl of sugar. There were delicate teacups inside an oak-and-glass cabinet, Sandy saw, but Barbara ignored them.

"What do you think?" she asked, holding up two mugs. One carried a picture of a cartoon puppy and the other bore the legend 1-800-MUFFLER.

Sandy suppressed a laugh.

"Wicked, aren't I?" Barbara said. "I'll be right back."

And she was as good as her word, Sandy noted with illicit pleasure.

"You just met Alden and Bennet. The two babies. Malcolm and Ralph are around somewhere. They each have a lodge on the estate. It's just the boys, this weekend. They sent the wives away. We girls are allowed to help, you understand. But, eventually, the boys all get together in a room and..."

Barbara waved an imaginary cigarette at the fireplace.

"Do you want a drink?"

"Um..."

"Come on, it's past five o'clock."

"All right, then."

"What do you want?"

"Whatever you're having."

"Really? Okay..."

And pretty quickly Sandy decided to put her notes aside for now and, instead, listen to Barbara talk.

Barbara felt a little *edged out* of the campaign, now that everything was fully under Ray Krall's direct control. But that was okay; she'd had her fun and they were rolling towards victory. Assuming, that was, there weren't any more *China gaffes*. Sandy should have been in the room when Krall heard about *that!* And yet nobody had been fired. Anyway, Barbara would ease back into her art dealing, maybe dabble again in real estate. Whatever took her fancy. Sure, she'd be helping Willard with his transition and his appointments. Did Sandy want a top-up? No? And — maybe, just maybe — Barbara herself might be in line for a top appointment in due course. Did she have something in mind? Well, that would be telling. But Willard generally got around to making the right decision. Eventually. When logic finally kicked in and...

But what about Sandy? Was she enjoying the campaign? Sandy said she was, but it was harder work than she'd thought.

"And how'd you like Josh's apartment?"

Sandy thought about the surveillance system that Teri had disabled.

"It's the future, I guess."

"The future? Well, it's not to my taste."

"I don't think Teri likes it, either."

"Teri?"

"Teresa Wolf."

"The girl that Gloria hired? Milly's little crush from college? She was up there?"

"Well, she kind of invited herself. But that's okay. We're friends. I guess."

Barbara put her glass down.

"I'm sure there was something about that girl. I forget what. I meant to look into it but... What do you think of her? Is she *sound*, would you say? You know, reliable? Trustworthy?"

"Oh, yes. I would say so."

"Sure about that? It would save me the effort of checking up and —"

"Definitely. She's young, though."

"True. She can't help that."

Barbara picked up her glass again.

"My guess is you're a good judge of character."

By rights, Sandy felt, she ought to be. And she'd had to learn fast in the village. But one of the things she'd learned was that people surprised you. And not often for the better.

"What about Mr. Prince's sons?" she asked, feeling emboldened by whatever it was she was drinking.

"What about them?"

"Do they work for the Fund?"

"No, no, no. Heaven forfend."

"So who actually —"

"You'd be surprised how few people you need these days. The computers do the work. Did you see that ridiculous car outside?"

"The red one?"

"That belongs to Mr. Giordano. Our *system architect*. But I shouldn't be so snooty. Where would we be without him? Well, not *you*, obviously, dear. But you know what I mean."

Sandy observed that just because you were talented, it didn't follow that you had taste. Barbara heartily agreed, and treated Sandy to some shocking examples from her own experience.

"But then what," Sandy asked, "do Mr. Prince's sons do?"

"Do? Whatever they want. Let's see. One of them likes horses. And women. Another one has a boat. I think he parties his way around the Mediterranean. One of them is arty. He puts money into movies. As far as I know, he doesn't take any *out*. The last one — what does he do? I'm not sure. Something to do with big game hunting? Answer your question?"

"Well, you make it sound —"

"Yes, I know. I should have mentioned that they all devote a great deal of their time to philanthropy. There. I said it."

There was a knock on the kitchen door.

"Ray!"

"Ladies."

"We were just talking about that car."

"I seen it. How come *he's* here?"

"Don't ask me."

"This weekend is the campaign. Ain't nothing to do with him."

"Ask Willard."

Krall looked at Sandy.

"Where're you gonna be, Sandy? Case I need you. Right here?"

"Yes."

"The boys found her in the library," Barbara said. "Sent her for *tea*."

Krall rubbed his nose.

"Did they now? Seen Megan anywhere?"

"No. Good luck with your strategy."

"Uh-huh. Okay. Thanks."

Krall loped off down the hall.

"Does he have a thing for you?" Barbara asked.

Sandy shook her head.

"Uh-uh. No way."

Barbara seemed disappointed. But didn't she see how cynical and manipulative Krall was? Sandy wondered if it would be okay to share her worries. But her chance was blown away by the arrival, in a state of excitement, of Megan and Milly.

But it wasn't a good state of excitement, Sandy quickly saw. Megan looked out of sorts, her face flushed.

"He did it again, mom!" Milly said.

"Malcolm?"

"It's okay, I'm all right," Megan said.

"No, it's *not* okay," Barbara said. "Megan, listen. You just tell him to stick it —"

"She can't do that, mom. You know how it is."

128

"You want me to do something? I don't have a problem —"

"No," Megan said. "Let it go. Please. Nothing really happened. I'm honestly okay. Let's all just calm down. Really."

"Are you sure?" Barbara said. "Damn their strategy. I'll go in there right now and —"

"Mom, she's okay."

"Fine. All right. Sit down, both of you. I'll get you a drink."

Barbara got to her feet. Then she turned to Sandy.

"Welcome to the family."

CHAPTER 20

Sandy Quayle did not find out exactly what Malcolm Prince had done, or had tried to do, to Megan. The talk in the kitchen quickly turned to Megan's new apartment and her plans for decorating it. Malcolm was not mentioned again. Perhaps the incident, whatever it was, had not been so serious. It was hard to believe that one of Mr. Prince's sons would behave so badly as to... Perhaps there had simply been a misunderstanding. But Barbara's mood, Sandy noticed, had darkened; she let Megan and Milly lead the conversation.

Milly confirmed to her mother that Teresa Wolfe was working out *just fine*, and was *blogging up a storm*, to the campaign's great benefit. And she reminisced about the fun times they'd had together at college. Teresa had been quite a *scatterbrain*. Sandy thought it sounded wonderful.

And then Megan explained how tweaks to the *system*, based largely on real-time analysis of Sandy's targets' responses, had encouraged the campaign to believe that the only demographic groups immune to its message were *low-income minorities* and *self-described lifelong liberals* over the age of fifty with higher degrees.

Barbara said there would always be some people who didn't get it.

Then Ray Krall appeared at the door again.

"Sandy, would you assist us, please?"

Krall led Sandy back to the library and offered her a chair in front of a bookcase by the fireplace. Sandy was grateful for this; a log fire had been lit, and she'd been feeling chilled in the kitchen in her thin suit.

Seated around the library table were twelve men. Sandy recognized Alden and Bennet, the younger Prince brothers. They didn't look her way. And the two older brothers were easy to spot. But which one was Malcolm? All four of them looked morose. Mr. Prince sat at the end of the table, dressed in a blue sweater and an open-necked white shirt. It was the first time that Sandy had seen him without a smile on his face. Even at their first encounter, up on the golf course, there had been a warmth in his expression. And you never saw a picture of him without that confident, compassionate, can-do beam that made you feel like he was a part of *your* family.

But then, this was a *strategy session*. It was meant to be serious! And the other seven men at the table looked like they thought so, too.

Krall didn't sit. He paced about the room, talking and gesturing, his arms ready like a wrestler or raised up like a preacher, returning at intervals to a whiteboard that he'd set up on the other side of the fireplace. From time to time he'd tell his audience to refer to a page in the folders in front of them, which would provoke a reluctant bout of languid page-ruffling that seemed to rile him.

"So we keep coming back to two things," Krall said. "Message discipline and empathy."

He strode to his whiteboard and wiped it clean.

"Let's start with the first."

He wrote a single word on the board. From where she sat, Sandy could not read it.

"I do not want to hear anybody using that word," Krall said. "I do not want to see it in any campaign material. Now, I know that it hits the sweet spot with some folk. Like maybe you all here. That ain't the point. Maybe this is your true agenda? I don't care. That's not my concern. My concern is to win the election, and you don't do that by scaring people."

A ripple of protest rose up but Krall quashed it.

"I hear what you're saying. Let me explain something. You're right to talk about fear. And sure, we use fear all the time. It's practically our number one weapon. But you need your voters to fear the *other* guy, okay? Because he or she is going to help *those people*, right? Remember we talked about *those people?* We're a third-party insurgency. We're pushing the envelope. Whatever you think, some of you, it is not a done deal at this point. People *have* to feel comfortable with us. So you *cannot* use that word, and then tell people they've got nothing to fear. It just don't work. We have the numbers."

Krall pointed to his whiteboard.

"That, my friends, is a thousand-dollar word. You need to be speaking in a language that most folk can afford."

Krall paused. Was he waiting for a reaction? All he got was some mumbled assent and a sour smile from one of the younger Prince brothers. Mr. Prince stared down at his folder, his hands palm-down on the table either side of it. Krall glanced at Sandy and made a gesture that seemed to mean *not long now*.

"One more thing on this topic," he said. "This is mainly for Josh, but some of you others need to listen up, too."

Josh, Sandy thought. Josh Merriweather? Which one was he?

"You need to stop talking about this NPP thing," Krall said. "Now I am well aware, Josh, that you are the campaign's most generous individual contributor."

He was looking at a young man with tousled blond hair and steel-rimmed glasses, who wore a navy-blue blazer over a gray T-shirt. The shirt bore a logo, but Sandy couldn't quite make it out — just the word *frontier*.

"But," Krall went on, "that don't give you the right to go off message. Are we all agreed about that? I hope so."

The young man — Josh — nodded.

"See, you don't have to lay out your entire program in advance. Here's an example. Let's say you want to privatize Social Security. Maybe you do. I don't

care. Now, you don't say nothing, until you're elected. Then you say, oh look —
we've just found this big ol' problem. But don't worry, we've already figured out
the solution. Make sense?"

Another nod.

"So no *trade pact* talk, okay? People hear *trade pact*, they think layoffs. They
think wage cuts. They think cheap foreign labor. And so on. Which is broadly
correct, not that it matters."

Krall paused for a moment and scratched his eyebrow.

"By the way, I've looked at this thing, and it ain't no *trade pact*. I studied law
and I don't know *what* it is. Some kind of extra-territorial legal shit. If it's
important to you, fine. Just don't talk about it."

Sandy thought she saw a smile flicker across Josh's face.

"Now we come to item number two," Krall said. "Which is empathy. You all
know what that is, right? It's what this campaign is missing."

He glanced at Sandy. *Here we go*, she thought.

"I'd like to introduce you to Sandy Quayle, right here. She's one of our best
people on the campaign phone bank. A couple of you might have met her already."

Krall turned his gaze on Alden and Bennet, but got no reaction. Sandy sat up
straight in her seat.

"Now we set Sandy to work on some of our toughest demographics," Krall
said. "And the results were amazing."

Sandy felt herself become an object of interest. Faces tilted up. Chairs turned.
Josh Merriweather adjusted his glasses and stared at her. The Prince twins stole
a glance. But Mr. Prince didn't look up from his folder.

"Let me tell you what empathy is *not*," Krall said. "It is not *are you better off
now than you were four years ago*. It is not *I feel your pain*. It is not *I am a firm
believer in compassionate conservatism*. It is not *we need to help all of our people*.
And it sure ain't *we are the people we've been fuckin' waiting for*. People see
through that shit in seconds."

He paused. Sandy held her breath.

"Tell them what it is, Sandy."

She thought for a moment. What a strange question! She'd expected Krall to
ask her to describe how she got the best out of the system, or perhaps to recall
some of her more memorable conversations. But, language aside, Krall's request
deserved a response, didn't it? And everyone — except Mr. Prince — was staring
at her.

"It's when you believe — no, it's when you *know* that you're no better than
anyone else. It's when you know that you're the same as everyone else."

There was silence.

Krall looked at his watch.

"Okay, I would like to leave you all with that thought," he said. "Now, I
understand there's a dinner going on, and some of you need to get ready, so we'll
adjourn until tomorrow."

There was the briefest pause, and then folders snapped shut, chairs scraped
against the dark oak floor and the room began to empty. Only Mr. Prince did not
move.

Krall touched Sandy's shoulder.

"Thank you for that."

"Oh, you're welcome. I didn't know if —"

"You were perfect. Are you hungry by any chance?"

She realized that she was.

"Yes. I'm eating in the kitchen with —"

"Aw, you don't want to do that."

"No?"

"How about you come out with me?"

"But aren't you going to the banquet?"

"Is that what they're calling it? No, I didn't get an invite."

"Oh."

Sandy glanced at Krall's whiteboard. The *thousand-dollar* word he had written was *Liberty*.

"So come on, Sandy. We're going out to dinner. And then we're gonna to see a show."

A *show?*

Krall led Sandy out to the courtyard and opened the passenger door of his BMW for her. She noticed that the red sports car was still parked alongside.

"Where are we going?"

"Place I always go, when I'm up here."

It turned out to be *Jack's Diner*, which was located on the main highway, between a gas station and a marine supply store. Jack, or someone, must have known that Krall was coming because, although the restaurant was busy, the best seats in the house, in a private booth at the back, had been reserved.

Krall offered Sandy a menu.

"You order whatever takes your fancy, Sandy. Goes without saying."

Sandy ordered a chicken Caesar salad, a barely-remembered treat from the old days. Krall ordered baby-back ribs with Cajun sauce.

"I hope you didn't mind what I did back there."

"No. It was okay. I'm don't know that I quite understand..."

"Nah, it's just these people. They think they know everything, but they don't. They hire me — and I'm not complaining or nothing — but then they think it's job done. But it ain't. They don't get that. They're so used to just buying whatever they want, and I... Oh, I beg your pardon. If I start to rail on them again, will you stop me?"

"Yes, all right."

The food came quickly; Sandy suspected Krall would turn out to be a big tipper. She looked at the waitresses as they hustled about the restaurant. Each one reminded her of Maria, at the waffle house. *We are all the same*, she thought. But some people want to tell us we're not. One day we'll learn and God will be pleased with us — though God had better be prepared to be patient. What did Mr. Prince think? He knew the truth, didn't he? Was that why he looked so sad, sitting at that table with his sons, and Josh Merriweather, and those other men?

While they ate, Krall told Sandy a little about his life. He'd been born in Louisiana, but had grown up in North Carolina, where his father worked for a tobacco company. Both his parents had died young. As a result, Krall had never smoked. At age seventeen, he'd lost his younger sister, his only sibling, in a car wreck. He'd won a bunch of scholarships and studied at Duke — law and public administration — and had gone into politics around the time that Charlotte got its first black mayor. He hadn't been pretty enough or rich enough to succeed as a politician in his own right, but he'd discovered his talent for campaigning. He'd worked for both parties, but now he was non-aligned. *These people*, however —

But Sandy stopped him right there.

"Thank you. You want dessert?"

"Oh, no thanks."

She was already beginning to put back the weight she'd lost.

"You don't mind if I do?"

"Not at all. What was that you said about a show?"

Krall rubbed his nose.

"Yeah. Well, I better warn you. It ain't Broadway. Might even be X-rated."

He reached down to his briefcase and took out a laptop computer.

"Why don't you just move around here, so you can see."

Sandy shuffled herself around the booth and Krall started up his computer. While they waited, he ordered his dessert — Mississippi Mud Pie. How did *he* keep the weight off?

Krall poked and clicked at his computer.

"Here we go. As young Mr. Merriweather would tell us, I am sure, we are living in an age of technology."

On the screen was a video image. From a high angle, the camera looked down at a long table. About twenty people were eating dinner — and in some style, Sandy thought.

"That's what we're missing," Krall said. "That's the *banquet*."

Sandy looked closer. The Prince brothers were there, and Josh Merriweather. But not Mr. Prince; there was an empty chair at one end of the table.

Krall turned the sound down.

"It's all just yakkety-yak. Too bad we can't make out what they're sayin'. But let's see who we got."

Krall's dessert arrived. He attacked it with a fork.

"Ray," Sandy said. "Do they *know?*"

"Nah," Krall said, his mouth full. "Least I hope not."

"But the Secret Service —"

"He's not President yet. They won't sweep for him 'til he is. He's still a politician. Heck, he ain't even that."

"But..."

"What? Are you thinkin' this is *unethical*, or somethin'?"

"Isn't it?"

"Don't rightly know. Kind of a gray area, in my opinion. Fact is, though, I can't win this election unless I know what's goin' on with these people. For example..."

Krall zoomed the picture to focus on two sixty-ish men with short, white hair. They were talking to one of the older Prince brothers.

"These two, they're your *society generals*. You heard about them? We want their endorsement. They go on all the talk shows. People seem to think they won a war, or something. Which, as I recall, they did not. But they do move in the right circles, and they have fancy wives, and *affairs* or *mistresses*, as they like to call 'em. They're in all the magazines. So the question is, what do we give 'em?"

"Who are they talking to?"

"That's Malcolm."

Malcolm! Sandy moved her face closer to the screen.

"Oh, you heard about *him*, too?"

Sandy didn't answer. She looked at Malcolm. His face was pink and shiny, happy; he looked to be enjoying his time with the generals.

"If they're talking to him, that means they want in," Krall said. "They want to be in the Fund. Good. We can arrange that."

Sandy leaned back.

"That's..."

"Corrupt? Nah, just kind of grubby. The minimum investment is supposed to be ten million. I don't think our military friends have that. Maybe somebody'll loan it to 'em."

Sandy thought of asking if Mr. Prince had any idea of what was being done in his name, but she dismissed the idea. How could he? As for Krall, she had begun to warm to him. But his cynicism, however necessary, made her heart sink.

Krall had focused in on two other men, who appeared to be sharing a joke together. They looked about seventy years old, and seemed more at ease than the generals. As Sandy watched, the other senior Prince brother joined in.

"Ralph," Krall said.

"And who are those two?"

"Senators. We got one from each party. That's fair and balanced. I like that. These guys are going to jump ship at the last moment and give us a boost. Plus they have some pretty good inside dirt on our opponents. We're savin' that up, too."

"And what's their reward?"

"Well, they all want to be in the Fund. But we're not going there with these two. They can be ambassador to who-gives-a... Uh, sorry."

"Why are you showing me all this?"

Krall sighed and pushed away his empty dessert plate.

"I thought you deserved to know. Plus I got nobody else."

She looked at him. Where did empathy end, and cynicism begin? She had no idea.

"Let's take a look at the library."

Krall flipped to a different view. Sandy recognized the library. The fire had gone out and the vase of flowers was in disarray again.

"Nobody there," Krall said. "Nothing happening. Let's try the last one."

He flipped again. This time the angle was the same but the room was much smaller. Sandy saw Mr. Prince sitting behind a desk, facing the camera. He wore what Sandy took to be his smart banqueting clothes. His face looked like stone. A man with untidy, thinning hair, wearing a dark denim jacket, stood with his back to the camera.

"Huh?" Krall said. "What's this?"

There was no sound. Krall fiddled with his computer.

"It's workin' fine. They're just not talking."

"Who is that?"

"You got me, Sandy. No, wait… It's gotta be Ferrari guy, what's his name? Giordano."

"The system architect?"

"Yeah, him."

They waited and watched. Then Giordano moved, and the rustle of his jacket almost blew Krall's speakers.

"Shit!"

Krall turned the sound down. Giordano was speaking.

"I'm done. It's over, okay? Do you hear me?"

Sandy watched as Prince's mouth opened — and then closed again without a sound.

"Are you getting this? I'm finished. Just send the fuckin' money, okay? Just send the fuckin' money and we're done. Yeah? Or I'm putting the whole thing in the fuckin' mail to you-know-who, okay? I'm outta here. And don't look for me, 'cause you're not going to find me. *Just send the fuckin' money.*"

Giordano vanished from the picture. Prince sat immobile and silent.

Krall let out a long, slow breath and scratched his eyebrow.

"You hear what I just heard, Sandy?"

CHAPTER 21

Ricky Ponton swung with unpracticed indolence in his personal hammock, high above his very own rosewood veranda, taking a cool and proprietorial pleasure in the accoutrements of a data-centric, twenty-first-century super-villain: The evening breeze ruffling the surface of his private, fish-free swimming pool; the exclusive sunset panorama that bathed his private bay in purple and gold; his powerful boat, slumbering in its powerful boathouse; the price-on-application mansion at his back, with its curving, Corsican marble staircase, and its chandeliers full of electric fake candles; and the rustling of his personal lemurs, or whatever they were, all around him in his wholly-owned personal jungle.

He felt in control, more or less. Challenges remained, to be sure, not least of which was the river of bills and pessimism flooding his way from Kerri's lawyers in London. He wasn't going to give up on her, no matter what it cost; the price of betrayal was too ugly to him. But there were other things he could take some satisfaction in. And, for now at least, nobody was demanding his passport or peeing into his tent.

Ricky craned his neck: Yes, there was Mr. Yu, with his notebook, cataloguing Ricky's garden. He was an odd bloke, Ricky felt, but you couldn't help liking him. Patient and gentle — but also shrewd and calculating. He had more secrets to yield; that was evident. The gardening was a contrived interlude.

And it wasn't as if Mr. Yu, unlike Mr. Lin, had disappointed so far. The look on Jay's face had been worth the trouble he'd put Ricky through. And the delay inherent in Big Data's encrypted video link had only enhanced the pleasure: Ricky could anticipate what was coming, and watch it all sink in.

Sure, Jay had been expecting some kind of Chinese jiggery-pokery in Madagascar. Maybe a radar installation. Or suspicious enhancements to the port on the east coast. But not the largest naval base in the world. With a full-length runway. And the possibility of anti-ship ballistic missiles.

Jay's world, Ricky speculated, had been well and truly rocked. Never mind the *string of pearls*. How would Jay explain this particular *jewel* to his alleged patron, the venerable ANC hero, Walter Gabo?

And then, beyond the shock and awe, there was the question of what exactly to do with Mr. Yu's data — his maps, blueprints, charts, technical specs, engineering estimates, Party memos, orders for construction materiel, PowerPoint presentations and all the rest. Jay's instinct had been to blow the whole thing wide open, without delay. But Ricky, tempered by bitter experience, had felt obliged to point out the pros and cons.

Now, if Ricky remembered correctly, Jay had claimed that his objective was, on behalf of Walter and the peace-loving peoples of southern Africa, to keep the lower half of the continent free of big-power political interference, and the proxy wars that had accompanied such meddling over the past two centuries. *Great*, Ricky had said. *With you on that.* But what would the Americans do, immediately upon learning that China intended to fulfil its obligations as a Great Power by policing, say, the Indian Ocean? With aircraft carriers and anti-ship missiles?

Ah. Guess you have a point there, Ricky. Sheesh.

Would they not instantly offer *aid* to South Africa, Mozambique and even Zimbabwe? You know, the sort of aid that you can't refuse, and that takes over your airspace? How's Walter going to like that?

Okay, Ricky, I get it.

South Africa could end up garrisoned by the Yanks, just like South Korea.

That's enough, Ricky.

So here's your problem, Ricky told Jay. It's the Madagascans. Somehow you've got to persuade them — or whoever seems to be in power at the time, that is — to veto the Chinese plans. Probably not so easy, given the amount of money involved. And you've got to do it before the Americans spot that four-kilometer-long runway on their satellites.

Shit!

I'm on your side, Ricky had said. Look, I've just moved in, I like the place, and I don't want a military base just up the coast. It's going to impact my property values and frighten my lemurs.

Oh, for Christ's sake...

Thus for Big Data, Ricky had resolved, this was one secret too far. Yes, the people of southern Africa had a *right to know*. But, if Jay could come up with a viable plan, then maybe they would only have to know just how close they had come.

Jesus. I'll think about it. What else have we got?

Ricky had then recounted the tale of Kirk and Spock, omitting only the bit where Kirk had characterized Ricky as a *sniveling little shit*. Jay said he thought something weird was going on. Ricky said he thought so too. They agreed that they had no idea what.

Then Ricky had concluded the session with a prediction.

Mr. Yu. I think he's got something else. Something bigger.

Bigger than the freaking naval base?

Could be.

Well, you let me know when you find out, okay?

No problem. Oh, and send some more money, will you? My pool needs cleaning.

Fuck you, Ricky.

All in all, it had gone rather well, Ricky thought. But there had been one issue that he'd glossed over. Kirk and Spock, he thought, were full of bluster. They were a threat, but probably not a major one, so long as he published their corporate dirt (minus the personal sleaze). Xin Jiao, on the other hand, represented the official might of the People's Liberation Army. She had demonstrated her expertise in industrial-strength hackery. If Ricky were to offend her — by exposing the naval base, for example — what would she *not* do to Big Data Underground, or to Ricky personally?

Then again, the data she'd given Ricky — due back from Norway any time now — was, by Jiao's reckoning, likely to upset some very powerful corporations. If you were going to poke tigers with sticks, perhaps it was best to poke them one at a time.

By now the sun had all but melted into the Mozambique Channel. That meant it was dinner time. He dismounted from his hammock.

Ricky found Mr. Yu waiting for him in the dining room. Mr. Yu liked his food.

"I talked to our American friend this morning," Ricky said.

"Oh yes?"

"We're going to hold off on the base, for now."

"Probably wise."

"We think someone needs to talk the Madagascans out of it."

Mr. Yu helped himself to grilled fish.

"Good luck with that!"

Ricky elected to try the vegetable curry with rice.

"Any ideas?"

"Maybe."

"Hm. Okay. How's the fish?"

"Good."

They ate in silence. When they were finished, Mr. Yu suggested a walk in the garden. The breeze had dropped and the lemurs seemed to have retired for the night. A blanket of cloud had begun to roll in from the south-east.

"Could be a storm tonight," Mr. Yu said. "You know that most of the cyclones that form in the Indian Ocean hit Madagascar?"

"Do they?"

"There is often great damage. But your house is well-built."

"Uh-huh. How would a cyclone affect the base?"

"The dock is designed to withstand cyclones. The ships will actually be safer out there."

They strolled into Ricky's rock garden.

"So this is your home, now?" Mr. Yu asked.

"Yes."

"How long will you stay?"

"Oh, I'm in no hurry to move on."

"No family?"

"No."

They entered a grove of palm trees.

"What about you?" Ricky said.

"No hurry, either."

No problem, Ricky thought. He wasn't short of space. And without Mr. Yu he would only have the staff and the lemurs for company.

"Family?"

Mr. Yu stopped.

"They are in Chongqing. They are safe. But they are being watched."

"Because of you?"

"No. Because of my daughter."

Ricky waited.

"She is in America. She went there to study. But I have not heard from her. She has disappeared."

"Have you tried to —"

"They tell me she has gone away with friends. But that is not true. She would have told me."

"I'm sorry... So what do you think —"

"The rain is coming. We should go inside. Then I will tell you."

Ricky led the way to the enclosed terrace that ran along the northern edge of his sprawling, multi-level mansion. From here, on high, you could look down over the roof of the boathouse to the creek, and the mangroves on its far side. A faint smudge on the horizon was, most likely, smoke from his neighbors' cooking fires. They'd better hurry, he thought; the sky was darkening and the stars were going out. The first heavy drops of rain were spattering on his glass and wrought-iron roof.

Mr. Yu sat in one of the terrace's over-sized wicker chairs.

"Beer?" Ricky asked.

"Thank you."

Ricky fetched the drinks, sat down next to Mr. Yu, and waited. Mr. Yu appeared to be marshalling his thoughts.

"What do you know about the city of Chongqing?"

"Big place," Ricky said. "Thirty-three million people. Nearly ten million more than Australia. Lots of foreign investment. Interesting politics."

"You know about our former Party Secretary?"

"Yes."

The city's erstwhile Party Secretary had become an embarrassment to the central party elite, and a supposed threat to political stability. He had accordingly been deposed on grounds of *serious discipline violations*, and subsequently accused of corruption. Of which, like anyone of his status, he was egregiously guilty. There was also the matter of the murder of a foreign businessman.

"Do you understand," Mr. Yu said, "how popular he was with the ordinary people?"

"Tell me."

"He refurbished the apartment towers where the poorer people live."

"Sounds like a good thing."

"He planted trees to make the city greener and improve the air."

"Definitely a good thing."

"The police who direct our traffic. They are the prettiest girls. They wear white uniforms. And makeup."

"Wouldn't work in Sydney, but hey..."

"He ran political campaigns. One was called *Sing Red*. Many people joined choirs, in order to sing Maoist propaganda songs. They wore Maoist uniforms. There was a Maoist revival."

"Not so sure about that."

"There was another campaign. It was called *Smash Black*. Very popular. Our Party Secretary pursued organized crime. There were thousands of investigations. Of his rivals and opponents. The law was abused. The police were used for political purposes."

"Right."

"After his fall, the activities of his family were exposed..."

"Nepotism."

"Yes, it is very hard to expose this in China. So then there was disillusion. But, you see, there had been a popular movement. Where is this energy to go? Those who offer us capitalism are corrupt. Those who say they wish to return us to communism are corrupt. Where is our outlet? Where is our hope?"

Ricky didn't have a good response to that one, so he just sucked on his beer.

"The old people are fatalistic," Mr. Yu said. "They are just glad that they have a nicer apartment. But young people are frustrated — I mean the middle-class, educated ones."

"Like your daughter?"

"Yes, like my daughter."

"What's her name?"

"Chen."

"Why are the young people frustrated? Apart from the corruption and the nepotism?"

"They think their future is being stolen."

"How, exactly?"

"They see the way that big Chinese companies like Weihan are becoming more powerful than the Party. They see them embrace Western capitalism, and entwine themselves into the international system, which they call *neo-liberal*. But they see no political progress. They thought that China would move slowly towards democracy, because that was the only way that it could prosper as a rich country. But this may not be so. They fear that China will have America's capitalism. And America will have China's politics."

Ricky put his empty bottle down on the Corsican marble floor of his terrace. Rain thundered on the glass above his head. The creek and the mangroves were obscured by a shimmering gray curtain of water.

"You said you would like to see democracy in China," Mr. Yu said.

"I did say that, yes."

"Well, Mr. Ponton, your chance has arrived."

CHAPTER 22

Teri Wolfe sat at her desk in the scullery. It was Sunday, and the apartment was quiet. Everybody important, plus Sandy and Milly, had decamped to the Hamptons. Nothing much of anything was happening. The naval crisis had subsided, apparently of its own accord, and had yielded its place in the news to another bridge collapse.

But Gloria had ordered Teri to produce a blog post entitled *Why Generation Y is All About Freedom*. Teri was struggling. She'd looked up *Generation Y* and concluded it probably meant her. Was she all about freedom? Jeez...

People are all always asking me, she wrote.

But what? What were they always asking her? Why do you waste all your money? Why don't you get a boyfriend? Can I get a brownie with that?

People are always asking me how our generation can get ahead of the game. Well, let me tell you, it's all about...

About what? Freedom. Of course. Obvious.

...it's all about Freedom. What do I mean by that?

What *did* she mean? Ngaarrgh!

Just then her phone blipped — her crappy, personal one. There was a text message from Robin. Perhaps he had some red-hot revelations to share! Dirty secrets painstakingly unearthed from the *raw trading data* she'd cunningly purloined from Fat Willy's private system. This spy shit wasn't so hard after all. In fact it was kind of fun. Sexy, almost. She would have to come up with a *persona*, though. *Teri Wolfe* wasn't bad. But it wasn't quite *Pussy Galore* or *Plenty O'Toole*. Something to think about later.

She opened the message: *park now stupid*.

Huh.

Park now stupid? Well, technically you could interpret that two ways, but...

Leaving her laptop running, she got up from her desk — or scullery bench, to be precise — and tip-toed out into the kitchen hall. All was quiet. She progressed to the vestibule and peeked down the corridor that led to Gloria's office. Gloria's door was closed. Teri made a dash to the cubby hole to retrieve her coat, and then hit the stairs.

Twenty minutes later she was at the rink. Robin was waiting for her.

"So what's up?" she said.

Robin glowered at her.

"Didn't you even check?"

"Check what?"

He produced the memory stick she'd given him and brandished it in front of her face.

"There's nothing!"

"Sure there is. *tradback.dat*. It's all there."

"The file is empty."

"Are you sure?"

He performed a little mime of exasperation — not exactly *spy cool*, she thought.

"The file is completely empty. There is no data in it. None."

"Oh. But it said backup complete."

"Walk me through what you did."

Well, this was humiliating. He obviously thought she *was* stupid. Which was not the case. But she told him anyway.

"All right. Yeah. Well, something's screwed up."

Or someone, she thought.

"Maybe there isn't any trading data."

"Of course there is. How could there not be any trading data? You're going to have to try again."

"What!"

"Go back and do it again."

"Do I have to?"

"Yes."

It wasn't the spy shit; it was Sandy. The second betrayal would be worse than the first. It wouldn't be a regrettable mistake. It would be a pattern of behavior.

"Remember, you owe me," Robin said, his voice calmer.

"Owe you?"

"You lost that video."

"Yeah, but if I hadn't..."

No, she couldn't really argue *that*.

"So, have you found her yet?"

"No."

"I'm sorry. What was her name again?"

"Chen."

"Hm. Look, I'll see what I can do, okay? I'm not promising."

"Okay. Sorry if..."

"It's fine. Take care."

"You too."

She began the hike back to the apartment. And on the way, an idea occurred to her. It was the kind of concept, she speculated, that would come naturally to a seasoned spy. You had to be alert to opportunity — the unguarded file; the break-in; the honey-trap; and the brazen impersonation.

Back at her bench in the scullery, she took out her laminated campaign ID and, in her blogging program, matched the font in which her name was shown.

Then she printed out *Milly van Dornen* on plain white paper. Next, with the aid of scissors and a sharp knife from the kitchen, she insinuated her new identity inside the ID so that it overlaid her old one. Okay, close up it didn't look too convincing. She went back to the kitchen and lit one of the burners on the range. Then she held the ID close to the flame until it began to discolor and curl up.

Then, having checked once again that the coast was clear, Gloria-wise, she exited the building, turned up the collar of her coat, spy-style, and jumped a downtown train.

On the journey, she reviewed her meticulously-planned exploit, subjecting every detail to merciless scrutiny and concluding that it was near-as-damn flawless.

It was Sunday. The ninth floor of the building on Water Street where the NACF was located would probably be empty; there was no trading on Sunday and, besides, everybody was out on the Island, even that immensely creepy Giordano guy, who supposedly programmed all of Fat Willy's consistent profits. Milly was out of the way. Barbara, also.

Now, there was a slight problem in that Milly did not work on the ninth floor. She weaved her PR web, or whatever she actually did, at Prince's business office somewhere in midtown. That was where lucky would-be inductees went to plead their case for admission to the Fund, on bended knee before the Prince Regent himself. No doubt Milly made them sweat in the lobby beforehand. However it was plausible that Prince would send Milly downtown on some errand or other. But what?

The Times had been demanding that Prince release his tax returns. Had he sent Milly downtown to fetch them? No. Totally improbable. There was *no way* Fat Willy was giving up those bad babies.

He'd forgotten to water the rubber plant? No, these people had no time for nature.

It was his silver wedding anniversary and he'd left his wife's present — a valuable emerald necklace once owned by Princess Diana — by the photocopier. No, too easy to check.

The Secret Service had demanded a list of all persons working in the Water Street building, in order to perform an in-depth security vetting, and Teri — whoops, Milly! — had been sent by the campaign to get the NACF's personnel list. This wheeze had the advantages of plausibility, urgency, non-checkability, and might just intimidate Reception a bit. After all, who *didn't* want to cooperate with the Secret Service?

But the trickiest issue was how to get the elevator to stop at the ninth floor. When you punched the button, it refused to say lit. So how did *that* work? Did you need some special gizmo? If it was one of those fingerprint or facial recognition things then Teri was screwed. But spies were nothing if not risk-takers. And it had been put about that Prince, despite his undisguisable wealth, was a man of frugal habits. No one who had seen the inside of the apartment on Park Avenue would entertain such nonsense, of course, but Teri's limited experience in the corporate world had taught her that frugality was definitely in vogue when it came to fixtures and fittings. Prince almost certainly hadn't shelled out for facial recognition.

By the time she got off the train, she felt she could have used a jolt of rocket fuel. But the Coffee Truck didn't cater to tourists and wasn't on duty on Sundays. So she simply made a mental flip into James Bond mode — *Jane* Bond? — and penetrated the lobby.

The guy at Reception — *Dave*, according to his name tag — gave Teri the typical once-over then asked how he could help. Teri went into her spiel.

"Secret Service?" Dave said. "I don't *think* we've heard anything about that."

"Well, it's secret. That's the thing."

"Let me just check..."

Dave peered at his computer.

"Anything like that, we normally get a memo."

"I don't think these guys do memos. They're kind of scary, if you know what I mean."

"Scary? Well, I —"

"You don't want to get on the wrong side of them. Trust me."

"Mm. So you want the ninth floor?"

"Yes."

"Do you work there?"

"No. Midtown office."

"Okay. Well, you need to be on the list. Give me your ID."

Teri handed it over.

"Jesus! What happened to this?"

Teri gave an exaggerated sigh.

"Stupid boyfriend! Set fire to my kitchen. Trying to fix the range. Gotta love him, though."

"So your name is... *Miffy?*"

"Milly."

"*Miffy...* something *Horner?*"

"Milly van Dornen."

"Really? Cute name. Okay, let's see. Ah. There you are. I see there's a Barbara, also."

"That's my mom. She's great."

"Looks like you've never visited us here before."

"Uh, no."

"No photo on file."

"Oh, really?"

"That's unusual."

"Yeah, but it's kind of an emergency. Like I said. National security."

"Well, I guess in that case... You got your radio tag?"

Radio tag!

"Uh, no. That thing is scorched. It's toast."

"The boyfriend?"

"It was all in the same bag on the counter."

"We'll need to know the serial number, so we can deactivate it."

"But it's history."

"We still need it."

"Can I get back to you?"

"By tomorrow, okay?"

"Sure."

Dave gave Teri one last, searching look. She brazened it out.

"So how long do you need in there?"

"Fifteen minutes?"

"To get a list? I can give you ten."

"Okay. I'll run."

"Off you go, then."

A flutter of excitement and a glow of triumph in her spy's heart, Teri ran to the elevator bank. A car stood open. She piled in and hit the number nine button. It stayed lit. The doors closed and the elevator began to rise. The mission was *go!*

At the ninth floor, the doors opened and Teri stepped out into a lobby of opaque glass. In front of her were sliding doors, but there were no handles to pull or buttons to press. A security camera gazed down at her from above the door.

"I'll open the doors for you." It was Dave's voice. "You got nine minutes."

There came a *clunk*, and the doors slid apart. Teri advanced.

She entered what she immediately recognized as a trading room: About twenty desks in four rows, kitted out with multiple monitors, keyboards, printers — the works.

But she also sensed that something wasn't right. It really was *too quiet*. There was no machinery running at all. Teri had never been in an office where stuff didn't get left on. All these traders had bothered to turn off their screens? There had to be servers somewhere, didn't there? But there was silence. The lights were off. The air-conditioning was off.

Then she noticed something that was definitely strange: Some of Prince's traders were still using old-fangled CRTs — the bulky tube monitors that went out in the early 2000's. Wow — talk about *frugal*. Didn't the traders complain?

Now she only had eight minutes. She had to grab some paperwork to keep Dave happy. Was he watching her? There were no cameras visible in the trading room. It made sense, kind of; Prince's *bespoke strategy* was priceless, after all.

But her true mission was to snatch something of interest to Robin — ideally, trading records. If she could satisfy him, she could get out of screwing Sandy over again.

She selected a desk at random and pulled open all the drawers. They were empty. *Weird.* Were these the tidiest, most security-conscious testosterone-fueled bonus babies ever? Then she spotted something else. She drew her finger across the top of the desk. There was a thick layer of dust. She looked at the carpet-tiled floor. It was filthy, too. Didn't Prince want to pay for cleaners? It was just possible to discern a single set of footprints in the muck; they led to a glass-walled office at the right-hand end of the trading floor.

Seven minutes left. She checked three more desks. They were all the same. Then she made for the office in the corner.

The desk here was clean, and there was an up-to-date computer on it. Otherwise the office was bare: No clutter, no pictures on the walls, nothing in the waste bin. But, in the top drawer of the desk, she found something. It was a simple, cheap, spiral-bound notebook. She flipped through it. Only the first five pages had been used. The first page contained a list of what looked like passwords. On the second page were two columns of numbers; those in the right-hand column were dollar amounts, some running into the hundreds of millions. The remaining three pages contained a list of banks and bank account numbers — in London, the Cayman Islands, Zug in Switzerland, Luxembourg, Bermuda, Liechtenstein and Buenos Aires — along with online account login information.

Teri had six minutes left. She took out her phone and carefully photographed each page.

Five minutes. She still needed some paperwork. The office contained a metal stationery cabinet. She opened it. It was full of glossy brochures. She picked one up. *New American Century Fund*, she read, *Uncompromising Values in a Changing World*. It was a PR puff for the Fund. Had Milly written it? There were no figures, just the usual varnished prose. The cover showed Willard Prince standing on the steps of Federal Hall, just across from the NYSE, arms folded, feet apart, a beam of ineffable prosperity on his face.

There were some brown envelopes on the top shelf. Teri took one and stuffed the brochure inside.

Three minutes.

She slumped into the chair behind the desk and gazed out on to the trading floor. *Uncompromising Values?* What the hell was she looking at here? *A Changing World?* How about changing those monitors?

A cold clarity descended on her. She put the notebook back in its place and slid the drawer shut. Then she picked up her envelope and walked back into the trading room, traversing each and every row of desks, taking pictures on her phone. Just for the hell of it, she made a second pass, this time spotting a book on the floor under one of the desks. She picked it up and blew the dust off it. *Windows 98 Bible*, she read. It looked as if Mr. Prince's system architect wasn't quite keeping up.

One minute left.

She made for the lobby, lingering for a moment in the doorway. And she decided to ask herself this question: What had she really just witnessed? It looked like a friggin' *Potemkin Village*, that's what. And if it wasn't a big, steaming plate of bogus, then *WTF?*

And what exactly was going on with Mr. Willard Gaffney Regent Prince?

Her time was up. She called the elevator and descended.

In Reception, she waved her brown envelope at Dave and blew him a kiss. Then she scooted before he could say anything.

At the entrance to the subway, she paused and took out her phone. First she checked that she really had gotten her pictures. Next she sent a message to Robin: *park now stupid xxx.*

Then she boarded an uptown train and, as she rattled north towards the Park, she wondered whether her useless slacker life had finally taken a turn for the better.

Or for the worse.

CHAPTER 23

As the morning sun rose above his jungle, Ricky Ponton's rain-washed terrace began to steam. The air was fresh but loaded with moisture and tropical scents. A reluctant breeze licked at the endemic bushes in his garden. Leaves drifted on the surface of his pool. Ricky's limestone mansion, La Cachette, had withstood its drenching, but its many roofs were now littered with broken branches and palm fronds; would his staff remove them? He hoped his lemurs had found somewhere safe and dry for the night.

He sat alone at a small ebony table with his coffee. Mr. Yu was sleeping in. They'd been up half the night together.

And now Ricky had some decisions to make.

Norway had called in assistance from Iceland and Brazil. The verification — insofar as it was possible — and identity protection work on both Jiao's data and Kirk and Spock's trove had been completed. It was hard to say who was worst: He thought he would have to give one prize to Jiao's Chinese corporations for nepotism, environmental crime, and sheer brutality; and another prize to Kirk and Spock's American corporations for political corruption, tax evasion, and general international malignity. As for the personal transgressions of Kirk and Spock's corporate executives — should Ricky find them amusing or depressing? Either way, they were not fit for publication. Big Data Underground had a reputation to preserve, and it wasn't Ricky's personal plaything.

Then there was Mr. Yu's material. Jay and Ricky had agreed, with Mr. Yu's assent, not to expose Chinese plans for the largest naval base in the world — yet. But the true size of the Chinese military budget was a matter of eminent public concern.

Here, then, were at least three tigers that Ricky could poke with a stick. You could argue that there were two more.

First, there was Weihan, the network infrastructure giant. It was shut out of the US, thanks to the sterling patriotism of America's two houses of Congress. But it provided much of the world with its Internet hardware, and dominated China. Its servers, notorious for the *backdoors* with which they were allegedly constructed, were an existential problem for Big Data. They could not be avoided.

Their ability to spy on anyone and anything at any time could only be mitigated by cumbersome encryption, and metadata often remained exposed. (And, one day, powerful quantum computers, owned only by governments or the largest corporations, might render encryption useless.)

Jiao's revelations concerning Weihan, Ricky thought, might be the second most dangerous of the tigers. It turned out that, via a web of front companies and cross-ownership schemes, stretching from Shanghai to the Caribbean, Weihan, the privatized Chinese public corporation, had sold thirty-two per cent of itself to large American global corporations, and to certain ultra-high-net-worth individuals. Jiao hadn't been able to identify all of these individuals, but one name stood out: Josh Merriweather.

And what was the most dangerous tiger? By far?

The *Chinese Spring*.

What was it that Mr. Yu had said?

You say you are an activist, but you are not.

And then Ricky had mumbled some excuse to the effect that he *had* been an activist, but it had turned out to be too bloody difficult, and...

You are passive, Mr. Yu had said. *People give you information and you publish it.*

True. But look at what he and people like him had accomplished: Everyone now knew that the entire world was bugged from top to bottom. And in places like Germany, though not England or Australia, people actually cared.

People may care, Mr. Yu had said, *but nothing has changed.*

The people of Egypt, Iran or Saudi Arabia, he had pointed out, had little to thank Ricky for. But now...

Mr. Ponton, your chance has arrived.

Mr. Yu's daughter, Chen, had gone missing in America. She had been a prominent, if necessarily discreet, voice in a diffuse and leaderless movement that called itself, in western countries, the *Chinese Spring*. In China itself, it went under other names. It was a movement of young, aspirational, but frustrated people. Middle class? Of course. Yet so were most of those other revolutionaries who had gathered in the city squares of the oppressed world. But the Chinese Spring had no square in which to gather — none, at least, in which they did not fear slaughter.

They needed a *virtual square*, a means by which to communicate and organize safely. Both in the western countries and in China itself.

Big Data Underground could be that virtual square.

Ricky would be an *activist* again. An activist in the greatest democratic cause in the history of the world. Would Ricky like to think about it, or could Mr. Yu take his enthusiastic cooperation for granted?

What had Ricky said?

It was embarrassing to recall. He hoped his lemurs had not heard him tell Mr. Yu that he'd have to check with Norway and Iceland to see what they thought. Later though, as the storm began to ease in the early hours, Ricky had done the right thing. He had signed up, in principle.

And it was probably Chen who had convinced him.

Mr. Yu believed that his daughter had been abducted by a private security and military logistics company called Fairmeadow Solutions. He did not know on whose account they had acted or who was paying the bill. Ricky said he knew a lot about Fairmeadow, and its prior incarnations; whenever it got caught, it changed its name. How and when had they grabbed her? Mr. Yu said that Chen had attended a demonstration in Battery Park in New York City.

What demo was that? Ricky had asked.

The Robin Hood Party.

Robin Hood — those bloody idiots?

Mr. Yu wasn't sure that the Robin Hood Party was comprised solely of idiots. He *was* sure that her involvement in the Chinese Spring was the reason for Chen's abduction.

Chen, and those like her, he had pointed out, did not admire American so-called democracy. They had their own ideas. They were not anti-capitalist. But they were opposed to plutocracy.

They favored the rule of law; free speech; human rights; ethnic, religious and cultural harmony; a mixed economy; social insurance; freedom of information; environmental protection; term limits; and tightly-controlled election spending.

What a bloody radical bunch!

As he sat on the terrace of his plutocrat's mansion, sipping his coffee, Ricky contemplated what he was about to do. According to Mr. Yu, Chen's comrades, in their moderate, reasonable way, wanted to take on both Beijing's unyielding autocrats and Washington's rock-ribbed establishment. At the same time. And they wanted to do it on Ricky's turf.

That being the case, he might as well poke all five tigers at once. Why not? Perhaps the first four would distract from the one that really mattered.

He finished his coffee, got up from his table and tramped into the house. He washed his cup in the kitchen, bade a cheery *good morning* to his cook, who had already made a start on lunch, and shut himself in his study.

Then he logged in to BDU and checked his email. There was nothing to concern him apart from a burst pipe in the São Paulo data center. He opened up his control panel and examined the four items awaiting his approval: Jiao's material; Kirk and Spock's; the Chinese military budget; Weihan.

Four clicks and he was done.

CHAPTER 24

S andy Quayle could not stop thinking about Mr. Giordano. She could not *speak* about Mr. Giordano, because Ray Krall had pleaded for her silence — he hadn't intended to drag Sandy into any kind of mess, he said — and she had acquiesced. Besides, Krall had pointed out, in what sounded to Sandy like the hickory-smoked tones of a southern lawyer, *what we just witnessed, Sandy, despite what we may think we saw, was highly ambiguous, would you not agree?*

She had agreed. But what was *not* ambiguous, Sandy insisted to herself, was that Mr. Prince was in trouble. And that Mr. Giordano had threatened him. Afterwards, Mr. Prince had sat immobile at his desk for nine minutes. He hadn't turned to his computer. He had not picked up the phone. Sandy thought he looked like a man who believed he had no one to whom he could turn — not even his Campaign Director. Krall had waited until Mr. Prince had gotten up and left the study before checking his other two cameras and shutting down his computer. Then he'd paid the check, leaving a large tip, and they'd driven back to the compound without speaking. Sandy spent a sleepless night in her unhappy bedroom. It felt cold and abandoned. She would have welcomed a ghost.

Sunday at Breedon Manor had expired without incident. There were subdued meals in the kitchen. The red sports car had gone. Krall spent the day in his strategy sessions. Milly went shopping. Megan asked Sandy to spend the day with her. They explored the estate together, under a blustery sky, and Megan told Sandy all about her plans for the apartment and her future with Hartley.

Barbara did not appear until it was time to drive back to the city. The journey passed almost in silence. Sandy wondered whether Barbara knew about Mr. Giordano. She felt sure that Megan and Milly did not.

As the Escalade approached the Aspire Building, Barbara turned on the radio. One of the major-party candidates, they heard, had been embarrassed by the discovery that gardeners employed at his California beach house were *illegals*. And Prince had moved to a three-point lead in the polls. Barbara had laughed — but not with her usual ebullience, Sandy thought.

Now, on a cold, gray Monday morning, as Sandy and Megan waited for the car to take them downtown, Sandy watched the news on FNN. The Chinese moon mission had reached a crucial stage: With the attachment of one last module, the assembly of the craft would be complete. It would then leave Earth orbit and begin its history-making journey. But FNN's experts expressed skepticism that it would succeed, citing recent quality-control problems in Chinese shoe factories. They were vehement. Sandy turned the TV off.

Megan activated Josh Merriweather's video telescope. Teri had left it pointed at the rink.

"Look at that," Megan said. "People out there already."

"But we have to work."

"Sure do. Back to the grind."

Reception called. The car had arrived.

Sandy did not feel ready for work. She had slept badly again, and the image of Mr. Giordano's blue denim jacket and the anger and hatred in his voice had haunted her dreams. And she did not feel well. There was a stiffness in her left leg. She hoped it was only the damp air at the beach, or the chilliness of her sad and unslept-in bedroom.

As they rode downtown, Sandy decided it was okay to ask God a personal question. She was rebuilding her relationship with Him, after all, and there was no reason to suppose that He would mind.

So what would He do, Sandy respectfully wanted to know, if he knew of a person suffering under some burden or torment, whose position forbade him from seeking help or solace in the way that a person normally would? And let's say that this person was already dedicated to God's will — saving America, no less — and was beset by enemies eager to exploit any weakness. And let's say, also, that this person had a friend, at a distance but known to him, who would have to break a promise to bear witness, or share his pain, or generally be a Good Samaritan.

And perhaps God would take into account that this person had a very busy schedule and might have to be approached via a third party, such as the friend just mentioned.

God didn't immediately get back to Sandy — his schedule had to be pretty busy, too — so Sandy looked out of the limo's rain-streaked windows while she waited.

Even here, in what was, for now, the capital city of the world, she thought, people looked harried, frantic, and careworn. She saw women struggling with overstuffed, worn-out shopping bags, like the one Sandy herself used to have. There were old men, layered in thrift-store clothing, some with shopping carts, who looked like they had no destination but merely a residual will to keep moving. They reminded her of Hunter Bill. And there were the city's workers, people with jobs and obligations, like Megan and Sandy: They looked the most fearful of all. Sandy wasn't sure whether the present economic crisis was the same economic crisis that held sway when she first moved into the village. Probably, it didn't matter a whole lot.

Could Mr. Prince really mend things? And not just the economy, but people, too? Well, if he couldn't, Sandy would like to know who could. Because she was putting herself out there with him, and she couldn't afford to fail.

When they arrived at Water Street, Ray Krall was waiting for them.

"Megan — there's some guy on the desk asking about Milly. Can you talk to him? Thank you kindly. Sandy — no phones for you today, you're with me. We're doing a Town Hall. Then we got debate prep. I need to have your feedback. You okay with that?"

She said she was. Actually, she hadn't been looking forward to the phones today. There was too much on her mind.

"We have a bus coming," Krall said. "Then we're heading over to Jersey. We got a whole bunch of Amber Pike's people showing up. Goes without sayin' we need her support. But I want you to stop us before we give the store away. You know what I mean?"

"Who's Amber Pike?"

"Who *is* she? You mean you've never... Okay, here's the bus. Let's go, people!"

Sandy found Barbara at the front of the bus. Barbara took her purse off the seat next to her and motioned for Sandy to sit. And Sandy quickly learned that Amber Pike was a *populist flake* with *folksy manners* and a back yard full of *over-cultivated resentments*. She was a failed politician, a TV blowhard, a huckster in a Valentino suit and a *dimwit*. She looked nice, and very *American*, in a *tacky* kind of way. And she had a lot of followers. The campaign needed their votes.

"So this is the marvelous Sandy! The miracle-worker — in person, as it were!"

Sandy looked up. Leaning over her was a disheveled man in a raincoat. He had messy hair and pungent breath. She thought he smelled even more of cigarettes than Barbara did.

"Got a moment for the foreign press, have we?"

"You!" Barbara said. "What's your name?"

"Nigel Weese, London Globe."

He leaned across Sandy's lap and tapped his laminated ID.

"See? We're doing a special on Prince's problem with working-class —"

"Oh, you're Flint's little helper, aren't you?" Barbara said. "Or maybe his brain. Whatever. Back of the bus! Now!"

"Look, I just wanted a quote from super Sandy here. And we all think she's doing a —"

"Back of the bus. Go! "

"A bit of gratitude wouldn't go amiss, you know. We helped you out of that Chinese mess. Our proprietor made up his mind, you see. Now we're on your side. He likes to play golf, by the way. Hasn't had the pleasure with your chap yet. If you could see your way —"

"If you don't go to the back of the bus and sit down, I'll —"

"All right, all right. No need to get shirty. I'm going. Sandy, love, we'll do it another time, all right? Oh, and while we're at it — Mrs. van Dornen, do you know anything about a gentleman by the name of Peter Giordano?"

Barbara stood up.

"Ray!"

At the sound of Krall's name, Weese stepped back.

"Um, no need to bother Mr. Krall, ladies. We'll just leave it there, shall we? Yes, I think so."

And, in a flap and a rustle, he was gone.

"Who *was* that?" Sandy asked.

Barbara groaned.

"Just some little... You let me know if he bothers you again, okay?"

"Okay. But why did he... Oh."

"Why did he what, dear?"

"Oh, nothing. I'm sorry. He got me all confused."

"That's how they like to work. Just forget about it."

"Yes, I will."

Then Ray Krall boarded the bus. The doors closed, and the bus began to wend its way through the streets of lower Manhattan.

When they entered a tunnel, Sandy checked to see if there had been a message back from God. But there hadn't. She would have to be patient. That was okay. She was used to that.

The bus emerged into the light and wound its way on to the New Jersey Turnpike. They drove for half an hour before pulling into the parking lot of a VFW hall. The lot was already full. They had trouble parking.

"Looks like Amber got her people out," Barbara said, without enthusiasm.

Krall stood up at the front of the bus.

"Okay, we're running late. So everybody go right on in. Barbara, Sandy — you're with me."

Krall led the way across the parking lot to a bus decorated with flags and painted in red, white and blue. On its side Sandy read *Amber Pike True American Tour*. It was guarded by two of the Secret Service agents Sandy had seen at Breedon Manor. Parked adjacent were two black SUVs belonging to Fairmeadow Security.

"Guess Willard's already here," Krall said. "Now, I wonder what they've been talkin' about."

"Hunting and fishing?" Barbara said.

Krall cracked a half-smile and gave Sandy a conspiratorial glance.

"Willard ain't never hunted nothing."

"Can you fix that?"

"If I have to. Wait here."

Krall went ahead. There was a short conversation in which Krall pointed to Sandy and the agents nodded. Then they were permitted to board Amber's bus.

The bus was empty, Sandy saw, but for two people sitting at a compact conference table. Mr. Prince looked calm and thoughtful, she decided. However troubled he might be, he had inner strength. He wore a dark gray suit with a white shirt and a pale yellow tie. At the other side of the table was a woman of Sandy's age, or a little younger. She was dressed in a dark-blue skirt suit that, to Sandy, looked expensively uncomfortable; a striped, pale-pink shirt; and a double-strand pearl necklace. She wore large rings and over-sized glasses, and her red-brown hair fell to her shoulders in extravagant curls. Her nails were glossy red and her lips, glossy pink. Sandy thought she looked *high-maintenance*, and not just in the way that someone who'd lived in the woods for years might think.

"Good morning, Mr. Prince, sir," Krall said. "Great to see you again, Amber. Lookin' good, as always. Now, y'all know Barbara. This here's Sandy. Today, she's acting as my special assistant. Guess we'll sit here."

He meant a three-seater couch opposite the conference table. They sat.

This was the closest Sandy had ever been to Mr. Prince; he was almost near enough to touch. Was this God's answer? Had He brought Sandy here for a purpose? Well, she supposed so. But what *exactly* was He suggesting? Sometimes she wished He'd make Himself clearer.

"We have been having such a great conversation, between us two here, that is so good to have between us," Amber said.

"That's great to hear," Krall said. "I like the sound of that. Amber, we really appreciate it."

"With all that future in America, and the small farms, and how this will be a new administration, restoring decency, and of course the children."

"Yeah, that's pretty much how we see it too. Uh..."

There was a pause. Amber had an odd way of speaking, Sandy thought. She glanced at Barbara; her face was set in an expression of weary indulgence — as if, Sandy imagined, Milly had brought home the wrong sort of boyfriend, and not for the first time. But be careful, Sandy, she told herself; if Amber says something funny, *don't you dare laugh!*

"Ray?"

Mr. Prince had spoken.

"Yes, sir?"

"Are we going to win this thing?"

"Yes, sir. I believe so, yes."

"You're sure?"

"Sure as I can be, sir. The polls —"

"No doubt?"

"No, sir. Excepting some last-minute..."

"It's very important. That we win."

"Absolutely. No question."

Mr. Prince turned to Barbara. Barbara shrugged.

"It's like I keep telling you," she said.

Mr. Prince looked down at the table in front of him.

"All right, then. Good."

Then he looked up again and turned to Sandy.

"*You* think so too?"

"Oh, I do, yes. Sir."

Another pause.

"Well, if you all think so..."

They waited. Mr. Prince leaned back in his chair and folded his hands together on the table.

"But then we are being so concerned," Amber said, "all across America, here, that our moon with China rearing up, and so also our flag which is up there."

"What?" Krall said.

"Oh, it's the moon mission," Sandy said. "That's what she — it's the Chinese moon mission. Really, I know that a lot of people are worried. What if they take our flag?"

"Why would they do that? Are they even landing in the same —"

"Ray, she's right," Barbara said. "Forget logic. Just deal with it."

"How? And how come I never heard about this?"

"You're too busy. This is why we have Sandy."

Krall sighed.

"Barbara, you are correct, as usual. It goes on the list."

He turned back to Amber.

"Amber, we need to have some substantive idea of your itinerary, your talking points, your media schedule and so on. You know, in the run-up. Assuming you're completely behind us now."

"Yes, that is so true that we are all completely behind us, and you, and also the talking points that we will give you."

"Okay, and the other stuff?"

"And the other stuff, also."

Krall glanced at Barbara. One of Barbara's eyebrows edged up.

"Amber," Krall said, "we think it would be good if *you* took the lead in this meeting, what with so many of your folks bein' here today. Is that okay? Are you with me?"

"I am okay with me, yes. Being such an honor, obviously, for Willard Prince, our next President, and America also."

Krall rubbed his hands together.

"All right, then! Uh, Mr. Prince, sir, if you're ready to —"

Sandy jumped in her seat as someone thumped on the window behind her head. She turned. It was one of the Secret Service agents. He was shouting, but she couldn't make out what he was saying. And he had his gun in his hand.

Krall ran to the front of the bus and yanked the door open.

"What the —"

"Where's your driver?"

"I, uh..."

"Can you drive this thing?"

"I guess, but —"

"Get it moving. Follow that black SUV, you hear?"

"What's happening?"

"Security incident. Get moving! *Now!*"

Amber stood up.

"What is this we are having?"

Barbara grabbed Amber by the arm and pulled her to the floor.

"Keep down! Crawl to the back. Get behind a seat. *And keep your head down!*"

"Ow! My knees! And get your hand off of my butt."

"Shut up. And get down the back. You too, Sandy."

Sandy hit the floor. The bus was moving — lurching and jerking. Krall was a good driver, she knew. But he'd never driven a bus. There was a bump as they hit a curb. Then they juddered across the rough grassy median between the hall

160

and the highway. Sandy, on hands and knees now, shoved Amber's discarded, red-soled high-heels aside and shuffled after her to the back of the bus.

Krall accelerated. Sandy could hear sirens in the distance. *Security incident!* What did that mean? And where was Mr. Prince? Was he safe? She stopped and turned her head. There he was — under the conference table. He had curled up into a ball. Barbara lay alongside on her stomach.

She was holding his hand.

CHAPTER 25

Teri Wolfe had only just completed her overdue blog assignment for Gloria — Teri wrote that her generation ought to celebrate their freedom to enjoy not just one but an entire *portfolio* of different careers — when Robin's message had arrived: *park now smartass xx.*

Gloria had seemed satisfied with Teri's homework, despite its being pure garbage, so Teri felt sufficiently emboldened to request a coffee break. Her temporary freedom granted, she grabbed her coat and ran out into the rain.

Once again, Robin awaited her at the rink. As she jogged towards him, Teri picked up on a certain agitation. Good, she wondered, or bad? *Smartass xx* sounded more good than bad, unless he thought he was going somewhere with the *xx*, but you never seemed to know with Robin.

Nevertheless, she felt that the pictures she'd given him yesterday — of Fat Willy's *Marie Celeste* of a trading room and his dollar-store Rolodex — were pretty hot stuff, as spy shit went.

"So," she said, as she panted to a halt in front of him and brushed her wet hair out of her eyes. "Smartass? What's that all about?"

Yup, she thought, he's certainly excited — practically bouncing from foot to foot, like it's Spring Break tomorrow and he's stud *numero uno* on the football team.

"This could be really huge," he said.

"Oh yeah?"

"Dynamite."

"Really?"

"Could blow everything wide open."

"You think so? Everything?"

He spread his arms wide, as if to embrace the entire city, or the lower section of the Park at least.

"So what do you think we're looking at here?" she asked.

He ran his hands through his hair — or tried to; it was really too short.

"Malfeasance."

And this said in such an ominous way that she couldn't help but purse her lips.

"Possibly on a grand scale."

"Uh-huh. Can we get a little more specific?"

"Well, we have a guy who can —"

"You got yourselves a tame banker."

"Right, and he says..."

"What?"

"Well, it's kind of complicated. But the bottom line is, it doesn't add up. All those accounts, the way he's moving money around..."

"You mean in a *malfeasy* kind of way?"

"Yeah, exactly. Then there's the trading records that don't seem to exist..."

"I mentioned that. But you pooh-poohed."

"I did?"

"You most certainly did."

"Well, I —"

"You're dealing with a *smartass*, remember?"

He gave a short, satirical snort.

"That's true."

"Look, is he doing something wrong? Something unethical? Something illegal?"

Robin took a deep breath and exhaled slowly.

"The way we see it, it could very wrong. Very unethical. And very illegal."

"It *could* be?"

He started in again on his little foot-to-foot jig.

"Just stand still, will you?"

"Okay."

"Good. Now, listen. Simple question: Have we got proof?"

"Not quite."

"Okay. Here's another one: what *exactly* do you think he's doing?"

"Well, our guy says it could be... He, I mean Prince... He could be... You know, I don't think I want to say it out loud until we're sure?"

That seemed reasonable, she thought. No rush to judgment. No prejudicial speculation. Just something unspeakably delicious, just out of reach, and a superstitious desire not to jinx it.

"So how do we prove it?"

"The proof," he said, "has got to be in London."

"Why London?"

"Follow the money."

"Ha! That's funny."

"It's true, though. It looks like the money all goes through London. And our guy says nobody seems to know where Prince gets his trades executed. In New York, I mean."

Teri thought for a moment.

"Okay, maybe there's an explanation. He runs everything out of London. But he doesn't want people to know. You know, because it's the New *American* Century Fund, and he claims he only ever invests in quality American stocks and all that crap. But he's actually going crazy in Europe or Russia or wherever. He's

164

doing derivatives, whatever they are. Or he's shorting Argentina, whatever that means. So the trading room is bogus, but it's just for show. No biggie, in other words."

"No biggie?"

Robin took a moment to gaze across the immensity of the Park as if he were thinking of buying it.

"No biggie?" he repeated. "Here's what our guy says. If it's what we think it is, there could be money missing. A *lot* of money."

"Like, how much?"

"Between a hundred and two hundred."

"Two hundred million dollars!"

"*Billion*, smartass! *Billion!*"

Teri felt the Park swoon on her behalf under her feet. What *had* she done!

"And he's in London," Robin said, "because he thinks he can get away with it there."

"Wait, wait, wait," Teri said. "Your guy. Has he actually been inside all those accounts?"

"Of course he has. How else would he figure all this out? You gave us the login info."

Teri tipped her head back so that the rain hit her full in the face.

"Shit!"

"And I guess you ought to be aware that..."

"What?"

"Well, we changed all the passwords."

"You *changed* —"

"To preserve the evidence. Plus freeze his assets."

"You *froze* his *assets?*"

"Sure. And, anyway, there's a whole other dimension to this."

"Huh?"

"It's not just about fancy white-collar crime. It's not just about rich people stealing from other rich people."

Teri stared at him. Was this going where she thought it was going?

"So where," Robin demanded, "do you think all that money came from in the first place?"

She felt an upwelling of politically-suspect nausea in her stomach.

"Oh shit, oh shit..."

"Seriously! Think about it!"

"Oh shit..."

"You know what this guy represents. You know who's backing him. And you know what'll happen if he wins. Which he will, if he's not stopped."

"So stop him! Call the cops! Call the FBI!"

"Oh, we'll stop him all right. Just not yet."

"*Not yet?* What are you going to do?"

He gave her a crazy, crooked smile. Rain dripped from his nose.

"We're the Robin Hood Party. What do you *think* we're going to do?"

"Oh shit..."

"Stop saying that. Look, we need your help. Two things."

"Oh sh—"

"You've got to get into the London part of the system. We need some customer statements. You got that? *Customer statements.* Our guys says if he sees a bunch of statements he'll be sure. There'll be *proof.*"

"Proof?"

"That's right. Proof. We want proof, don't we?"

"Gotta have proof."

"Exactly. And the other thing is... Well, we need Prince's itinerary. This stupid *Bus Across America* tour he's doing. It's secret. But we want you to get it."

"Secret bus tour. Right."

Had she heard about a secret bus tour? No. She hadn't. That was because she wasn't a spy at all. She was barely a grown-up. She was a stupid, dumb *blogger-girl* who'd gone and got herself into a shit-load of trouble.

"Er, you know what?" she said. "I think I'm kind of out of my depth a bit here? I wish you well, and all. You want to take from the rich, give to the poor, all that shit? I'm basically okay with that. But, you know, I've got my own problems, and I can't really handle any more. So I'm going to have to take a pass on this. Sorry."

There was an awkward pause. She flicked her hair out of her eyes again.

"I don't think you can really walk away from it," he said.

"Can't I?"

"Don't think so."

"No?"

He shook his head, slowly.

"What's your real name?"

"My real name is Nile. Nile Tyson."

And there you had it, she thought. No blood, no oaths — just a small exchange of data. And the bonds of conspiracy had been sealed.

Then her fancy campaign phone rang. Her heart raced. It was Gloria.

"Teresa! Get back here right now. Something's happened."

"What? What's happened?"

"Just get back here."

Nile was looking at his phone.

"An incident..." he said. "Campaign stop, town hall meeting, shots fired, Prince safe, undisclosed location, two women missing..."

He looked at Teri.

"Jesus. You better get back."

She turned and ran.

Back at the apartment, things looked like they were falling to pieces, Teri thought. In the absence of Krall, Barbara and Prince himself, there was a strong smell of *leadership vacuum.*

In the kitchen, Milly tried to fend off the relentless enquiries of Flint Gunner, his creepy sidekick and a whole bunch of their pals. Who'd let them in? Why had nobody taken their cameras? What was to prevent Prince's bespoke interiors from being splashed across the tabloids?

In her office, Gloria sat at her desk, her hairdo aquiver, a phone in either hand, not knowing who to call. When she saw Teri, however, her instructions were clear and concise: *Do something to help!*

In the hallways, serious, fit-looking men in suits ran to and fro — Secret Service agents, Teri surmised.

In the scullery, a cop wearing rubber gloves was wrapping Teri's laptop in polythene. Should she say something? Maybe not.

In Prince's study, Teri caught a glimpse of the Mayor. He and his entourage — or as many of them as would fit — were updating themselves by watching FNN.

And, in the library, Teri found Megan. Prince's rarely-seen younger brothers were there, too — the one who ran a private-equity empire and the one who was said to *broker deals* for Middle-Eastern potentates. They were yelling at Megan, who looked close to tears.

But it wasn't their elder brother they were all wound up about. They wanted to know *where the fuck* that *bastard* Peter Giordano was.

CHAPTER 26

andy Quayle had to slow down. Amber Pike could not keep up with her. They were walking on a rough, gravel trail, and Amber had no shoes. She had abandoned her red-soled *Louboutins*, as she called them, in the bus; a heel had snapped off in the accident.

Poor Amber, Sandy thought. She'd come out of it much the worst: a cut over her left eye, a bruise on her left cheek, scraped knees, ruined pantyhose, broken glasses, and her skirt split down the seam at the back. By contrast, Sandy had suffered nothing more than a bruised shoulder. Her leg still felt numb, but that was nothing to do with the accident.

She would have offered Amber her own shoes, but Amber's feet were too big.

Where were they? Well, they'd driven only for fifteen or twenty minutes before the accident, but they'd spent that time on the floor of the bus, huddled together behind the seats at the back. Ray had been told to follow the black SUV that belonged to Fairmeadow Security. He'd driven at great speed. And he'd gone off the road — this gravel track — into a ditch. It looked like *Amber Pike's True American Tour* was wrecked beyond repair.

Sandy didn't recall the accident itself — had she blacked out? She remembered Amber shaking her, and she remembered climbing out of the bus and wondering what had happened to Ray, Barbara, and Mr. Prince.

And wondering why they were in the middle of a forest.

Amber's phone worked; she could get a decent signal. But when she tried to call, all they could hear was noise. They tried text messages and email, but nothing worked. Sandy didn't have a phone; unlike Teri, she was a volunteer, not an employee, so she hadn't been given a campaign phone.

They reasoned that, having been hidden at the back of the bus, they had simply been overlooked in the heat of the moment. Someone had taken the others away — Fairmeadow, presumably. They would realize their mistake and come back for Amber and Sandy. Probably. But, just in case, they had decided to walk on, in the direction that the bus had been pointing. The cut above Amber's eye needed attention.

169

"So, do you know what happened back there?" Amber said. "At the Town Hall?"

"Not really. I just heard *security incident.*"

"Because I thought I heard gunshots. You know, when we were hittin' the highway? And I *know* what a gun sounds like. That was a large-caliber semi."

"Oh! I hope nobody was hurt..."

"Well, you know, that hall was full, so..."

"Oh."

"Probably just some crazy person. We do get a few. You know, at our rallies, and also our Town Halls, like this."

"Do you?"

Sandy noted that Amber could speak quite coherently, when she wasn't trying to impress anyone.

"How are your feet?"

"Oh, not so bad. We used to run around barefoot when we were kids, so..."

"You didn't live in the city, then?"

"Nah, we kinda lived in the woods. Like *this*, only with junk and hobos and stuff. How about you?"

"Oh, something like that. Do you think Mr. Prince is okay?"

"Guess we'll find out soon enough."

"But what if he had to..."

"Pull out of the race? Yeah, *that* would make *some people* happy!"

"I hope Ray and Barbara weren't hurt."

"Yeah, but you know what? There's a reason for everything. Isn't that what God tells us? He spared you and me. So that just shows that there's, you know, a purpose. Don't you think?"

"Yes, I do. I do think that. I really want to believe that, Amber."

God had saved them for a purpose. He must surely have saved Mr. Prince too; and Sandy could only hope that Ray and Barbara were also part of the plan. God hadn't saved Amber's shoes, but perhaps that was because He didn't like them very much. Sandy could understand that.

"So where do you think we are?"

"I'm guessing this is part of Fairmeadow's facility. They have this... I guess they call it a regional command center. It's right next to that big new prison they run for the state."

"Prison?"

"Well, they do a lot things. They are very successful in our growth sectors. As we all know."

Sandy remembered the eviction from the village — the *goons* with their clubs, and the Sheriff sitting in his car in the shadows.

"Yes, I know."

"Oh, but you must be pals with Josh Merriweather, right?"

"Not really."

"He just put a bunch of money into Fairmeadow Data. Well, it's nothing to him, obviously!"

"I suppose not."

They approached a fork in the road. There were no signs.

"Which way?" Sandy said.

"Let me try my phone again."

She tried — no luck.

"Let's try left. You would think they woulda come lookin' by now, wouldn't ya?"

On they trudged.

"Amber," Sandy said. "Do you think Mr. Prince can save America?"

Amber stopped. She tried to hike up her skirt, which, being beltless, was slipping down. There came the sound of ripping linen.

"Ah, shoot. You know, Sandy, what can I tell you? Somebody has to. The overspending, the taking away of our liberty, all the debt that we are putting on our children, here in America, and then the weakness, and the socialism, and the foreign enemies. And China rearing up, also, like I said."

They began to walk again.

"So I guess that's why they formed the Committee. You know, because of the gridlock and not being bipartisan. And the not reaching out. And the people hate that, in America. But you know, Sandy, if you stand up against the elites and the establishment, they will tear you down. They're going through your garbage and they're, like, *critiquing* what you wear? And raggin' on your children? Is that fair? In America? Anyway, the point about the Committee is, it can stand up to the elites. You got Josh Merriweather, who is one of our great tech pioneers, and invented the DirtBaggr app. And DumpChat, also. And you got the guy with all those casinos, and then there's the coal guy and the chemical guy, and I guess the rest of them are Wall Street."

They walked on. The forest became denser.

"So, if *they* can't save America," Amber said, "Who can?"

"Ray asked me if I thought America was in decline."

"I don't think he really gets it."

They walked another hundred yards, then Amber stopped.

"I think this is the wrong way. They'll be looking for us back there."

"No, there's something ahead — look."

"My glasses are broken."

"There's a clearing. I think there's a building."

"Okay, let's check it out."

As they got closer, Sandy could see that there was a long, low, concrete building. It had very small windows. In front, there was an empty parking lot. Around the perimeter she saw a heavy chain-link fence, about twelve feet tall. In each corner was a steel tower, fitted with lights and cameras. A single gate was padlocked shut. There were no signs.

"Huh," Amber said. "So what is this?"

"You said they ran prisons."

"Yeah, but this is..."

"What is it?"

"Maybe we should go back."

Sandy walked up to the fence and peered through it without touching it. The building's small windows were barred. All were dark. But at one she thought she saw a face — a small, female face.

"Hey, Sandy — come on. This is the wrong way."

"No, wait a moment. I think there's someone in there. And..."

"Sandy?"

"We came here for a reason."

"No, we just got lost."

"Amber, I think this is beginning to make sense."

"Not to me. If this is some kind of law-enforcement —"

"Fairmeadow aren't the law."

Amber made a face.

"Technically."

"This doesn't feel right to me."

"*Feel* right?"

If there were some kind of test awaiting her here, Sandy thought, then Amber deserved to be tested, too.

"You see, I've been waiting to hear back from God..."

"You *talk* to God?"

Sandy did something she didn't like to do: she frowned.

"Why, yes, Amber, don't *you?*"

Amber wrinkled her nose. Her broken glasses slid down.

"Well, ya — but you're makin' it sound like you're chattin' away all the time."

"I'm not *chatting*. It's not like that at all."

"No, I just mean —"

"When you're at peace, the word comes to you. It's just *there*."

"Well, yeah. And that is how it comes to me, also."

Amber paused and pushed her glasses back up her nose.

"So. Are you gettin' anything now?"

Sandy looked to see if the face she'd seen at the window was still there. It was. She thought she could see a hand waving.

"Amber," she said, "we need to get through this fence."

"Through that? There's no way."

If only Hunter Bill were here now, Sandy thought; there were few fences that could keep him out.

"Let's look."

Sandy led Amber on a circuit around the fence. Sure, she thought, it looked formidable — to someone lacking Bill's resourcefulness. But it didn't appear to be electrified, and the bottom edge of the fence disappeared into dirt, not concrete. Had Fairmeadow skimped? She didn't expect to find a neatly-cut hole, such as the one Bill had carved in the fence that protected the Stimsonville Country Club golf course. But Sandy knew from her time in the village that wild animals would dig their way under almost any barrier if they thought food lay on the other side. And people did too, sometimes.

On the opposite side of the compound, where the forest was closest and there were no windows in the building, Sandy found what she was looking for: garbage cans, and a scooped-out gap under the fence. It wasn't big enough for Sandy, let alone Amber. So there was work to be done. Sandy found a pointed stick, got down on her knees, and began to dig.

"Uh, what are you doing?" Amber said.

172

"You can help if you want."

"How?"

"Scoop the dirt out."

"What with?"

"Your hands."

Amber looked at her hands.

"You know, these nails? Do you know what I had to —"

"It's up to you."

"I'm gonna have to take my rings off."

"If you want."

"Are you sure about this?"

"Why else would we be here?"

"Oh, you're not givin' me that old —"

"Old what?"

"Nothin'. Move over."

Amber lowered herself to the ground and set to work.

After ten minutes, Sandy figured the hole was big enough for her. But she kept digging until it was big enough for Amber, too. Then, while Amber held up the bottom edge of the fence, Sandy shuffled underneath on her back.

"Now you," she said. "Maybe take your jacket off."

"It's not big enough."

"Try it."

"I'm gonna get stuck under there, and then somebody's gonna show up with a camera and —"

"You'll be fine. Breathe in."

Amber took off her jacket and passed it under the fence to Sandy. Then she lay down on her back and wriggled under while Sandy pulled up on the fence.

"See! No problem."

"This suit is ruined."

"Yes. I'm sorry."

"Now what?"

"This way."

Sandy led Amber to the front of the building and located the window at which she'd seen the face. But it was a foot above Amber's head and eighteen inches above Sandy's, so they had to build a pile of rocks.

"You first," Sandy said. "You're taller. I don't know why you need those shoes."

"No? Well, let me tell you, those shoes send a message. They say —"

"I know what they say. Get up and see who's in there."

"Me? Aw, shoot."

Amber climbed up. Sandy steadied her from behind.

"Move your hands up a bit."

"Okay. What can you see?"

"Uh, there's a girl in there. Not lookin' too happy. Yellin' something."

"What?"

"I can't hear. There's glass. Behind the bars."

"Here. Smash it."

Sandy handed Amber a heavy, pointed rock.

"Go ahead."

"Uh..."

"Do it!"

Amber broke the glass.

"Great. Now there's glass in my hair as well as dirt."

"Who is she?"

"I'll ask her. *Who are you?*"

Sandy waited. She could hear the girl's voice, but her words were indistinct.

"Okay," Amber said. "Her name is Chen Yu. She says she's been kidnapped. Uh, they're going to send her back to China. And she's very scared."

"Is there anyone else in there?"

"No. She says she was in Battery Park, and Fairmeadow came, and they dragged her into a van, and they brought her here."

"What have they done to her?"

"Wait, I'll ask."

Sandy felt her spirit strengthen, even as her arms weakened in the effort of propping Amber up against the window. How could they get this poor girl out? What could she possibly have done?

"They've threatened her, but they haven't touched her. They want her to name people. People in the *Chinese Spring*."

"Chinese Spring?"

"She wants something to write with. Have you got anything?"

"No. Give her your phone, Amber. Let her record herself."

"Okay."

Amber passed her phone between the bars.

"Use this."

They waited. Ten minutes passed; the girl had plenty to say, it seemed. Then Sandy heard the sound of a vehicle approaching. Of course — the cameras had seen them.

"Amber!"

"What?"

"They're coming. Get your phone back and get down."

A black Fairmeadow SUV emerged from the tree cover and accelerated down the track towards them. It skidded to a halt in front of the gate.

"Okay," Amber said. "Got it. Help me down."

Two men in military fatigues jumped out of the car. One unlocked the gate. The other held a rifle across his chest. Then the SUV roared through the gate and pulled up four yards from them. A third man climbed out. He pulled a gun from the holster on his hip and advanced towards them.

"Get down," he said. "Down on the ground."

Amber turned to Sandy.

"I'm not gettin' down there again. Fuck 'em."

"Face down! Now! Both of you!"

Amber took a wobbly step forward.

"Now what *are* you doin' with this girl in here?"

"That's none of your — I *told* you to get down!"

"Do you *know* who I am?"

174

"I don't give a flying... Oh, wait..."

Sandy looked at Amber: but for the missing shoes, the dirt and glass in her hair, the cuts and the bruises, the muddy blouse and the ripped skirt, she was precisely the package as advertised. And this guy just didn't know what to make of it. He put his gun away.

"Just... Just wait there."

He went back to his vehicle and got on the radio.

And Sandy now understood why God had given her such an unlikely partner. New orders came quickly.

"Mrs. Pike? Would you get in the car, please? And your, uh, *you too.*"

"We should have been rescued from that bus," Amber said. "You left us there. You think we're goin' anywhere with you? Well, you're just goin' to have to think again, that's what. I'm callin' a taxi."

"Please just get in the car, Mrs. Pike. My orders are to —"

"This here's America, mister. Did you know that?"

"Yes, I know that."

"And we have a constitution in America. Did you know *that?*"

"Mrs. Pike. Please just get in the car."

"Me and Sandy here? We are going to sue your ass. And your company's ass."

"Mrs. Pike. You broke into a secure location. We have no choice but to —"

"You know who you sound like?"

Amber folded her arms and tipped her head to one side. Then she wagged her forefinger.

"You sound just like the socialists, with the not having any choice, and the Big Government orders. And then lockin' girls up in the woods, and —"

"Amber," Sandy said, "there's someone else coming."

It was another black Fairmeadow SUV. But its only occupant was Ray Krall. He pulled up between Amber and Sandy and the first car. Then, calmly, he stepped out and flung open the back door.

"Amber and Sandy — in the back, please. The rest of you, y'all can head on back. Nothin' else to see here."

Amber grabbed Sandy's hand.

"Come on."

"Hey, hey — wait a minute!"

"No, *you* wait a minute," Krall said. "My name is Ray Krall. I'm the director of the Prince campaign. These ladies are comin' with me. You got a problem with that, you talk to Willard Prince or you talk to Josh Merriweather. Okay? You got that?"

A moment of indecision.

"You can get on the radio if you want," Krall said.

No response.

"Okay. We're heading back to the city. Ladies — if you will?"

Amber climbed into the back of Krall's car. She seemed to struggle, so Sandy gave her a push.

"Hey, that's enough of that."

Then Amber gave Sandy her hand and pulled her up. Krall spun the car around and they took off out of the compound and down the track. They blew past

175

Amber's *True American* bus, still stuck in its ditch. And five minutes later they were back on the public highway.

"Okay," Krall said. "Now, would you like to tell me what the hell you were doing? Because, whatever it was, that ain't the place to be doing it."

"Oh, we just got lost," Amber said. "And then we thought we found someone who needed help."

"That's it?"

"That's it."

"Sandy?"

"Yes, that's right. We didn't mean any harm."

Krall didn't reply. *He doesn't want to talk about this*, Sandy thought. *And he hates Fairmeadow.*

"Amber," Krall said. "You're not lookin' your best. We'll go to Aspire. They have a doctor's office there."

Amber shrugged.

"Ray?" Sandy said. "Barbara and Mr. Prince..."

"They're okay. Willard's gonna be just fine."

"What happened? At the —"

"At the Town Hall? Just a crazy guy. He got on stage, grabbed the mic. Yellin' stuff about Prince and China. Old guy. Wild hair, big ol' coat. Looked like he lived in the woods, so they tell me."

"Amber said she heard shots."

"Yeah."

"So he had a gun?"

"No. No, he didn't have a gun. But they *thought* he did. So when he reached inside that coat..."

"What?"

"They shot him."

Sandy closed her eyes. It couldn't be, could it? How could God let *that* happen? What purpose could *that* possibly serve?

"So what *did* he have in his coat?" Amber said.

Krall sighed.

"The Wall Street Journal. All folded up. Some editorial or something about China. Big red ring around it."

Sandy opened her eyes.

"What was his name?"

"Uh, William something. Nesmith?"

Hunter Bill.

Krall and Amber began to talk about the election, and Sandy heard Amber slip back into her red-soled, broken-tongued, TV-ready persona.

And Sandy slipped away, too — back to the village.

Hunter Bill offered her a rabbit, and this time she took it. She carried it into the woods and found a grassy hollow. Then she buried it and placed a flower on top of its grave. And then she just sat, with no thoughts to think and no prayers to say.

Amber nudged her. They were in the underground parking garage at the Aspire Building. Krall had just gotten out of the car.

"Do you want this?" Amber asked.
She meant her phone. Sandy took it.
"Thank you."

CHAPTER 27

Having left Mr. Yu behind to manage his estate, supervise his staff, catalog his garden and tend to his lemurs, Ricky Ponton, the newly-self-appointed Bringer of Democracy to the world's largest economy, flew back alone to Tana, capital city of the lucky country scheduled to host the world's biggest naval base. He'd run low on cash and had elected to take Jay, the well-capitalized ex-spy, for all he was worth, while the opportunity dangled and before the bloke disappeared like a Manly sea mist.

Because Ricky adored La Cachette. He loved Madagascar. He thought he was developing a fondness for the lemurs. And, most of all, he prized having a sanctuary; and he relished being the master of it.

As the plane ascended, abandoning Ricky's verdant littoral for the despoliation of the highlands, Ricky contemplated the future of Freedom. Big Data Underground still had a chance, he thought, if certain conditions were met.

Somehow, there had to be a push-back against Weihan and its fellow pioneers on the transglobal digital frontier. Corporate control of the Internet would suffocate BDU; there would be no *net neutrality* for Ricky. There was irony — not much to Ricky's taste, in this case — in that government control of the network worked to Big Data's advantage: The spies wanted information to flow, so that they could tap it; the capitalists wanted to *enclose* the digital commons, in order to profit from it. A fight between Ricky and the spies was a fair match; a contest with the plutocrats — like Josh Merriweather — was no contest. Jiao, the cynical Party loyalist understood that. So did Kirk and Spock, the clownish but patriotic defenders of the old order.

There was another condition. The supply of high-value whistle-blowers had begun to dry up. Why? Well, look what happened to them. In the land of the free, they lived an isolated, slow-breathing death in open-ended military confinement; in the land of *habeas corpus*, deprived of legal corporeality, they tried to kill themselves softly, like Kerri, before secret evidence run up by secret courts dispatched them to a harder end.

Or, if they were lucky, they got to go to Russia.

But now Ricky had found his sanctuary. He would stay as long as he could — so long as the politics remained manageable and the money lasted. And maybe even beyond that.

But how would his future guests travel? There would need to be some kind of escape route or *rat run*. Would Jay help Ricky organize it? Maybe — but the bloke had his own agenda, and even *he* had to run out of money at some point, didn't he? Ricky's whistle-blowers, leakers, renegades, turncoats and traitors would have to make their way to Africa. Then it was simply a matter of getting to the coast and crossing the Mozambique Channel. A risky but romantic ride on a dhow out of Zanzibar? Not bad.

Unless that bloody naval base got in the way.

Mr. Yu thought that, were it to succeed, the Chinese Spring would destroy the authority of the Party. But it would not necessarily lessen Chinese military ambitions. Could Ricky point to any notable examples of pacifism among the mature democracies of the west? Furthermore, Mr. Yu said, if the Party could no longer control the military, who would? Ricky ought to think about it, because his organization was now actively assisting in the demise of the Party.

Too right, he thought — Ricky the *activist*, once more. Not up in court for trespass at Greenham Common, but toying with the fate of nations.

Norway and Iceland had moved fast. Big Data's secure communications network had been cloned and then reconfigured for its new Chinese clients and their world-wide supporters. Activity had spiked at once. Contingency funds had already been diverted to a new server farm.

But what about the base? Mr. Yu had hinted, dryly, at a solution. Someone would have to broker a secret deal between the Chinese and American militaries. *Like who?* Ricky had asked. Mr. Yu had smiled and gone out to watch the lemurs.

As Ricky's plane descended into Antananarivo, he wondered idly how much of a splash Big Data's newest revelations had made.

After he'd collected his Nissan four-wheel-drive, now mud-free and squeaky-clean, and had driven to his hotel, he found out.

While Jiao's run-down of the corruptions of Chinese capitalists, and Kirk and Spock's inventory of the vile deeds of American corporations got plenty of attention in the business-oriented media, it was Mr. Yu's military-budget bombshell that dominated. NATO and the European Union had convened summit meetings. The British Parliament had been recalled for an urgent and self-important debate. The Australian Parliament had tabled a vote of censure, but then changed its mind on the advice of mineral interests. Japan, South Korea and the Philippines wanted to know what America had to say for itself, now that their warnings had been vindicated.

And the US Presidential Election had blown a Hummer-sized gasket. Prince, in particular, was said to be in a jam.

But they were all getting ahead of themselves, Ricky thought. They didn't know about the naval base yet. How was Jiao taking it all? Luckily, he probably wouldn't have to find out. And, right now, the Chinese Spring might find a distraction useful.

Satisfied with the results of his hard work, Ricky set about loading up on cash. He recruited assistants from the hotel and purchased eight large holdalls. (The airplane company had calculated that this was Ricky's baggage limit.) The first bank branch he visited didn't have enough *ariary* on hand, so arrangements were made with two further branches. On return to the hotel, Ricky selected a top-floor room for himself and his money, and paid for two guards to sit outside.

Then he set out on foot to find a pharmacy where he could buy the powerful stomach medicine that the food-loving Mr. Yu had requested. This was easily accomplished, despite Ricky's shaky French.

But his sense of achievement didn't last long. On exiting the store, he spotted a black SUV parked on the opposite side of the boulevard. Darkened windows. American license plates — but Texas, not Maryland. It wasn't Kirk and Spock; their vehicle had carried government decals and other bureaucratic regalia. This car was clean. Texas? Home of Fairmeadow?

The car was pointed in the direction of the defunct railway terminus, to Ricky's left. Ricky turned right and walked briskly uphill. The air was thick with smoke blown in from the burning grass of the southern plateau, and he began to cough. When he glanced over his shoulder, he saw that the car had moved off. At the top of the boulevard, he crossed the street and ducked into a covered market.

The grass smoke, the captured fug of traffic fumes, and the sweet, charred stench of burning meat combined with the sweat and the excited din of the place to muffle his fear and make him feel as if he were bobbing in ocean of pure, dollar-a-day, human energy. Silently, he thanked his fellow shoppers for their unwitting support.

Ricky eased himself through the crowd to the center of the market, and found a spot where he could just about see his way to three of the market's exits. Then he pretended to browse a stall of Chinese-made rock-and-roll memorabilia. while on the look-out for anyone tall, white, foreign or armed. The stall-owner pressed him to examine an audio statuette of Elvis in his late-period pomp. Ricky smiled and nodded. Elvis looked a little too, well, *Chinese*, but never mind. The stall-owner commandeered Ricky's attention — *look, see!* A decisive button-press. *Glory, glory, hallelujah...*

A quick check of the exits: All clear, but too soon to abandon the relative safety of the market.

His truth is marching on...

Ricky shook his head.

"No thanks. Not much of an Elvis fan."

As nimble as any Valley start-up, the stall-owner switched his marketing strategy.

"Regardez! Ici!"

A model car — one of those red 2CVs, hand-made out of beer cans and wire, that you saw everywhere. But this one had *Route 66* written on the side. And the picture on the bonnet might have been John Lennon. Ricky had nothing against these developing-world cultural mash-ups — they were pleasantly subversive, he thought — but it just wasn't the right time.

To the left: A tall white guy in khakis, black T-shirt and sunglasses that he hadn't taken off despite the gloom and violent shadows of the market. Short on hair, big on biceps. *Shit.* Why didn't they just drop the drama and wear their Fairmeadow IDs and baseball caps?

181

"Reagan Pruett!"

Okay, so it wasn't Lennon after all. Who was Reagan Pruett?

"Nice, but no thanks."

To the right: A second guy, of the same general description as the first. And ahead: The only way out. Ricky went for it.

Outside, temporarily blinded by the sun, Ricky tripped over a cage of chickens. A flurry of clucking and remonstrance. Ricky picked himself up.

"Sorry, sorry! Excusez-moi!"

He ran through the crowd, brushing the feathers from his jeans as he ran. Now a choice: Down the boulevard, with its wide, open spaces — or up one of Tana's hills, via a long, steep flight of steps, up into the old city and the diplomatic zone? He chose *up*.

He made it half way before he realized his mistake. The air was foul. His lungs ached. At the foot of the steps, the two Fairmeadow guys stood, watching. They were fitter than Ricky, and probably fifteen years younger. They could have caught him up easily. But they weren't bothered. Which meant they knew what was waiting for Ricky at the top of the steps.

There was nowhere else to go; on either side, brick or concrete walls ran from top to bottom. Set into them, here and there, were wooden doors and iron gates. Ricky tried the nearest three; they were locked.

He sat down and tried to get his breath back. *Fuck it*. Let them come and get him. The two guys at the bottom looked at one another. A brief, guarded discussion. Then they started up, slowly. No weapons; they didn't take Ricky to be much of a threat.

"Mr. Ponton!"

A voice from behind and on high. A *female* voice. Huh?

"Mr. *Ponton!*"

Ricky shifted on his filthy step and looked up. At the top, in pink sneakers, white ankle socks, denim hot pants and what appeared to be a *Coldplay Tokyo 2014* T-shirt: Xin Jiao, the People's Liberation Army's secret weapon in the Sino-American cyber wars.

Earlier in the day, Ricky had been complacent enough to congratulate himself on not having to brave Jiao's wrath in respect of the military budget blow-up. Things looked different, now. Kirk and Spock would have seen the logic. Below, the Fairmeadow guys were legging it. Ricky realized he might not get to Jiao before they got to him.

"Mr. Ponton, please!"

Ricky hauled himself to his feet and barreled on upwards. Somehow, he found the strength he needed. Jiao wasn't precisely the answer to his prayers, but she would do in a pinch.

When he got to the top, the Fairmeadow guys were only thirty steps behind.

Jiao looked determined, but not exactly pleased.

"Get in!"

Ricky looked from side to side, his lungs pumping, his windpipe burning.

"Get in what?"

"The *car!*"

"What car?"

"*That* car!"

She pointed. Ricky looked down the hill. He saw an ancient Citroën — a 2CV! — painted in red and yellow, and one of Jiao's backing-band helpers standing by the open driver's door, waving at Ricky furiously.

"Are you serious?"

"*Get in! In the back!*"

He did as he was told. The car sagged under his weight. From behind, a single gunshot rang out and echoed across Tana's historic hillsides.

And then Jiao was in the front passenger seat and the car took off downhill, lurching crazily on the curves.

"Did you *shoot* at them?"

"Yes. They were too close."

"Did you *hit* them?"

"No. We don't want any trouble."

"No *trouble!*"

"You are trouble enough for us, Mr. Ponton."

The car swung around another curve. A Y-shaped junction loomed. Charging uphill from the right was the black SUV — or else another one like it.

Jiao slapped her driver on the shoulder with her free hand — she still held her gun in the other; where did she stash it when she wasn't using it?

"Up, up!"

The car careered to the left and screamed its way uphill again. Ricky grabbed hold of the edge of his seat. The cushion came away in his hands. In the car's cracked wing-mirror, he saw the SUV gaining on them.

At the top of the hill, they swung left again, past a large, stately house in colonial style, protected by steel fencing and wary soldiers – the Presidential Palace, Ricky figured.

Then they tore down a tree-lined avenue.

"Oh, there was a massacre here," Ricky said.

"Shut up."

The SUV had all but caught up. Jiao's driver forced the Citroën uphill again, into a narrow, walled lane that led to a dusty hilltop square. On the far side stood an empty stone palace — nothing left of it but its fire-blackened bones. Three small children sat in the dirt in front of it. The boys stared. The girl waved, cautiously.

"That way!" Jiao said.

The driver seemed to hesitate.

"Go on!"

They rumbled across the cobbles of the square and on to a rough, descending road, which turned into a dirt track, that turned into a footpath.

Ricky turned and looked back. The SUV had stopped where the dirt track ran out.

"These cars can go anywhere," Jiao said. "Those can't."

They wound their way downhill, past the backs of tumbledown houses, between vegetable patches, over ditches. Way down to his right, Ricky could see rice paddies, terracing, and *zebu* — the cows that many Malagasy regarded as their most valuable assets.

Eventually, they issued out on to a paved road that took them down to the boulevard again.

"So where are we going?" Ricky asked.

"The station."

They plied their way through the traffic to the far end of the boulevard and pulled up at the gates to the plaza in front of the old railway terminus. Jiao had put her gun away — Ricky could only wonder *where* — in order to negotiate, sweetly, in Mandarin, with the guards on the gate. Then they drove inside and the guards shut the gate behind them.

The terminus, grand enough for a minor European city but sadly train-free, had been turned into a tourist attraction — hence the guards — but not a very inspiring one. There was a coffee bar and a boutique that sold clothing, bags and knick-knacks. There were no other visitors.

"We would have gone to the embassy," Jiao said. "But we need neutral territory."

"Neutral territory?"

"Be quiet, Mr. Ponton. I am not very pleased with *you*."

All right, he thought, *I'll zip it*. The girl was armed and cross. But what was all that about *neutral territory?*

"Do you want a coffee?"

He nodded.

"It's over there."

Ricky crossed to the coffee bar, bought himself an espresso, and then sat down at a table, opposite Jiao.

"Where is he?" Jiao demanded.

"Who?"

Her brow furrowed and she pursed her lips.

Oops, he thought.

"Your new friend. Mr. Yu."

"He's minding the lemurs."

"He tells lies."

"Does he? So what's the true budget, then?"

"Never mind the budget. The budget is not the issue. *We* don't know what the budget is. *Nobody* does."

"Nobody?"

She sighed and rolled her eyes.

"It's like... How much money have the banks lent? *Nobody knows!*"

Ricky swallowed his espresso. She was going to ask him about the *Chinese Spring*, wasn't she?

"You've been talking to the Americans," she said.

"Have I? Which Americans?"

"They gave you the *dirt* you published. The American companies."

"Oh, those Americans. What about them?"

Jiao pointed to a corner of the terminus, to the right of the coffee bar.

"There is a pay-phone. Go call them. Tell them to come here. Now."

"Er, I'm not sure that's..."

Jiao pulled a scrap of paper and a plastic card from the back pocket of her shorts.

"Here. This is the number of the American embassy in Tana. We think your friends are DIA. Use this phone card. Go!"

Ricky took the card and the number and ambled across to the phone. How was this going to work, he wondered. Who should he ask for?

He asked for Kirk and Spock.

It wasn't an easy conversation, but after he mentioned the Defense Intelligence Agency, it felt as if he were being taken seriously. He was told that his request would be passed on for consideration by the appropriate office.

"Are they coming?"

"I don't know."

"We will wait. I need to talk to you about some things."

CHAPTER 28

Teri Wolfe had obeyed Gloria's commandment to the letter; she had *done something to help*. First she had rescued Megan from the rage and the verbal intimidation of the younger Prince brothers. This she achieved by falsifying a summons from Ray Krall — and deceit had come so easily to her lately, hadn't it? Krall had, she declared, demanded Megan's assistance *right now!*

The Prince brothers had stared at Teri as if they'd ordered dinner and she wasn't what they'd asked for. Then they'd cursed Krall out and thundered from the library in the direction of Gloria's office. Gloria, Teri felt, was made of sterner, more vitriol-resistant stuff than Megan, but even so...

Then Teri had smuggled Megan into the servants' quarters and squeezed her into the cubby-hole.

"You'll be safe here for a while."

"Um, thanks. Kind of small, though, isn't it? Do you, like, sleep here?"

"So what's up with Peter Giordano?"

Peter Giordano was, according to Megan (and just about everybody), the computer genius behind Prince's *bespoke strategy*, the "Man with the Golden Algorithm", as *Forbes* had it. He was also a creep and a drunk and a *toucher* — not that such truths were to be spoken in front of the Prince family, but Megan felt like getting a couple of things off her chest. What else? Well, the Prince brothers were a pair of shits, if you really wanted to know. Krall had pleaded with Willard to keep them out of the country during the election but, well, you just saw for yourself... So what had happened to Giordano? Megan didn't know; he'd just disappeared, without warning, without trace. Everybody said he was irreplaceable, so what would it mean for the Fund?

Teri had some thoughts on that. But she didn't share them with Megan.

Next, and still in help mode, Teri had braved the kitchen, where Milly, the Girl with the Golden Résumé, remained besieged by Gunner and his content-hungry hordes.

"Look, Flint, it's our feisty Teresa again. The new girl, remember?"

"Maybe she knows something, Nige."

187

"Wouldn't be surprised if she did, Flint. She's a sharp one, she is."

"Think she's in on it?"

"What, the kidnapping? Well, Flint, we do know her sympathies, don't we?"

"You bet."

"Researched her, didn't we?"

"Researched her good, Nige."

Kidnapping? Sympathies?

Once again, Teri had resorted to her weapon of choice. Krall, she announced, was heading hot-foot back to the apartment. He was moments away. And he was not in the best of moods. Now, that *might* be because he'd been watching the coverage on Freedom News. Teri couldn't say. But Krall had expressed enormous interest in discussing the nature of this coverage with Flint Gunner, in person. And the same went for Gunner's esteemed international colleague, whatever his name was. And, indeed, for the entire kitchen press corps in its truth-seeking totality.

There was a rush for the exits. Teri wondered aloud if Mr. Gunner and Mr. — what was the name? *Weasel?* — would be so good as to remain behind and await Mr. Krall's pleasure? Oh, it was Mr. *Weese*, was it? Whatever. Please, gentlemen — take a seat...

"Uh, are we done here, Nige? 'Cause, uh, you know how..."

"Well, what do you think, Flint? Back to the studio?"

"That's what I'm thinking, Nige. They need us there."

"Perhaps you're right."

"Yeah."

"We'll catch up with Teresa later, won't we?"

"Sure will."

And thus Teri had found herself alone in the kitchen with Milly. It wasn't possible to fit both Megan and Milly in the cubby-hole at the same time, so Teri had taken Milly to the scullery. She was relieved to observe that her laptop had been restored, though it did seem a bit *sticky*.

Anyway, what was all that about a *kidnapping?*

According to Milly, Freedom News had reported a rumor that Amber Pike had been taken hostage by a disgruntled campaign worker who had *links* to Islamic terrorism. By the time they'd turned on Teri's laptop, however, the story had already been discounted, owing to *flaws* in some of the *details* of the initial reporting. But *some were still asking* if the *alleged gunman* at the Town Hall could have had such links.

Milly thought that Mr. Prince would not be deterred; he knew what he had to do.

And now, as she shivered in the cold outside the Aspire Building, trying to pump up courage for what *she* had to do, two thoughts occurred to Teri: First, that she had been right on the money about Krall and FNN, without even knowing it; and, second, that there was little to prevent Gunner and Weese from updating Barbara on the subject of Teri's *sympathies*. Shit!

But Milly, at least, had pledged her allegiance; she'd been so grateful to Teri for being liberated from the media mob.

"Teresa, you're my best friend forever."

Right. Until she found out that Teri had stolen her identity and was about to wreck her cushy career as PR girl and high-priced greeter at Fat Willy's midtown Ponzi Palace.

Whoa.

Whoa!

Just *hold on* a moment there, Teri.

Cool it.

Yeah, really!

You just used the P-word.

The word that Nile recoiled from. The word that he had declined to enunciate. Okay, you only *thought* it. You didn't say it out loud. But still...

Don't jinx it, Teri.

Get the proof.

Go into Sandy's apartment *right now*, lie to her, and get the *proof*.

*

S andy looked rough, Teri thought, and old. Her faced sagged. But there was a hint of something in her eyes — a beaten-down determination? And she seemed preoccupied.

"Glad you're okay," Teri said. "You *are* okay, aren't you?"

Sandy looked up at Teri from the far side of Josh Merriweather's U-shaped couch.

"Oh, I'm fine."

Teri gestured in the direction of the Prince apartment.

"It was a zoo back there. For a while."

"A zoo?"

"You wouldn't believe it. Those reporter guys got in. They had Milly surrounded, you know? I had to rescue her."

"Did you?"

"Oh, yeah. Did you hear what they were saying about you?"

"What? What were they saying? Who?"

"You know, Gunner? Freedom News? They said you were a terrorist, or something, and you'd kidnapped Amber. You didn't, did you?"

Sandy clasped her hands together.

"No! Of course not! Why would they say that?"

"It's what they do. Don't worry about it. They're on to something else now."

"But they used to be so reliable..."

"Reliable! They're about the most— Nah, never mind about them. So what happened to you?"

Sandy stared down at Josh Merriweather's exotic-looking hardwood floor.

"Ray doesn't want me to talk about it."

"Why not?"

"He said it could affect the campaign."

"How?"

Sandy looked up and shrugged.

"But you can tell *me*," Teri said. "I'm part of the campaign."

Half-true, she thought, though perhaps not for much longer.

"He made me promise."

Well, that was that, Teri thought. Solemn Sandy wasn't going to break a promise, even one made to a rogue like Krall. So it was time to cut the small talk and move on to the main item on Teri's treacherous agenda: Getting Sandy out of the way temporarily, and grabbing her security key. Right there in front of Teri, on Josh Merriweather's smart coffee table, was Sandy's bag. It looked kind of bashed up — as if it had been in a car wreck. Would the key still work? Anyway, the issue was how to get Sandy out of the room...

But Sandy was looking at her.

"Teri?"

"Yes?"

"You know how things work, don't you?"

Hah! She sure did — only too well, sister! But what was Sandy really getting at?

"I mean these fancy smartphones."

"Sure. You having a problem with yours?"

"No. No, it's not mine. It's... Could you help me?"

"Absolutely. Let's have a look at it."

Sandy hesitated. This was weird, Teri thought; what was Sandy up to with somebody else's phone? Then Sandy reached for her bag and unzipped it. She took out her security key, and placed it on the table.

"Oh no, that's not it. Silly."

She dipped in again and took out a fancy cell phone. It was a model similar to Teri's campaign phone. Sandy held it in both hands.

"I didn't promise Ray... He doesn't know about this."

"Okay. So..."

"Do you know how these work?"

"Uh-huh."

There was a pause. Again, Sandy appeared to hesitate.

"So... What do you want to do on it?"

"Teri, will you promise me..."

"Promise you what?"

"Oh, I don't know. This is so difficult. I don't know how to do this..."

Okay, Teri thought, *distress level* mounting here — so say something soothing and take charge of the situation.

"It's okay, Sandy. Whatever it is, we can work through it together."

"Do you think we can?"

"Can I have a look at that?"

Teri took hold of the phone and eased it from Sandy's grip. The phone didn't have a PIN-lock or any other security, and nothing about it looked unusual. Then again, there was a Bible-related app and another one that had something to do with guns. And there was none of the stuff that people usually had — the Times, sports, stupid games, cat videos. Most of the bookmarks were for right-wing blogs. Teri was about to hit the phone's email when a wobbly, tremulous feeling overcame her.

"Uh, Sandy? *Whose* phone is this?"

"Oh, it's Amber's."

"Amber Pike?"

"Yes."

"You've got Amber Pike's phone?"

"Yes. I guess she has another one."

"Quite possibly. But *this one* is hers?"

"I just told you it was."

Sandy seemed on edge again. Take it down a bit, Teri thought.

"I'm sorry, so you did. No problem. Just wanted things to be clear."

Except they weren't. So tread carefully...

"So, um, what was it you wanted —"

"She *gave* me that."

"Okay..."

"Because there is something important on it."

"Right..."

"And I would like you, Teri, to find it for me. And, if you can, to make a copy of it."

"Ah. Okay. And it's... What is it, exactly?"

"A video."

A video! Teri dug down into the video folder. There was a single clip, from earlier in the day — around about the time that Sandy wasn't kidnapping Amber. Teri tapped *Play*.

A small, female face, in shaky close-up. Long black hair. Frightened expression.

My name is Chen Yu.

Teri hit *Pause*.

Wait. Chen? Did she really say that?

Rewind.

Play.

My name is Chen Yu.

Pause.

Teri looked up at Sandy. The edginess had gone and the determination was back.

"Teri, this girl is in trouble. She is suffering. We have to help her. It's our duty."

Sandy pointed at the phone, arm outstretched, as if this very gesture was latent with meaning.

"God wants us to, Teri. Do you understand?"

Did she? Teri bit her lip and nodded while she tried to figure it out.

Here was Chen Yu, in a selfie video, looking pretty scared. Chen Yu was Nile Tyson's girlfriend — the self-styled Robin Hood's *Maid Marion*, if you will. Actually, if you thought about that, it was a pretty neat multicultural reinterpretation, but never mind about that now. Because Chen must have been more than just the love interest, right? Fairmeadow had snatched *her* and ignored *him*. It had all been very plain to see on Teri's now infamous, and unfortunately lost, French Roast video. *Was* Chen more important? And why did Fairmeadow — and whoever it was who was picking up their tab — take the Robin Hood Party so seriously? They'd been causing trouble and getting up the nose of elite opinion for some time now — to much ruling-class derision and little practical effect.

Then there was the puzzle of how Chen had got herself on to Amber Pike's phone, and why Amber had given her phone to Sandy. These mysteries defied imagination. Why not just watch the video?

"Teri?" Sandy seemed impatient. "What is she saying?"

"Uh, hang on..."

Teri plugged the phone into Josh Merriweather's next-generation multimedia center. Chen's anxious, frozen image appeared on Merriweather's jumbo screen.

Play.

It was a manifesto.

And it had nothing to do with the Robin Hood Party.

Chen said it was likely that, within days, she would be returned, forcibly and secretly, to China. Since she was neither a world-famous artist nor a religious dignitary, she fully expected that she would never be heard from again.

But she had something to say now.

She believed in science, but she did not trust it.

She trusted technology, but she did not believe in it.

She did not trust herself, nor any individual, group, class, sect or party.

History was to be understood, and then defied.

The opportunities of humanity were limited and contingent.

Authority derived from consent, not from power.

Wisdom was the scarcest commodity.

Freedom was not a condition but a struggle.

Politics was inevitable, and desirable.

Capitalism and democracy were opposites, and yet there was no choice but to reconcile them.

Technology could choose its historical fate by picking a side: The capitalists or the democrats.

Capitalism, unrestrained and allied with technology, would exhaust the Earth.

Okay, it was possible that greed alone could wreck the planet, Chen said, but *to really fuck it up you needed a computer.*

Teri glanced at Sandy. Was she getting this? Because Teri sure wasn't. Sandy seemed entranced.

But now Chen dropped the grand-perspective stuff and got real.

She was proud to say that she had committed herself to the movement known as the *Chinese Spring.* Yes, it was a stupid name — but it was important that people in the western countries got the point. Because their support was essential. And the opportunity was *now*, and it was limited and contingent.

A new order was coming. The people of America and the other western countries ought to know this, because their experiment with popular democracy was almost over. The people of China, by contrast, would never get to experiment at all. Capital and technology had advanced, almost, to the point at which this new order could be effected and made permanent.

The New Pacific Partnership would be the legal framework. Willard Prince — or those who controlled him — had committed to it. The treaty, supposedly a *trade pact* that excluded China, would, in effect, be a Sino-American unification.

The Chinese economy would merge with, or absorb, the American economy. Chinese and American law would become one. Governance would be elevated to a transnational level, at which corporations were uniquely privileged.

Democracy, such as it was, would die.

Unless.

The American people could refuse. But they had never heard of the New Pacific Partnership, they thought Willard Prince was an American patriot, and most of them didn't vote anyway.

So, in this very last moment before the experiment ended, it was up to the Chinese Spring, and the people around the world who supported it, to seize the opportunity.

In the end, numbers mattered.

At this point Chen stopped and looked to her right, apparently distracted by something unseen. Then she turned her face back to the camera.

"You can't kill us all."

The video ended.

Teri looked at Sandy. Sandy appeared to have fallen into a trance — or religious ecstasy? — and was staring up at Josh Merriweather's glass-domed ceiling.

Teri unplugged the phone and flopped down on the couch. Okay, she thought, the first thing was *not to panic*. Yes, it seemed as though she was probably in even deeper shit now than she was ten minutes ago, but the main thing was not to panic. How about a calm, logical assessment of —

"Teri?"

Sandy had checked out of the astral plane.

"What?"

"I know what we have to do."

"You do?"

"Yes. I think I knew all along."

"Well, okay, but —"

"Is Mr. Prince at home now?"

"You mean at the apartment? Yeah, I think he's supposed to be back by now."

"Well, then. I must go and talk to him."

"Talk to him? Uh, Sandy, I'm not sure that's —"

"He will make sure that this poor girl is taken care of."

"Um, Sandy — did you, ah, did you *hear* what she just said?"

"She's suffering. Mr. Prince won't allow that."

"No, no, you see... The thing is, what she's saying —"

"I'm just going to get my coat. Is it raining out there?"

"Sandy, listen, there's like a couple of things you don't know about..."

"About what? What is there to know?"

"About Mr. Prince."

Sandy's face registered disapproval — haughtiness, almost, Teri thought.

"Well, if you're talking about Mr. Giordano, Teri, then let me tell you that, yes, Mr. Prince *was* very hurt. But he was steadfast. He overcame. And I probably shouldn't tell you this, but since you brought it up — Barbara is his *rock*. She gives him strength. I've seen it with my own eyes, Teri. And if Mrs. Prince is unable —"

"Wait, wait, wait. Back up. You said *Giordano.*"

Now Sandy looked peevish. Where was all this attitude coming from all of a sudden?

"Yes, I did. So?"

"Prince was *hurt?* Because Giordano disappeared?"

"Well, I'm not surprised if he wanted to disappear after what he did."

"Huh? What *did* he do, Sandy?"

"Well, he threatened Mr. Prince."

"Threatened! Why? What did he say?"

Sandy screwed up her face.

"I can't repeat that."

Oh, come on, Sandy!

"Okay, but what was the gist?"

"The gist? He demanded money, Teri. If he didn't get it, he was going to put the *whole thing* in the *something mail* to *you-know-who.*"

The whole thing in the fucking mail to you-know-who. Nile and his tame banker were right. But this wasn't *proof,* it was just Sandy talking. *Jesus!*

"But how do you know this, Sandy?"

"Well, it was Ray. When we were at the Manor. He took me out to dinner, after that business with Megan, and he had his computer, and..."

"What?"

"Well, they were in Mr. Prince's office. And that's where it happened."

Teri closed her eyes and ran this new information through her slacker brain a second time.

"Are you saying that Ray *bugged* Prince's private office?"

"Yes. But there was a reason for it."

"Really? Well, okay, but what else did Giordano say?"

"Just that it was *over* and *finished* and *done.* And he was *outta here.*"

Wow!

"Okay. Okay. Uh, Sandy..."

"Yes?"

"What did you think he was referring to?"

"I've no idea."

"Did Ray say anything?"

"No. Now, I'm getting my coat. Are you coming with me?"

"Um, actually, no. I've just got so much to... Look, it's better if you go on your own, really. You don't want me around. He'll listen to you."

Sandy seemed disappointed.

"All right."

She fetched her coat from Josh Merriweather's cloakroom and made for the door to the elevator.

"Wait!" Teri said.

"What?"

"Where is she?"

"Chen?"

"Yeah."

Sandy hesitated. Was that a frown?

"She's at the Fairmeadow compound. In New Jersey. Near the new state prison. On her own. In the forest."

Sandy let herself out of the apartment. The door clicked shut behind her.

Teri pulled out her campaign phone. She looked up Ray Krall's number and let her thumb hover over the call button. Then she tapped.

"This is Ray. Who's calling?"

"This is Teri? I work for Gloria?"

"Just one moment."

The line went quiet. Then he was back.

"Okay, I gotcha now. What can I do for you?"

"It's about Sandy Quayle."

"What about her?"

"Uh, she's... She's kind of gone rogue."

There was a pause.

"Aw, shit!"

"It's about this Giordano guy, and also —"

"She tell you about that?"

"Yes, but there's also —"

"Is she on her way to Willard?"

"Yes. But —"

"Okay. I'll deal with it. Thank you, Teri."

"No problem. But the other —"

"Where are you, by the way?"

"Aspire Building."

"All righty. Well, you stay there, y'hear? 'Til I get there."

"Okay. But —"

The line went dead.

Shit! She'd tried to tell Krall about Chen, but... No, wait. Maybe it was better to check with Nile first. Oh yeah, and before Krall got to the apartment...

Teri grabbed Sandy's security key and made for Merriweather's office. She cranked up his computer and plugged the key in. Sandy's menu appeared. But now there was only one option: *Prince for President.*

Fuck! What did that mean? Had Fairmeadow Data Security spotted her prior intrusion? Was Prince's whole Fund system down on account of its *architect* having scrammed? She pulled out the key and shut the computer down. So what about the *proof* now? So close and yet...

But she had to tell Nile about Chen. He'd never mentioned a *Chinese Spring.* He probably had no idea. Chen hadn't trusted him; the Robin Hood Party must have looked like kids' stuff from her point of view. And there she was, sitting out there in Jersey, alone, waiting for...

Could she call him now? No, he'd said that wasn't safe. It would have to be another meeting in the park. But what about Krall? Could she blow him off? No, not really; she needed to know where he stood.

She took out her personal phone and sent the message.

park now urgent pls wait 4 me xxx.

Then she activated Merriweather's video telescope. It still pointed at the rink. Despite the dark, there was enough lamplight for her to recognize Nile's shape and gait when he showed up.

And Krall or no Krall, if she saw that shape leave the rink, she was *outta here.*

CHAPTER 29

Kirk and Spock must have hauled themselves out of a meeting, Ricky thought, because they were wearing suits and ties. Well, okay, they'd loosened their ties and taken off their jackets, because the air-con in the old railway terminus had begun to struggle as the heat built outside, but, with both of them over six feet tall and Kirk on the portly side of plump, they offered a striking contrast with the elfin Jiao in her hotpants and hipster T-shirt.

Ricky had thought it might be tricky for him to convince the two Americans that this girl really did speak for the People's Liberation Army. But he needn't have worried. She took care of *that* all on her own.

And so here they all were, on *neutral territory*. How far-sighted Mr. Yu had been, Ricky mused, to conjure up the concept of a secret deal between the American and Chinese militaries. And how bloody amused he must now be feeling, sunning himself in Ricky's garden and taking snaps of Ricky's lemurs, given that the task of brokering the fucker had fallen to Ricky.

Such a subtle bloke, Mr. Yu, always a couple of strides ahead and downright sneaky with it. But then bereft, too. Of course he had calculated that no deal Ricky brokered could possibly be concluded without the name of his daughter at least entering the negotiations.

The problem was, Ricky was not your born negotiator. He was a take-it-or-leave-it guy, a loner, an anti-authoritarian, never a bluffer, and a poor conciliator. He didn't *stroke* people; he wound them up. He would have to juice his match skills.

And it wasn't going to be a two-dog fight, either. Ricky had his own fur in the game — albeit one in which two Wolfhounds and a miniature Pit-bull shaped up against a scrappy Terrier.

Ricky had little sense as to what manner of deal Kirk and Spock would accept, and, given the shifting winds and unpredictable seasons of the American military-political eco-system, not much idea of what they could deliver. But he was pretty confident he knew where Jiao was coming from. Because she'd been haranguing him for the last thirty minutes.

Didn't Ricky understand how important the Party was to stability in China? Did he have any idea at all of what *instability* in China would mean? Under what other dispensation did Ricky suppose China's peaceful rise to prosperity could have been managed? Had Ricky been to India or Russia? If he had, he would have seen for himself the results of *shock-therapy* and *laissez-faire* and so-called democracy in countries that had no political cadres and were the playthings of rapacious oligarchs. Had Ricky seen the state of Africa, with its kleptocrats, its tribalism and its *instability?*

China stood at a critical point in its history, Jiao said. It had the biggest economy in the world. But a gigantic transition now had to be made — from a tumultuous period of epic investment and high growth to a calmer new era of domestic consumption, moderate growth and capital account liberalization. And this had to be achieved against headwinds of American profligacy, European complacency, Japanese truculence and Russian mischief. If the Chinese economy were to implode in the process of this epochal change, then it would take the rest of the world down with it.

Only the Party stood any chance of managing this transformation. So just who did Ricky Ponton think he was to stand in its way?

Oh, did Ricky mention corruption? Really? *Corruption?* Yes, fine, Australia was the cleanest country in the G20, and ninth overall, but there were at least three cities in China with bigger populations than Australia's, and nobody — nobody in the world — was tougher in cracking down on corruption than the CCP. Hadn't Ricky heard about the former Party Secretary in Chongqing? Oh, he had. Well, that was only one example.

And if Ricky was up to any funny games with Mr. Yu, he would regret it. The budget thing was bad enough. But if, for example, Ricky had any other military secrets up his sweaty, irresponsible sleeve, then he'd do well to tell Jiao about them right now.

Not really. Just the naval base. We put that on hold.

Naval base? What naval base?

And that was where she'd really got going. Ricky hadn't seen it coming, because he'd assumed that Jiao must have known all about the naval base. But she didn't. Whoops. She'd made him tell all.

Right, then. So not only was Ricky ignorant of the *economic* peril that Jiao was fighting, he was clueless about the *military* threat, too. This was all too typical of the flabby, lazy, post-imperialist patterns of thought indulged in by western, liberal so-called intellectuals.

Didn't Ricky understand that, just as America and Britain had their neo-conservative warmongers, so China had its ultra-nationalist militarists? They were the bane of Jiao's life. Just like the neo-cons, they wanted a fight, or, more realistically, a *cold war-type* scenario, in which they got to play out their games. China's war party got high on historical grievance — against Britain, Japan and America — and it was only the fact that they weren't complete idiots that made them slightly less dangerous than their western counterparts. Jiao's job — or part of it — was to keep these would-be brawlers apart. And Ricky really wasn't helping, was he?

Oh right, Ricky had said, so all these peculiar naval crises that kept cropping up — it was the warmongers having a pop at each other?

Wrong again.

Hadn't Ricky observed how exquisitely-calibrated these incidents had been? Nobody had been hurt. Damage had been minimal. The subsequent kiss-and-make-up on the part of the military commanders involved had been carefully publicized. And the reaction of the American public and their politicians had been what? Had Ricky noticed? Had he been paying attention, or was he too busy pleasuring himself with the pointless exposure of petty crimes and misdemeanors?

Ouch!

And to what end did Ricky think Jiao had made him summon the two Americans he comically referred to as Kirk and Spock? Didn't Ricky get it now?

Uh, not quite.

How could Ricky be so stupid? Wasn't it obvious? The objective was to create a backlash against China on the part of the American public and their politicians. But only a *mild* backlash. Why? To create *just enough* anti-China feeling in the US to avert a Prince Presidency. But not so much as to empower the militarists.

Hang on moment, Ricky had said. Prince? That rich guy? Isn't he all about abolishing taxes on the one per cent and standing up to China?

Yes to the first, no to the second, according to Jiao. Prince and his plutocratic backers had formed a secret alliance with China's new class of *capitalist oligarchs*. What they intended was a form of merger. Their primary victim would be the Party. And Jiao believed she had already explained the consequences of such a calamity, hadn't she?

Oh! So then all this Sino-American corporate dirt...

Correct. Jiao and her American counterparts — not Kirk and Spock specifically, but others like them — had come to an understanding — an informal alliance, you could say. What they favored was the *status quo*: Independent sovereignty, political stability and friendly military competition — well, mostly.

Ricky remembered the question he'd asked himself in Hong Kong: Why was the Party afraid of its own capitalists? Now he'd been given the answer.

And so you used—

Yes, Ricky had been *used*. What poetic justice! Not only that, but Ricky had missed the main event: Had he heard about the New Pacific Partnership?

Er...

Well, why didn't he look it up in his own database when he had a spare moment? Even those dopes in the Robin Hood Party had got it figured out.

At that point Jiao had sat down. She crossed her legs, folded her arms and smiled faintly in Ricky's direction — it was a mixture of contempt and pity, Ricky thought. Why wasn't he angry? He had lost control. Had he ever really been in control at all? Now he was compromised. But he couldn't summon the rage he would once have felt. Who was to blame for this loss of potency? Was it La Cachette? Was it the lemurs?

Or was it Mr. Yu and his priceless daughter? Well, here was something to think about: Jiao hadn't mentioned the Chinese Spring. Why not?

Jiao had said one more thing before Kirk and Spock arrived. The naval base on Madagascar would be a huge mistake. China didn't want to police the world, and shouldn't try. What a foolish idea! Look at the mess the Americans had made of it.

"So may we ask what this meeting is about?" Spock said.

"And why the fuck is *this guy* here?" Kirk added, meaning Ricky.

CHAPTER 30

O n the short, chilly walk to Park Avenue, Sandy Quayle wondered whether she ought to buy a proper winter coat. Out of her thousand dollars, seven hundred and fifty-three remained. Plus seventy-two cents. She still found it difficult to envisage her life beyond the end of the election and Mr. Prince's elevation to the White House. There had been talk downtown about the *transition team*, and jobs in the new administration. But, while good things certainly awaited all those bright, confident young women at the Campaign HQ — Teri and Megan especially — Sandy failed to imagine any kind of job that might be offered to her. And no one had else had either, it seemed.

Should she fear that she was about to fall again? Surely not. She had grasped her chance, when it had been offered to her. She had *worked* to repay her luck, or grace — whatever it really was. There was no going back. But should she be worried about her health?

Well, in any case, a winter coat might be a wise investment. And perhaps if she were warmer, that stiffness in her leg would go away. But there was a problem. What she needed was a thrift store or an outlet mall. But in *this* neighborhood... Well, you were probably lucky if you could get a coat at all for seven hundred and fifty-three dollars.

She had intended to attempt a short-cut across the Park, but she saw a solitary young man in a hoody loitering by the rink and decided to go the long way instead.

Sandy hadn't understood much of what Chen Yu had said.

The poor girl was clearly distressed — all that nonsense about *technology* and *capitalism*. But you only had to look in her eyes to know that she was sincere, and that she was suffering. And who could possibly be against a Chinese Spring? It sounded like the most wonderful thing.

Sandy wasn't sure, but she thought that *something* had almost happened once in China. People had rebelled against tyranny. But the Communists, of course, were having none of that. And they had spilled the blood of the innocent. What would they do to Chen, if they got their hands on her?

Chen was so brave. And spiritual, too — even Amber had seen it. Chen hadn't mentioned God, but perhaps she felt that she didn't need to provoke the Communists any more that she already had.

And who had hired Fairmeadow to kidnap Chen? The Communists themselves? Or their spies in America? Sandy had already decided that she didn't think an awful lot of Fairmeadow. She was with Ray Krall on *that*. And Josh Merriweather would surely be furious when he found out. Wouldn't he?

Sandy understood that although Mr. Prince had made standing up to China a major plank of his platform, he had been very clear that there ought to be no animosity between the American and Chinese peoples. It was China's rulers who angered him, with their ideology, their cruelty and their refusal to grant their people freedom.

No doubt, in private, their godlessness irked him too; but he was wise enough to know that, as President, he would have to bite his tongue and conduct relations with these same heathens. And Mr. Prince had said that the people of America and China should, in the future, make common cause in the interests of global prosperity and stability. Though that did not mean, of course, that Mr. Prince required China's help in saving America.

When Mr. Prince heard of Chen's plight, he would act. How could he not? Sandy wished now that she'd brought Amber's phone with her, instead of leaving it with Teri. But then it was important that Teri copy Chen's video testament — this was a technical task beyond Sandy's competence. And Sandy did not doubt that she would be able to touch Mr. Prince's heart.

By the time she reached the Park Avenue block where Mr. Prince's building stood, Sandy was shivering. She hoped that Mr. Prince's doorman would remember her.

"Sandy!"

She recognized the voice; it was Barbara. She pulled up alongside Sandy in the Escalade.

"You look frozen, my dear! Where are you going?"

"Oh, I have to see Mr. Prince. There's something he needs to know."

"Well, I dare say that's true. But you can't see him now — he's holed up with Merriweather and the others. Good heavens, look at you! Get in the car and warm up."

And such was the authority in Barbara's oaky voice that Sandy found herself in the passenger seat before she'd quite made the decision to obey.

"We'll go to my place, we'll get you a nice drink, and we'll have a little chat — yes?"

"All right."

"And if there's anything that Willard needs to know, I'll make sure he hears it. Deal?"

"Okay."

Barbara's townhouse felt much more like a *home*, Sandy thought, than Mr. Prince's apartment. There were no Secret Service agents, no stuffy library, no staff quarters and no pesky servant girls.

"Well, I do actually live here, you know," Barbara said.

Barbara's living room — or *salon*, as she called it, humorously — was sparse but comfortable; modern, but also classy, Sandy thought. There was a single, small photograph of Barbara's husband. He'd passed away ten years ago, Sandy learned. Barbara didn't mention his name.

Barbara fetched a bottle of red wine — Sandy thought it was French, not Californian — and poured Sandy a large glass, even though Sandy had asked for tea.

"Well, now. What's on your mind?"

Sandy told her story. Barbara didn't touch her wine until Sandy had finished.

"Sandy, have you talked to anyone else about this?"

"No, just Amber."

"I don't think we need to worry too much about *her*."

"Oh, and Teri, of course. She's making a copy. Of the video."

"Teri?"

"Yes."

"She knows all about this?"

"Yes. She saw the video. I had to get her to —"

"She was at the apartment?"

"Yes."

"What was she doing there?"

"She came round to see if I was okay."

Barbara topped up her glass.

"Is that right, now?"

Sandy nodded.

"I've been hearing some things about that girl. Have you heard anything? Has she said anything to you about herself?"

Why was Barbara talking about Teri, when Chen needed help?

"Not really. Couldn't we just call Mr. Prince? From here?"

Barbara sighed.

"Sandy, trust me. It's not quite as easy as that."

"But Chen —"

"No, dear. I understand. I really do. You're such a sweetheart. I wish I had your sense of obligation. Leave it with me. I know what to do. I'll be talking to Willard later."

"Tonight?"

A pause. Then a sip.

"Yes, dear. Later tonight."

"He'll make sure that —"

"He'll do the right thing. As he nearly always does. Why are you rubbing your leg like that?"

Sandy hadn't realized that she was.

"Oh, it's just a little stiff."

"Are you feeling well? You should have warmed up by now, but you still look pale."

"I guess I'm a little off-color."

"Well, we don't want you coming down with anything. I can make you an appointment with my doctor, if you like."

"Oh, no, I don't think... I mean —"

"Well you just let me know, all right? So where is that girl right now?"

"Teri? I left her at the apartment."

"She's there on her own?"

"Yes."

"Okay. Has she been there before?"

"Once or twice."

"Not quite as thick as thieves, then, the two of you?"

"Not really."

Barbara took a long draw on her wine. Sandy took a sip of hers; it tasted musty and sulfurous.

"You don't have any daughters that age, do you?"

"No."

"I suppose we were lucky with Milly. She *could* have more ambition, that's obvious, but her generation expects everything to be... Even Merriweather seems to have *lucked* into whatever it is he actually does."

Sandy wanted to talk about Chen, but it felt as though Barbara had already closed the subject down. And Sandy was afraid of appearing presumptuous. Barbara was very protective of Mr. Prince; everyone seemed to accept that, though nobody spoke about it — any more than they mentioned Mrs. Prince. Barbara *would* tell Mr. Prince about Chen, wouldn't she? It was a matter of Christian compassion, plain and simple. And surely Mr. Prince would want to do everything he could to encourage and to hearten the Chinese Spring?

"Drink up, dear. It'll do you good. Things are going well, we're four points up now; I think we can enjoy ourselves a little."

Sandy wanted to protest that she could not feel at peace with herself so long as Chen remained a prisoner, but she could think of no polite or respectful way in which to pierce Barbara's lofty composure.

"Does that girl have a passport?"

"Teri? I don't know. Why?"

"Ray's decided to move up Willard's foreign policy tour. He wants to get it out of the way before another of these silly crises blows up. I'll have to lay down the law with Gloria. We'll get little Teresa out of town for a few days. You won't miss her, will you?"

"No, I guess not."

"It's just the usual — London, Poland, Israel. Oh, and Australia this time, for some reason. The voters don't give a damn, of course. But we have to keep the *opinion-formers* happy. They want to see *leadership*. I hope Ray knows what he's doing."

"Well, I think he *does*."

"We're paying him enough."

Barbara took another mouthful of wine.

"Yes, we'll get that girl where I can keep an eye on her. Now promise me, Sandy, that you *will* see a doctor."

"I promise."

"You've got one over at Aspire, haven't you? I think mine might charge less, but it's up to you..."

Barbara could be right about that, Sandy thought. It had cost nine hundred dollars to patch up Amber's cuts and bruises.

Then Barbara's phone rang.

"Ray?" A pause. "No, no, it's fine. She's here... No, I told you, it's fine... She's okay. Well, as a matter of fact, the poor thing looks a little... You're going where?" A long pause. "All right. Let me know. Bye."

Barbara finished her glass and refilled it.

"Where were we?"

"Perhaps I should go home now," Sandy said.

"But you haven't finished your... Are you sure you're feeling okay? Perhaps you ought to stay here tonight. What do you say?"

"Oh, I don't want to —"

"I'm sure we can make you comfortable. I have to go out, but Milly will be here."

"Well..."

"Good. That's decided then."

Sandy picked up her glass but didn't drink.

"You're going out?"

Barbara put down her wine and gave Sandy a long, lingering glance — a blurry mixture of triumph and resignation.

"My dear, since it's you... We're on our way. We're on our way, and I don't deny the thrill of it. But Willard... Well, someone has to — what's the phrase? Something about courage and screwing? Was it Shakespeare? Whatever. You know what I mean. From time to time... He needs a little *bucking up.* You know what they say — behind every strong... No, forget I said that."

Barbara drank again. Sandy wondered if this might not be the first bottle of the day.

"Sometimes, little things get to him. Are you like that? I'm not. Anyway, I don't know why he's so out-of-sorts about this guy at the Fund. I told him, don't believe your own hype. These computer people are two-a-penny. Find someone else and stop worrying."

Barbara must have meant Mr. Giordano, Sandy thought. But it didn't sound like she'd gotten the whole picture. Perhaps Mr. Prince didn't confide in Barbara as much as she thought. Should Sandy tell Barbara what she knew? Well, Ray obviously hadn't told her anything — how could he? And so how could Sandy? Besides, Barbara seemed to have forgotten about Chen already. Sandy wasn't sure that she would be able to forgive that.

"*It's not as easy as that*, he says. So I have to put him straight. *You* are the New American Century Fund, Willard. I know that, you know that, America knows that. Just keep on doing whatever you're doing. I mean you'd better! For God's sake, I have my entire net worth invested with you. Apart from the real estate, the artworks and whatever. So, anyway..."

Sandy stood.

"Would you excuse me? I need the bathroom."

"Sure. Downstairs on the left."

Sandy hobbled downstairs and hid herself in the bathroom. What was she to do? Stay in Barbara's house? No, she refused to do that. It wasn't just Chen, it was the way Barbara talked about Mr. Prince. In front of Sandy! And her attitude to Teri. But it was a long walk back to the Aspire building from Barbara's townhouse. What about a taxi? Sandy had enough money. But could she actually just *run out* on Barbara? What would Barbara tell Mr. Prince? Sandy could be dismissed from the campaign.

Would Ray help her? Perhaps, but she wasn't sure. Plus he wasn't here and Sandy had no phone. Unable to think of anything, she let herself out of the bathroom.

And ran straight into Barbara's daughter, Milly.

"Oh — hi, Sandy! Hey, you will not *believe* this. Those two guys followed me home. They're outside now. Where's mom? Upstairs?"

"Which two guys, Milly?"

"You know — Gunner and that creepy friend of his."

"They're journalists, aren't they?"

"Yeah, right. That's what they *call* themselves. Is mom upstairs?"

"Yes."

"Okay. Whatever you do, don't open the door to them."

Milly bounded up the townhouse's broad, curving staircase in search of her mother.

Sandy went to the front door and opened it.

"Well, if it isn't mystic Sandy, channeler of the popular mood and the spin-doctor's secret weapon! Wanna come out and have a chat, love? Course you do."

CHAPTER 31

Teri Wolfe hadn't waited. She'd seen Nile's shape appear on Josh Merriweather's video telescope, and she'd been *outta there*. Krall could wait. Maybe she couldn't trust him anyway. In fact, screw him.

"This is Amber Pike's friggin' phone? Are you serious?"

"Watch the video, Nile."

And he did.

Well, she thought, it was ever thus. Boy meets girl. Yadda, yadda, and so on. Boy discovers that girl is into something much bigger and much more important than he ever knew. He's not the big-shot, she is. His world is well and truly rocked. Turns out he's actually pretty small beer, and she's the real deal. Happened all the time.

"Where is she?"

"Jersey. Fairmeadow compound."

"Okay. Okay. What we have to do... We need to..."

"What? Swoop on Fairmeadow with your whistles and your toy drone? Those guys are armed, from what I hear. They're kind of mean. I can tell you *that* for free."

"Yeah, but..."

"Call the cops?"

"Like they'll listen to us."

"Good point."

"Plus who do you think has a hotline into Trenton?"

Trenton again. The fount of all evil.

"Do you want to know what I think?" Teri said.

Nile shrugged.

"Why not? Go ahead."

"Well first, you've got to get this video out. Get it out fast, and worldwide. And you've got to make sure it doesn't get edited or screwed around with. Forget the networks. Forget cable. Forget the Times and the Guardian. Get it to Big Data. You can't trust anyone else with this."

"Yeah. Yeah, you're right. Okay, what else?"

"Well, if you're feeling brave... Get your pals together and blockade the entrance to the compound. Sounds like there's only one way in and out. I guess you guys have some crappy old cars, don't you? Don't go on their property and it's a legitimate protest."

"As if that means anything these days."

"I'm just saying. One more thing. Take a good look at Amber's phone. See what else you can find on it."

"Oh, great! I mean, can you imagine the shit! Yee-ha!"

"Don't get over-excited."

"So what about this other woman — this Sandy? She's with the Prince campaign, right? We could —"

"Leave her out of it."

"Really?"

"Yeah, really. Completely. Understand?"

"Sure, okay."

"All right, listen. I've got some other stuff for you. About Prince."

"You got proof!"

"No, hang on. Calm down. I couldn't get in. They've cut off access, for some reason. I couldn't get you any customer statements."

"Oh."

"But there's this. Prince's computer guy. Giordano. He's gone. Disappeared."

"Coincidence?"

"To tell the truth, Miss Marple, I don't friggin' know. But before he went, he threatened Prince. It was, like, *send me the money or I squeal to the Feds*. Words to that effect."

"That's the proof!"

"No, it's not. And I only heard it from someone. Your guy wants to see the numbers, remember? Follow the money, you said."

"Yeah, okay. Shit. So what do we do?"

"Ah, well. You got me there. Let me think."

As she pondered, Teri tipped her head up in order to seek inspiration among the fleeting clouds of the night sky. They appeared to be rushing away to the east, as if voting with their fluffy feet in advance of Prince's seemingly inevitable victory. And she found herself staring up at the Aspire Building.

Uh-oh. Wait a minute. Had she left that stupid telescope on? Was Krall up there now, glaring down at her? Sheesh.

"What are you looking at?"

"Uh, Nile? How about we take a walk?"

"Why?"

"Why not? Exercise, stupid."

They began to walk. Teri steered towards Central Park South, veering abruptly towards Columbus Circle once they were out of any possible line of sight from the Aspire Building. They should have done this *spy shit* in summer, when there were still leaves on the trees, damn it!

Teri's campaign phone blipped. It was a message from Krall: *where are u? DO NOT TALK TO ANYONE!*

"What's that?"

"Nothing. Boyfriend."

"Boyfriend?"

And was that some kind of satirical sniff from Nile? Never mind.

"Customer statements," Teri said. "Doesn't your guy know someone who's in the Fund?"

"Says not. Pretty exclusive. How about you?"

"You are totally kidding. Oh, wait..."

They stopped.

"What?"

"Hm. You know what? I *do* know someone. Kind of."

"Who?"

"Remember that whole coffee shop thing?"

"Your friend. From college."

"Right, Milly. Her mom. Barbara van Dornen."

"Never heard of her."

"You wouldn't have. But she's close to Prince. *Very* close, if you know what I mean. And she's in the Fund."

"Huh. Think she *knows?*"

"Well... It's possible. But I would say not."

"Where does she live?"

"Townhouse, upper east side."

"There you go! Problem solved."

"Er, when you say problem solved —"

"You just go there, and you kind of rummage around until you find the statements."

"Rummage around?"

"Sure."

Teri folded her arms.

"Okay. Two things. First, this is a big house we're talking about. You can't just *rummage around*. Second, she's gonna catch me."

"You can do it. Think cat burglar."

"Listen, this is not some friggin' movie with Gregory Peck and Audrey Hepburn. I don't want to mess with this woman. She is seriously scary. Oh, and there's a third thing."

"What?"

"I think she already suspects me."

"What, about breaking into —"

"No, just in general. It's only a feeling."

"Look, Teri. This is just too good an opportunity. Those statements are practically sitting there on a silver platter waiting for you to grab them. Just get your friend to invite you round."

"Too much peril."

They began to walk again.

Not only was it too perilous, Teri thought, but it would mean betraying Milly yet again. What was the score? Sandy twice, Milly... Oh, forget it.

"Fine," Nile said. "I leave it with you. If you can come up with anything better, then..."

Teri let that last incitement hang in the frigid air. They progressed in silence to Columbus Circle.

"All right. I got stuff to do," Nile said. "Give me the phone."

She handed it over and he was gone.

So what now? Back to the cubby-hole? How long could she avoid Krall? And what pack of lies could she possibly conjure to cover up her assignation with Nile — assuming Krall hadn't seen it all from Merriweather's apartment. Oh, and that thing recorded video too, didn't it? Not good.

She crossed to Broadway and made her way south, aiming to give the Aspire Building a wide berth.

Had Krall intercepted Sandy before she'd gotten to Prince? Teri hoped so. It wasn't that Prince didn't deserve to have Chen shoved in his face; these plutocrats liked to pretend it wasn't brute force that kept them rich. It was Sandy. Imagine the disillusionment. She'd heard the whole of Chen's manifesto, and she'd seen in person what they'd done to her — and she still didn't get it. She still believed. In friggin' Fat Willy, of all people. One day there would be a meltdown. And it would be ugly.

It was hard not to dwell on these thoughts. And, distracted, Teri took a left without really thinking about where she was.

"Hey."

A voice behind her. She glanced over her shoulder. It was Krall. He wore a suit but was tieless. He stood by the open driver's door of his black BMW, which idled on the ramp that led down into the Aspire Building's parking garage.

"Come here."

She hesitated. Krall ordinarily wore the ghost of a smile on his face, even under stress. But not now.

"I said, come here."

He couldn't pull anything here, could he? In the middle of midtown, in a street full of taxis and busy restaurants? In front of the very people from whose sight he was employed to remove any and all social or economic ugliness, let alone violence. If he tried something, she would fight back.

"Get in the car."

Teri edged towards the black BMW.

"For Christ's sake, Teri. I ain't gonna do nothing to you. Just get in the car."

She got in and closed the door. Krall climbed carefully into the driver's seat, clicked his door shut and fastened his seatbelt.

"Put your belt on. I'll take you back to the apartment."

"Listen, I —"

"Hold it right there. Don't say anything."

She bit her lip.

"Now you listen to me, Teri. And you listen good. I don't know what you and your little friend are up to. You got me? I don't know, and I don't care to know. I just want to make two things clear to you, okay? One, whatever you're doing, you leave Sandy out of it, y'hear? And two..."

He twisted his mouth, as if he were chewing tobacco and was about to spit it out.

"Whatever crazy, fucked-up thing you're planning, it better not hit the fan before November 8."

He paused, and looked at her over the top of the glasses he wore for driving.

"Now, I'm serious about that, Teri. I'm real serious. Do we understand each other?"

Teri nodded.

Krall's phone blipped. He held his gaze on Teri for a long moment, then picked it up.

"Huh. Wonder what that's about. Well, shoot. Looks like you're comin' to London with us. Better buy an umbrella. And put your fuckin' seatbelt on."

CHAPTER 32

T he grand, arched windows in the old railway terminus had begun to steam up. Ricky thought it was bloody lucky they hadn't shattered, such had been the acrimony of the negotiations.

And it was just as well that Jiao's minders had turned away a minibus full of French tourists; the elderly station could barely contain the combustible presence of two present-day neo-colonial marauders, let alone the bemused descendants of its resource-hungry creators. What would the average rice-growing, locust-fearing Malagasy family in their west-facing mud house have made of it all?

Kirk and Spock had accused Jiao of hacking into American corporations, stealing their trade secrets, and then handing them over to Chinese competitors. Jiao had demonstrated her incredulity at the hypocrisy of this — the Americans were well known, thanks to Ricky, to be bugging the entire world for their own nefarious purposes, and a hundred years ago hadn't *they* stolen all *their* technology from the British? — by rolling her eyes and kicking over a chair.

Then Jiao had accused Kirk and Spock of the ultimate hypocrisy: They sent their ships, planes and submarines into China's backyard, the East and South China seas — but imagine the reaction were a Chinese sub to surface in the Gulf of Mexico!

Kirk and Spock responded by criticizing China's *stealth takeover* of Africa. Jiao pointed out that the Pentagon's gung-ho and irresponsible Africom operations were spilling over from one country to another, destabilizing the continent and provoking far more fundamentalist extremism than they had any hope of repressing.

Ricky had proposed that, as far as Africa went, perhaps they could all agree that, whatever the Americans or the Chinese were up to in Africa, the Europeans had behaved far worse. This point had been generally accepted and the temperature had cooled a bit.

Jiao had then attempted a take-down of American macro-economic policy, but Kirk and Spock clearly didn't get what she meant by *global imbalances* or the *sterilization of liquidity*, and the heat had gone out of that attack pretty quickly.

"Look," Ricky said. "I haven't got all day. I've got to get back to my lemurs. I thought the whole idea was to agree a deal. So crap or get off the pot, okay? I'm willing to help, up to a point, providing the price is right. So how about it?"

"What did he say?" Kirk said.

Spock raised an eyebrow.

"I believe he indicated a willingness to facilitate matters. But he suggests that he might name a price for his services."

"*Price?* Fucking little creep..."

Ricky saw Kirk coming, but couldn't get out of the way in time. He found himself on the floor with his neck wedged in the angle of Kirk's elbow and Kirk's knee in the small of his back. It took Spock plus two of Jiao's helpers to free him.

"However much of a creep he may be," Spock observed, once Ricky had recovered enough to crawl to a chair and park himself, for safety, between Jiao's two largest assistants, "Mr. Ponton has made a valid point. To dismiss his offer would be a mistake."

Jiao flicked her hair and rubbed her eyes.

"We must have a deal. Now. There is no other way."

"Fine," Kirk said. "Let's have a deal. What are we going to do about Prince?"

Jiao sighed.

"We hoped to use Mr. Ponton. But we can find no dirt, no scandal. Except for what is normal in the financial industry."

"Neither can we."

"Mr. Ponton?"

"Wish I could help. Sorry. There's nothing."

"No whistle-blowers? No dis... What is it?"

"I believe you refer to the phenomenon," Spock said, "of the *disgruntled employee.*"

"That is it. Mr. Ponton?"

"I've got nothing. Sorry. Get me something and I'll put it out. Otherwise, he's a boring rich guy. End of story."

"This man must not be President. We cannot give up. What about this other man Merriweather?"

"Nothing there, either," Ricky said. "Except for Weihan."

"American voters don't understand Weihan."

"Alas, no," Spock said. "At least, not yet."

There was a pause, during which Kirk scowled at Ricky and Jiao contemplated the station's grubby glass dome.

"Then we must concentrate on military affairs," Jiao said.

"Okay," Kirk said, "but let's throw *this guy* out. He's useless."

"No, Mr. Ponton is essential," Jiao said. "He has already contributed. Perhaps not so helpfully. You know this. He gave us your entire so-called Enhanced Air-Sea Battle scenario. In which you attack China from Australian territory."

Ricky saw Spock place a restraining hand on Kirk's arm.

"Unfortunately," Jiao said, "Mr. Ponton's source has since fallen into your hands. That is his problem. But it is also ours, because our hawks have become excited. And it is yours, too. Because Mr. Ponton is in possession of information that will cause *your* hawks to..."

Jiao consulted privately with one of her minders.

"Yes, to shit themselves. Mr. Ponton?"

Did Jiao have a plan, or was she making it up as she went? Ricky had to assume she was talking about the Madagascar base.

"Er, yeah. That's more or less right."

"And whatever we might do to Mr. Ponton, now or perhaps a little later, we cannot prevent his organization from releasing this information. Can we, Mr. Ponton?"

"Well, I guess not."

Was she promising them something?

"Tell Mr. Kirk what it is."

Ricky looked at Kirk. Then he turned to Jiao.

"No, you tell him."

Jiao described the Madagascar naval base and offered her opinion as to the impression it was likely to make on the delicate sensibilities of Washington neo-conservatives, were they to learn of it.

"That is indubitably the case," Spock said.

"Jesus Christ," Kirk said. "They'll go fucking ape-shit."

Ricky shifted in his chair and exchanged glances with his protectors. Everyone seemed to be waiting for him to respond.

"I won't release it," he said. "If you give me Kerri back."

Spock tilted his head, as if he found this proposal intriguing.

"No way," Kirk said. "She's in London. None of our business."

"Like you're not telling the Brits what to do."

"Back off from Australia," Jiao said, "and I will see that the base is not built. The plans will be destroyed."

Spock perked up.

"Can you do that?"

"Maybe. Can you?"

"It is possible."

"Then that is the first part of the deal."

Kirk seemed skeptical, Ricky thought. But Spock placed a reassuring hand on his partner's shoulder.

"Agreed. But we must not forget Mr. Ponton."

Kirk hadn't.

"Why don't we just take the bastard out back and —"

"If," Spock said, "Mr. Ponton were to offer himself up to the British authorities, then it is possible that pressure might be brought to bear that would result in the release of Ms. Law."

"There's no way in hell he's doing that," Kirk said. "Two-faced fucking coward."

"No hang on a moment," Ricky said. "Run that by me again..."

Spock walked to a far corner of the station atrium, close to the gift shop, and motioned for Ricky to join him.

"Are you truly willing," Spock said, "to exchange yourself for Ms. Law? You must surely understand what that would entail?"

Yes, he understood. Ricky was responsible for Kerri. To exchange himself for her would be just. But what happened afterwards would be... *Was* he willing?

215

He would swap his verdant sanctuary for bare, exemplary entombment; his tropical sun for a harsh, fluorescent night. Was there a greater good? Yes, there probably was; but Ricky Ponton had already served his purpose, and had turned out to be, as he'd always assumed, very disposable.

"There are things," Spock said, glancing at Kirk, "of which my colleague is not aware. We must satisfy him. But then we may move forward and make our own arrangements."

"Huh?"

"Destroy all data pertaining to the base. Go to London. Surrender yourself there. Ms. Law will be released. Do you have friends who can take care of her?"

"Maybe. But then..."

"A few of us are aware of a movement known as the Chinese Spring. Have you heard of it?"

"Yes."

"My colleague and Ms. Xin have not. I think we should keep it that way."

"I agree. So —"

"Don't you think that it would solve all our problems?"

"Not Jiao's."

"No."

"What about *Kirk* over there?"

On the far side of the atrium Kirk glared with cold hostility while Jiao buffed her fingernails.

"Don't worry about him. Can you help?"

"What if I do?"

"Then your reunion with Ms. Law will be a happy one."

"You can arrange that?"

"Probably."

"I can trust you?"

"What do you expect me to say? I don't like Prince. I don't like the Party. I don't think the military should be abused and I don't believe in war. I'm an old-fashioned democrat, I suppose."

London was the last place in the world that Ricky wanted to be — apart, probably, from Russia. But now he understood that he had to go.

"There's a young woman called Chen Yu. Do you know anything about her?"

Spock shook his head.

"Wait a moment."

He took out his phone and stepped out of earshot, into the gift shop. When he returned, he shook his head again.

"She's a student in New York. She's gone missing. That's all we know."

"I'll go to London," Ricky said. "But you need to find her."

CHAPTER 33

W hy had they brought her here? The din was oppressive, the lighting harsh, the atmosphere fetid with indulgence. The men were drunk, the women dressed like...

Sandy Quayle thought that if there were banquets in Hell, they must surely be like this.

It was the annual Boilerplate Dinner. She knew this because it said so on the *Schedule of Speakers* that lay on the white linen tablecloth in front of her, next to the menu and a wine list whose prices could not possibly be real. They were in the ballroom of a midtown hotel — Sandy did not know which one — and Flint Gunner and Nigel Weese had dragged her to a small table reserved in Gunner's name, apparently in pride of place. A third chair had been stolen from a lesser table.

"They have a do like this down in Washington," Weese said. "The President comes and tells jokes. Not that he or his party have got much to laugh about right now, obviously, ha-ha. But it's all a bit *starchy*, if you know what I mean. We're a bit more laid-back here. Unbuttoned, as it were. But not necessarily unplugged."

"But why —"

"You don't mind, do you, Sandy? We wouldn't miss it for the world, would we, Flint?"

"No way, Nige."

"You've got all evening to unburden yourself, Sandy. So just sit back and enjoy. Unbutton 'em if you want. Nobody here'll mind. And the bill's on us. Or Flint, rather."

This was a mistake. She should not have allowed them to hustle her into a taxi. Yes, she'd felt upset — betrayed — that Barbara had waved Chen's plight away as if it were a problem with the laundry that could be left for the housekeeper to deal with in the morning. But what could Sandy expect here — amid this grotesque carnival of cynicism and lewdness?

"I'm sorry," she said, pushing her chair back. "I don't think... I mean, I made a —"

"No, don't go," Weese said, grabbing her wrist. "We've only just got here. The entertainment hasn't started yet! And don't worry about Flint here. I know he looks like a gorilla with hemorrhoids, but he doesn't bite. Do you, Flint?"

Gunner leered.

"Well, not unless he's invited to, that is. Very polite, he is. Religious background and all that."

Sandy tugged but Weese did not release his grip. For a moment she thought of screaming, but she knew she didn't have the strength. She gave in. Her temples were beginning to pulse with the noise, the pain in her leg felt worse, and a weary nausea had begun to rise in her stomach.

"That's better. Relax. You're in for a treat. We've even got Bickle on later."

Who was *Bickle?*

A roar went up. Gunner made a noise like the air-horn on an eighteen-wheeler. A plump man in a tux, with slicked-back hair and a grin like sin, had hauled himself on to the stage. As he swaggered to the lectern, a fast-cut sequence of images played out behind him, on a video screen twenty feet high: Casinos; a bridge full of traffic; a giant pizza with flags in it; a vast construction site; cheerleaders at a football game... Sandy didn't know what to make of it.

"He's not on our team, but we don't care tonight, do we, Flint? All rivalries put aside. Very civilized."

The plump man began to tell a joke; it had something to do with a female school-teacher and a fire hydrant. Sandy put her hands to her ears.

Gunner was ordering food from a waiter — a tired-looking girl who reminded Sandy of Maria at the waffle house.

"We always have the surf-'n'-turf," Weese said. "Make that three, Flint."

"Sure thing, Nige."

"And a cocktail for the lady. One of those... You know the one."

"You sure, Nige?"

"Yes, go on. It's only one night a year, isn't it?"

The plump man delivered his punchline. Laughter rolled around the ballroom.

"So Sandy, love, what's up with that spiky little friend of yours?"

"What?"

"You know, tarty tearaway Teresa. What's she been up to?"

"Up to?"

"Yes. Come on, Sandy. You know — what's she been saying, where's she been going, who's she been palling around with?"

"I don't... I can't —"

"Tell you all about herself, did she? No? Can't say I'm surprised. What do you think, Flint?"

"Girl's an interpoler, Nige."

"He means interloper. He started early, Flint did. As you can probably tell."

The plump man wound up his bit, declaring, to scattered applause and drunken jeers, that, much as he admired Prince's entrepreneurial achievements and high ethical standards, if the new President actually prevented Weihan from devouring a single American corporation, then he, Mr. Haven't-Touched-a-Doughnut-in-Five-Years, would personally devour every last dog-burger in Shanghai.

"The way we see it," Weese said, "she used her best chum from college to wangle her way on to the campaign, then she proceeded to wrap her tentacles around you, in a manner of speaking. No, not tentacles, that's too fishy. What's the right metaphor, Flint?"

"The right what, Nige?"

"Silken threads. That's more like it. Ask you for any favors, did she?"

"No," Sandy said. "I don't know why you —"

"I mean, the idea that this girl *actually supports* Prince for President... Based on what we know about her..."

A tall glass materialized in front of Sandy. It contained a green liquid and was stuffed with fruit. Paper umbrellas had been jammed into a chunk of pineapple. There was a white substance all around the rim. Salt — or something else?

"Based on... What do you —"

"Oh look, it's what's-his-face. I like this chap. Very amusing. Wouldn't turn my back on him."

A second speaker ascended to the stage, to an accompaniment of cackling and ironic applause.

"What's his name, Flint?"

"Who cares. Joe Asshole. Fuckin' liberal."

Suppose she downed her filthy drink, Sandy thought — perhaps she would pass out. She would wake up in bed. Or in the hospital. Or on the street. The hospital would be best, wouldn't it? She felt weaker by the moment. The ragging, keening noise of the room filled her ears and made her feel as if she were drowning in vulgarity and derision.

Joe Asshole directed an obscene gesture at one corner of the ballroom and began to speak.

"Sandy?" Weese said. "Still with us? You haven't touched your drink. We were talking about young Teresa, our little Friend of the Poor. Though not in the *Mother Teresa* sense, obviously. Didn't let her use your computer, by any chance, did you?"

"No. No, I don't know what you mean."

A flash of impatience on Weese's grinning countenance. *I won't tell you anything*, Sandy thought. Oh — but what, then, to do about Chen? Because all that mattered was...

They talk about decline, Joe Asshole said. *They say America's in decline. It's irreversible, they tell us. Well, let me tell you something...*

"Nothing but trouble, computers, if you ask me. I prefer the old ways, myself. We used to manage. Kids, though, they know what they're doing, don't they? They're *computer-literate*, that's what they are. Are you computer-literate, Sandy? You still haven't touched your drink. They sent Flint on a course. Don't know why, he's got assistants for all that stuff. Haven't you, Flint?"

"Fuck are you talking about, Nige?"

So they built more bridges in the last five years than we did in the last hundred. That's great. But all their bridges go someplace. Only in America can you build a bridge to nowhere...

"I mean, take that young chap Merriweather. Everybody says he's a genius, but nobody seems to have a clue what he does. Got lots of ideas, apparently.

Innovative, radical, and what have you. I don't mean radical like our Teri. Did you know she was radical?"

"Radical? What do you —"

"I suppose some people might say *extremist*. Drink up. Would you say extremist, Flint?"

"Big time."

Sandy decided that the only escape available lay in the green concoction before her. She drank. The white power on the rim of the glass tasted both sweet and salty — and also bitter.

Okay, so a few of them fell down recently. It happens. But that's the beauty of the American system. You're allowed to fail. You build a bridge in China and it falls down, it's so long, pal...

"Did you know our Teri has a little friend?"

"Well, I... Yes, her boyfriend, and they —"

"Boyfriend? Think you're barking up the wrong parade there, love, but never mind. It's what we call a pattern of radicalization."

"Pattern?"

"A young man of color. Mention him at all, did she?"

Do you have kids in school? I do. Are your kids learning shit? No? Mine neither. I guess we're way down the league these days. But is that a problem? Is it? Okay, we can't do biology. We can do the controversy. We can't do physics or geology, but we can do the controversy. History? That's controversial. Math? Too hard. Okay, so we've got controversy and we've got sports. But like I say, where's the problem? If we need to know that other shit, we can ask the Chinese.

"No," Sandy said. "She didn't mention him."

"Pity."

Weese yanked a Champagne bottle from a silver cooler and refilled his glass. It overflowed on to the tablecloth.

"Flint? Top-up?"

"Sure. You're doin' fucking great, Nige. Just wanted you to know that."

"Oh, do shut up."

"*No problemo*, Nige. Kinda enjoying Joe Asshole. He's funny."

"I'm trying to make progress here, if you don't mind."

"Yeah. You go, girl."

Weese turned back to Sandy.

"Just ignore him. Where were we? Oh, right..."

So how about all these naval crises, huh? What's that all about? We can look down from space and read the tattoo on our sexy neighbor's ass, but we can't see a fuckin' Chinese frigate fifty yards away?

Sandy took another slug of her drink. It was beginning to work, she thought. The half-glass of wine she'd had at Barbara's townhouse probably helped. Sharp edges were beginning to blur. Weese's nasal voice had started to merge into the bubbling clamor of the ballroom.

"How's the drink? Nice, isn't it? Should probably just have the one. So how's Mrs. van Dornen these days?"

"Barbara?"

"Oh, so it's first-names, is it? You *are* privileged. Teri and *Barbara* — one foot at each end of the social ladder, so to speak. Having a little soirée, were you? Discussing anything important?"

So is anybody here in the market right now? Okay, quite a few of you. What about you, sir? You look like a member of the point-zero-one per cent. What's that? You're in the New American Century Fund? Jesus, what are you doing at a crappy shindig like this? Only kidding, only kidding. I know this guy — he's down to his last ten million like the rest of us.

Sandy must have given something away in her expression or her body-language — she felt she was losing control now — because Weese leaned across the table and brought his face close to hers. She could smell his breath.

"So there *was* something important! Anything to do with Mr. Giordano?"

New American Century Fund, huh? That's gotta be the place to be, right? Can't get safer than that. Anybody worried about these rumors? You know, like, a couple o' banks on the edge? Midnight sessions at the Fed? Yeah? Okay, some people over here. Listen folks, don't worry. I got it on reliable authority: We have another crash, Willard Prince is going bail us all out, personally. He happens to know a nice little country he can mortgage to the Chinese.

Sandy shook her head. But this made her dizzy, so she stopped.

"No."

So is anybody here sad about the middle class? Anyone? Does anyone here remember the middle class? No?

"Okay. What about Mrs. Prince, Sandy? People are very worried about Mrs. Prince. Did Mrs. van Dornen say anything about Mrs. Prince?"

Sandy took another gulp of her drink. The ballroom had begun to spin. But, if she concentrated hard enough, she could slow it down.

"Sandy?"

Well, they warned me you were a tough crowd. I've been first on the bill at some of our finest educational establishments — Angola, San Quentin, Rikers, you name it. I felt more love there, I have to tell you. But let's move on. Let me ask you this: What's the difference between the American Dream and the Chinese Dream? Any suggestions?

"Sandy?"

"What?"

"It's about Mrs. Prince, love. We're all wondering how she's doing."

"How she's doing?"

"That's right. Does she have a little problem, perhaps? What do you think, Sandy?"

"Problem? Barbara?"

"No, Sandy. Mrs. Prince?"

"She's seeing him tonight. Said she was going to tell him, but I don't know..."

"What? Who's seeing who, Sandy?"

"Oh, I really can't..."

Okay, okay, that's all very inventive, not to say obscene. You want to know what the answer is? Fine. Here it is. The American Dream — and don't tell me you don't know this shit — is that, whoever you are and wherever you come from, you have a fair shot at a good life. You put in the work and nobody can stop you realizing your potential. You're not a slave. Nobody keeps you down. You and your family reap the full and just reward for your effort. And your children will do better still. Am I right?

"Sandy?"

The Chinese Dream, on the other hand, is not a dream at all. It's a fucking nightmare. And if you vote for Prince, you're walking right into it. Good luck with that. Okay, I gotta go. Thanks for listening. You've been a lousy audience and I hope you get what's coming to you. Thanks and goodnight!

A commotion of jeers and cackling. Gunner brought his fist down on the table, upsetting Weese's Champagne.

"Guy's a dick."

"Flint! Look what you've done now!"

"Order another one."

"Bloody hell, Flint!"

Sandy gave up her struggle and allowed the room to rotate freely. The nausea in her stomach seemed to have risen to her throat. But the pain in her leg had gone away. She closed her eyes.

"Sandy! Wake up! Your dinner's here, love."

In front of her, so wide that it teetered over the edge of the table, was a silver platter piled high with food: Lobster, crab, shrimp, steak, ribs, pulled pork, onion rings, fries, mayonnaise...

Sandy twisted her head to the left and threw up over the ballroom carpet. An amplified acoustic guitar started up.

"She just barfed, Nige."

"Oh, for fuck's sake. Get a waiter over here, Flint. Sandy, are you all right, love? Have some water."

A female voice chimed in with the guitar. A wistful country song with a harsh edge.

"Just clear that up for us, will you? No, she's all right. No, leave the food for now."

Somehow there was cool water in Sandy's mouth. She swallowed. The song seemed to go on and on. The singer's lover had abandoned her and taken all her money, leaving her destitute. But she was going to make a new start, all on her own, in the big city.

The song finished.

"Very pretty, I thought," Weese said.

"Reagan Pruett. She's hot."

"Yes, Flint. She is. Changed the lyrics, though, didn't she? Did you hear that? Very clever."

"Huh?"

"She said she was *packin' up her small-town life* and heading for *Hong Kong Town*. Not *New York Town*. As in the original. That's irony, that is."

"Whatever. She gonna eat that?"

"I don't think so. Help yourself."

Sandy looked up. Her bleary vision cleared momentarily, and she saw a tall, blockish man with yellow, wispy hair and a rubbery face stump up on to the stage.

222

"Here he is," Weese said, "Barry Bickle, the famous real estate mogul. Or should I say *infamous*, Flint?"

"Hey, the guy made some mistakes. But, you know what? It was just with the facts, okay? You can't argue with his... With his..."

"His argument?"

"Yeah. And fuck you too, Nige."

"Eat your bloody lobster."

"What about her, Nige? You finished with her? She looks out of it."

"Not quite."

Sandy watched the blockish man. There was something ungainly about him; perhaps he was much older than he was trying to look. And there seemed to be more energy in him than his wonky frame could properly contain. He flexed his jaw and began to speak.

I have come here tonight to say that I am proud to support Willard Prince for President. Did you hear what I just said? Barry Bickle endorses Willard Prince for President!

Cheers and catcalls; applause, both ironic and hysterical.

"Sandy? All right now? We were talking about Mrs. van Dornen. Or possibly Mrs. Prince. Someone's seeing someone tonight? Remember?"

Sandy watched Bickle. He couldn't keep still, but there seemed to be no point to his restlessness beyond the assertion of his physical presence.

"Is someone seeing Mr. Prince tonight, Sandy?"

This is big. This is a big announcement. You're gonna be reading about this tomorrow. The Bickle Organization is throwing everything we got behind Prince.

"Barbara."

"Flint! Did you hear that?"

"Maybe you were right, Nige. Wife's in the tank, so he's nailing —"

"Shh!"

The Committee to Save America, they asked me to help. This is a while back. I was the first person they came to. I said, I need to take a look, okay? Because if there's anybody who knows how to save America, it's me. It's no secret. I got speeches. By the dozen. I got articles. I go on Freedom News I don't know how many times. Sometimes they don't even pay me, okay? I've been doing this for years, so there's nothing I don't know.

It was true, kind of, Sandy thought. She remembered Bickle now — that boiling face, that wagging finger. Johnny-boy used to watch him on Freedom News. Johnny-boy was a fan. He was going to be the next Bickle. Well, the Bickle of Stimsonville, at least. Anyone could do it. If they really wanted it. Just look at Bickle.

And let me tell you. I looked. I took a good, hard look. And you know what? I was impressed. And I am never impressed, that's a fact.

"Nige, she's not looking good."

"Sandy? Have some more water. Here."

So I said, Willard, here's my decision. I've had my money in your fund for I don't even know how long. I'm very satisfied. I'm paying for consistency. I'm getting consistency. I like that. I feel I can trust you.

Sandy drank her water. It sank pleasantly down into the woozy vagueness of her body. Why had Johnny-boy ever admired this man? He was a — what was the word? Charlatan?

"Er, Nige?"

"Not now, Flint. Look at me, Sandy."

Willard, I said, here is my decision. You believe that America is the future. Nobody believes that more than me, but you come close. The old parties are all about big government. I talk to people all the time and they tell me they hate that. Look at China, they say. America's gotta compete. We gotta get government out of the way.

"Nige. He's here."

"Who?"

"Krall."

"Oh, bollocks."

So this is my decision, Willard. I want you to be the next President of the United States.

Cheers, hollering, laughter, a mad scream from somewhere far away.

"He's comin' over, Nige."

"Shit."

How did it get so warm in here? Sandy touched her face. It was hot. But her hands were cold. How could that be? She rubbed her eyes and tried to focus. Was that Ray coming towards her?

And there he is. This is the guy we hired. As you know, I am a busy man. But I think we got the next best thing. Ladies and gentleman, there he is, our Campaign Director, Mr. Ray Krall. I want you to give it up right now.

Applause, whoops, high-fives.

That smell again. Weese was in her face.

"Listen, Sandy. I'm sorry you're not feeling well. Perhaps it was a bit much, bringing you here and all. In hindsight, as it were. But I did get the distinct impression — correct me if I'm wrong — that there was something important you wanted to tell us. Was there, Sandy? Was there something important?"

Something important. Chen.

"You see, Barbara wouldn't... All she wants is freedom. But they..."

"Who wants freedom, Sandy?"

"Fairmeadow locked her up and..."

"Fairmeadow? They locked —"

"Chen Yu."

"Who's that, Sandy?"

"Chinese girl. All locked up."

"Why did they lock her up, Sandy?"

"The Communists."

"She's not making any sense, Nige. Watch out!"

The ballroom began to spin again. But now it went up and down as well. The floor dropped away beneath Sandy's feet.

She felt a pressure around her waist. Then the table exploded and people began to shout and laugh. A clatter and a smash. A soft thud. The crack of splintering wood. A deranged merriment. Laughing and cursing.

Then it all receded. She closed her eyes.

Cold. Then warm again. A soft thump, then a click. A hand on her shoulder, shaking her.

"Sandy?"

Krall's voice.

"We're gonna get you checked out. Been on some bad dates myself, but... Aw, Jesus, I sure hope you ain't said nothing in front of those bastards."

CHAPTER 34

The apartment was quiet, but for the ever-present background hum that signified the normal operation of the shields protecting it against radiation from the low-income belt.

All staff, including even Gloria, had been given the night off, it appeared. There remained only one Secret Service guy in the vestibule, and another in the kitchen, drinking coffee and struggling to find something to read in Prince's copy of *International Wealth*.

These were the two who followed Prince everywhere. So Fat Willy had to be on the premises, presumably in his private suite. Teri was told to go directly to her cubby-hole. The pointed look that accompanied this instruction suggested to her that Prince was entertaining a very special visitor. Well, either that or these guys were winding her up to relieve the boredom. Whatever. She had some thinking to do.

For example: What the hell was going on with Krall?

Krall knew about Teri and Nile. But did he know who Nile was? That wasn't clear. Krall thought that Teri and Nile were planning *some shit*. But he didn't want to know anything about it, and he didn't care when it *hit the fan*, so long as it wasn't before election day. Did he have any concept of what Teri and Nile believed Prince was doing? It didn't seem that way. All Krall seemed to care about was winning the election — and never mind what might happen immediately afterwards.

And Sandy. He cared about Sandy. That, Teri thought, was just as well. Somebody needed to. But Sandy — and Amber Pike! — were responsible for the Chen Yu video. That put them on the wrong side of Fairmeadow — and whoever Fairmeadow happened to be servicing right now. Amber could look after herself. But Sandy? Did Krall know about the video? Who else had Sandy talked to?

Teri's personal phone blipped. A message from Nile: *blockade is on r u coming?*

Well wasn't that just typical? How did he expect her to get from the upper east side to the wilds of Jersey at this time of night? Subway downtown, PATH to Jersey City, then a bus? Yeah, right. But she absolutely had to go, didn't she? Sure, she could hunker down here in the cubby-hole and read about it in the morning. But how pathetic was that? Did she regret getting fired from Bean Village for checking out the Robin Hooders in Battery Park? Hell, no. And what, to be blunt, was the point of Teri Wolfe at all — otherwise nothing but a slacker radical and a generational statistic — if not to stand athwart History, video camera at the ready, shouting *wow!*

There had to be a way. Ah! She picked up her phone.

"Milly?"

"Hey, Teri."

"Where are you?"

"At home."

"Mom there?"

"No, she went out."

"Where?"

"Didn't say."

"She take the car?"

"Uh, let me see... No, it's out there. Why?"

"Wanna have some fun?"

"What kind of fun?"

"Just kind of a scene going on."

"What, like a party?"

"Well, kind of... More of a scene, really."

"Who's gonna be there?"

"Oh, just some crazy friends of mine."

"From the coffee shop?"

"No! It's a whole different set. Pretty upscale. You'll like them. They're really cool."

A pause.

"I guess you want me to drive."

"That would be great."

"Mom doesn't like me driving her car. It's kind of big, you know? Last time I put this little tiny scratch on it, and she's like, oh look what you did, that's fifteen hundred dollars..."

"You'll be fine."

"So where is this thing?"

"Jersey."

"Who goes to Jersey?"

"Brooklyn's over, Milly."

"It is?"

"So are we going?"

"Well... Okay."

"Pick me up outside the apartment?"

"Sure."

Okay, so once again Teri had not been entirely straight with Milly. But what else was Teri supposed to do? Besides, Milly would, most probably, be in for a night to remember. Just not the kind she was expecting.

Teri sent Nile a reply — *c u there* — then grabbed her coat and made for the vestibule.

"Where are you going, Ms. Wolfe?"

"Party. Over in Jersey. Could be a riot."

"You have yourself a ball."

She waited outside for six minutes before the Escalade lumbered up to the curb, Milly's head just visible above the dashboard.

"Are you sure about this, Teri? I mean, Jersey? Really?"

"Oh, yeah. This is like one of those *flash* things, you know? So, like, anything might happen?"

"You know I'm not into drugs, right?"

"It's nothing like that. More like performance art."

"Okay, I could be into that. Mom only likes art you can collect. What are you doing?"

"Programming your satnav."

Teri scrolled the map, zoomed and tapped three times.

"We're going to a *prison?*"

"Uh, *no*, Milly. It's like next door. Off we go. What time's your mom home?"

"She said late."

"Cool. Want the voice on?"

"Uh-huh."

Tap.

Right turn in two hundred yards.

Milly edged the Escalade out into the traffic. Horns blared.

"Oh, I meant to tell you?"

"What?"

"About Sandy? Something weird happened."

"Like what?"

"Well, she was at the house and —"

"*Your* house?"

"Yeah. And —"

"Why?"

"How should I know? Anyway, those two guys followed me home. You know, Gunner and..."

"Weese."

"Whoever. But then Sandy, she goes off with them. And then Mom freaks out. And I'm like, I *told* her not to open the door! And then she's on the phone to Ray, and it's like it's this *big thing* and it's all my fault..."

Oh God, Teri thought. *That* wasn't going to end well. You could only hope that Krall found her in time. Surely Sandy wouldn't tell those two slime-balls about Chen? Would she?

"Milly," she said. "Don't let it get to you. They're all stressed out about the election. It'll all be over soon. It really will."

*

A s they approached the location of the Fairmeadow compound, a blank space on the map adjacent to the state prison, a traffic-jam icon popped up on the satnav.

Warning! Queuing traffic ahead!

Milly slowed the car.

"Huh! Wonder what that's about."

"Yeah, I dunno. Accident maybe?"

Oh, what a sly bitch she was! She would have to be extra nice to Milly in future to make up for this.

Ahead, the highway was blocked in both directions. There had to be dozens, perhaps hundreds, of cars. Teri had expected VW Beetles, crusty Mustangs, hand-painted Buicks, and maybe a pink Caddy or a converted ambulance. Which just went to show how you really had to keep your stupid political fantasies under control. What she saw were Hondas, Volvos, Jaguars and Land Rovers. Directly ahead of them was a red Prius with a bumper sticker that read *Frack Off! No to Shale!* Like Milly, the Robin Hooders had borrowed their parents' cars.

"You know what," Teri said. "You wait here, I'll go down and see what's happening."

"Can't we just turn around?"

"There's a concrete barrier along the median. Look."

"Oh."

"I'll be right back."

That was likely to be, at best, a gross exaggeration, wasn't it? But never mind. Teri edged her way along the highway, hugging herself against the cold. As she progressed, it became ever clearer that this was a Robin Hood crowd: Banners, chants, those ubiquitous whistles. Rhythmic honking of car horns. People standing on top of their vehicles drinking coffee from Bean Village cups. No sign of the toy drone; perhaps it lacked the night-vision equipment required for nocturnal missions.

At the entrance to the Fairmeadow compound, which, Teri was pleased to note, had been neatly sealed off with crime-scene tape, she found a scrum of raucous protestors, at the heart of which was Nile. By his side was a tall Indian girl in skinny jeans and a black leather jacket.

"Hey, Teri! Thanks for coming! This is Meera."

"Hi Meera."

"She's our tame banker."

Okay, that was unexpected. Wow.

"I thought you said you had a *guy.*"

"No. Don't think I said that."

"Okay, so what's happening?"

"Not much, yet. But if you look up there..."

A helicopter, high up, circling, its searchlight picking out the length of the jam along the highway.

"Is that Fairmeadow?"

"Yeah."

"Is Chen still here?"

"We don't know."

Teri glanced at the helicopter.

"What's to stop them taking her out in one of those?"

"This area's all trees. And there are power lines. Maybe they could do it, but it would be dangerous. Especially at night. This is about publicity. We put out a news alert, but nobody's shown up yet."

Teri saw that some of the largest banners bore the image of Chen's face, taken from the video. These Robin Hooders worked fast.

"Hey, you know what?" Nile said.

"What?"

"Remember you told me to check out Amber's phone? Guess what we found?"

"NRA membership?"

"No. The itinerary. Prince's secret bus tour. Guess Amber must be speaking at some of the stops."

"Okey doke. That's one thing off my to-do list."

"Meera's got some ideas. She's in charge of the money."

"The money? You're really going to blow Prince's wad?"

"Once Teri gets the proof. Right, Meera?"

"Once we have the proof," Meera said. "We're going to spread the wealth around."

"Cool."

"So how would you like to help me with that, Teri?"

There *was* something appealing about the idea of redistributing Prince's stash. But was it a practical proposition?

"He must know by now that someone's hijacked his accounts, right?"

"He must. But have you noticed something?"

"No. What?"

"Nothing. Nothing's happened, as far as we can tell. He can't call the cops, obviously. And he can't complain to his banks, because these are dodgy, arms-length accounts to begin with. They'll tell him it's his problem. We've moved some of the money, anyway."

"How much?"

"About six billion. It's just a fraction of what's there. And a tiny fraction of what's *supposed* to be there."

"*Six billion?*"

"Yeah. Plus, according to you, he's lost this guy Giordano, who was running the whole thing for him. What's he going to do? Who's he going to tell? His brothers might be in on it. He might tell them. But he must be totally freaking out. He's a few steps away from the Oval Office, and there's *this* hanging over him. It's got to be bad for the nerves."

"Okay," Teri said. "Two questions. One, can we really get away with this? And when do we pull the plug?"

"Get away with it?" Nile said. "Maybe. Maybe not. But I think the question we should ask is, what would Robin Hood do? And as for pulling the plug, we figured maybe a few days before election day, assuming you get —"

"The proof. Okay. But let's say we do that. What happens? Prince goes *splat*. One of the other guys wins. What changes?"

See, Teri thought, that right there was the problem with your Robin Hooders. All good intentions, no depth of strategy. Nile and Meera looked at each other.

There was a considerable amount of foot-shuffling and lip-biting. Plus pensiveness, and that kind of thing.

"Let me propose an alternative," Teri said.

Some chastened nodding.

"Wait until a while *after* he wins. Let things settle down a bit. It's gonna be a big change — a third party candidate, Mr. Committee to Save America, and all that. Let the political system begin to reconfigure itself. Let the guys who are backing him think they've *won*. Let the media suck up to him. Let the people who voted for him think they're the people they've been waiting for, or however you want to put it."

"And then?"

"Let Prince think he's gotten away with it. Then blow him up. Maybe on Inauguration Day. So then people go nuts. It's like headless chicken time. Nobody knows what to do. We break the system."

Nile and Meera looked at each other again.

"I think I like it," Nile said. "Meera?"

"Me too."

"You're gonna use Big Data?"

"That's what we figured," Nile said. "But..."

"Did you upload Chen's video?"

"No. We tried. But uploads aren't working right now. They say on the web site they're looking into it."

"Are they under attack?"

"If they were, they wouldn't necessarily say so."

Big Data had been attacked before. But each big revelation brought a new, more ferocious assault. Since no one else could be relied on to disseminate Chen's video across China, its survival was essential.

Above them, there were now two helicopters. They held themselves in a static formation above the entrance to the Fairmeadow compound, their searchlights directed at the knot of protestors on the edge of the highway. Teri could feel the downdraft from their blades on the back of her neck. Then her phone rang.

"Milly?"

"So what's happening down there?"

"Well, there's a demonstration, that's what."

"What kind of demonstration?"

"Uh, actually it's Robin Hood."

"Oh my God! Teri!"

"It's all right, I'm okay."

"Teri, get back here!"

"Actually, I thought I might —"

"You can't be with those people!"

"No. But the thing is —"

"Teri, the police are gonna come. You'll get in trouble!"

"All right, all right. I'm coming. Just stay in the car, okay?"

"I'm locking the doors. *Please*, Teri!"

Teri ended the call. Something was happening inside the compound. Way back in the forest, lights were blinking. It looked like a column of vehicles moving

232

down towards the entrance. Nile had joined a human chain that spanned the entire width of the ramp that led down to the highway. Meera hung back, taking pictures with a video camera. The helicopters had descended. Their thumping noise now made shouting futile, and Teri had to screen her eyes from flying dirt and grit.

She ran to the side of ramp, where overhanging pine trees offered some shelter. Lights flashed inside the compound. The electric gates slid open. Two heavy, armored trucks accelerated towards the ramp. The human chain broke apart and its members scattered. Teri ducked back into the trees along the highway's edge. The armored trucks tore down the ramp towards the parked cars on the roadway.

Banners flung down on the road; people jumping, falling, running.

The trucks began to shunt the cars aside or crush them against the concrete barrier on the median. One of the helicopters began to descend.

The demonstration was over. Most people were running. But Teri could see Nile and Meera on the far side of the ramp. Meera tugged at Nile's arm, but he resisted.

A black SUV swept out of the compound and skidded to a halt on the ramp. The armored trucks had cleared a thirty-yard section of the road. Down came the helicopter.

The rear door on the SUV slid open. Two men in black fatigues jumped out. They held Chen between them, her feet off the ground. Teri crouched down. She could still see Nile on the far side of the ramp, but Meera was gone.

The helicopter touched down. Its door swung open. The two men ducked and ran towards it. Chen's feet dragged along the ground.

And then Nile. He was in the headlights of the SUV, he was behind her, he had his arms around her waist. One of the men pushed him away. He came back. A kick to the ground. Back again, his hand on Chen's collar. Shoved away again. And then a flash to Teri's left and Nile sitting on the road.

The helicopter rising. Nile sitting on the road, still. And then the helicopter fading up into the night and Teri's ears ringing on until all she can hear is the idling of the trucks — and Meera's voice behind her.

"Take this."

Amber's phone in Teri's hand.

"Run."

One last glance. Nile sitting in the middle of the road, amid the debris of the wrecked cars. Nile collapsing gently on to his side, as if blown over by the breeze. Nile with his right cheek on the road. Then the two men in black, and one of them crouching down. A couple of words into a radio, but no sense of urgency.

Meera had gone.

Teri ran.

*

She got there just in time. Milly was in a panic. The police had started to clear the highway; everybody had to turn around and drive back on the wrong side. Milly shunted the Escalade to and fro; there was a low, metallic shriek as she scraped the barrier.

"Oh, shit. Oh shit."

They drove a hundred yards before they were stopped at a makeshift checkpoint. Milly buzzed her window down. The beam of a flashlight inside the car. Then they were waved on. They didn't look like Robin Hooders. And they were in Barbara's Escalade.

"Teri? What happened back there?"

What happened? What could she tell Milly about that? What could she tell Milly about anything?

"Teri?"

How could the Robin Hooders be so stupid and yet so right?

What about that? Or she could tell Milly that the scrape on her mom's car wasn't really the worst thing that...

"Teri!"

"Just drive, Milly."

"Are you okay?"

"Drive back to your house."

"I knew this was a mistake. Mom's gonna —"

"Yes. It was."

"She's gonna make me pay for it."

Teri closed her eyes and didn't open them again until they were parked outside the townhouse. She tried to think, to reason — but she couldn't. Her mind would admit nothing but the image of Nile sitting in the middle of the road, chin lifted slightly as if in surprise at something, one shoulder dropping before the rest of him did, taken aback, one last time, by the unexpected.

She got out of the car and, while Milly wailed over the ding in her mom's car, she sent one final message: *park now, stupid xxx.*

Then they went inside. Milly said she was going to bed. But Teri could stay if she wanted.

Barbara hadn't returned. So Teri went through the house until she found the room that Barbara used as an office. Then she searched Barbara's desk until she found the key to her filing cabinet. She rifled through Barbara's files until she found the one that contained her statements from the New American Century Fund. She laid these out on Barbara's desk and photographed them with her phone — all twenty-two of them.

Then she put everything back where'd she found it and left the house.

When she got back to the apartment it was past two in the morning. The same Secret Service guy was in the vestibule.

"Good party?"

"Not really."

"That's a shame. Don't forget, you're on the plane with us tomorrow."

"Plane?"

"London. You've got three hours. Better get some sleep."

"Sleep?"

"You look like you need it."

"Yeah."

Her phone blipped. She froze.

"I think you got a message."

She lifted her phone and looked: *it's you + me now. meera.*

CHAPTER 35

Ricky Ponton was pleasantly surprised to find that Jay Percival, the former American spy who had so successfully and profitably outsourced himself to the southern African espionage market, had not, for once, been exaggerating, obfuscating or downright lying when he had claimed to be a leading service-provider to Walter Gabo, the ANC elder statesman and dedicated fan of South African sovereignty.

Had this not been the case, Ricky would not now have been in possession of a South African diplomatic passport in which he masqueraded as one Jan du Toit. Jay had chosen to pass himself off as Marius Goosen. Walter had said that they wouldn't last ten minutes in Johannesburg, but, as far as accents went, the Brits couldn't tell a South African from an Australian.

And that was how Ricky Ponton, in an historic switcheroo, came to be standing *inside* the South African embassy in Trafalgar Square, staring *out*.

"They actually pissed in your tent?" Walter said.

"They did."

"Then, on behalf of the Republic, I thank your for your sacrifice."

"Mate, you're welcome."

Walter approved of Ricky's decision to support the Chinese Spring via Big Data Underground. From a strictly African point of view, he said, Chinese democracy would, most likely, only enhance Africa's complex and evolving relationship with China. And as for the Chinese people themselves, the favor Ricky was doing them made his pee-soaked night in the Square look like small beer.

Jay's opinion was that Ricky's choice could be best characterized as *brave*. And, though Ricky apparently had, to his great credit, nixed the Madagascar naval base, the deal he had done with the guy who called himself *Spock* — and Jay had a shrewd idea as to who that might actually be — could only be characterized as *nuts*. If, however, Ricky insisted on going through with it, Jay would help. Who said there was no gratitude in geopolitics?

But, getting back to the *brave* thing, Jay said, even if Ricky had a billion Chinese citizens on his side, and right-thinking people all around the world, his enemies were formidable. Obviously, democracy in China was not compatible with Party rule. But neither was it compatible with what everyone expected to happen on November 8.

Now, Jay would have been skeptical, to say the least, about the idea that Prince's secretly reworked New Pacific Partnership was intended to impose a kind of Sino-American economic, political and legal union, under corporate control, were it not that Kirk and Spock — assuming they were who Jay thought they were — clearly believed it. And Xin Jiao too, for that matter. So even if Ricky wasn't scared of Jiao — and he probably should be — then he might want to consider what resources would be directed against him once Prince became President.

In short, Jay said, it wouldn't just be Jiao and the Party who would try to kill the Chinese Spring. Prince's gang would, too. And, with Merriweather's help, they would take down Big Data, if they could.

"So how resilient do you think you are?"

"We've been holding up against Jiao's people. I don't know that Merriweather would be any worse."

"What if someone gave him access to all that cyber-warfare shit that the military has?"

"Yeah. Well, that would be different."

In fact, Ricky thought, it could be fatal. How fast could the Chinese Spring mobilize? They wouldn't have much time, and they couldn't spend it all messaging each other on Big Data. If only there were some spur to action — an inspiration, a rallying point, an emblematic event, a catalyst, a final straw. Something that the idiots in the mainstream media would call *iconic*.

"So what's the plan for today?" Jay said.

"A little sight-seeing," Ricky said. "Coffee with a friend."

"Spock?"

"Uh-huh."

"That guy's more of a politician than an operative. You better watch your own back."

"If he's who you think he is."

"Correct."

"What are *you* doing?"

"You don't want to know."

"Yes, I do."

"Well, Ricky, it's better if you don't, okay?"

Ricky smiled and shrugged. Jay didn't seem quite so cocky here in London as he had done in Australia, or on the phone to Madagascar from Namibia. He'd lost some of his swagger. And Ricky knew how he felt. There was something enervating about the place: A feeling that it had been built for secret power, and that power — such as it might be these days — remained elusive, intractable and unaccountable. In Ricky's memories of the old days, there were interminable debates about how to confront power. But *it* always knew how to confront *you*.

"Hey," Jay said. "Something to be aware of, in case you hadn't heard. The Chinese PM's in town. Big delegation. Tea at Buckingham Palace. Major suck-up offensive. The Brits are broke and they've heard that the Chinese are loaded. I guess I don't need to explain the political sensitivities?"

"No. I get it."

"Walter's a cool guy, but there's a limit to what he and I —"

"I get it, Jay."

"All righty. You have yourself a good time, then. Be safe out there."

He intended to be. But, figuring that he would never do this again, and duly disguised in baseball hat and sunglasses, he ventured out into a sharp, gray, brittle day and headed south down Whitehall. He paused outside the Ministry of Defence, and then again outside the Foreign and Commonwealth Office and wondered if, even now, some committee or task force within were reviewing a report on Ricky Ponton's last known whereabouts, or dozing through a PowerPoint presentation on strategies for disrupting his network or neutralizing his activities.

He conjured up a vision of the people on the committee or task force, and imagined them waking up, a few hours ago, in Esher or Tunbridge Wells. There they were, grabbing a bowl of muesli; petting the dog; dropping the kids off at school; reading the free paper on the train; updating their social media about the upcoming ski trip to Italy; settling in at their desks with a take-away coffee; checking their email; and then getting psyched up to damn Ricky and all his works, with an eye on the annual performance review and the attendant career satisfaction. And, once the project was brought to a successful conclusion, how could there not be a post-implementation office party?

On he walked. In honor of the Chinese, presumably, the gates to Downing Street were heavily guarded. A small pro-Tibet demonstration was ostentatiously contained in Parliament Square.

The Palace of Westminster, Ricky thought, looked okay, if you were into fake Gothic. But the fabric of the building, he'd read in his in-flight magazine on the way from Jo'burg, was in a state of irreparable decay. Nevertheless, it was being repaired, probably forever and at great expense. Symbolic, or what? Perhaps the Chinese could chip in.

Venturing a little further, he paid his respects to the stuffy MI5 building, on the northern bank of the Thames, and also its gaudy MI6 equivalent to the south.

Hi guys. Look out the window, why don't you?

Then he reversed himself and crossed Westminster Bridge to the South Bank, heading east. The towers of the City looked insubstantial in the gray light. But, just as in Hong Kong, Ricky thought, you could feel the presence and the sheer pressure of money — though not the sense of *future*. The Brits wanted London to become a colonial financial outpost of the new Chinese empire. *Role reversal*, you might say. Well, if Prince got his NPP, the Brits might get what they wished for. And then some.

Ricky ducked into a coffee shop underneath the Royal Festival Hall, logged in to Big Data and checked his dashboard. Iceland reported that the video upload subsystem was down. Someone in Shanghai had successfully mapped the server configuration — because of the size of video content, fewer servers were used than in the document upload subsystem, which was consequently less vulnerable — and had launched a denial-of-service attack, the usual crude-but-effective tactic. Iceland's network people were working on a reconfiguration; it would take a day or two.

Norway said that routine probing, originating in Maryland and Utah, had been stepped up in recent days, but didn't look like anything to be concerned about.

And Brazil reported that the plumbing issue in São Paulo had been resolved.

There was a single item on Ricky's action list: The activation of the secure messaging system that was Big Data's gift to the Chinese Spring. An email from Mr. Yu confirmed that the word had gone out. Expectations were high. And did Ricky have any news of Chen?

He would reply to Mr. Yu after his meeting with Spock. But he would activate the messaging system now. *Tap.* It was done. Had he sparked a revolution? Perhaps. It felt good to be in control.

Ricky left the coffee shop and walked as far as the Tate Modern art gallery. There he crossed the footbridge back to the northern bank of the river and St. Paul's.

This modern city seemed to mock his memory of it. The London he remembered from his angry youth was dirty, louche and mildly dangerous. It had smelled of petrol, cabbage and cigarettes. The urban landscape had been one of sooty brick, moldering monuments, decrepit trains and filthy pubs. Yet there had been a cynical but self-accepting energy amid the decay and the desuetude — among the population at large, if not their rulers. The rulers, needless to say, hadn't changed at all, but the people had — at least here, in the rich center. They seemed almost happy in their frantic, shiny self-deceptions. Superficially, the city had been cleaned up and repurposed towards the pursuit of American-style happiness — money, in other words. The stench now was of wealth, not of rubbish. The rubbish, and the people associated with it, had been removed.

But something of that old smell remained, trapped underground, threatening to leak out and combust one day.

Ricky walked all the way to Regent's Park, where he found Spock waiting for him in the Rose Garden.

Spock gestured to the northwest.

"I have just had lunch with our ambassador. He has an impressive house."

Ricky remembered the house. It sat, hidden by trees, in the corner of the Park, next to the big mosque. He'd been arrested outside, once.

"Talk about anything interesting?"

"The possibility of another naval confrontation. The worrying state of the financial markets. The complete absence of foreign policy expertise among the Prince campaign's backers and advisors."

"How was the food?"

"We ordered pizza. It was quite good. Shall we walk?"

"Okay."

Ricky surveyed the Rose Garden. Two dog-walkers, a twenty-something female jogger, and an elderly Indian lady in a wheelchair with a helper pushing. He was pretty sure he hadn't seen any of them before. So far, so good, then. Vigilance, as per Jay's injunction, was probably a good idea.

"First off," he said. "I need to ask about Chen. On a personal level. Any news? Did you find her?"

"There *is* news," Spock said. "But it's not *good* news."

Ricky rubbed his temples. He had *so* wanted to give Mr. Yu some good news.

"What happened?"

"She's on her way back to China."

"Not voluntarily?"

"I believe not."

"Where was she?"

"She was detained at a facility in New Jersey."

"What facility?"

"It belongs to Fairmeadow Security."

"Fairmeadow? They're a private company. How can they *detain* anyone? On American soil?"

Spock turned to Ricky and raised his eyebrows.

"Anything else?" Ricky said.

"There was a demonstration outside. A young man was killed. He attacked Fairmeadow personnel. They were forced to defend themselves."

Mr. Yu had mentioned a boyfriend. This just got worse.

"A demonstration? So someone knew she was there?"

"Apparently. There is much confusion. There are outlandish theories."

"Any chance of getting her back?"

"None."

They walked on, past gray herons immobile along the banks of a stream, reaching the boating lake. A Pakistani family fed bread to a flock of geese while an excitable gang of Japanese schoolgirls watched and took pictures on their phones.

"So," Ricky said. "Do we have a plan?"

"Indeed we do. But let us begin with the *big picture*."

They made a detour around a convocation of pigeons.

"Congress," Spock said, "has held hearings. About you, Mr. Ponton. Some of our most distinguished Representatives and Senators have made their opinion of you very clear. They know what they would like to do with you. Or to you. And their enthusiasm in this connection appears to be, unusually, entirely sincere."

"I heart them, too."

"And the President has been repeatedly embarrassed by your revelations."

"He's right to be."

"Of course, we shall have a new President shortly. But it is clear to the meanest observer that none of the possible incumbents lacks a similar capacity. Certainly not Mr. Prince."

"Meet the new boss."

"Then there is the intelligence community. For many of them, the exposure of their secrets is almost a personal matter."

"Maybe they should get out more."

"And, in the background, there is what we might call the *media drumbeat*. Have you heard what they say about you on Freedom News?"

"No," Ricky said, untruthfully.

"In short," Spock said, "there are *lists* out there. And you are at the top of a lot of them."

So what was new?

"But let us now turn to more local considerations. The British intelligence services are, in the general case, eager to please or impress their US counterparts. This is for historical, political, cultural and financial reasons. So long as there is no great impact on their self-regard. Perhaps I should say self-*respect*."

"Say what you like."

"*You* would make an exquisite prize for them, Mr. Ponton. Their account, so to speak, would be thereafter be greatly in credit."

"Cash in the bank."

"Thus it may be easy to tempt them, in circumstances that might ordinarily occasion suspicion."

"Okay, now I think you're losing me."

They turned right by a busy café and crossed a bridge. Ricky took the opportunity to glance back at the path by the lake. No grim-faced men in trench coats and trilbies. No blind match-sellers. No large women in burkas with wires coming out of their ears. Nothing to worry about.

"But before we discuss the mechanics of the operation, let us be clear as to the exchange involved."

"Operation?"

"On our part, we will see that Ms. Law is released. You will become responsible for her. It would be wise to remove her to another country as soon as possible. And we will endeavor to ensure that you yourself are detained only briefly."

"Endeavor? Briefly?"

"For your part — and I believe you have already begun; is that correct? — you will use your network to assist the Chinese Spring. Please understand that our objective here is to avert a Prince presidency and the unwelcome changes it would bring. In principle, we are in favor of Chinese democracy. In practice — and we need only look in the mirror, I think — we are agnostic."

"I agree. We have a deal."

"Wait. There's more. Our feeling is that our mission, in future, will be to manage military relations between ourselves and the Chinese in a mature, responsible way. We assume here that Willard Prince does not win, and that we have a... A *normal* President. Furthermore, we believe that this task would proceed more smoothly were such relations to enjoy a certain benign neglect on your part."

Benign neglect?

"You mean you want me to censor myself?"

"Yes."

"What if I don't?"

"Then you become fair game again."

"Okay, fine. You want neglect, you can have it. Let's talk about the mechanics."

They began to walk uphill. To their left, Ricky noted the fences, trees and electronic devices that protected the US Ambassador's residence. Had they put their pizzas through a scanner?

"There are several elements to the plan," Spock said.

They exited the Park and crossed the Outer Circle. Ricky glanced back at the entrance to the Ambassador's house. There were only two policemen on duty; was the Ambassador feeling lucky, or did the Chinese take precedence? Ricky and Spock crossed the footbridge over the Regent's Canal and stopped at the zebra crossing on Prince Albert Road.

"I hope this isn't going to be too complicated," Ricky said, as they waited for a white van to pass.

"Not at all. It is, in fact, quite elegant."

The van shot over the crossing but then pulled in sharply to the left. A second van stopped to the right of the crossing.

"We can cross now," Spock said.

"No hang on, there's something funny —"

The rear doors of the first van flew open. Inside were three men in khaki jumpsuits and balaclavas.

"Is that part of the plan?"

Spock raised an eyebrow.

"No," he said. "It is not."

CHAPTER 36

REALITY CHECK.

I t's dark. Teri Wolfe is hunkered down in her seat under a blanket that she's pulled up to her chin. The droning of the engines, plus dinner and unlimited free booze, has sent everybody else — except maybe Krall — off to sleep. They're all at thirty thousand feet, hurtling towards jolly old London, except that nothing seems very jolly.

All the gang is here. Except Merriweather. He's got his own plane. The coal guy, the chemical guy, the casino guy and the Wall Street guys have elected to fly with him.

And except Sandy. What's happened to her? Krall has been evasive.

Prince has been closeted in his cabin. Has he been boning up on foreign policy? If so, why the shouting? And what do Barbara or the Prince brothers know about foreign policy?

The press pack is sequestered in the gloom at the back of the plane, on the far side of Prince's den. Gunner and Weese are lurking there, though how they hitched a ride is a mystery: The look on Krall's face when he sees them is enough to set off the emergency oxygen supply. They're keeping a low profile. Which is good. Because Teri's scared of them, even if Krall isn't.

Nile is dead. Teri's pretty sure about that. She saw it with her own eyes, and Meera confirmed it. No more madcap meetings in the Park. No more snarky text messages. Meera's a serious girl. Everything's serious now.

Amber's been on TV. Sure, she was in the bus crash at the Fairmeadow compound. She's never denied that, hell no. But she knows nothing about a Chinese girl. Chen *who?* Also somebody stole her phone, god damn it!

Teri knows that's a lie. *Someone's* had a word with Amber. Amber gave her phone to Sandy. Who gave it to Teri. Who gave it to Nile. From whom it was retrieved by Meera. Who gave it back to Teri. Teri has it in her hand now. It's still got Chen's video on it. And it's got photos of twenty-two of Barbara van Dornen's monthly statements from Prince's mind-blowing, jaw-dropping, world-destroying, epoch-defining Ponzi scheme, the New American Century

Fund. If only Teri can get those statements to Meera, she'll be able to prove that Prince has stolen two hundred billion dollars. Give or take.

And the Robin Hood Party have got their grubby Arcadian mitts on about six out of those two hundred. Meera says she has some *ideas*. And she wants Teri to help her.

Krall knows that Teri and her *little friend* were planning some *shit*. But he doesn't want to know anything about it — so long as it doesn't stop him winning the election. Does he know that Nile was Teri's little friend? Is he actually *encouraging* her? If not, how come he hasn't thrown her off the plane? Or the campaign, at least?

Barbara has been giving Teri the eye. But it's not because of the statements; she doesn't know about that. And it's not because of the ding on her car; that's gotten Milly grounded. Maybe it's Barbara that Teri needs to worry about. Not Krall. Not Weese or Gunner.

Teri is so tired. If only she could sleep, like the Secret Service guy said.

But, no. She can't.

REALITY CHECK, CONTINUED.

So what the hell does Teri Wolfe really think she's doing? She shouldn't be on this plane. It's not her place. She really has no business messing with History. It's all Milly's fault. Teri was doing fine at the coffee shop. Okay, not actually as fine as Pedro and Aliyah, and she shouldn't really have been their boss, but hey — they understood what *that* was about. Teri could have survived in the food service industry, couldn't she? Year after year, grinding away until, at long last, she met... Another over-educated loser like herself? Jesus, if it hadn't been for the French Roast...

But Mom and Dad already believe their daughter's a deadbeat. Living in that *disgusting* apartment in Bayonne with Alicia and *Burgandy!* How is she *ever* going to pay off those loans? She's sleeping on the *couch*, for God's sake! Just tell us, please — what did we do to deserve this?

Mom, Dad — it's ninety-four thousand dollars. Of course I'm never going to pay it off. I'm not supposed to. This is the way we live now. Dad's not earning any more now than he did in 1980. I know you don't want to believe that, but it's true. Read what that guy in the Times says. Canada and South Korea are richer than we are. People like us, I mean. So go ahead and rent out my room, I don't mind. It makes sense. I never wanted to hurt you. None of this is our fault.

But what if I could do something about it? Would you like that? Would you think better of me?

Because I *could*.

I just need to send those statements to Meera. Meera? No, you haven't met her yet. But you'll like her. I think I do.

So what if I *did?* Let's imagine...

So here it comes. *It*. The Big Reveal. Folks, there's something you need to know about your new President. The guy you just voted for. Because you're sick of the system, and you wanted Change and you've given up on Hope. Because you're afraid of the Chinese. Because the other two parties are so corrupt it hurts, and here's Mr. New American Century who looks like he would get you one hell of a deal on a beachside vacation home, if only you could afford one. So here's

246

the *real* deal, folks: You're looking at the Greatest Ponzi King of All Time. How do you feel about that? Do you want to stick? Play again? Burn down the whole friggin' casino?

And, by the way, this news is brought to you by Teri Wolfe, a feckless blogger-girl who has nothing else to offer you but the worst possible confirmation of your fears. (And you don't even know about that Chinese thing yet!) How do you feel about her? Grateful? Bemused? Grudgingly accepting? She's going to need a job now, probably, so if anyone out there needs a...

No, wait. Maybe you feel angry. This isn't what you wanted to hear. You refuse to believe, despite Meera's slam-dunk numbers. You want to go on living in denial. What happens to Teri then?

All right, enough with the reality check. It kind of sucks.

So how about Prince? How would he deal with *his*, when it came? He, and his menacing, palpitating brothers, had no idea what Teri guarded on the slim device she cradled in her clammy palm. Chen's video, if it could only be uploaded to Big Data, would surely ignite the Chinese Spring. Which, in turn, would dynamite the Prince campaign, given its cognitive dissonance, world-class contortions and brazen mendacity on the China issue. Perhaps that — or something like it — was what Krall feared.

But the Ponzi thing — *forget about it!*

It wouldn't be the White House that the Prince clan was looking at — but a house of a very different nature. Wouldn't it? Wasn't that what happened when you stole from the rich? When you stole from the poor it was called a *bailout*. Or so the Robin Hood people said.

A thin triangle of light appeared on the storage bin above Teri's head. She took a peek over the back of her seat. Prince had emerged from his cabin. He was half-undressed, in pajama pants and a white vest. His hair was all mussed up. Teri shrank back under her blanket. Prince made his way slowly and carefully down the aisle, steadying himself against each seatback, even though the plane was flying smoothly and there was no turbulence. When he reached the front row, he stopped. This, Teri knew, was where Barbara sat. Prince stood still and looked down at Barbara. She didn't respond; she had to be asleep. Prince's shoulders slumped. He rubbed his eyes.

For perhaps three minutes he stood like this. Then Teri saw Krall emerge from his seat, take Prince by the arm, and guide him gently back up the aisle. He ushered Prince into his cabin and quietly clicked the door shut.

Krall headed back to his seat. But before he sat, he turned and looked in Teri's direction, catching her eye. There was a moment of indecision, then he beckoned to Teri and moved towards the front of the plane again. Teri got up and followed. Krall waited for her.

When she caught up with him, he pushed open the door to one of the toilets and gestured for her to enter. She took a step back. He leaned forward and brought his mouth close to her ear.

"It ain't nothin' like that, Teri. We need to talk in private. Okay?"

"Okay."

She stepped into the toilet and turned about. He squeezed in after her and fastened the door. They were chest-to-chest — or, more accurately, Teri's face was in Krall's chest. Krall banged his elbow on the washbasin.

"Ow! Shit!"

"You okay?"

"Yeah. I said we should have had a bigger plane — you know, with, like, a conference room? But Willard didn't want to pay for it. He's gotten kind of tight with the money, for some reason."

"Really?"

"Uh-huh. But that's not the main problem. As I think you saw."

"Is he losing it?"

"Not sure I'd say that. But somethin' is eatin' him. I guess you wouldn't happen to know what, would you?"

"Nope. Don't think so."

"Could it be anythin' to do with Sandy?"

"Sandy? No way. I mean, how?"

"See, Teri, I'm kind of protective of Sandy."

"Well, yeah. Me too."

"Glad we agree. Don't want nothin' happening to her."

Teri shook her head.

"But I need her, Teri. She has made the difference in this campaign. I'm not exaggerating. I need her up until the debates, and then for the focus groups afterwards. And that's it. Then she's out of here, and I'm gonna take care of her. That's what we both want, right? I'm gonna make sure she's okay. Don't ask me how. Just believe. There's things about her you don't know. Do you trust me?"

Not totally, Teri thought. But in Sandy's case...

"Yes."

"Good. Now let me ask you this. Those two guys — Gunner and that shit-eating pal of his. They got a hold of her and took her to this — well, it don't matter about that. I think she said something. I think they got something out of her. But I don't know what. Now you called me, remember? You said Sandy had *gone rogue*. She wanted to go see Willard. And I was looking for her, but I couldn't find her. Turns out she fetched up at Barbara's house. So did she tell Barbara somethin'?"

"I dunno. What does Barbara say?"

"She says Sandy was just talkin' nonsense. That's all. Do you know why she wanted to see Willard?"

Teri eased herself down and sat on the rim of the toilet. Now she was looking directly at Krall's belt buckle, a heavy bronze oval featuring a picture of a horse — a mustang?

Sandy had wanted to tell Prince about Chen and the Chinese Spring. She hadn't understood that she would have been telling exactly the wrong person. Teri had only called Krall out of desperation. Sandy might have told Krall instead; Teri had simply guessed that she wouldn't. But had she told Barbara? Either Barbara really had thought that Sandy was talking nonsense, or else Barbara's default instinct — to protect Prince — had kicked in. Did Barbara know what Prince's true China agenda was? Probably not.

But Teri couldn't trust Krall with the Chinese Spring. He wanted to win his election. A democratic uprising in China would blow Prince out of the water.

"I don't know. She was worked up about something. She had a tough day, right? Maybe Amber..."

Teri could feel Krall staring at the top of her head. She looked down at the scuffed toes of his urban-cowboy ankle boots.

"Amber? Jesus, maybe that's it. She's been on TV... You can tell she's lyin' her tight little ass off about somethin'. But what?"

"I don't know."

"Maybe Gunner and that other creep know. Maybe Sandy told them. They're meant to be on our side now, but..."

They *were*, Teri thought. They'd said so. Suppose Sandy had told them about Chen. What would they have done?

Krall fell silent. He seemed to be thinking; his cowboy toes were twitching. Teri tore off a strip of toilet paper and dabbed her eyes.

"Can I ask you something?" she said.

"Sure. What?"

"Where's Sandy now?"

"She's at my place. I'm havin' my doc check her out."

"Okay, that's good."

"Yeah."

A pause.

"Do you really want Prince to win?"

A long, long pause. The toes stopped twitching and seemed to curl up inside their holsters.

"I told you, Teri. I want to win this election. After that... It's not my concern."

"Do you really care about Sandy? You're exploiting her."

"Yes, I'm exploiting her. But I'm goin' to make it up her. Like I said."

"Do you really not care what I do? After the election?"

A long intake of breath.

"I'm lookin' forward to it. Anything else?"

"No."

"Then we're done. For now."

Krall twisted around so that he could unlock the toilet door. There was a distinct *thunk*. He stepped out and she followed, waiting in the aisle until he'd sunk back into his seat.

Something stirred at the rear of the cabin. She looked. Was that Weese? Had Weese seen Teri and Krall coming out of the toilet together?

Shit! No, make that *fuck him*. She glared down the aisle for a moment, then walked slowly back to her seat.

*

The rest of the flight passed without incident. It was only after they landed that the incidents started and kept on coming.

On the way from the airport, Prince's motorcade took a wrong turn and ended up snarled in the middle of a Hindu street festival, which occasioned some bad

249

feeling but also provided opportunities for professional motor-cycle-borne photographers and amateur video uploaders.

On Park Lane, it turned out that hotel rooms reserved for the Prince entourage had been given instead to a larger-than-expected contingent of economists from the two largest Chinese state-owned banks. Alternative, and inferior, accommodation had to be obtained at short notice.

In Mayfair, at an afternoon reception held for Prince by hedge fund managers, Prince apparently fell victim to a rogue cucumber sandwich and was obliged to spend most of the session in the bathroom. Krall told Teri that, yes, it *really was* the sandwich.

In St. John's Wood, addressing a rally of expatriate voters at the American School, Prince, who had been wandering distractedly close to the edge of the stage as if searching for his missing poodle, fell off, in the middle of a peroration on the subject of children being the future, and twisted his ankle.

On the BBC, while being interviewed on the subject of future American security guarantees with respect to those former eastern bloc nations that might or might not aspire to NATO membership, Prince mispronounced the first name of the Corporation's top international correspondent and appeared not to know the names of the Polish Prime Minister, the Ukrainian President, the Belorussian President, the Russian Foreign Minister and the British Foreign Secretary.

At a Gala Dinner organized by City bankers in the heart of the financial district, Prince inadvertently insulted the Mayor of London by asserting that small government was best, and London proved it because it clearly prospered without any. He proceeded accidentally to dis a significant section of the city's population by observing that, while New York had been built by immigrants, the ones who'd only got *this far* hadn't done so badly either.

In a pub in Soho, Krall told Teri that, *ass-clenching* as the day had been, none of this mattered, because the only foreigners that American voters cared about these days were female celebrities, preferable Royal, and the Chinese.

And since Gloria was too preoccupied with Prince's ankle to bother her, Teri was able to blog away happily about each of these occurrences, keen to show that Prince could take a little adversity when he had to.

CHAPTER 37

Ricky Ponton could tell that Spock — he'd been obliged to confess to a real name that sounded like *Ken Freihardt*, but Ricky preferred to stick with the familiar — was not happy. He was trying not to show it and, in fact, was doing a pretty good job, in the circumstances, of maintaining his composure. Still, Ricky could tell.

Spock's *elegant* plan had gone *tits up* before even getting off the ground; he and Ricky were sitting in a windowless dungeon — possibly the basement of an Indian restaurant, to judge by the smell — trussed up in plastic restraints; and their captors could barely restrain themselves from gloating at the *exquisite prize* they'd grabbed for themselves.

"You are royally fucked, lads, do you know that?"

"Allow me to repeat," Spock said. "I am an employee of the Defense Intelligence Agency of the United States. You are making a most unfortunate mistake by detaining me here."

"Yeah, well, we're checking, aren't we? You've got no ID, mate. So just hold your horses."

"I can give you the appropriate number to call."

"We know who to call."

"With respect, you —"

"What are you doing with *him*, then? Eh? Answer that!"

This was a question to which Spock, with all the dignity he could muster, declined to respond.

"Doesn't look good, does it, sunshine?"

No, Ricky thought. And from his own point of view, it looked a hell of lot worse. Luton Airport, a favorite with the rendition crowd, was a fifty-minute sprint up the M1. He could be on a private jet to Norfolk, Virginia before Big Data's supporters had even agreed a text for their online petition. Did he blame Spock? Not really. Jay had warned Ricky. He had been right.

But now the leader of the snatch squad re-entered the dungeon. It appeared that there was a problem.

"It's got out *already*. Look."

A tablet computer showing headline news. A picture of Ricky in mid-snatch. LEAKS BOSS GRABBED ON LONDON STREET.

"They want to know how it happened. Anyone? How the fuck did this happen?"

Incredulity. Shaking of heads. Tapping of boots on oily, damp brick floor.

"This is a fucking disaster! Do you want to know what's happened, right? The Yanks want him. And now the fucking Chinese are demanding him. They're in a fucking *press conference* with the fucking Prime Minister right now! What are we supposed to do? Saw the fucker in half?"

Ricky could see their dilemma. And so too, to judge by the merest upturn at the corner of his mouth, did Spock.

There was an interlude in which the leader paced the length of the basement, shaking his head while his troops kicked their heels in a corner.

"It's no good. I'm going to have to get a ruling."

The leader got his phone out and dialed a number from memory.

"Yeah, it's me. What? No, we're still at location X... Yes, he's here. There's also a bloke who says... Yes, we *know* about that. That's why I'm... What? No, of course we followed... Look, I need a ruling. Are we going to location Z or... From the top? Right. Well, when... Yes, I *know* he's in a press conference. Can't someone pass him a note or... They're asking him questions? Well, what's he saying? Christ... All right. Yeah, you get back to me. Bye. Fuck!"

Ricky inferred that the PM had been put on the spot, in front of the TV cameras, and that his predicament had become sticky. He glanced at Spock, who, as Ricky anticipated, raised his eyebrows.

But now there was a commotion on the stairs leading down into the dungeon. Ricky thought he heard an American accent — a familiar one?

Jay Percival burst into the basement. Behind him were two of Walter's minders. In an apparent attempt to look the part, they were wearing suits, ties and shades instead of the chinos and short-sleeved shirts they usually wore.

Deftly avoiding the slimy patches on the floor, Jay approached the leader and flashed a small, black wallet in his face. Ricky saw the leader's eyes swivel from left to right, his lips moving as he read. Then he took a good, hard look at Jay's face, before returning his gaze to Jay's ID.

"Hi there," Jay said. "Good work! We'll take it from here."

He gestured to Walter's men. They began to move towards Ricky.

"Much appreciated," Jay said. "You all have a nice day, now!"

"No, no, no," the leader said. "Hang on a moment. You got here bloody fast, didn't you?"

"Sure did."

"But how did you —"

"Oh, come on. Like we don't know what you're doing."

"Yeah, well. Be that as it may, the thing is —"

"Look, the guy's ours, right? You *were* going to hand him over, weren't you? Why wait?"

"That would seem logical," Spock said, perking up a bit.

"*You...* You just shut it, okay?"

"I really think we're done here," Jay said.

"Look, you don't understand. We've got a problem. The Chinese want him as well."

"Okay. I can appreciate that. But are the Chinese here now? I don't see them."

"Well, no. But —"

"Let me ask you this. Whose, uh, *help* does your service most depend on? Ours or theirs?"

"Well, yours. Obviously."

"So it kind of looks to me as if the decision is made for you."

"Yeah, okay. Right. When you put it like that. But I've got to check with —"

"I'm not waiting around here, pal. It's now or never. Hand over the goods or pay the price."

"Yeah, but the PM... You know how it works. The *embarrassment*. There'll be a ton of shit coming down, and..."

"I know. It's tough. I feel your pain, guys. What're you gonna do, huh?"

A mood of resignation. Muttering. Clucking of tongues.

"All right. Take the bastard. Have your sodding way with him."

Ricky on his feet. Jay feigning surprise at discovering Spock down there on the floor, also.

"Oh, and we'll take this guy off your hands, too. Nice to see you again, Ken. Looking good."

A gracious if defeated nod from Spock. Then Ricky and Spock on their feet, still trussed, and Walter's men making a decent show of dragging them out of the basement. In the street, a black minivan with diplomatic plates.

Ricky turned to Spock.

"The elegant plan? Any chance?"

Spock shook his head.

"I fear not."

"Move it," Jay said. "Get in the car. It's gonna take them about ten minutes to figure out what just happened to them. My ID is five years out of date. When they check it... Well, let's just say that the PM's day is about to get even worse."

Ricky let Walter's guys bundle him into the car.

"Where're we going?"

"Back to the embassy. Nowhere else we can go. Looks like it's siege time again, folks."

CHAPTER 38

The hall was packed – expensively so, Teri Wolfe thought. She sat in the second row, at the right-hand end. She'd chosen this seat because Flint Gunner and Nigel Weese had seated themselves in the back row, on the far left. When she glanced over her shoulder to check that they hadn't moved, Weese spotted her and gave her a lascivious smirk.

Barbara, Gloria and Megan sat directly in front of Teri, in the first row. Josh Merriweather and his crew had occupied real estate a couples of rows back from the front on the left. Krall was onstage with Prince and what looked, to Teri, like the best bunch of top-table think-tankers and foreign-policy re-treads that Krall had been able to purchase.

Prince was giving a press conference at the headquarters of an investment bank. It wasn't going well.

Did Prince think another financial crash was coming?

Well, sure, there was a little *froth* in the markets, and maybe some folk had gotten a little more *exuberant* than was justified by the fundamentals, but Prince believed that the American economy was essentially sound, and any misallocation of capital would be rectified in due course by the normal market mechanisms.

But what about all the *toxic assets* that some people said the *shadow banking system* had been piling up and throwing around — yet again?

Prince thought that some assets were of higher quality than others, but the market priced them accordingly and risk was thus allocated appropriately and generally spread around the system in an efficient manner. And the correct term, in any case, would be *troubled*, not *toxic*. People needed to avoid talking the market down. Next question?

Well, nearly every other investment fund was down for the quarter, but the New American Century Fund was posting the same consistent advance it had done for the last five quarters. What was Prince's secret?

A ripple of discomfort spread through the room. Teri detected seat-shifting and throat-clearing. It was almost as if someone had farted. Onstage, Krall was studying the floor. Come on, Willy Boy, she thought. Tell us your secret.

Prince said that the New American Century Fund had always been run according to the most conservative principles and therefore its selection of securities, combined with sophisticated hedging strategies and (of course!) its highly-regarded, computer-driven bespoke algorithms, guaranteed, under almost any market scenario, returns of a modest but agreeable consistency. You only had to look at the Fund's track record over the years.

As Teri focused in on Prince's face, he folded his arms, leaned back in his chair, and, rotating his gaze from one side of the room to the other and back again, bestowed on his audience *the smile*: The effulgent, plutocratic beam that you saw on his election posters; that blast of sunny, prosperous all-American ease that broke down your barriers; the friendly, fatal gleam that, like an electro-magnetic pulse shot out into the low-income belts, wiped the brains of people like Sandy Quayle and took them down.

You could almost see how he did it, Teri thought. He was the leader of a cult — the cult of endless money.

Next question.

Did Prince have any comment to make about the capture — just minutes ago and a few streets away — of Ricky Ponton, the fugitive boss of Big Data Underground?

Prince didn't want to comment, except to say that he hoped and trusted that justice would be done.

Teri felt in her pocket. Amber's phone was still there, its secrets intact but still secret. If this guy Ponton was heading for a lifetime in military custody, would Big Data survive? Their video upload system was still down; she'd tried again at the hotel. How was she going to get Chen's manifesto to them?

Then Krall asked if there were any questions about foreign policy. At first it seemed not; but then someone at the back piped up.

"We're getting reports of a dangerous situation developing in the vicinity of the Spratly Islands. Would Mr. Prince like to comment?"

What was Weese up to? Teri figured she was thinking the same thing as everybody else in the audience: Where on Earth were the Spratly Islands; what kind of dangerous situation could possibly be developing there; and how the hell could Prince answer, given that yesterday he couldn't even get the Prime Minister's last name right. But then she saw Krall lean across and whisper in Prince's ear.

Prince said that there had long been a dispute between China and the Philippines over the Spratlys, particularly in relation to the Second Thomas Shoal — and Fiery Cross Reef, too, for that matter — but the presence of an American warship in that part of the South China Sea was, he was given to understand, merely a precaution against aggression. From *any* quarter. And the Prince administration would, of course, stand ready to facilitate and assist negotiations at any time.

Wow, Teri thought. You could see how Krall earned the big bucks. Planted question, impressive answer; neat. A murmur of approbation ran around the room. But was that really what was going on in the South China Sea?

Weese had another question.

"And speaking of China, how can Mr. Prince reassure American voters that enhanced economic cooperation with China will bring good jobs and higher wages back to America?"

"Well, Mr. Weese, I'm very glad you asked that question."

Teri looked at Krall. He was biting his lip. *Oops*, she thought. Prince knows Weese's name, but not the Prime Minister's?

Prince said that it was vital to remove the obstacles that prevented American companies from competing with, and in, China. Moreover, it was important that the US and China agreed a common framework for the future, so that disputes could be avoided, or quickly resolved, to the obvious benefit of everyone. China was maturing rapidly, as an economy, and perhaps in other ways too, and there was much that China could learn from the American way of doing things. And, while not succumbing to false modesty, it wasn't entirely beyond the realm of the possible to suggest that America might even learn something from China, too. Plus when Mr. Weese said *cooperation*, what he really meant was *tough but friendly competition*, of course.

Teri glanced at the Merriweather contingent: Blank expressions everywhere, but a slight narrowing of Josh's baby-blue eyes.

"One last question," Weese said. "And you can take this as seriously as you like. What do you think of the Robin Hood Party?"

Back came the beam, this time supplemented by an indulgent guffaw.

"I think we've all seen that movie, haven't we? My message would be: Take off the tights, go get a job. We're gonna make sure there's one waiting for you."

A ripple of amusement. Krall looking pleased.

"Anyone else?" he said. "Freedom News? Got anything for us, Mr. Gunner?"

Gunner stood up to speak, but an unsolicited question rang out from the middle of the audience.

"What about the Chinese Spring? Do you support them or not?"

The beam extinguished from Prince's face like the lights in a poor neighborhood hit by a rolling blackout. Krall on his feet, concern on his face; does he know what this gate-crasher's talking about?

"Answer the question!"

Excitement at the back. Merriweather watching Prince. Krall trying to take control.

"Sit down, please. No questions from the public. Media only."

"Do you support democracy in China? Yes or no?"

Krall gestured to towards the back of the room. It was over quickly: A clean-looking young man with a goatee escorted to the exit by two of Fairmeadow's local employees. No resistance, but a touching, repeated demand for Prince to answer the question — *please!*

Teri turned around to find Barbara staring at her.

"What?"

"Mm? Oh, nothing."

Krall made a lackluster apology, ignored Gunner's renewed attempt to ask his question, and wound the meeting up by reminding everyone that there would be another chance to ask questions after Prince's meeting with the Governor of the Bank of England.

On her way out, Teri was waylaid by Gloria.

"Write something about how young people in Europe want their own version of the Prince Plan for Youth Jobs. Don't mention that, uh, interruption."

"Sure. Okay."

And before she could make it out on to the street, she was waylaid again — this time by Gunner and Weese.

"Here she is, Flint. Little Miss Mile-High."

"Yeah, Nige. Wowser."

"Make a lovely little column-filler, wouldn't it?"

"You bet."

"Lucky for her we're under orders, that's all I can say."

"Don't rock the boat."

"That's right. Until it's all over. But you've got the pictures, haven't you, Flint?"

"Sure do. Kinda dark, though."

"Don't worry. We'll get the computer boffins on to it. Image enhancement and all that."

"Think we should interview her, Nige?"

"Quiz her on her nocturnal activities, you mean? Bit prurient, wouldn't you say?"

"Bit what, Nige?"

"Besides, you can't blame a girl for wanting to advance her career, can you?"

"Hell, no."

"Then again, some people would argue that there is a legitimate public interest."

"Is there?"

Teri tried to push past, but Weese blocked her way.

"After all, Mr. Krall is a public figure. People are entitled to know whether or not he is a man of *upstanding* moral fiber."

"Oh, yeah."

"So Teri, love. Tell us. Did you leave the seat up or down?"

She pushed again. Weese pushed back.

"And how about this so-called Chinese Spring? Know anything about that, do we?"

"Let me past."

"Does the name *Chen* mean anything?"

Given the wet, chilly weather in London, Teri had chosen to wear her heavy platform boots. It was a fortunate choice. She gave Weese a precision-guided blow to the ankle and broke free.

"Ow! Jesus!"

"Ha! She got you good, Nige."

"Shut the fuck up, Flint."

Out in the street, Teri ran two blocks as fast as she could in her deadly boots. Then she stopped in a store doorway to get her breath back. Where was she? She took out Amber's phone and opened its street-map app. Okay, she was on Leadenhall Street. She needed to get to Hampstead High Street. Where was that? She searched. All right, it was a couple of miles to the north-west. Although her *adequate* salary had yet to make itself known, Teri had been given a *per diem* in local currency, so she hailed a black cab.

The premises she wanted to find weren't on the High Street itself — they would have seemed out-of-place amid the pricey boutiques and chi-chi coffee-bars. She found the address she was looking for down a steep, cobbled alleyway lined by what she took to be mews houses. The lower floor housed a vintage clothing store. And above, according to the faded label next to the door buzzer, were the offices of Prince Securities (London) LLP.

Teri looked up. The windows were dirty; the blinds were closed. Was there anyone at home? It didn't look like it. Then she felt something warm and furry rub against her leg.

"That's Buster. You can pet him, if you like. He's a sweetie."

A tall, thin, sixty-something woman in the shop doorway, dressed a little bit too much like a flower-child from half a century ago. And a large, ginger cat with green eyes. Teri crouched down and scratched it behind the ears.

"Hey, Buster!"

"Do you have a cat?"

"I'd love to, but where I live..."

"I know it's difficult for you youngsters. Sometimes I think our generation had it too good."

"Oh, I don't know. Aren't things always supposed to get better?"

"I think they used to tell us that. American?"

"Yup."

"Looking for the Prince people?"

Teri gave Buster one last mega-scratch and stood up.

"Uh, kind of."

She pointed to the upper floor.

"Anyone at home?"

"Hasn't been anyone there for months. Far as I know."

"Oh. Perhaps I've come to the wrong place. I'm supposed to pick up some paperwork."

"Try the buzzer and see."

"Er, yeah. Okay."

Teri detached herself from Buster. Then she braced herself and hit the door buzzer. And waited. Nothing.

"No, I didn't think there was anyone in. Have you come far?"

"From New York."

"Really? Good heavens. Is it important?"

"Yeah, kind of."

"Well... No, Buster, *don't* eat that! Put it down! That's right. What was I saying? Oh, yes. Look dear, you like cats, you look trustworthy. Such a long way to come! Have a look under that big flowerpot."

Teri looked: A single key, attached to a New American Century Fund key ring.

"Ah!"

"Don't tell anyone I told you."

"No, don't worry."

"These Prince people. Are they anything to do with this chap who wants to be President?"

"It's the same family, yes."

"Well, it's up to you, of course. I can't help feeling there's something a bit odd about him. Probably just me."

"No, I don't think so."

"Really? Oh well. Hope you find what you're looking for. I've got to get back to work. Buster! Come along!"

"Thanks! That was really helpful. Bye, Buster!"

The offices of Prince Securities (London) LLP consisted of two rooms, a toilet and a kitchenette. As Teri had expected, there was little sign of serious business activity, let alone a stock-trading operation. The place was a mess: Dirty, untidy, a single outdated computer, paperwork everywhere. But wherever Prince's fake statements were printed, it wasn't here. Maybe Giordano ran them off in his basement. It occurred to her to sort through and photograph each document, but it hardly seemed necessary. So she simply took pictures of the two rooms on Amber's phone.

Then she sat down at the only desk in the office and thought about the decision she had to make.

Out of what was probably a naïve sense of precaution, she had turned off mobile reception on Amber's phone. And, although she knew that she couldn't change the phone's unique hardware serial number, she had switched the SIM for a pay-as-you-go number that she hoped might confuse things a bit. That Amber's phone had continued to operate happily long after she'd reported it "stolen" surely had to be considered a big, red, flashing light.

So Prince's London office was, if anything, even more bogus than his New York setup. There really was no doubt any more. Which meant, in turn, that Teri had every reason to send Barbara's statements to Meera *right now*. Twenty-two image files. Transmitted, unencrypted, via an anonymous cell phone account, from Amber's "stolen" handset to Meera's personal phone in New York. It had to be risky. Image files could be parsed, and text extracted. Did Meera want to take the risk? Teri sent her a text message from her personal phone: *ready for the big one?*

Ten minutes later, the reply came: *ready*.

Teri activated mobile reception on Amber's phone and emailed each statement as a separate attachment. Then she sent a selection of the photos she'd just taken of Prince's London office. When she was done, she turned off mobile reception again and left the office, replacing the key under the large flowerpot. She looked for Buster, but he'd moved on.

Then she ran to the Tube station at the top of the High Street and took the Northern Line south to Charing Cross, emerging into watery daylight to find herself in the midst of a riot.

CHAPTER 39

S andy Quayle thought she'd never seen a more peaceful place. Or anywhere quite so beautiful, pristine and well-ordered. Even the plants in the garden were labelled: Creosote Bush, Cholla, Brittlebush, Barrel Cactus, California Fan Palm, varieties of Yucca and Aloe, Echeveria, White Sage, Rough Horsetail, Angel Trumpet, Cat's Claw, Desert Petunia, Madagascar Palm, Desert Smoke Tree.

"So do you have any shades?" Milly said.

"Shades?"

"Sunglasses."

"No."

"We'll have to get you some. I've got to run into town later."

They were at Mr. Prince's California vacation home in the Coachella Valley, just south-east of Palm Springs. According to Milly, the house was to host a pre-election *retreat*, in which the inner circle of the Prince Campaign would review strategy, discuss last-minute tactics and prepare for the debates. Milly said that the debates would not normally take place so close to the actual election, but Krall had fought hard for the change, and had been successful.

Sandy and Milly were part of a small advance party, whose job it was to prepare everything before the big-wigs got back from Europe. Or Australia, or wherever.

The house was a vast, single-story, flat-roofed, glass-sided pavilion. Milly said it was *modernist*, the work of a famous Spanish architect. Mr. Prince had been very savvy; the market value of the house had quadrupled in the fifteen years that Mr. Prince had owned it. And you didn't need to worry too much about earthquakes, Milly told Sandy. The house had specially-engineered foundations. So if there happened to be, like, a *tectonic event?* Well, you could rest assured that Mr. Prince was going to be sitting pretty at the end of it.

Sandy said she hoped that was so.

The garden was divided by a central axis, a pebbly path punctuated by large fountains in a style that Sandy thought must be Spanish Colonial rather than modernist. To either side there were herbaceous borders and bright-green lawns. Sprinklers ran constantly. At one end of this axis was the *garden lounge*, an airy, spacious, comfortable room in which Milly said most of the *working sessions* would take place. The garden lounge let out on to a raised terrace. If you stood there and looked west along the main path, you could see, beyond the garden, a golf course. And beyond that, the mountains.

The house was located, Milly explained, on a private estate. Mr. Prince owned an equity share in the golf course.

Milly knew that Sandy had been unwell, so Sandy's main job was to relax and recuperate. Those, in fact, were Krall's orders. But Milly had been given a *shit-load* of work to do — not least by her mom, who'd been on Milly's case for reasons that Milly didn't care to go into. Anyway, if Sandy felt up to it, Milly would appreciate a little assistance.

"I think I'll be up to it."

"Cool. Can you help me set up the computers and stuff?"

"I'll try."

"Okay, so the rest of the guys are coming tomorrow, and I've got to drive into town and go shopping. You know there's, like, *no food* in the kitchen? And Ray's got have his *beer*, and Willard's got to have this particular brand of *oatmeal*, and Megan says she's *trialing* veganism? Which is bullshit, by the way. And Josh can't have gluten. Actually, that's serious. He could die."

"You should make a list."

"Yeah. That's a good idea. Anything for you — apart from the shades?"

"No."

Okay, so catch you later. Take it easy."

"I will."

Sandy wandered through the garden, her eyes screwed up against the sun. Milly was right about the glasses. Flaming Katy, Oleander, Golden Lotus Banana, Monkey Hand Tree, Washingtonia — there seemed to be no end to the richness and abundance of Mr. Prince's desert garden. What did it take to accomplish this in such a harsh, arid and otherwise brutal place? Such fragile beauty! A constant labor of love, and artifice. And if there were gardens in Heaven — there surely must be! — could they compete with this?

Sandy stepped up into the shade on the terrace by the garden lounge, sat on a bench, and tried to collect her thoughts. Her memory of the last couple of days was fuzzy. She'd been in a terrible, noisy place, with hundreds of people. There had been something frightening about it — and perhaps wicked, too. Someone had taken her there. Who? And someone else had sung a strange, sad song. Then the room had begun to spin, and she'd felt sick to her stomach.

She remembered that Ray had appeared out of nowhere and had taken her to his rented apartment downtown, close to the Campaign HQ. A doctor had come. Some simple tests had been performed. She'd been given medication; she wasn't sure what for, exactly. And the test results were... Where? Did Ray have them?

Ray had left for Europe, taking Teri with him — which seemed a little surprising to Sandy. Teri was a nice girl and all but her *blog*, or whatever it was, had hardly set people talking down at Campaign HQ. Unlike Sandy's contribution. Not that Sandy wanted to go to Europe. Not at all; everything was so crazy over there. The government told you what to eat for breakfast.

And then Milly had taken Sandy back to the Aspire building so that she could pack for the trip to California. Milly had been in a snit about something. It sounded like she'd fallen out with Teri. But that was what girls did.

Sandy had never been to California before. Hunter Bill used to assert that California was a *basket case*. He'd obviously never come *here*. And now, of course, he never would. But perhaps he was looking down at her? Was he shaking his head at this foolish adventure of hers?

Sandy, don't you see where this is all gonna end up? Don't you read the Journal?

Well, it wasn't so foolish, she'd have him know. Willard Prince was going to be President and Sandy had already played a significant part in his triumph. Ray said so. He said that Sandy had made all the difference. That was probably a kindly exaggeration, but even so.

Mr. Prince is going to be President, Bill.

And America would be saved. Most probably.

The shadows beneath the cactus and palm trees had dwindled almost to nothing. Even in the shade, the heat was building. Sandy went into the garden lounge, where it was cool, Milly having turned on the central air-conditioning as soon as they had arrived. She sat on a couch and turned on the TV. It had been left on the Freedom News Channel.

There were wildfires in California — the fall had been unusually dry — but nowhere near Palm Springs. In Texas, a train had derailed, spilling chemicals; a town had been evacuated. The Chairman of the New York Fed said that yesterday's drop on both the Dow Jones and the NASDAQ was due to technical factors, and not investor panic. But the Fed would continue to monitor the situation. In a brief interview at a campaign stop in Ohio, Amber Pike said that she was fully behind Prince for President, as were all her supporters, also. She had a new suit on, Sandy noted; she looked nice.

There had been a riot in the center of London, but there was disagreement about the cause. London? Was that where Mr. Prince was now? Sandy hoped he was safe. Or perhaps he was in Poland.

Political commentators were agreed that the turn-around in the fortunes of the Prince Campaign was unprecedented. Somehow, Willard Prince had captured the public mood in a way that the two old parties simply could not. People were now asking if there was any way that Prince could be stopped.

The Chinese moon mission had successfully passed another milestone: The main craft had now achieved moon orbit, and the lander, with its huge rover, was being prepared. But FNN's panel of experts doubted that such a massive machine could be landed safely, despite the moon's low gravity, citing a baby-milk scandal in Chengdu.

Sandy wondered what had happened to Chen. Had Barbara told Mr. Prince, after all? If not, then surely Amber would have said something; she was now fully on board with the Prince Campaign, after all. Chen was probably free already; Sandy could not believe that she was still a prisoner. Not in America. No doubt she would be released quietly; Mr. Prince would not want to confront the Communists until he was ready. Chen would be a formidable weapon for him. And Josh Merriweather would see to it that the CEO of Fairmeadow Security got fired.

All the same, it would be nice to know for sure. How could Sandy find out? Perhaps she could try asking Ray when he got back.

As Sandy explored the house, she wondered how often Mr. Prince would be able to visit in future. Imagine being stuck in Washington — that sink of iniquity — when you could be here! But perhaps this airy, untainted mansion would become Mr. Prince's *Western White House*. Sandy hoped so; there was something reassuring in the very sound of it. And if you had to wrack your brain to think of ways to save America, where better to ponder than in Mr. Prince's perfect desert garden?

The house was busier than Sandy expected. Everywhere, she found concerted activity: Cleaners, interior decorators, flower-arrangers, computer technicians, security consultants, picture-hangers, a pool-maintenance crew and, of course, gardeners. Milly had said that, given the ever-present threat posed by unauthorized recording equipment, all domestic staff had been told not to report for work during the retreat. That explained the present bustle. And also why Milly had been put in charge of catering. She wasn't wild about that, she lamented, but what could you do?

Sandy wandered from the library back down the main hall, and noticed that the double doors to the pool lounge, hitherto closed, were now open. Peeking inside, Sandy caught sight of a thin, elegant woman sitting at a glass-topped table by the steps that led down to the pool. She looked to be in her early sixties and wore wide-legged, silky black pants and a gold, sleeveless top. On the table was a wine bottle, and a single, large glass of red wine. It was ten-fifteen in the morning.

Sandy must have lingered in the doorway too long, because the woman turned and stared at her, a look of puzzlement on her face. For a long moment, Sandy felt as if she'd violated some sacred precinct. But then the mood changed in an instant.

"I know *you*. Come in!"

Sandy hesitated.

"Hey, you're good. Come on in. Sit down with me."

Sandy did as she was told. Close up, she could see that the woman's shoulder-length hair was a natural gray. And it was wet, pushed back behind the woman's ears as if she'd just gotten out of the shower.

The woman nodded at the wine bottle.

"Would you...?"

"No thanks."

"Good for you. You're Sandy, aren't you? I'm Eleanor."

Eleanor Prince. Mr. Prince's missing wife.

"Oh! I didn't expect to..."

"No, I'm supposed to be shipped off to Palm Beach while they hold their... Whatever it is. Should have gone yesterday, but... Well, I guess it didn't happen. Maybe today."

"Palm Beach?"

"Yes, we have a house down there, don't we? I think we do. Between you and me, I'd rather stay here. I cope better with the dry heat. But I guess we all have to do our bit. You certainly have, from what I hear. They never stop talking about you."

Sandy wondered whether Milly knew that Mrs. Prince was in residence. Milly hadn't said anything.

"And they tell me we're going to win. How does it look to you?"

"Ray thinks so. But he says a lot depends on the debates."

Eleanor took a gulp of wine. Then she reached into her bag and took out a box of pills. She swallowed two with another sip from her glass.

"Oh, now I see. That's why you're here."

"Yes. I think so."

"You're going to give Willard the common touch. I think that's just wonderful. No offense, you understand."

Sandy chose not to be offended.

"It can be hard to touch someone else's heart, even if your own is full."

"Really? Maybe that's right. I never thought of Willard's heart as being full of anything. But there you go..."

Talking to Eleanor was not so hard, Sandy thought. Eleanor was intelligent. She seemed to listen and understand. Why were people so uptight about her?

"I suppose you'll have to get used to being First Lady," Sandy said, feeling somewhat bolder.

"Me?"

A weak smile and a one-shouldered shrug.

"You know, that's not something that I can really envisage."

"Oh, but there'll be so many good things you can do. You know, for the children. Or the veterans. Or people who are suffering from their health."

"I'll be a great role model."

"Or there's the young people. I've been working with some of them. I think they need to find their way. You could teach them about financial responsibility."

"Oh, that would be perfect. Financial responsibility! They're right about you! You *are* a genius."

Was that sarcasm, or just the wine talking? Sandy decided it was neither; Eleanor liked to talk *witty*. As for the wine, well, drinking a bottle on your own at ten in the morning was not something that any respectable person in Sandy's admittedly limited social sphere would have done. Even Hunter Bill didn't start until after lunch. But Eleanor was not, and probably never had been, remotely a member of Sandy's socio-economic bracket. And if the rich were different — Sandy now knew for certain that they *were* — then it wasn't just that they had more money.

Moreover, Sandy now doubted all the barely-spoken insinuations that hung in the air at the Campaign HQ downtown. Even if Eleanor did have a problem, she wasn't a drunk, a basket-case, a wreck or a zombie.

In which case, what exactly was she?

"Can I ask you a question?" Eleanor said. "You don't have to answer."

"Okay."

"Do you get on with your children, if you have any?"

"We didn't have any."

"Why not?"

"Well, I think we thought... We were going to wait until the money —"

"Money?"

"Until we were more... I don't know. Secure, I guess?"

"Did you get to be secure?"

"Not really."

"What about your husband?"

"Oh, he's gone."

"Gone?"

"Yes."

Sandy hoped that Eleanor could read her body language. She didn't want to be rude, but...

"I shouldn't be prying. But maybe you're better off."

"Yes."

"Excuse me one moment."

Eleanor took out another tube of pills and inspected the label.

"Now, is this the right one? Blue label in the morning. Or was it green? What the hell."

She popped two more.

"You know what's funny?"

"What?"

"You talk of being *secure*. Suppose you had more money than you knew what to do with. But you just couldn't figure out exactly where it was coming from. Would you still be secure?"

"I don't know. What do you mean?"

Eleanor took another long draw from her glass, tipped her head back and closed her eyes. Sandy saw that she was rubbing the thumb of her free hand against her forefinger, as if on the nervous cusp of some decision.

"I'll tell you what I mean, but it's just between us, okay?"

"Sure."

"I challenged Peter. I said, explain this to me. And I showed him the spreadsheet I made. And he says, Eleanor, you don't know what you're doing. It's way too complicated for you. Look at you, with your puny little PC and your Excel. Leave it all to us. Don't worry."

"Peter?"

"Yes. I said, look, Peter — I *studied* math, I *studied* finance. This doesn't make any sense."

"Peter Giordano?"

"Yes, that's right. So then —"

"But he's..."

A long pause. Eleanor putting her glass down carefully on the table.

"Sandy, do you *know* something about him?"

"Didn't Ray tell you?"

"No. Why would he know anything about Peter?"

"Well, okay, but didn't..."

"Didn't what?"

"Didn't Mr. Prince..."

"Willard? What *are* you talking about, Sandy?"

"I don't know that I can tell you."

"I say you *can*."

*

S andy Quayle sat on a bench on the garden lounge terrace. Beyond Mr. Prince's desert garden, his golf course, and his mountains, the sun was setting. Night seemed to slide down into the valley from its slopes like some viscous, numbing drug seeping into the contours of a frazzled brain. Sandy welcomed it.

She thought about how she'd told Eleanor all about Peter Giordano and what she and Krall had witnessed: The shouting, the obscenities and the threats. The *money*. The being *finished*.

Then she recalled Milly's return to the house; her fright at finding Eleanor there; and her panic when a driver and a *nurse* arrived to take Eleanor to the airport.

And, finally, Sandy dwelled on her last, frantic exchange with the troubled Mrs. Prince, as they hauled her to her limo:

Eleanor, do you know anything about a girl called Chen Yu?

What, the Chinese trouble-maker? Honey, they shipped her back to Shanghai. In chains, would you believe?

CHAPTER 40

T eri Wolfe had never participated in a riot before. Then again, she had never visited London before. Perhaps they had them all the time. This one, however, had an international flavor: It had been convened by the local chapter of the Robin Hood Party. As per usual there was no mistaking them: Check out those red-and-green banners and those jaunty-but-sinister masks.

And, familiar as she had become with the general mind-set and temperament of the Robin-Hooders, Teri figured that they'd begun the day, with righteous brio and in high spirits, with a noisy but peaceful demo, and then something had gone wrong. Did it have anything to do with the differently-masked contingent whose main priority seemed to be to rearrange the street furniture, redecorate the buildings around Trafalgar Square, tip cars over and generally burn stuff down? Perhaps it had been these hangers-on — provocateurs? — who'd provoked the cops into showing up in such numbers, with their helmets, shields and water-cannon. It probably hadn't been the small group of China pro-democracy protestors now marooned in the center of the square at the base of Nelson's Column.

So now missiles flew, voices roared, and smoke drifted.

But, whatever the ultimate causes of this mob scene, it clearly wasn't a good place for Teri to be right now. She tried to flee back into the Underground station, only to find the entrance shuttered.

So where now? The riot had filled Trafalgar Square and was spilling out into adjacent streets. The wide avenue to Teri's right had been blocked by police vans. They had steel grilles across their windshields and bull bars up front. But it looked like the best option.

She ran.

The cops grabbed her, rammed her up against the side of a van and began to search her. One pulled Amber's phone from her pocket. She protested. They seemed to react to her accent.

"Tourist?"

"Yes."

"What are you doing here?"

"I just got off the subway."

"You're not allowed to be here. Go back to your hotel and stay there. Now!"

"My phone?"

They gave it back. She started to run again — and ran straight into Gunner and Weese, who had been hiding behind a TV satellite truck.

"I tell you, Flint. This one, trouble wherever she goes."

"Yeah. Think she started it?"

"Not really, Flint. But we *do* know her sympathies."

"She's got that attitude."

Teri gave Weese a meaningful glare and tapped the side of her boot against the pavement. Weese lurched backwards. He seemed wobbly and off-balance. Was it Teri's blow to his shin, or had he come straight from the pub? His cheeks were flushed.

"Seriously though, love, they've been looking for you. Where've you been?"

"Nowhere. Sight-seeing."

"Maybe she hooked up with that traitor guy," Gunner said.

"What, our Ricky?" Weese said. "The pious Mr. Ponton? Hardly likely, Flint. By all accounts he looks down on your anti-capitalist rabble. Very superior, he is."

Why were they talking about the boss of Big Data?

"Your guys fucked up, Nige."

"No need to rub it in, Flint."

"PM's gettin' his ass kicked."

"I dare say he is, Flint. Couldn't happen to a nicer fellow."

Tempting though it was to put the boot into Weese again, Teri elected to take the subtle approach.

"What are you idiots talking about?"

"Haven't you heard, love? It's all over town."

"What?"

"Our Rolls-Royce security service detained Mr. Ponton. And then immediately released him into the hands of an imposter."

"Friggin' useless —"

"Yes, all right, Flint. Anyway, his whereabouts are presently unknown."

"Gonna be hell to pay."

"Yes, Flint. If he is not recaptured, that will very likely be the case. Then again, we had a tip-off, didn't we?"

"Careful, Nige."

"What?"

Gunner nodded, indicating Teri.

"Oh, come off it, Flint. We like to have our little jokes, yes we do. But, let's face it, when it comes down to it, she's basically harmless, isn't she? Probably going to be kicked off the campaign soon anyway."

"Nige, I'm warning you."

"Warning me? Christ..."

"You cross that line, Nige, and..."

"And what?"

"You'll leave me no choice."

Weese exhaled noisily and looked up and down the street. He seemed deflated.

"Bloody hell, Flint."

"Don't make me do it, Nige."

"All right, all right. For Pete's sake, Flint. Oh look, someone wants you."

A woman with a clipboard had exited the satellite truck. Gunner strode off to talk to her. Weese watched him go. Then, with great caution, his habitual smirk lighting up again, he approached Teri.

"You see, we're hoping for a scoop."

Weese pointed to a building at the end of the street, near the square. Teri had seen it earlier; it was the South African embassy.

"We think he might try to sneak in there. Seeking sanctuary, as it were. Shame about the riot."

"Why there?"

Weese winked and tapped the side of his nose.

Gunner was watching them. Teri decided it was time to go.

"Take care, love. Watch out for the Molotov cocktails!"

Glancing back over her shoulder, Teri could see that the riot had engulfed the embassy. The police had formed themselves into a wall of shields, and were edging towards it. No one would be going in or out for a while. She walked on, not sure what to do.

What if Weese was right? Suppose he got his *scoop*. Could Big Data survive the capture of its creator and public face?

Yes, that face! The cringe-inducing mug-shot you saw on TV or in the newspapers. It was familiar enough to Teri, and to most people, probably. And Weese wasn't wrong; it did look way too pious. But perhaps what you saw was simply an unfortunate blend of too little physical beauty — that round, squashed dial and those small sticking-out ears — and too much moral determination. But if he was weird, so what? If it took a weirdo to defend freedom, privacy and transparency, so be it. The true weirdness was on the other side.

On she walked, not sure where she was going. She could have gone back to the hotel — she thought she knew the way — but she could feel that old Teri-Wolfe-on-the-cusp-of-history thing reasserting itself. And you know what? This time there was something to it. It wasn't a total fantasy. She had Chen's video in her pocket. And, any time now, she'd be getting that final confirmation from Meera.

But none of this, well, *unsettling* material could be trusted to the establishment media. It would be ignored, edited, spun, glossed, downplayed, distorted, blocked by lawyers or delayed by government officials — whom the media outlets would, out of professional courtesy and downright fear, consult before publication. Nor could someone like Teri publish it alone. Only Big Data had the necessary credibility, and also the resources to rebut and withstand attacks. And the fearlessness.

The streets had emptied. Teri stopped and looked around. No traffic. Anxious faces at windows, but nobody on the sidewalks. The sound of sirens. She really ought to get away from here, she thought; she felt exposed.

She turned in the direction of the hotel and ran down a narrow side-street. Half-way down she stopped. A dark-colored minivan blocked the roadway. It wasn't moving, but the engine was running. Despite the depth of the gloom here, it had no lights on. Two men in the front. Three in the back.

She backed up a couple of steps. Who were they? Hard-core professional looters waiting to move in? Actual provocateurs? A Fairmeadow-style snatch squad? Undercover cops? But then a bright light — the headlights of a fire truck? — shone up the street from the far end, throwing the minivan into silhouette. And, in the middle of the back seat...

Really? Could it be? Those *ears*...

She edged forward again. The minivan didn't move. There were no sidewalks in the street; it was too narrow. So she flattened herself against the brick wall on the driver's side and edged past. The occupants of the car ignored her. They looked away. Hiding their faces!

Teri walked a few steps past the minivan, then turned and looked back. Middle seat, in the back. Slumped down. Little round head. Sticking-out ears. It was *him*.

She went back and tapped on the window of the left-hand rear passenger door. Nothing happened. She rapped a little harder. Nothing. A third time. The window buzzed down.

"Hi," she said.

"What do you want?"

She leaned in and directed her question at the small, hunched shape in the middle seat.

"Excuse me, but are you Ricky Ponton?"

There was a delay — it was probably only seconds, but it seemed longer. Then she found herself penned in against the brick wall, two guys on either side of her. And, alone now in the car, there he was: The second-most-wanted criminal in the world. Looking kind of sheepish and surprised.

"Uh, guys," she said, "if you were heading down to the embassy over there... Well, my advice is, forget it. It's literally a riot scene. Cops everywhere. Plus they're expecting you. You know that guy Gunner from Freedom News? Big, square head? Well, *he's* there. He got a *tip-off*."

A short silence. Had she stunned them? She thought so. Then a thin, wiry man in shiny black shoes spoke up in an accent that Teri identified as Southern but not Deep South.

"Well, thank you kindly for the information, miss. But *who are you?*"

"Me? I'm Teri. Teri Wolfe. I work for the Prince Campaign."

Okay, so now she really *had* stunned them.

"The *Prince Campaign?* So what are you doing..."

"Oh, I kind of got caught up... Happens to me a lot. Listen, do you guys need somewhere to hole up? Because I know a really good place."

"You do?"

"Oh sure. It's tucked away. Nobody there. Except Buster."

"Buster?"

"He's a cat."

Another pause.

"Uh, Miss Wolfe... Are you serious, or are you —"

"Yes! I'm serious. It's in Hampstead."

"Okay... That might work. What kind of —"

"It's an office. But nobody uses it."

A hushed discussion began. Two Americans, she thought, and two South Africans. Plus Ricky. She leaned into the car again.

"Um, Mr... Can I call you Ricky? You, like, seem kind of familiar..."

"Yes, whatever. Ricky."

"See, the thing is, Ricky, this is pretty amazing luck meeting with you like this because —"

"Luck?"

"Yes, because I've got something for you."

"Sure you have."

"No, really. You'll see. I mean, I can come with you, right?"

He didn't seem hugely keen on that.

"What do you think, Jay?"

So *Jay* was the shiny-shoed Southerner who appeared to be in charge here.

"She's a crazy cat-lover. What the hell. We can't stay here."

He turned to Teri.

"You're gonna have to get in the back."

"Okay."

So then everybody got back in the car. Teri flipped the tailgate, climbed in, and yanked it shut again. Ricky ducked down and the car moved off, slowly.

They made it up to Hampstead with little difficulty; some of the roads were blocked, but Jay seemed to know his way around town. He took the car on a circuitous route. It was four-thirty by the time they got there, and already getting dark.

Teri released herself from the minivan's cargo bay and retrieved the key from under the flowerpot. The air was cold and damp; she could almost feel the dew of the morning beginning to condense. Not surprisingly, Buster had chosen to take himself indoors.

"So what is this place?" Jay said.

"Oh, this is Willard Prince's London office? But he doesn't use it."

"Willard Prince? This place?"

"Yeah. I see you're surprised."

"And he doesn't use it?"

"Ah, well. Kind of a long story. Don't worry, I'll explain."

Teri unlocked the door. Jay, Ricky, and the other American followed her upstairs. The two South Africans drove off in the mini-van.

Ricky seemed indifferent, or perhaps just tired — he slumped down in a corner and closed his eyes — but Teri could tell that the Americans were impressed.

"One would not expect the London office of a major investment fund to look like *this*."

"This is Ken, by the way," Jay said. "Also known as *Spock*."

Spock? Never mind.

"Well, yeah," Teri said. "Tell me about it. You should see the one in New York — oh, excuse me."

Teri's personal phone had blipped. It was a message from Meera. The message. She opened it.

Meera had written quite a lot. And there was an annoying amount of math. Teri jumped to the executive summary. Even here there was much technical waffle about *correlations* and *beta*, but the bottom line was pretty clear: The *probability* that all — or even five per cent — of those consistently winning trades in Barbara van Dornen's NACF account were legit was about one in a very, *very* large number.

A number so big, according to Meera, that it was greater than the number of electrons in the known universe.

It was official. Willard Prince was the Ponzi King of all time. And also the next President of the United States.

"Um, Ricky? Jay? Ken? Gentlemen, something kind of cool just happened. Why don't you take a seat? I've got a story to tell you."

CHAPTER 41

Ricky Ponton believed that he knew a thing or two about whistle-blowers. They were serious, tortured souls who suffered from an elevated sense of personal and public morality. Because of this, they were frequently regarded by their peers as loners, sticklers, monomaniacs or obsessives.

And they were fatalistic, for good reason. They knew that, once *outed*, they could expect to be smeared, denigrated, demonized and lied about by the powers they'd offended, and by those instruments that sucked up to power, or appeased it, or feared it. For that reason, most of Ricky's clients chose to out themselves, early on and on their own terms. The older ones gave up any hope of an easy or comfortable retirement; they knew that they could lose their families, and that, even were they to escape imprisonment, lawsuits and official harassment could reduce them to poverty. Yet it was the bravery of the younger ones, who sacrificed their entire lives, that always struck Ricky in the gut.

But this girl, Teri Wolfe, who really did seem to work for the Prince Campaign, was not like any whistle-blower Ricky had ever encountered. He struggled to get his head around what she seemed to have done. And whether she really understood what it would mean for her.

However, Ricky would have to put that aside for now. Action was necessary. Chen's video manifesto had to be uploaded to Big Data.

He looked at the single, outmoded computer with which Prince's London office had seen fit to equip itself. Was it even connected to the network? As a precaution, Ricky had ventured out to meet Spock without a phone or any electronic equipment. And it wasn't safe to use either Jay's phone or Spock's — let alone any of the three that Teri carried.

Then he examined the office's walls and ceiling. What were the chances? Well, it didn't matter. Video surveillance was so easy and ubiquitous now that it wasn't even worth asking the question.

"Look," he said, indicating the computer, "I've got some work to do here. Can someone find me a blanket?"

This request precipitated a ransacking of Prince's London quarters — both main rooms, the kitchenette and the bathroom — out of which a blue bath towel bearing the NACF logo was produced.

"That'll do."

The computer asked Ricky for a username and password. He entered *admin* for the username and guessed the password on the fifteenth attempt. This was a machine that nobody cared about. It was connected to the network, but not by fiber and the upload speed was slow. Too bad. It might take several hours to upload Chen's video.

He pulled the towel over his head, making sure to hide both the keyboard and the monitor. Then he logged into Big Data and downloaded the secure video-upload client that he kept for his own emergency use.

"Teri? Take the memory card out of Amber's phone and plug it in *here*... Okay, thanks."

Ricky started the upload; thanks to Prince's parsimony, it would take two hours and seventeen minutes. He checked his messages. Norway and Iceland were under sustained attack, but holding up. Brazil had been down for three hours but was back up again. Mr. Yu had sent another message.

"Teri? Where is Chen now?"

"They took her away in the helicopter. That's all I know."

Ricky hesitated. What could he say? He told Mr. Yu that his daughter had made a video, which Ricky was in the process of uploading, and that he hoped to have more information later. Then he looked at the metrics page for the secure messaging system Big Data had built for the Chinese Spring. Twenty-eight million messages had been exchanged, half of them originating in China. Volumes were mounting by the hour. He checked Big Data's main newsfeed for Asia. There were large demonstrations in Central in Hong Kong. The PLA was said to have been put on alert.

Ricky logged out of Big Data and ducked out from under his towel, leaving it draped over the monitor. Jay and Spock had been engaged in a whispered conversation. Now they stopped to look at him.

"Our assessment," Spock said, "is that the reaction we may expect from your Chinese associate will not be one of great equanimity."

"Ken's right," Jay said. "Jiao's gonna freak."

Ricky shrugged.

"Too bad."

Jay and Spock looked at each other.

"She could take it out on Chen," Jay said.

"Only if Chen's in China."

"Where else do you think she's gonna be?"

Ricky adjusted his towel. Chen was a classic whistle-blower type. And she knew what to expect. She'd said as much to camera. He fiddled with the towel again. For about a minute no one spoke.

"I can't stay here much longer," Teri said. "I'm supposed to be at some Bank of England meeting. So what I'm wondering is, what about the other thing?"

This question provoked a debate. Ricky said nothing. He tried to follow their arguments, but, in this particular moment, he found he didn't care whether Prince was exposed and destroyed, or whether he sold America out to the Chinese and went on to win four more years. Ricky was about to do to Chen what he had done to Kerri. If anything, it was worse. And Spock's *elegant* plan had been a bust, and Kerri would never even know that Ricky had tried.

"What is your feeling, Mr. Ponton?"

"Hm?"

"The question," Spock said, "is one of timing."

"Timing?"

"The New Pacific Partnership will fail in either case. That is *my* primary concern. But you, Mr. Ponton, have the option of employing Ms. Wolfe's material to destroy Willard Prince either now, or else after the election. When he is President. My recommendation would be *now*. But Ms. Wolfe favors the second option. She hopes for something that we might term political *creative destruction*. She is perhaps too optimistic."

That was it, Ricky thought. The girl was a romantic. She'd hooked up with the Robin Hood Party and bought into their fantasies. It was as fetching a display of innocence as you could hope for. Sure, all credit to her for providing the Chinese Spring with what could well be the *spark* that it required — perhaps its *defining moment* and its *iconic* image — and *bravo* for sinking the Prince Plutocracy before it even got its carried-interest boots on. Good for her. She was, after what appeared to be her own scatty style, a minor miracle. Perhaps she even thought she was saving America. As for Ricky — he thought she was doomed. It was just that, unlike Ricky's turncoats and traitors, she didn't know it.

"What do you think, Jay?"

"Either's good with me."

"You know what," Ricky said, dialing a number on Prince's desk phone, "I'm going to call Jiao. See what she thinks."

Jay and Spock looked at each other again.

"Who's Jiao?" Teri said.

"Don't ask," Jay said.

Jiao was, of course, asleep. Ricky got her out of bed. She sounded angry, and perhaps a little fearful. And she immediately threatened Ricky with dire but unspecified consequences, should he have anything to do with a sudden upsurge in anti-Party agitation across China, and especially in Hong Kong. But she softened considerably on learning that Ricky had got the goods on Prince after all, and insisted on hearing every detail.

"So what's your vote, Jiao?"

"Kill him now."

"Your vote is for now?"

"Yes!"

"Okay. I'll add up the votes and we'll see."

"*Votes?* What are you talking about? There are no votes. Do it now!"

"How about laying off my servers, then?"

"Um, yeah, don't worry about that."

"I want you to say to me that you owe me."

"What?"

"You owe me."

"Yes, okay. Let me get back to sleep."

"Say it."

"I owe you!"

"Okay. Don't forget. Whatever happens."

"I won't. Bye."

She hung up. It was useless, he thought. But he'd made his point.

"So it's now?" Jay said.

Ricky took a peek under his towel. Still over an hour to go.

"No. Let her sweat. Let's see how it goes with Chen."

Then Teri announced that she had to leave. Ricky copied all her Prince-related data onto Prince's antique PC and started another secure upload. Then he made her memorize a Big Data login that her comrades in the Robin Hood Party could use to upload the account information they'd stolen from Prince's offshore banks. And he told her to use it to keep in touch with him; she wasn't to attempt to contact him in any other way.

"Goodbye and good luck," he said. "And thank you."

"No problem! This is cool, isn't it? Making history?"

He smiled. And she was gone.

Jay and Spock were silent. Ricky tweaked his towel and checked his upload again. Still working. He heard Jay sigh behind him.

"This is what you do, isn't it?"

"Yes. It is."

Then Jay's phone rang. He answered and listened in silence for about a minute. Then he hung up.

"Okay, two things. First, Walter's figured out a way to get us back into the embassy."

Spock seemed interested.

"How?"

"He didn't say. We just need to be *prepared*."

"What was the other thing?"

"The Spratly Islands. Someone went and let off a ship-to-ship missile. And sunk a Chinese destroyer."

CHAPTER 42

Sandy Quayle believed that the dry electrical storm which had rumbled and crackled all night above Mr. Prince's desert gardens, golf course and mountains must have been a portent of *something*. In the morning, the air still felt dense and charged. And Sandy, having slept little, found herself laboring under a dull headache and a heaviness of spirit.

But Milly was all nervous energy. Stuff had happened! Plans had been ripped up! It was all because of that ship sinking. What ship? Hadn't Sandy heard? An American warship had sunk a Chinese ship! Near some islands! Its commander had gone rogue or crazy — or maybe not, because now they were saying it was a computer malfunction.

Anyhow, Mr. Prince had been forced to cancel his Foreign Policy Tour — which was kind of a shame, because it had been going so well — and fly back to Washington for a crisis summit. The outgoing President had virtually *pleaded* for Mr. Prince's help in calming the situation and smoothing things over diplomatically. Because, obviously, Mr. Prince was respected in China in a way that the current President, you know, with the lousy ratings, the weakness and all the scandals, wasn't.

So anyway, what this meant was that the retreat was going to start early, but without Mr. Prince. Krall and the others were on their way. Milly and Sandy had work to do; the domestic staff had already been told not to report.

They cleaned and tidied and prepared the bedrooms. Milly called the caterers to reschedule deliveries, and rearranged the furniture in the public rooms. Sandy raked the paths in the garden and cleared leaves from the pool. Campaign workers from Los Angeles delivered laptops and audio-visual equipment, then left for a nearby hotel where they were to set up a temporary campaign office. Together, Milly and Sandy set up the laptops and the audio-visual gear in the garden lounge. Sandy made sure that all the bathrooms were sparkling.

During the afternoon, the house began to fill up. Sandy spotted Mr. Prince's brothers and sons; they were staying in the adobe guesthouses that overlooked the golf course, Milly said. The sons looked happy, Sandy thought. Punchy, even. But the brothers just looked like they want to punch someone.

Josh Merriweather and the members of the Committee to Save America arrived by helicopter — the golf club had a helipad, Milly informed Sandy — and took over the pool lounge. Sandy thought she recognized the coal guy and the casino guy. The others looked much alike.

And then, finally, Megan and Ray Krall rolled up together in a taxi. Megan was delighted to see Sandy again. But Sandy thought Krall looked exhausted.

"Hey, Sandy. How're you holdin' up?"

"Oh, I'm fine."

"Uh-huh. Listen, I'm gonna get me a beer, then I'll see you in the garden lounge. You want somethin'?"

"No thanks."

Sandy sat on a couch in the garden lounge and waited. After ten minutes, Krall entered, beer in hand. He kicked the door shut with his heel, dumped his backpack on the coffee table in front of Sandy, and then collapsed onto the couch beside her.

"I truly *hate* the Foreign Policy Tour," he said. "It's always a disaster. Guess we got off light, this time, though. Thanks to Captain Hair-Trigger."

He sucked on his beer, wiped his mouth on his sleeve and took a long, studious look at the garden lounge, from one end to the other.

"You think Josh has got this place wired?"

"Wired? You mean like —"

"Well, it don't matter at this point. Gonna have to get used to it anyway. So. You wanna do some debate prep?"

"Okay."

"I don't know how we're supposed to do it without Willard, but... I guess I'll pretend to be him. We'll look at some likely questions, and the answers I've written, and you can tell me how they sound, okay?"

"All right."

Krall unzipped his backpack and pulled out a pink folder.

"Here. How about you just take a quick look through that while I finish my beer?"

Sandy opened the folder and took out a loose stack of paper. There didn't seem to be any questions on the top sheet. In fact, the first few pages seemed to contain nothing but emails. Someone had been through them with a yellow highlighter. And there were handwritten notes in the margins.

Krall drank his beer, staring out into the garden, as if distracted or deep in thought.

Sandy flicked through the rest of her stack. Nothing but emails. No sign of anything that looked like a Q&A. She glanced at Krall. He didn't seem to notice. So she looked down at the page in her hand and began to read.

These were personal messages, she thought. They had little to do with the election, and she saw no mention of issues or policy. And some of the highlighted sections were *very* personal. She flicked through the next few pages, looking at the sender and receiver addresses. Many of these were unknown to her, but not the names of Mr. Prince's two opponents.

"Ray?"

"Mm?"

"What is this?"

Krall looked at the page Sandy was holding.

"Aw, shoot. That's the wrong file. Uh, you want to give me that back and I'll give you the —"

"Are you reading their email?"

Krall took a moment to finish his beer. Then he burped.

"Kind of looks that way don't it? Uh, this here's the right —"

"Is that legal?"

"Well, you're asking a difficult question there, Sandy."

"How did you get this?"

"Now, you're gonna have to ask Josh about *that*. Way too technical for me."

"What else are you doing?"

"This stuff goes on, Sandy. I kind of wish it didn't, but..."

"Why do you even need to do it? We're... You're winning anyway, aren't you?"

Krall gathered up the email print-outs, stuffed them back into their folder and slipped it into his backpack.

Sandy felt the air around her fizzle with an oppressive static. It made her head hurt.

"Why?" she said. "You said *I'd* made all the difference."

"That's true. A big difference. But... In this game, well, some shots are too good not to take. I mean... Sandy, that guy *really was* employing illegals."

"You bugged him."

"He was being hypocritical."

"And you bugged Mr. Prince."

"I thought I explained that. And if I hadn't, we wouldn't have known about that guy Giordano, and —"

"Eleanor didn't know about that. She didn't trust him. She didn't know where the money —"

"Eleanor?"

"Peter told her she didn't understand. But that's wrong, because she studied finance and —"

"Wait a moment. You *talked* to Eleanor?"

"Yes."

"When?"

"Yesterday."

"She was *here?*"

"Ray, she told me about Chen."

Sandy got up out of her seat and stumbled against the coffee table. She felt dizzy. Out of the corner of her eye she could she Krall watching her.

"Sandy, listen. I only just found out about that. There was nothin' I could do. Those two guys — Gunner and the other one — they found out somehow, and they... Well, I guess they told somebody."

Sandy made for the door on to the terrace, steadying herself against Milly's carefully arranged furniture as she went.

"Sandy?"

"I don't know if I want to do this any more. Does Mr. Prince know about *any* of this?"

281

"Aw, c'mon, Sandy. Listen, did you say anything to Eleanor about —"

"I don't remember. I need some air. Excuse me, please."

"Sure. Look, uh, there's one other thing… Your… Nah, I guess we better do that later."

Sandy slid open the glass door to the terrace and stepped outside, closing the door behind her. Krall did not follow. She took out the sunglasses Milly had bought for her, slipped them on, and picked her way unsteadily out into Mr. Prince's desert garden.

The sprinklers fizzed and the air seemed to hum. In her ears, a leaden atmosphere pressed against the uneven pulse of her heartbeat.

She wandered, losing herself first in the singing gardens, then in the grassy margins and shady recesses of the golf course and, finally, in the scrub and thorn of the mountains' edge.

*

S andy returned to Mr. Prince's desert pavilion at dusk. The light was fading fast but the sand, pebbles, rocks and dirt of the garden still radiated heat. During her hours in the wilderness, Sandy had put her fears aside and prayed for guidance but, as yet, none had come. Thus she was not at peace — not with Ray Krall, not with the Campaign, not with herself. Moreover, she was tired, and she felt dirty. And her headache had not gone away. She thought she would take her medication, shower, and try to sleep.

But her haphazard route back to the house had brought her to the pool garden. Now, as she watched, low-level lights illuminated, all around the edge of the pool. Uplighters clicked on beneath the palms. And carefully-angled spotlights snapped on in order to pick out the sculptures and artworks that hid amongst the foliage. Some of these were abstract; and some, Sandy thought, must have been inspired by indigenous folk-art.

The pool and the garden were empty of people; it looked as though Josh Merriweather and his fellow saviors had retired to the pool lounge. Sandy could hear their voices.

She changed her mind. Instead of returning to her room, she sat at a table by the side of the pool. The garden was beautiful at night. And the pool was a mirror for the stars. Yes, she thought, I get the message: God's going to get back to me, of course he is. He's busy. But in the meantime, he's saying *look what I created, Sandy — isn't it wonderful?* There were worse ways to be *on hold*, she thought.

Someone had left a document on the table. It looked like a sales brochure or a corporate report. Presumably, a member of Josh's party had been reading it. Sandy picked it up. *The New Pacific Partnership,* she read. *Securing the Future: The Corporation as Super-Citizen.* What did that mean?

Sandy flipped the document open. On the first page she found an *Introduction*, by Josh Merriweather. There was a picture of Josh, dressed in khakis, and a denim shirt with rolled-up sleeves over a T-shirt that bore the word *Disrupt*. He had mussed-up hair, a scratchy, juvenile beard, and those blue eyes. The caption beneath the photo described him as a *cyber-visionary*, a *social entrepreneur* and a *big-data futurist*. He was also the inventor-creator of DumpChat and DirtBaggr, and a major investor in the cutting-edge Fairmeadow Group.

Josh's *Introduction* didn't make any sense to Sandy, so she closed the document and put it back on the table. Then she looked at the pool again. A warm breeze riffled through the garden and rippled the surface of the water. She felt a sudden, wanton desire, a pleasurable urge for which she felt instantly guilty. Could she? Would anyone mind? Was there any reason not to?

Well, of course, she had no swimsuit, but the thin, linen shorts and cotton T-shirt that Milly had found for Sandy wouldn't weigh her down. And they would dry out pretty quickly too, wouldn't they? She got up and ventured down the wide, curved steps of the pool until the water came up to her knees. The temperature was perfect. She waded in further. The water brushed her thighs. When was the last time she'd been in a swimming pool? Was it when she and Johnny-boy were in Cancun, and he'd confessed that the hot-tub business had been bust for three months and he'd borrowed the money for the vacation?

She lunged forward into the water and struck out, freestyle, for the far end, surprised to find that she could still swim after all. At the deep end, by the foot of the steps that led up into the pool lounge, she trod water until she got her breath back. The effort had intensified her headache, but the rest of her body felt weightless and refreshed. Even the ache in her leg, which had returned during her sojourn in the wilderness, seemed to dissolve away, though the swelling remained.

And from behind her, up in the pool lounge, there came the sound of a single voice. It was soft, warm and measured, and yet there was an edge and an insistence to it. It was Josh's voice, she decided, even though she'd hardly heard him speak before. He was talking to the Committee members, she supposed. It sounded like a lecture — composed, dense and technical. She tuned out from the meaning of the words — which was not at all transparent to her anyway — but permitted Josh's melodious voice and honey-sweet tone to collect in her ears each time her gentle laps brought her to his end of the pool.

"We talk about inalienable rights, but rights have to be earned in our modern world, where we must compete for resources and attention. And who can say that the corporation, that spans the globe, that creates jobs by the thousand, that generates wealth and donates its technology, often for free — who can say that such a corporation has not earned rights? Even superior rights?"

Sandy wondered whether anyone would ever get to see Chen's video testament. What had Teri done with it? That girl had smarts and initiative, but did she really know what she was doing? It was hard to imagine a ditzy little thing like her going up against the Communists.

"We believe in free speech. And when we talk about free speech we mean many things. We mean your social choices, your online profile, your personal network and your rankings. Your consumer niche, your credit score. Your religious or political affiliation. All of these things make you what you are. They are choices. And the sincerest expression of choice is what you do with your money. Therefore money, or capital, is the purest expression of free speech that our society has yet discovered."

What would happen to Eleanor when she got to Palm Beach? Would she get the help she needed? Perhaps Barbara would go to her. Sandy hoped she'd done the right thing in telling Eleanor about Peter Giordano. It looked as though Eleanor had been right all along, and Mr. Prince had been too trusting.

"We will protect free speech. But we will go even further, and enable unlimited free speech. We will ensure that everything that is said, or even thought, can be heard. By anyone. Anywhere. At any time. And for all time. Except for privileged corporate communications, and subject to national security and the standard sign-up agreement."

Sandy was disappointed in Ray Krall. She didn't believe there was wickedness in his heart. But he had allowed himself to be led astray by personal ambition. And he had been corrupted by big-government politics and *business-as-usual*. On Freedom News, they used to talk about it all the time. Sandy hadn't really understood what they meant until now. Mr. Prince would try to change all that. And if Josh Merriweather really was the visionary that everyone seemed to think he was, then he had better help too, hadn't he?

"What we have gotten used to calling *democracy* is as out-of-date and obsolete as MS-DOS. Look at your smartphone. Think about what it can do. And now think about the last time you went down to the VFW or the Junior High to vote. Pretty low-tech, wouldn't you say? But the key thing is this: What effect did your vote have? Not much, I think you'd say. But we are going to change that. Nobody knows what you think or what you desire more than the modern networked corporation. No politician or congress or parliament can respond to the will of the people like we can. That's the first big lesson I learnt at DirtBaggr."

Sandy decided that she would not leave the campaign yet. And she would continue to help Ray win the election for Mr. Prince, in any way that she could. That was her mission, after all. And who was she to suppose that she would be able to fulfil her mission without sacrifice?

"Sometimes you hear talk about *people power*. There's a belief out there, that you'll come across sometimes, that says change has to be *bottom-up* to succeed, or to be legitimate. The idea is that, somehow, people are going to come together spontaneously and, somehow, reconfigure the whole system. And, somehow, this reconfigured system is going to be better. You notice how many times I have to say *somehow*. Because this is hopelessly inefficient, and we simply cannot allow it. It's destructive, I'll give you that. But it's not creative. It's the wrong kind of *disruption*, if you will. All of the capital that we've built up — of whatever kind — could be lost. If you're going to reconfigure the system, you've got to do it based on the data. And it's only the people who *have* the data who are qualified to do it. In fact, they — that is, we — have the *responsibility* to do it."

"Hey, Sandy."

Krall was standing at the shallow end of the pool. Sandy stopped swimming and waded to the foot of the steps.

"Are you okay?"

"Mostly."

"What about the leg?"

"Still aches."

"You finished with your swim?"

"I guess."

"Wanna sit with me a while?"

"Okay."

Sandy climbed out of the pool and dripped her way over to the table where Krall sat — the same one that Sandy had occupied earlier. Krall picked up Josh's report and flicked through it.

"Bullshit."

He flung it away. It landed in the pool.

"Sandy, you remember when we were at my place? We had the doc come?"

"Yes."

"Uh, Sandy, this ain't exactly my business but... Well, I guess you were real sick a while back?"

"Yes."

"Okay. Well, did they tell you... Did they warn you..."

"That it could come back? Yes, I remember they said that."

Krall was looking at her. Briefly, she met his gaze.

"Doc says you need to start treatment now."

"Does he?"

"Sandy, I know you don't have insurance. But I want you to know that ain't a problem."

"Isn't it?"

"No. I'm going to take care of it."

"They said it would be expensive."

"Don't matter. Plus, if Willard wins, I'm gettin' that bonus I told you about."

"I don't know."

"You don't... C'mon, Sandy. Don't say that."

"It doesn't feel right."

"You have to start now, Sandy. The doc says it's got into your bones. Please? You want me to beg, I will."

If this was another test, Sandy thought, it was a cruel one. But a test was a test. When God wanted to give you a gift, he used someone like Mr. Prince. Not a man like Ray Krall.

"I can't take your money, Ray."

She got up and dripped her way back to her room.

CHAPTER 43

I t turned out, for some reason, that the Spratly Crisis Summit, convened in Washington to defuse diplomatic tensions exploded by the sinking of a Chinese warship by an American missile, was unable to find any use for the tart and waspish stylings of a self-absorbed, twenty-something blogger-girl.

Thus Teri Wolfe was dispatched directly from London back to New York, while the Court of the Prince Regent headed to the nation's capital in order to rally to the Commander-in-Chief's side, while not publicly exploiting the outgoing administration's embarrassment. Prince had even offered to suspend his campaign, though not even the meanest insider, like Teri, took this to imply that Ray Krall would be suspending *his*.

Back in the cubby-hole in the servants' quarters on Park Avenue, Teri exchanged messages with Meera. A meeting was arranged, but not in the Park. Meera didn't want to go there; Teri was to come downtown. Meera would be waiting by the Coffee Truck.

y there?

u will c.

Teri snuck out of the apartment. The Secret Service guys weren't there, so it was only necessary to evade Gloria, whose potential contribution to Sino-American rapprochement had also been deemed slight.

Meera was pacing up and down by the Coffee Truck — which looked to be doing a roaring trade. In fact, Teri thought, there was a distinct *frisson* of excitement in the air. Excitement? Or...

"Don't worry," Meera said. "Our money is safe."

"Our money?"

"Any place with sand, palm trees and anonymous corporations. Anywhere that the one per cent stash their loot. We're there. RHP Investments. Sherwood Asset Management. Marian Capital. Get it? We're using the system's own strength against it. Like judo, or whatever. Want coffee?"

"Oh, yeah. Please. Uh, so you've been busy?"

"Yup."

"Well, me too. I actually met Ricky Ponton."

287

"You did? Wow! Go girl! How did you manage it?"

"Oh, I kind of tracked him down and helped him out of a tight spot."

"So what was he like?"

"Kind of a grump, actually. Looks better on TV. But it was really cool."

"So you gave him the stuff?"

"Uh-huh. He's releasing the video. But we've got to send him the rest of the Ponzi data. He gave me a login. You've got to memorize it. You can't write it down."

"Okay. Hit me."

Meera's memory was impressive, Teri thought. Perhaps it was her banker training. Or maybe not — questioned on oath, your typical banker couldn't recall *anything*.

They drank their rocket-fuel coffee.

"So I think it's gonna happen today," Meera said. "That's why I dragged you down here."

"What?"

"The next crash. Check this out."

Meera had the Freedom News web site up on her phone. There was a video clip from Flint Gunner's Market Madness.

So what's your take on the current mayhem in the markets, Flint?

This sucker's going down, Nige.

"See?"

"Like they know what they're talking about."

"It's serious. And you know what? The market might expose Prince before we do. If it crashes and all his investors want out..."

"He hasn't got the money."

"Not even close."

"We've got it."

"No, Teri. We've only got a tiny fraction of it. Most of it is gone forever."

"Where?"

"Well, basically, he and his brothers and the rest of his family, and a few of their closest friends — they blew it all."

"But how could they blow *that much?*"

"I guess, over time, they got really good at it."

They finished their coffee.

"The fun really starts," Meera said, "when the investors realize that there never were any profits. At all. So when investor A takes cash out, they're actually taking it directly from investor B. You can imagine the lawsuits."

"Wow."

"Okay, so let's go somewhere private and I'll tell you about our plans."

"We have plans?"

"Sure. For the Prince Secret Bus Tour, remember?"

"Oh, that. Uh, what sort of plans?"

"Come on."

They holed up in a gloomy basement bar up on Broadway. Meera said they'd be able to watch the fun on the TV monitors and financial newsfeeds suspended from the bar's gaudy, gilded ceiling. The bar would remain empty, Meera predicted, until its regulars capitulated and swarmed in to numb their pain.

"Okay, so look at this."

Meera produced a spreadsheet print-out from her bag. Teri scanned it. At each stop along Prince's Bus Tour to Save America, Meera had planned what her column heading denoted as an *exploit*. Each of these was described in detail, as was the amount of money to be deployed. It looked like Meera intended to emulate the Prince family's spending style.

"What do you think?"

"You're really going to do all that?"

"*We* are, yes. You *are* going to be on the bus tour, right?"

"I think so."

"Because we'll need to coordinate. We need you on the inside. We need you on that bus."

"Er, okay. But..."

"I know you wouldn't want to let Nile down."

God, Teri thought — was Meera ruthless, or what?

"No."

"Good. Do you like our ideas?"

"Oh, they're amazing. How do you come up with stuff like that?"

"You just have to ask yourself what Robin Hood would do. You know, if he was around today."

"You know he's a fictional character, right?"

Meera grinned.

They bought themselves bottled water and salty snacks and settled in to watch the show.

Stock index futures were way down — a bad sign, according to Meera. Data from the repo market suggested that a credit crunch was underway. Over on FNN, Flint Gunner claimed to detect a *flight to quality*. Which was fine if you had access to, say, the New American Century Fund.

Meera told Teri all about how her grandparents had immigrated from Bombay, as it was in those days, and started a printing business in New Haven. The firm had lost out to larger competitors before her father could inherit it, and her parents had become academics, specializing in finance.

"Look," Teri said.

A Freedom News Alert: A wave of unrest was spreading across China. Local sources were saying that the immediate cause was a *video* distributed by Big Data Underground. But many people were asking if it might be work of an organized terrorist network, that being the firm view of the Chinese central government.

"You did that," Meera said.

"No, people don't take any notice of me. It was Chen."

Willard Prince had taken time out from the Spratly situation to appeal for calm and restraint on all sides, and to call for a strengthening of high-level contacts between the US and China. Asked about the turmoil in the markets, he said that no systemically-important institutions were at risk, and that the financial authorities stood ready to act if they were.

"Well are they or aren't they?" Meera said. "Does he think this sucker's going down or not?"

"More nuts?"

"Who's more nuts?"

"No, do you *want* more nuts?"

"Oh, okay."

Meera told Teri that she'd wanted to study computer science, but her parents had pushed her into doing an MBA so that she could get a high-paying job on Wall Street. But — guess what? — she'd discovered that the culture on the Street didn't really gibe well with a stroppy, tall, independent, liberal-minded girl of Indian heritage. Plus she'd realized that the markets were rigged from top to bottom. Willard Prince was just the Ponziest Ponzi of them all.

Then, at about eleven-thirty, it happened.

All of the main stock market indices crashed, in a welter of program trades, insider panics, high-frequency trading and emergency develeraging. Exchange circuit-breakers kicked in and out and then blew up like the electrical grid under attack from remorseless zombie space aliens.

Three large banks, said by none other than Willard Prince to be *not at risk* only an hour earlier, were rumored to be on the brink and seeking the assistance of the Fed, or the Treasury, or perhaps even Willard Prince himself.

TV anchors were out on Wall Street, accosting passers-by and asking them where they thought this would all end. Nobody knew. So they reported that the Coffee Truck was running out of coffee. Things were *that* bad.

"Okay," Meera said. "Now things get interesting. Let's see what Prince does. He can't afford more than a few redemptions from the fund. If they all want out, he's toast. Why don't you head back to your fancy apartment and listen out for rumors?"

"I live in a closet."

"And I'll go see if I can upload the rest of the Ponzi stuff to Big Data. Talk to you later."

Teri took the number one train back uptown. Some of her fellow riders look wild-eyed. The word was spreading: That *frisson* wasn't excitement any more; it was the sweet, delicious buzz of *financial panic*.

When she got back to the apartment, she found it more populated than before. The California retreat had been cut short because of the market meltdown. The Prince brothers had arrived. They looked furious. Milly was there, but she still wasn't talking to Teri, it seemed. Teri looked for Sandy, but there was no sign of her. Then Teri ran into Megan, who said that Gloria was looking for Teri and wanted to talk to her.

Teri tried to sneak past Gloria's office, but her door was open and Teri was spotted.

"Teresa! Come here, please."

Teri slunk into Gloria's office.

"Sit down."

Sit down? That didn't sound good. Especially given the way Gloria spat it out. Teri sat.

"Teresa, I've been reviewing some of your material. I must say it's not what I was expecting."

"It isn't?"

"No. Not at all. I thought you understood that the primary purpose of your, ah, *blog* — indeed its *only* purpose — was to increase support for Mr. Prince among people of your, ah, *generation*."

Was? Ominous.

"Oh, I understand. That's what I'm doing."

"Well the results are in, I'm afraid. I'm told that Mr. Prince is supported by only eight per cent of low-to-middle-income millennials."

"Oh. But that might actually be *good*."

"It was eleven per cent before you started *blogging*."

"Yes, but —"

"I'm not blaming you. Well, not entirely. And it's not so much the content, it's the tone. The attitude. And the way you sometimes refer to Mr. Prince as *Willy*."

Hey, she'd left out the *Fat!*

"I can tweak it. Just tell me —"

"I'm sorry, Teresa. The decision has been taken."

"Decision?"

"It comes directly from Barbara, I'm afraid. So it's entirely out of my hands."

Barbara! Milly!

"But..."

"You'll need to collect your things immediately."

"My things?"

"And I'll need your campaign phone back now."

Gloria held out her hand. Teri thought furiously; had she left anything incriminating on it? No, she didn't think so. She handed over the phone.

"And the charger."

"It's in the cubby-hole."

"The what?"

"My room."

"In that case you can just leave it there. I'll collect it later."

"Erm..."

"Yes?"

"Well, I was supposed to get some... You know, like a salary? It was going to be *adequate?*"

Gloria made a face. It was the sort of face, Teri thought, that Gloria might have made, had she been invited to strip naked and sit cross-legged on her desk, smoking a joint. *Not gonna happen*, in other words.

"That was entirely contingent upon satisfactory completion of the trial period."

"Oh."

"I'm very sorry, Teresa. But I'm sure you'll fall on your feet. Goodbye."

Teri tramped back to the servants' quarters and gathered her meager possessions together. In a fit of pique, for which she instantly felt guilty, she kicked the phone charger under the bed.

What now? Crash Josh Merriweather's pad at the Aspire building and bunk up with Sandy? Hardly. And where *was* Sandy, anyway? Or how about checking in at the Plaza? Teri's remaining resources might stretch to one night in the worst room. She had some British pounds left; would they take those?

What about crashing with Meera? Tricky. Meera had lamented to Teri, while they were watching Gunner freak out at the merest suggestion of another round of *bailouts*, that she'd had to move back in with her parents, out on Long Island. Teri on Long Island? Meh.

Money. What a ridiculous, annoying, vicious problem it was. But wait a moment. What had Meera said? *Our money is safe*. Our money. Six billion dollars. In the region of. But no, that would just be... What? A little, tiny bit of street justice? No, it was a non-starter. Meera would be scandalized. There was only one option. One, lousy, miserable option.

Back to Bayonne.

*

The first thing Teri noticed was that her apartment key no longer fitted the lock. She rang the bell. Luckily, there was someone at home. But it wasn't Alicia and it wasn't Burgandy.

"Who are you?"

"Yolanda. Who are you?"

"Teri. Is Alicia —"

"Are you that girl who used to live here?"

"No, I'm the girl that still does live here."

"No, you're not."

"What?"

"Your lease got canceled."

"What lease? Alicia's the one who —"

"That's right. She canceled you. You were behind on the rent."

"Look, I've got nowhere else to go."

"Should have thought of that."

"Are you on the couch?"

"Yeah. That stinky old couch."

"It stank long before I was here."

"So you say."

"Trust me."

A pause. Then *capitulation*.

"Okay. Fine. Let me in so I can take my stuff."

"It's right here."

Yolanda yanked a large, black garbage bag out from behind the door and dropped it at Teri's feet.

"That's your stuff."

The door slammed shut. Teri stared at the garbage bag.

She was too young, of course, to have witnessed it herself, but Teri had heard tell of a time when it was just about survivable to be a *bag lady* in New York City. Not these days, though. Someone had redrawn the line between poverty and crime.

She rummaged through the garbage bag and retrieved a few viable items of clothing, a couple of books, and her iron-age laptop. These she stuffed into her backpack. Then she hauled the garbage bag out of the building and tossed it into a handy dumpster. Wait — was it possible to sleep in a dumpster? Nah, what if she didn't wake up when the truck came?

Seriously, though — what now?

Well, what about mom and dad? Teri would have to trek upstate and hope that they hadn't rented her room out. Which they probably had. And she didn't think she could face them anyway. Plus she wasn't ready to give up on Meera and the *exploits*. Some of them sounded seriously cool.

An idea came to her. It was slightly desperate, and definitely a long shot, but if it worked it would be quite something.

Ray Krall.

Ah, but she didn't have his number on her personal phone; it had only been on the campaign phone that Gloria had repossessed. Teri hadn't memorized it. Okay, what about calling Megan? Teri *did* have Megan's number.

"Megan?"

"Hi Teri."

"Uh, can I ask you something? Do you have Ray's number?"

"I'm sorry, Teri. I'm not at liberty to provide that information."

"Huh? Why are you talking funny?"

Megan lowered her voice.

"Nobody's supposed to talk to you any more, Teri. Barbara sent a memo around. I'm sorry you got fired. I kind of liked your stuff. It was... Sassy."

Sassy?

"Yeah, thanks. I just need Ray's number, because —"

"I can't, Teri. They're recording all calls now. Sorry. I've got to go."

Megan hung up. Teri shivered. It was a cold afternoon, and a bitter night was forecast.

Was there anyone else Teri could call? Sandy didn't have a phone. Milly wasn't talking to Teri on account of the ding on her mom's car — and now it sounded as though Barbara had issued some kind of *fatwa* against Teri.

Krall had a place downtown, close to the Campaign HQ. But where, exactly? It had to be within walking distance, because Krall didn't drive to the office. Teri felt sure she would recognize Krall's car — the big, black BMW. She'd ridden in it. It had a *Tar Heels* bumper sticker. Not many of *those* in lower Manhattan! If she could find the car, she could waylay Krall when he returned to the apartment.

It was worth a try. Teri still hadn't figured out exactly where Krall was coming from regarding Prince and the *shit* that Krall had accused Teri and Nile of plotting. But he cared about Sandy, so maybe he wasn't a total hard-ass.

Teri hiked up her backpack, hugged herself against the cold, and began the trudge back to the train station.

CHAPTER 44

Ricky Ponton stank of the ocean. But it hardly mattered; he hadn't showered for three days. What irked him was that Jay and Spock still smelled — as far as Ricky could tell — of sunshine and daisies.

Walter Gabo's brilliant plan for returning the three of them to the relative diplomatic safety of the South African embassy, once the riot in the square had been put out, involved a large catering truck, a seafood buffet, and a non-existent embassy reception. It had been enough to get them past the police guard around the building. But it turned out that few of the embassy's junior staff had a taste for lobster or smoked salmon.

Ricky's sanctuary was a file storage room on the top floor, overlooking the square. It was ten square meters of dust and paperwork. There was a small desk. Someone had found him a laptop. There wasn't room for a bed, and it was already dark. Where would he sleep? How long would the South Africans put up with him? Walter said that diplomatic protocol demanded that they acknowledge Ricky's tendentious presence.

Sanctuary? He looked out of his foggy window and saw his younger self sitting by his tent under the sodium lights in the square. *You had it and you blew it.* No more bloody lemurs for Ricky.

It was all Spock's fault.

"Get the bastards on the phone," Ricky said. "Tell them they can have me. All they have to do is let Kerri go."

Spock said nothing.

"*They* already called *him*," Jay said. "There's not going to be a deal. They know you're here. Ken's been demoted. He's been recalled to Washington. They want him on a plane tonight."

"Is he going?"

Jay looked at Spock. Spock nodded.

"Yes. I'm sorry."

"I've got to leave, too, Ricky," Jay said. "It's way too hot here. And the guys at *the office*... Well, they're not returning my calls any more."

"Where are you going?"

"Jo'burg with Walter. Then Windhoek."

"And I'll still be sitting here a year from now?"

"It's gonna be over long before that, Ricky."

Ricky stared at them. Spock looked at the floor. But Jay met Ricky's gaze.

"All right. Go. Get out of here. We're done."

"We do appreciate everything you did, Ricky. Truly."

A shrug from Spock. Jay's wistful smile.

"And Ricky — if you're going to pull the plug on Prince, do it *now*. Okay? *Now*."

Ricky watched them leave. Then he got up and paced his new sanctuary like a captive beast, hoping that the stink of feral anger might overwhelm the stench of fish.

At length, he cooled off. But the odor remained. He turned on his laptop, logged in to Big Data and downloaded his secure remote dashboard. Brazil was down again, but Iceland and Norway were up, albeit under constant attack now. In his priority in-box was a single item.

An associate of the doomed, cat-loving, American hipster girl, going under the name of *Meera*, had uploaded a ton of financial data. It wasn't Ricky's specialty, so he forwarded it to Iceland for urgent attention.

But Meera's commentary was plain enough for a sweaty, stressed-out battler-kid stuck in a diplomatic attic: Here are Prince's offshore accounts, including those in London; here's where all the money comes in; here's where a little of it gets siphoned off into the New American Century Fund, to pay out on the small number of redemptions that Prince typically gets; here's where most of it gets flushed into a network of offshore cess-pools in order to be freshened up and fumigated before moving on; and here's where it trickles, splashes and surges into the personal accounts of the Prince family, some close family friends and some guy called Aylsham in London; and here's a summary of how much has gone missing, it's, oh, about a hundred and eighty-seven billion dollars; and we hope you find this of interest, Mr. Ponton.

Yes, he found it of interest. He also found it bloody annoying. It was petty corruption, albeit on a gargantuan scale. It was rich people stealing from rich people — those Robin Hood idiots got that bit right. But Big Data didn't exist to expose rich crooks with their hands in the till. Jesus bloody Christ, imagine the workload if it did! Big Data's job was to expose the Big Lie. A big lie such as, for example, the New Pacific Partnership.

But how could you expose something that was so deliberately technical and obscure that the great lied-to public couldn't begin to understand it? They didn't even understand how capturing metadata was *worse* than tapping the actual content of phone calls. Put alongside the NPP, Prince's crimes were pathetically unsophisticated.

But maybe there was a use for them. Ricky looked up the Prince Campaign web site. Then he poked around for a phone number. But, just as he was reaching for the phone, it rang.

"Yeah?"

"What do you think you are doing, Mr. Ponton?"

"Hello, Jiao. How'd you know where I was?"

"The BBC."

"Great. What do you want?"

"Why are you supporting terrorism?"

"Talk sense or fuck off."

"Do you understand how much blood there will be on your hands?"

"Not mine. Yours."

"Why are you making a martyr of this girl?"

"What?"

"This Yu Chen. You are responsible."

"No, I haven't even... Wait a moment."

Ricky checked Big Data's home page. There was a picture of Chen, and a link to her video. But there was also a picture of Mr. Yu. Underneath, he appeared to write in his own voice: He accused the Party of kidnapping Chen from America and *disappearing* her. He demanded that she be produced, and be shown to be alive. Ricky figured that Norway had approved the post while he'd been trapped with the cat-girl in Hampstead. It was within their rights and responsibilities to do so, particularly if Ricky were uncontactable.

Even so... But Ricky would have done the same for Kerri, wouldn't he?

"Well, *is* she a martyr?"

An angry torrent of Mandarin from Jiao.

"Take it down."

"I can't. We don't work like that."

"Why are you doing this? Why aren't you attacking Prince?"

"That's coming up."

"Do it now!"

"It has to be done properly. Why don't you let Chen go?"

"It is not possible."

"Just produce her, then."

A long silence.

"First you show the world she's unharmed," Ricky said. "Then we do Prince."

The line went dead. Ricky glanced out of the window. In the square, a detachment of paramilitary vehicles had lined up, headlights on, facing the embassy. It looked as though Ricky's siege might not be the polite affair he'd hoped for.

He picked up the phone and dialed a New York number. Then he got passed around like a hot potato or an unexploded bomb until he ended up in the right place.

"This is Ray Krall."

"And you know who I am."

"Sure do."

"I need to communicate with you securely."

"Okay."

"You're willing to do that?"

A pause.

"Yeah, I'm willing. How do we do it?"

"I can't give you the information you need over this line."

A laugh.

"No kidding."

"There's someone who can. Someone who might be quite close to you. I can't say who. Tell me if you know who it is."

A pause. Then a sigh.

"Yeah, I guess I know who."

"Get the information from that person. Then email me. I'll be waiting."

"Okay. Anything else?"

"No. Thanks."

Ricky hung up. And immediately had doubts: This guy Krall had been far too cool. He should have come across as affronted, angry or outraged. He shouldn't have zeroed in on the cat girl so quickly and so acceptingly. There was something going on there — but it didn't mean that Ricky couldn't blackmail Prince into freeing Kerri. Jiao could wait.

Ricky checked his newsfeeds. There was a curfew in Hong Kong. PLA forces had assembled north of Kowloon. Demonstrations in support of the Chinese Spring had spread across Europe and Asia. In the US, outbreaks of support were so far limited to the major coastal cities. According to Freedom News, *intelligence sources* had uncovered evidence that the Chinese Spring was being manipulated, if not directed, by old-guard Communists who were bent on a return to hardline Maoism. So what, Ricky wondered, did the next President of the United States have to say about it all? So far, nothing, it appeared.

Ricky sent a message to Mr. Yu. He apologized for failing to share his knowledge of Chen's condition. And he expressed his regret that Mr. Yu had not heard the worst from Ricky, personally. Mr. Yu should know that Ricky had told Xin Jiao to produce Chen, and also that Ricky believed he had some leverage.

Mr. Yu's reply came quickly. He did not blame Ricky for anything. It was his view that Beijing would be forced to give up his daughter. Mr. Yu believed that the Party's grip was about to fail. The Chinese Spring, as westerners called it, stood on the threshold of victory.

Ricky should also know that, while La Cachette, its staff, and Ricky's lemurs were just fine, in Tana there were rumors of an impending coup, backed by sections of the military, that might have an anti-Chinese character. Mr. Yu wanted Ricky's permission, should it come to it, to borrow Ricky's powerful boat; he envisaged a speedy, though risky, escape across the Channel to Mozambique.

Take the boat, Ricky replied. Keep it. I may not be coming back. And those bags full of *ariary* in the safe room? Give one to the staff and drop the others off at the village on your way to Africa.

Mr. Yu hoped that Ricky's *siege* would end happily.

Thanks, Ricky said. And good luck.

He took another look out of his single window. Some kind of mobile command center had parked itself in the middle of the square.

There was a knock at the door. It turned out to be supper: Smoked salmon sandwiches. Ricky slid open one of his desk drawers and stowed the food inside. Then he lay down on the thinly-carpeted floor and told himself he needed to sleep.

And he did.

When he awoke, three hours later, he found a new message from Mr. Yu. His daughter Chen had appeared on Chinese television, he said. She was fit, healthy and unharmed. She had appealed for calm and peace. Her video manifesto had been a mistake, she had said; it had been misunderstood. She had returned voluntarily from America, and would devote herself in future to patriotic duties.

But the problem, Mr. Yu said, was not what she had said, or her apparent change of heart.

The problem was, it wasn't her. Mr. Yu knew his daughter. The girl on TV was a fake. Mr. Yu understood what that meant. He wanted Ricky's permission to tell the world.

Ricky didn't understand why Mr. Yu thought he needed permission.

Do it, he wrote.

CHAPTER 45

By the time Teri Wolfe got to Water Street, she'd figured out the flaw in her plan. Because of the Spratly crisis and the financial crash, the Presidential Debates had been curtailed.

Congress and the outgoing administration apparently believed that the only force of nature that could stop both of those suckers going down was Fat Prince Willy. How could he be dickering with moderators or respectfully disagreeing with his opponents when Chinese missiles threatened and a new depression loomed? So there would be one debate, not three. And the schedule had changed.

Which meant that Krall would either be in attendance at tonight's debate, in the Great Hall of the Cooper Union, up on East 7th Street, or else watching it on TV in the comfort of his rented apartment. Teri would not be able to follow him home from the Campaign HQ.

What about the black BMW? Teri could prowl the streets of lower Manhattan for hours and not find it. It could be in an underground parking garage under one of those towers in Battery Park City.

She wandered south to Battery Park, the location of the Robin Hood encampment where she'd first seen Chen and Nile, and sat on a bench. It was one of those benches that were, by design, impossible to sleep on. But that didn't matter; she wasn't sleepy. And if she did sleep, she thought, she would freeze.

Meera had been counting on Teri to be her secret source inside the Prince Campaign as it undertook its absurd *Bus Tour to Save America*. Okay, it was actually called the *New Century Express*. Same difference. But Teri had gotten fired for mouthing off satirically on her blog and had thus let Meera down. How to break the news? What would Meera think of her? Would she be mean? And would it be over before it even started?

What a roaring success Teri Wolfe was. Everything she touched turned to...

She felt her chest tighten. Tears dribbled from her eyes and would have frozen on her cheeks but for their guilty heat. Nile was dead. Chen was in a Chinese prison, or worse. And where was Sandy? Teri had abused her trust, too, and left her in danger.

For perhaps twenty minutes she remained on the bench, staring into the darkness of the harbor and trying to blink away her tears. She didn't want to take her hands out of her pockets because she had no gloves. An icy rain began to fall. Unable to stop herself shivering, she got to her feet again and began to walk.

She marched north, past Castle Clinton and the Jewish museum, finding shelter under the trees in South Cove Park. She couldn't stay outside in this weather, she thought. And she was hungry; some food would warm her up. She thought there were restaurants, though probably not cheap ones, on South End Avenue and in the World Financial Center. Did she have any money?

Her pockets were full of the junk she'd scooped up from the cubby-hole in the process of her precipitate exit from Park Avenue. In amongst it were about thirty dollars in crumpled bills, plus Amber's phone (with battery removed) and Teri's own, crappy personal phone. It had switched off — probably because of a dead battery. She turned it on. It powered up, locked on to a signal, and beeped. One new text message. From Ray Krall. She barely had time to read it before the phone died.

where r u? need 2 c u. come 2 apt.

And there was the address: South End Avenue. She was standing in front of the very building.

*

K rall's rented apartment was a modest one-bed, but it was on the top floor and it looked out over the harbor to Liberty Island. The place was tidy. There was a laptop on the coffee table, but otherwise it looked as though Krall had hardly bothered to unpack. The TV was on, tuned to the channel showing the debate, but the sound was off. Krall wore sweatpants and a black T-shirt with a picture of a pit-bull.

"Attack dog. Get it? Want a beer?"

"Not really. Do you have any food?"

"Pizza's comin'. Want to watch the debate with me?"

"Okay. Why aren't you there?"

"Because I want to talk to you. Take your coat off. Sit down."

Teri peeled off her sodden coat. Krall took it from her and hung it up over the tub in the bathroom.

"You okay? Your face is all red."

"Yeah, I'm okay. Actually, no. No, I'm not. Because —"

"You got fired."

"Not just that."

"I guess not. Got anywhere to go?"

"No."

"Good thing you came here, then."

"I can stay?"

"Sure."

"You're going to sleep on the couch?"

"No. You are. You're young."

"Um, okay. Thanks."

"So sit down."

Teri sat on the couch. On the TV a group of debate-watchers were instructed in the use of a simple device that registered their reactions from moment to moment. Krall opened a can of beer and sat in a swiveling armchair.

"We're gonna lose this debate," he said. "But we're also gonna win it."

Teri wasn't in the mood for Krall's wisecracks, but he'd saved her from a night on the street, and pizza was on the way, so she felt he'd earned her indulgence.

"Oh? How come?"

"You'll see. It's happened before. This time's kinda different, though. Thanks to Sandy."

"Where *is* Sandy?"

"She's in a safe place. Don't want to say where. I had this place swept, but you can never be sure these days."

"Swept?"

"For bugs."

"Who do you think might be bugging you?"

"Well, just the usual folks. Plus our opponents. Plus Josh Merriweather. And those Weihan people. Hell, maybe even you and your Robin Hood pals."

Against her will, a broken laugh erupted from Teri's chilled lungs.

"You have no idea."

"They got a drone, right?"

"It's a toy. It's useless."

The pizza arrived. They ate. Teri warmed up, the tension fled her limbs and she began to feel *safe.*

"Can I have that beer now?"

"Sure. This'll be a three-beer debate, so you help yourself."

"Thanks. What did you want to talk to me about?"

"After the debate."

Krall turned up the sound. The debate started.

It was obvious to Teri that the first part of Krall's wisecrack was correct: Prince lost every argument. His two opponents had fact and figures — mostly misleading ones, according to Krall — at their fingertips. They could quote from congressional hearings or academic research. There seemed to be no statistic or trend that they had not mastered. They knew the names of every state governor and foreign leader. This one knew that imports of biofuels from Brazil were up sixteen per cent over two years. That one knew that prices of Chinese-made solar panels had fallen by twenty-three per cent in the last six months alone.

Prince appeared to know nothing.

Despite being a financial genius, he hardly seemed to know the first thing about fiscal or monetary policy. He didn't know the size of the federal government's debt, or its current annual deficit. Hadn't Krall gotten him to memorize a single number?

Prince's opponents seemed to sense weakness; they went for him. Prince had been the front-runner. Rather than attack each other, they wanted to take him down.

So why was Krall still smiling?

"They're killing him."

"No, they ain't."

"He can't answer any of the questions. They're ripping him apart."

"Looks okay, though, don't he?"

Teri studied Prince's face. He was smiling; he looked genial. Somehow, his opponents weren't getting to him. The rich uncle act was in full swing: Those self-effacing hand gestures; those little upward feints of the eyebrows; the openness; the generosity; the tolerance. But there was something else. Teri noticed that Prince, unlike his opponents, never said or implied that there was anything *wrong* with America that needed fixing. He was all optimism and modesty; or else patriotism and justified pride. Whereas the other two identified various and differing groups of malfeasants upon whom they intended to *crack down*, Prince seemed to despise no one and nothing.

When the subject of the financial crash came up, Prince simply asked for people to trust him. He said the same thing in respect of the Spratly crisis.

"I don't get it. He's losing."

"No, he ain't. Look at the graph. And listen to the sound and the rhythm."

"Huh?"

But then she saw it. The real-time graph at the bottom of the screen showed Prince's rating going *up* whenever he was attacked, and his opponents' going *down* whenever Prince responded with *aw-shucks* and can't-we-all-get-along and his heart full of sunshine.

And she noticed something else: Although Prince never mentioned God or religion, there was something in the tenor and roll of his speech that was almost evangelistic. It was nothing like the way he talked in private. But he didn't quite sound like a preacher. Instead, he sounded like Sandy Quayle.

"Now do you get it?"

"Shit!"

"So do our fellow citizens want to vote for anger and recrimination? Do they want to vote for bullies? Or do they want to vote for the underdog? For optimism, for civility, for success?"

"Underdog? Prince?"

"In this context."

"You *knew* he could never win the debates."

"Correct. Not in conventional terms."

"So you have him go on there and talk like Sandy."

"There's a little more to it. But that's basically it."

"You really are an evil genius."

"Aw, don't say that. Not evil."

The debate proceeded. And Krall was correct; it was a three-beer occasion. Or was it four? Anyway, the opinion of the after-show pundits was unanimous: Prince had been pummeled. But the graph said otherwise. And an instant online poll made Prince the victor.

"So much for fun," Krall said. "Now we need to get serious."

"What about?"

"I'm gonna turn the TV up, okay? And we're gonna whisper in each other's ear. Hang on."

The TV blared. The commentariat had *capitulated*, Teri observed, very shrewdly, and was undertaking the major effort required to justify Prince's victory and to pretend that it had been expected all along.

"What the hell were you playing at in London?"

"Uh, well... That's... No, no, Ray! You said you didn't want to know. You said that!"

"Okay. That's right. You are correct. Let me take that for you, you don't need to drink the rest of it. Let me rephrase. Who did you talk to?"

"It's a secret!"

A big old sigh from Ray. What a teaser — an *evil* teaser!

"Well, actually it ain't. Because I know you talked to Ricky Ponton."

"You know!"

"Yes, I do. Now —"

"He's funny looking."

"Aw, shit. Listen, Teri..."

"What? Listen where?"

Oh, he meant *pay attention*.

"He called me, okay? He wants to talk. For some reason. But we have to do it securely."

"Oh, *I* know."

"That's exactly right. Now, he says you have some information? Some kind of secret login?"

"Oh!"

Krall indicated his laptop.

"So, if you wouldn't mind, Teri..."

So Krall wanted to talk to funny-looking Ricky? Was that all right? Well, Krall was kind of weird-looking, too — so why not? Ah, but what if...

Teri peered up at the ceiling of Krall's apartment.

"What are you lookin' at?"

"No, no, Ray. You wait. Wait right here."

Teri stumbled into Krall's bare, orderly bedroom. Was that a blanket on the bed? Or was it a coverlet? Never mind, it would have to do. She dragged it from the bed into the living room.

"What in hell's name are you doin' with that?"

"This is what you have to do. Trust me."

She pulled the blanket over Krall's head and over his computer, then stood back to check her work. He looked kind of funny under there, didn't he? What now? Oh, right.

Teri dropped to her knees and crawled around the coffee table. Then she lifted up the edge of the blanket and scrambled up on to the couch next to Krall.

"Wow. Dark under here. Spooky."

"I guess you think this is really necessary?"

Teri nodded. The blanket drooped over her face. She adjusted it.

"Necessary. Really necessary."

"All right. Login, then."

"Okay. Ah."

Could she, in fact, remember the very long strings of letters, numbers and characters that Ricky had made her memorize? Oh, come on, Teri, come on! Start working, brain! How many beers had she had? Too many...

"Let's go, Teri."

"Yeah, we're going. Um..."

Then it came to her. She logged in.

"Yay!"

Krall angled the laptop away from Teri and towards himself. She leaned in order to see what he was typing. Okay, he'd started a chat session with Ricky. But it was hard to follow. Her eyes refused to focus, and their lids began to feel very heavy. Tap, tap, tap. Chat, chat, chat. Guys talking to each other...

"Are you asleep?"

Krall was standing over her; the blanket was on the couch.

"Huh? What? No."

"Yes, you were. You're lookin' tired. How about you just curl up under this thing?"

"Okay. Did you finish —"

"Uh-huh."

"What did he say?"

"He's got some kind of dirt on Willard. Says he'll hold back 'til after the election if he gets a favor. I said okay. Didn't think that was the kind of stuff he did. Have to say I'm disappointed."

"What favor?"

"Don't matter to you."

"What dirt?"

"Didn't say. You have any idea, little Miss Intrigue?"

"Er, not really."

"You and your little friends know somethin', don't you?"

Teri shrugged.

"Guess it's some kind of financial sleaze. Maybe Willard diddled his taxes. These guys usually do."

"That might be it."

"Nothin' important."

"Can you actually do this favor?"

"Maybe. Maybe not. It won't matter."

Teri stood up. For a moment she feel dizzy.

"You okay?"

"Oh, yeah. Can I ask you something?"

A tolerant sigh from Krall.

"Course you can, Teri."

"Do you really want Prince to win?"

A long pause, while Krall rearranged the blanket on the couch for Teri.

"No, Teri. I just want to win the election. Professional pride, an' all that. Fuck Prince."

"But, if he wins —"

"The system will very shortly fall apart. As it deserves to. I should know, Teri. It's been my whole working life. Plus, I get my bonus."

"That's kind of what the Robin Hood Party thinks."

"Do they, now?"

"It's what they're, like, working towards."

"Well, then. Let's wish 'em luck, shall we?"

CHAPTER 46

Teri Wolfe awoke on Ray Krall's rented couch to find that the arch-spinmeister and not-so-evil genius had already left for the office. But he had been so good as to leave out clean towels and a brand-new toothbrush for Teri. Which was fortunate, because her mouth felt like the inside of a dumpster. So did her head, but there was little to be done about that.

And Ray had left a note:

Gonna miss you on the bus. Maybe I'll send you postcards. Keep your damn phone charged!

She searched for it and found it plugged into an outlet in the kitchen. It was fully charged. And there was a message from Meera:

ready 2 roll?

Teri sat and stared at Meera's message for some five minutes. Then she decided it made more sense to shower and dress before replying.

Having showered and dressed, she sat with the phone in her lap for another six or seven minutes, before concluding that she really ought to eat breakfast before responding. So she raided Krall's refrigerator. Then she made coffee. The coffee was good, so she made some more. Then she cleaned her teeth again.

And only then did she sit down, think hard — or as hard as she could in her semi-wasted condition — and do what had to be done.

sorry can't roll got fired sorry.

Ten trembly, lip-biting minutes later, the answer came.

better come with me then. pearl st bean village @ 10

How did Meera know about Bean Village? Nile must have told her. But why there? If Meera's intent was significant or symbolic then, well, *great*. But its true import would have to wait until Teri's brain was fully functional again. She gathered her things together, threw Krall's note in the garbage, and slipped out of the apartment.

*

B oth Pedro and Aliyah were on duty, so Teri loitered outside the coffee shop, hidden from what she feared would be their piteous gaze. Just after ten, Meera rolled up in a rental car — a gray Honda station wagon. In the back was Meera's travel bag. And a heavy, metal briefcase with a padlock.

"I love a road trip," she said, as they drove off towards the Holland Tunnel. "And this one's going to be special."

"Sorry I got fired."

"Yeah, you already said. It's okay. It's not like you want to work for those people."

"No. They didn't even pay me."

"I'm shocked. What an outrage."

"It was my *tone*. That's what they didn't like."

"You need to learn to keep a civil tongue in your head, young lady."

"It was almost like that."

"So we might not be able track their bus route. If they change the itinerary. Too bad. But we can still have some fun."

"Oh, *maybe* we'll know where they're going."

"Really? How?"

"Just something Ray said."

Meera gave Teri a narrow-eyed look.

"What's the deal with him?"

"He's just an evil genius. Did you see the debate?"

"Yeah! Is Prince always like that?"

"No. Not at all. He was channeling Sandy."

"Who's Sandy?"

"Long story. Tell you later."

"Sure."

"So what's our first stop?"

"Delaware."

They crawled through the tunnel and drove for two hours before pulling in at a rest stop. When Teri checked her phone, she found a message from Ray Krall, consisting of nothing but an image of the Liberty Bell Center in Philadelphia.

"Forget Delaware," she told Meera. "We're going to Pennsylvania."

By evening, they'd found themselves a cheap motel on the north-eastern outskirts of Philadelphia.

"So is it one room or two?" Meera asked.

Teri stared at her.

"What I'm saying is, our funds are limited."

"But we've got six billion dollars."

"No, we don't, Teri. That's not *our* money."

"But we're going to spend it, aren't we?"

"Yes. But in a *good* way. Not on ourselves. It's the principle, okay?"

"Yes, all right. I can see that."

"Good. Well?"

"I guess we can share."

"It's a sensible economy."

"Yeah. Uh, Meera?"

"What?"

"What's in the briefcase?"

"Emergency cash. In case they shut down our accounts."

"How much?"

"Two fifty."

"Thousand?"

"Well, duh! Come on."

They checked in. Meera started up her laptop and set about mobilizing the local chapter of the Robin Hood Party. Teri checked the TV news for the latest on the Prince Campaign's activities.

The Spratly crisis had cooled. A faulty software upgrade was now officially blamed for the incident, following an independent investigation conducted in partnership by Fairmeadow Systems of the USA and Weihan of China. Willard Prince was given credit for working behind the scenes to facilitate this most diplomatic alliance. *Behind the scenes?* Sure, except that someone had made sure the backstage lights were on.

The financial crisis, on the other hand, had heated up. A *super-committee* had been set up by the outgoing administration. Its purpose was to *get out ahead of this thing*, according to the administration's soon-to-be-gone spokesperson. And Willard Prince — who better? — had been appointed to head it. His first act, it was said, had been to order the drawing up of a list of *systemically-important institutions*. And the Fed and Treasury had been ordered to ready their fire-hoses of unlimited liquidity.

With that accomplished, Prince had felt at liberty to commence his bus tour across America, aboard the *New Century Express*. Freedom News ran a *special* on the embarkation celebration — with all its associated hoopla, razzamatazz, high hopes and sturdy intentions. Amber Pike was there. And Prince's stately, bedecked armada of air-conditioned traffic-snarlers departed not, as you might have expected, from Park Avenue, but from Main Street, Stimsonville, in Prince's *home town.*

"Okay," Meera said. "Everybody's ready. Tomorrow, we strike."

And thus the pattern was set: Long days in the Honda; picture postcards from Krall; cheap motels; laptop and TV; bad food; Teri and Meera, side by side, every day and every night.

And here come the *exploits.*

*

I n Philadelphia, the Robin Hood Party upstages the Prince Campaign's *Liberty for All* event by assembling a noisy demonstration, complete with brass band, on the steps of the Museum of Art, whence it announces that the Party, under one of its new corporate guises, has made a major intervention in the *secondary debt market*. It has purchased two hundred million dollars' worth of debt for five cents on the dollar, and has *abolished* it, thus *liberating* thousands of indebted individuals from the gnawing chains of bank, credit-card and — most of all — medical debt. Five cents on the dollar means four billion dollars of personal debt, all owed by the nation's poorest — gone!

We're freeing the debt slaves, says Meera.

Teri wonders if something couldn't also be done about student debt. Because she's read that there's at least a trillion dollars of *that* out there — and it's not even all hers!

The Prince Campaign ignores the exploit — or, at least, strenuously insists that's what it's doing. Ray Krall says these kids have some nerve, but you *gotta admire their balls.*

Freedom News and the mainstream media dismiss the exploit as a meaningless stunt, but can't help but wonder where the money's coming from. It must be from that crazy, left-wing, European financier; how dare he!

Meera says *give me liberty or give me debt!*

Teri wonders if Meera still has college loans.

*

I n Columbus, Ohio, the Robin Hood Party shocks the world of the Corporate Citizen, and wrong-foots the Prince Campaign's *Rally for Research and Innovation* by staging a kidnapping. Or, rather, by buying a drug company whose star product is unaffordable to all but a few of those who could die without it. The Party voids its newly-acquired patent, reduces the price-per-pop from two thousand dollars to fifty cents and offers the thing free to anyone in Africa.

You can't put a price on life, says Meera. Well, not more than fifty cents, anyway.

Teri wonders about Sandy. She didn't look too healthy, last time Teri saw her. Is there something wrong? Is that why Krall is hiding her?

The Prince Campaign is visibly put out. One of the Prince brothers goes rogue and rages on camera that it's immoral *not* to squeeze the last drop of profit from your patent. Ray Krall, challenged to repeat the Campaign's official line that the American healthcare system is the best on Earth, doesn't want to comment.

Freedom News has been sued by the crazy, left-wing, European financier. But that doesn't change the fact that what the Robin Hooders are doing is subverting the very basis of capitalism. How can this not be illegal?

On *Flint Gunner's Market Madness*, Gunner knows where the blame lies.

So I hear this Robin Hood guy's from England, Nige. That means you guys are to blame.

I think you'll find that Hollywood played a major part in popularizing him and his exploits, Flint.

Yeah, them too.

The markets tank again. The super-committee starts to use the B-word. *Bailouts!*

*

I n the northern suburbs of Springfield, Illinois, The Robin Hood Party goes on a real estate binge. It buys a hundred million-dollar houses situated on a variety of upscale developments. And it signs over these homes to local homeless

312

families, couples and individuals. This distracts from the Prince Campaign's theme-of-the-day, which is the *Emancipation of the Entrepreneur*.

Hey, says Meera, if you don't have to live in your car any more — and, in some places, that's not even legal! — or on the street, or in a dangerous shelter, or even in one of those, like, tent cities — well, if that isn't a *new birth of freedom*, what is?

Teri thinks of the apartment in Bayonne and the one on Park Avenue, and decides that these mini-mansions aren't so bad, even if they're really ugly from the outside. She wouldn't mind one herself.

But questions are being asked — so TV viewers are told — about how the Robin Hood Party seems to know the Prince Campaign's secret itinerary. Ray Krall says he's taking the matter very seriously, and a full-scale investigation is underway.

Freedom News has reached an out-of-court settlement with the crazy, left-wing, European financier. The financier has donated his windfall to a food-bank charity. He would have given it to the Robin Hooders, he says — except they don't seem to need the money.

Teri wonders how Prince is holding up, in private. *He* must know where the money's coming from. Is it tearing him up inside? Is it some exquisite torture for him? But it looks like he's holding his nerve. How can that be? Does he have an exit strategy? What if he does? Teri can't imagine any possible way out for him, and yet... Should she tell Ricky Ponton to pull the plug *now*? *Yes*, she decides, sending him a secure and heartfelt message to that effect.

Freedom News has determined that the actions of the Robin Hood Party constitute *social and economic terrorism*. And many are now asking, it says, why the Federal Government has not added the Robin Hood Party to its list of Terrorist Organizations. After all, they've known about the organization for years but done nothing. Another scandal!

And this just in: The hardline leader of the most radical faction of the RHP goes under the nom-de-guerre of TerrorWolf!

TerrorWolf?

Oh shit, Teri thinks. How did *that* happen? Ray wouldn't, would he? Meera thinks it's a weird development, but not to worry.

*

I n Kansas City, Missouri, where the Prince Campaign is staging a mock-populist protest against the depredations of the Internal Revenue Service, the Robin Hood Party steals the limelight by bussing in hundreds of people from not-so-fancy Wyandotte and Jackson counties to the very-fancy-indeed Country Club Plaza district, where they are treated to five-course meals in the very best restaurants, and all the *free stuff* they desire from the Plaza's upscale shops, boutiques, delis and markets. Special packages are offered to the minimum-wage employees who can't afford to buy the basic goods sold in the very stores where they work.

Meera says that the IRS, doing Congress's dirty work for it, hands out plenty of *free stuff* to corporations in the form of loopholes, deductions, amnesties, and general looking-the-other-way. So a few free bags of groceries and a gourmet burger with Cajun curly fries are no big deal.

Teri's still a bit worried about the TerrorWolf thing. But she's becoming ever more intoxicated with the sheer thrill of this oh-so-special road-trip and its exploits. What an adventure! Teri and Meera forever!

Meanwhile, over on Freedom News, on *Flint Gunner's National Security Bunker Hour*, there's a new segment, introduced by scary graphics and an ominous, rumbling soundtrack: *The Hunt for TerrorWolf*.

So how would you characterize the deranged, paranoid and, for all we know, ultra-violent nature of this guy, Flint?

Guy's twisted, Nige. We've seen his type before. Gets his kicks from subverting the natural order.

But how do we stop him, Flint?

Oh, he's not gonna stop, Nige. No way. Not now. He's tasted blood.

So how do we stop the bleeding, Flint?

We take him out, Nige.

Flipping hastily to another channel, Teri learns that demonstrations in favor of the Chinese Spring have reached a new pitch and fervor all across Europe and Asia following the *iconic events* of a few days before. Hong Kong is under curfew and martial law. And Ricky Ponton remains under siege in Trafalgar Square in London — though rumor has it that legal maneuvers are afoot, and the South African embassy might yet be stormed by Special Forces.

There's news on the super-committee, whose job it is to *get out ahead of* the financial crisis. They've come up with something. It's called TARP III. Well, *they* don't call it that, but everybody else does. The Chair of the committee, one Willard Prince, has sketched out on a single sheet of paper what's needed. This sheet of paper has been sent to Congress and the outgoing President for immediate approval.

*

T en miles west of Denver, Colorado, in the Red Rocks Amphitheatre, with big screens outside for those who arrive too late for a seat inside, and on the same night as the Prince Campaign is struggling to fill Mile High Stadium for a *Celebration of American Culture*, the Robin Hood Party pays for a free concert for unemployed and low-income Coloradans. The show features local bands and singers, but the highlight is a set by Reagan Pruett, performing her recent sexy hit, followed by songs by Woody Guthrie, The Levellers and Billy Bragg. It's not clear that Reagan knows who these illustrious composers are, but, like Teri and Meera and most people, she's a sucker for a good tune. And a good sport, too — though not quite good enough to turn down the ten million dollars the RHP is paying her.

Meera thinks Reagan should have donated the money.

Teri thinks Reagan's cute.

Ray Krall says he thinks that Reagan Pruett is the New Face of Country and heck, there was no way in hell that we were gonna compete with *that*.

Freedom News reports an unsubstantiated rumor that the net is tightening around TerrorWolf.

Teri wishes they'd stop talking about TerrorWolf.

Meera laughs.

*

I n Phoenix, Arizona, while the Prince Campaign is holding a Business Forum in order to explain that opening the country to entrepreneurs and job-creators from the East is a *totally different* thing to opening the borders to the South, the Robin Hood Party reserves every available four- and five-star hotel room for the next six months, and offers the accommodation to refugees from violence in Central America. The State Government refuses the offer and the Federal Government ignores it. The rooms remain empty until the hotel chains realize they can get away with re-letting them.

Meera says that the RHP expected as much. So this was an exploit that didn't really help anyone much. It was inevitable that it would get harder.

Teri says how much money have we got left?

Meera says a hell of a lot.

Teri thinks there must be some way that the money could be used to effect *permanent* change.

Sure, Meera says. We could buy politicians. But *we'll* eventually run out of money. And the other side won't.

*

I n San Diego, California, as the Prince Campaign hosts its High-Tech Education Summit, the Robin Hood Party attempts to pay for poor kids to attend Bunningfield Academy, the elite college preparatory school. But their approaches are firmly rebuffed.

*

A nd thus the exploits, and Teri and Meera's very special road trip, were at an end. Over the next five days they drove all the way back to New York.

There were no messages for Teri from Ray Krall. Nor was there anything on Big Data's web site about Willard Prince.

The Chinese Spring continued to ramp up in Europe.

Then, on November 8, election day, it broke out all across China, in a howl of rage and frustration that, Teri thought, could easily match that of the Prince Brothers, were they to lose the vote in the electoral college.

In what Teri feared was the very last motel room she was to share with Meera, they stayed up late together to watch the result.

CHAPTER 47

Sandy Quayle felt off-balance and queasy. She struggled to repress a niggling, non-specific dread — a terrible conviction that something important had changed for good, and she was yet to find out what it was.

Perhaps it was just the unsettling spectacle of the Chinese astronauts landing on the moon — in their enormous craft, with its red flags on top and its monstrous, ten-wheeled rover slung underneath — at the same time as there were riots and massacres in their cities. Sandy wasn't quite old enough to remember, but hadn't it been utterly different in America in 1969?

Freedom News had tried to cover up the Chinese captions on the live feed from the moon, but of course you knew that they were there.

And Sandy feared the consequences of the latest financial crisis. There had to be many people now, who, like Sandy once upon a time, did not know, and were not prepared for, what they were about to experience. It was mysterious to Sandy — and surely even God had to struggle with all that gobbledygook about *liquidity* and *securitization* and *troubled assets* — why these cataclysms should come about so often. And yet now, even though it seemed that the worst was still to come, all the talk was of *recovery*, as if everybody *did* recover.

Nonetheless, in comparison, Sandy felt blessed.

The medication that Ray Krall's doctor had prescribed for her had lessened the pain in her leg to the point where she hardly noticed it. She was beginning to feel odd sensations in other parts of her body, but perhaps those were merely side-effects. And the calm and tranquility of Ray Krall's cabin, and the peaceable beauty of its Adirondack mountain setting, had raised her spirits a little.

Cabin? Well, it was really more of a small, rustic house. It had two bedrooms, one bathroom, a wood-burning stove for heat and hot water, and a hole in the downstairs ceiling so that warmth could rise into the upper story. It may have been built out of logs, but it was well-equipped with electronic gadgets, a freezer full of food, and top-notch security. And it was hidden from public view down a private drive lined with conifers.

There had been an early snowfall, and Sandy thought the landscape looked wonderful — spiritual, even. Ray had said that his job ended when the polls closed, and he would be driving up to the cabin as soon as he could get away. So Sandy kept an eye out for tire tracks in the snow, or a glimpse of the big, black BMW lumbering up the drive.

Although Ray had said that the cabin would be an ideal place for Sandy to rest and recuperate, she couldn't help but wonder if there was something more to Ray's desire to get her away from the campaign, and from New York. He seemed desperate for the election to be over. That was understandable. But why did he not show any excitement? Why did he seem fearful?

Sandy had followed the campaign closely on TV. She had had little else to do, after all. What had become of Eleanor Prince was very sad. And, no doubt, many people — and even his opponents, surely — had felt deeply for Mr. Prince in their hearts. Mr. Prince had paid for Eleanor to be admitted to the finest long-term rehabilitation clinic in America. He had pledged to order his lawyers to be generous in drawing up the separation agreement. And he had appealed to America to welcome Barbara van Dornen, his new life-partner, into their hearts. Well, Sandy knew that Barbara was devoted to Mr. Prince, so out of sadness came hope.

But Sandy didn't really think it was Eleanor's unhappiness or Mr. Prince's consequent grief that lay heavily on Ray's mind. It made her shiver to think of it... But perhaps it had to do with what had happened to Peter Giordano. The TV report had gotten his name all wrong, of course. But Sandy had recognized him instantly. If you drove all on your own, looking like a rich American tourist, in the mountains of Argentina, then perhaps you might expect to be murdered by robbers. For all Sandy knew, it happened all the time.

Was Ray superstitious? No, of course not. No more than Sandy was. But events like that gnawed at you, didn't they? Thus, while Sandy felt it might be presumptuous to speculate on, or question, God's ways, she would permit herself to observe that a wicked person who had threatened Mr. Prince — and in the most violent language — would not be capable of doing so again. Good riddance, in other words.

Moreover, Sandy thought that Mr. Prince had conducted himself with great dignity and restraint during the closing days of the campaign. The anger, the hatred, and all of those horrible provocations hadn't gotten to him. Perhaps he'd had to lean on Barbara and Ray for moral support. But he must also have seen that America's better angels were on his side.

That much had been obvious ever since the debate. How unfair Mr. Prince's opponents had been. All that sneering. The condescension. The smart-Alec *gotcha* questions. Hardly bothering to conceal their disdain and contempt. All but laughing in Mr. Prince's face. Didn't they understand how it all looked to ordinary Americans? They must have heard time and again about the resentment felt by honest citizens towards the self-dealing, out-of-touch elites — and yet they still didn't get it.

And how had Mr. Prince reacted? Had he fought back with the same dirty tactics? Not at all. He had risen above it — the insults, the barbs, the sneers, all of it. Kind of like Jesus, in a way. And he had spoken to the people in his own true voice. Sandy was tempted to say *His* own true voice, but she'd already had to warn herself against presumption.

318

Yet Mr. Prince must have known that he would have to suffer through trials to win the prize.

There had been the discovery that the Chinese Spring was not at all what it had at first appeared to be. Poor Chen had been deceived. And her deceivers had delivered the unhappy girl into purgatory, if not something worse. Sandy had felt this setback so keenly that she had lapsed into doubt and confusion for at least a day and a half. She, too, had been deceived. For a time Sandy herself had acted, albeit unknowingly, on the side of evil. Well, okay, she could atone. *That* came easily enough to her. But she still felt sick to her stomach to think that she'd been on the side of the worst of the Communists, who wanted to take over the Chinese Spring and subject China once again to the tyranny of what FNN's experts called *hardline Maoism*.

Politics was hard enough to understand in America, Sandy thought, let alone in a foreign country. But Mr. Prince had explained it as well as anyone could: The Communists were bad, and the Maoists were even worse. But, out of the present violence and turmoil, Mr. Prince said, he had faith that a new, better order would emerge. There were good people in China — visionaries, entrepreneurs, investors, businesspeople, and hard-working families — and *they* would be the future. Mr. Prince vowed to support them. His belief was unshakeable.

Then, on election day itself, there had been that terrible bomb attack on a school near Stimsonville — the very school attended by some of Mr. Prince's grandchildren. Fortunately, it was a private school and therefore had sufficient security to see off the attackers before any children or staff could be harmed. And it was all the work of TerrorWolf, who had been identified as the leader of the armed wing of the so-called Robin Hood Party.

Now, Sandy wasn't one of those people who saw evil everywhere. That was foolish; most people were merely weak. Yet she knew that it existed. What was more, she knew that if people like her held on to their faith then evil would ultimately be defeated.

And it was to that end, with God's will, and the best of America on his side, that Mr. Prince had won the election.

Sandy had watched the victory celebrations on TV. It was fun to pick out the people she knew — Barbara, Megan, Milly, Gloria, Josh Merriweather. Okay, she didn't *really* know Josh, but she'd lived in his apartment and gotten to know him in a weird, second-hand way. And there were the casino guy, the coal guy, the chemical guy and the Wall Street guys. Sandy didn't know *them* at all, not really. But they probably knew about her, didn't they? If what Ray said was true, they must.

Come to think of it, didn't Sandy deserve a small moment of honor at the party? She was the only significant member of the campaign team not present. Well, except for Teri. But then Teri hadn't been very important, and the rumor was that she'd been fired for helping herself to campaign funds. If true, that was a let-down. What would the boyfriend say? Sandy couldn't help but feel aggrieved at the trust she'd placed in the girl.

The Prince brothers were present. They weren't part of the campaign team, of course, but who would be churlish enough to deny them the chance to rejoice with their elder brother? For once, they all looked as if there was nothing to be angry about.

Mr. Prince had looked humble and yet magnificent in victory. Barbara had gleamed with pride; she stuck by Mr. Prince's side, clinging to his arm, throughout the coverage. Megan and Milly were girlishly exuberant. Even Gloria had cracked a smile.

Ray had looked a little drunk, to be plain about it. Sandy trusted that he would sober up before attempting the snowy drive up into the mountains.

And even though she hadn't been present at the party — she told herself it would really have been too much for her — Sandy took pleasure in what had been achieved.

That night she'd taken her medication and gone to bed happier.

CHAPTER 48

Teri Wolfe had led a life of unmet expectations, failed ambition, backsliding and disappointment, whose wrong-choice turning points were marked out and commemorated, as if with giant, sullen obelisks, by Big Mistakes. And she figured now that she'd just made the Two Biggest Ever.

It had all come together in a climactic screw-up at the motel in Jersey City, on the morning after the election results were declared, when the shock and the horror had begun to cool, condense and solidify.

Fat Willy wasn't going to wait until Inauguration Day in January to get stuck in.

In his *victory speech*, before his defeated rivals had even conceded, he'd announced a ramping up of TARP III, and the fast-tracking by Congress of enabling legislation for the New Pacific Partnership — this being essential to the *safeguarding of prosperity* in these difficult times. No demur from Congress. Not a bleat from the mainstream media. High-fives at Freedom News.

In the morning, Meera had nailed it: *This feels like a coup*.

Thus, Big Mistake Number One: Teri had discouraged Ricky Ponton from exposing Prince before the election. Okay, the Robin Hood Party had bought into that idea, too; and Krall hadn't forced the issue in his side-deal with Ricky. But now, just hours after his unprecedented victory, Prince already looked invincible. He was The Man, and unchallengeable. All opposition had capitulated. Would anyone even *listen* to the Ponzi story, supposing it still got out? And the New American Century Fund was *participating* in TARP III — because it was a *systemically-important* institution!

This was a move that even Meera couldn't get her head around: *Is the Prince of Ponzi bailing himself out with public money? Is that really happening? How can that be a thing?*

And then had come Big Mistake Number Two: The Disagreement. The Big Data site was down. So down, in fact, that it was in *Page Not Found* territory. Teri couldn't log in to her secure account. Therefore, Big Data was a bust, Teri said. Something had to be done *now*. And Krall was the only hope. Meera had disagreed.

"He's the enemy, Teri. He just got Prince elected!"

"No, that was Sandy."

"You keep talking about this *Sandy!* Who the hell —"

"Krall's not what you think. He kept telling us where the bus —"

"He *knew* we wouldn't make any difference. He was laughing at us."

"No, see, he thinks the system is going to crash and —"

"The system! The *system* just won, Teri. Big time!"

"— burn, and then..."

"Then what?"

A pause.

"Well, it doesn't really look like it's going to work out the way we —"

"No kidding! We have to stick with Big Data. They're the only people we can trust to —"

"Meera, Krall *hates* Prince. He told me so!"

"He's got a weird way of showing it."

"You're wrong."

"No, *you're* wrong!"

And there it was: The latest pillar of humiliation in a trail of monumental fuck-ups. Teri had stormed out of the motel and now stood, damp, dripping and yet frazzled, in front of the door to Ray Krall's rented apartment in Battery Park City.

Oh, yeah. And, for some reason — was it the student loans, the other debts, the unpaid but otherwise *adequate* salary, or was it sheer spite? — Teri had taken Meera's metal briefcase. It was horribly heavy. And Teri knew she shouldn't have done it. But it was too late. What did Ray think?

"Oh, it's you. What the fuck do you want?"

Krall's apartment was no longer neat and tidy. There were empty beer cans everywhere.

"Can I come in?"

"Why not?"

Teri swept the cans from Krall's couch and sat, placing the briefcase on the coffee table. Krall stared at it, but said nothing.

"I think we fucked up," he said, at length.

"Yeah, I think so, too," Teri said, trying to choose her words carefully but failing as usual, "but you don't know the half of it."

"It's like they've taken over already. It's an *instant* transition. They had it all ready. Everything and everybody... All lined up in advance. I never knew. They didn't tell me."

"The two old parties... It's like they're gone."

"Aw, shit, Teri — I worked with both of 'em. There was only ever one party in reality. But there had to be a *semblance*, you know? And, once in a while, someone broke through and..."

"You know Prince is a crook, right?"

"No kiddin'. You know what they're tellin' me? They ain't gonna pay my bonus. It's all because of these *criteria*... I don't know what the hell they're talkin' about."

"Yeah, I had that too."

"See, I was countin' on that. It's not your concern, but I got a lot of debts..."

"Me too."

"And then there's Sandy. I promised her…"

"What? Where is she?"

"I got this cabin. Up in the Adirondacks. She's there. I told her to wait for me."

Krall hadn't picked up on Teri's insinuation regarding Prince. But Sandy's plight took precedence, Teri decided.

"Ray, is she sick?"

"Yeah, she's real sick. I'm not sure she understands how bad she is. I told her I'd pay for her treatment. Course she's all, *I'm not takin' your money*, you know how she is. But now…"

"No insurance?"

"No. You know what gets me? Nobody else gives a shit about her. Except you, maybe. I had her… I found out stuff about her. She knows I know."

"What stuff?"

"Well, like she was homeless for years. The day before she walked into the campaign office in Stimsonville, she was livin' in this… I guess you'd call it a squatter camp. It was next to the Country Club — I think Prince is actually a member — so it got demolished."

"She was homeless?"

"Used to have a nice house. Lost it in one of these financial things. Got sick. Nearly died. Managed to get treatment just before her husband's insurance ran out."

"She never mentioned a husband."

"He killed himself. With a shotgun. In the garage."

Teri stared at the briefcase on the table, and found herself rubbing her eyes.

"There's more," Krall said. "But… Wait. What was that you said? I don't know the half, or somethin'?"

Well, Teri thought, could this be Big Mistake Number Three? Whatever. There could be no more holding back.

"Yeah, about that."

Krall waited for her to speak. She made a show of composing herself, shuffling about theatrically on her couch. Above Krall's bloodshot eyes, his forehead crinkled like corrugated cardboard, and his bald head seemed to glow under the apartment's tasteful but inexpensive lighting.

"What the hell is it?"

"Well, first off, you need to know that there is no doubt about this. We have the proof."

"Proof? Proof of what?"

"Okay. So, um, do you know what a Ponzi scheme is?"

Was Krall's head steaming already? It was probably going to, any moment now.

"Course I know what a fuckin' Ponzi scheme is. There's, like, about fifty of 'em every year."

"Not like this one."

So now Krall stared at Teri as if she were some bad fairy come to announce that his new puppy was in fact the Hound of Satan.

"What exactly are you sayin', Teri?"

"You know how everyone thinks the New American Century Fund is so great?"

"Oh, yeah. They *all* wanna be in it."

"It's a Ponzi scheme."

Another long pause, in which wisps of superheated moisture began to escape the gravitational pull of Krall's scalp.

"When you say..."

"Want me to say it again? It's a Ponzi scheme. A two hundred billion dollar Ponzi scheme."

Krall ran his hand over his scalp and wiped his palm on his shirt.

"And you have proof? You have it nailed down?"

"Totally."

"And so... *This* is the thing that you and your Robin Hood pals..."

"Right. The thing you said you didn't want to know about."

"Jesus fuckin' Christ, Teri! You're telling me NOW?"

"You said you didn't want to —"

"Aw, this is just fuckin' beautiful!"

Krall put both hands on his head and commenced what looked to Teri like a desperate dance of frustration, hopping about the apartment, cursing to himself, flinging and kicking empty beer cans.

"Big Data was going to release it all," Teri said, ducking.

Krall stopped.

"Ooh! So *that* was your plan! I get it. Absolutely fuckin' brilliant. You know what just happened?"

"What?"

"They gave Merriweather access to all this cyber-shit the military has. So you got the Pentagon, Fairmeadow and Weihan all gunning for Big Data. *And* the Chinese military. It's goin' down, Teri. And it ain't never comin' back up. That guy Ponton — I wouldn't want to be in his shoes."

"Ray. Can't *you* do something?"

"Me? I'm frozen out already. And I'm *sure* this fuckin' apartment is bugged."

Teri pushed a stray beer can off her couch.

"Yeah, but..."

"Listen, Teri. Prince is fuckin' God in Washington now. Nobody's gonna want to hear this. And the TARP thing? It's six *trillion* dollars, Teri. There's no oversight! It's written into the law! You think Prince's people won't be able to cream off a couple hundred billion?"

Yeah, she thought. Big, big mistakes. She got to her feet.

"Goin' somewhere?"

"I don't know."

"Maybe you should. You know that the Robin Hood Party has been designated a terrorist organization, I suppose?"

"No. When did that happen?"

"This morning."

Teri wasn't sure it mattered, but there was something she just had to ask.

"TerrorWolf. Was that you?"

Krall kicked a beer can all the way into the kitchen.

"Hell, no. Why would I do that?"

324

"Who, then?"

"You want me to guess? I'd say Barbara. She's the brains."

"Does anyone really think it's me?"

"If I was you, I wouldn't stick around to find out."

"Ray, I don't know what to do."

"That's obvious."

Teri sat down again, and the conversation stopped. After a minute or so, she realized that they were both staring at the briefcase.

"So what you got there? Kind of a fancy case."

"Money. I stole it."

"I believe that might be against the law."

"I'd say it depends."

"You are probably correct."

"I stole it from the Robin Hood Party."

"Okay."

"They stole it from Willard Prince."

"Really? I'm impressed."

"He stole it from his investors."

"Uh-huh."

"Who stole it from... Well, I guess we have to watch what we say. Now that Robin Hood is a terrorist."

"This is still America, Teri. You have the right to free speech. You just need to use it responsibly."

A pause.

"So. How much've you got there?"

"A quarter of a million. I think."

"Cool. Prince ain't never gonna miss that, right?"

Teri found herself smiling.

"You know who needs that kind of money?"

"Me."

"Sure. Me, too. But what's the correct answer?"

"Sandy."

"Wanna go see her?"

"Yes."

"Good. I'm sick of this place. Let's get in the car."

While Teri waited, Krall packed a holdall and then cleaned up all the beer cans, crushing them and putting them into a recycling bin. Then he picked up the heavy briefcase and led Teri down to the parking garage and the black BMW.

Yes, Teri thought: Two Big Mistakes. To be followed by an act of atonement.

CHAPTER 49

icky Ponton looked down on the square from his chattering, swaying, strapped-in perch eighty meters above it, and saw his younger self, in long hair and stained jeans, staring back up at him, arms aloft in a despairing gesture of *what-the-fuck?* Then the machine tilted forward and took off across the roofs of Charing Cross Station, before veering left to track the river. Young Ricky faded from view, never to return.

Two hours earlier, just after a small, hopeless, pro-Ricky demo had been broken up by battalions of riot police, Walter Gabo had informed Ricky of the decision from Pretoria. There was anger, regret, and sympathy, too. But the pressure from the Americans, the British and the Chinese was too much to resist. And the Brits had claimed to have discovered legal grounds upon which they could storm the embassy — something bogus, based on a cooked-up violation of the Vienna Conventions, according to Walter. Pretoria didn't want the loss of face involved in having its premises ransacked and its secrets, accidentally-on-purpose, stolen. So Ricky was requested to pack his trunk and move on.

The question had been *where?* (Even if the answer had hung, distressingly unspoken, in the stuffy, unwashed air of Ricky's file-cluttered, mattress-stuffed, takeaway-perfumed attic.) Jay Percival had been on the phone from Windhoek. He felt sorry for Ricky, apparently, and even acknowledged some minor responsibility for Ricky's plight. And he could do even better than that, he said. Okay, there was one small catch, but Jay didn't think Ricky was going to find a better deal out there, anywhere.

Norway couldn't take Ricky. Its NATO membership had been questioned. And police had occupied Big Data's server farm in Bergen and taken away all the hard drives.

Iceland wasn't in a position to offer accommodation either. All power had been cut off to the datacenter outside Reykjavík. And Iceland's vulnerable banking system needed access to the international capital markets.

Brazil might have been big enough, just about, to resist political intimidation. But its government had elected to shut down all of Big Data's operations as a pre-emptive concession. And, besides, nobody could figure out how to get Ricky there safely.

Which left only one — admittedly large — portion of the world's surface upon which Ricky could set foot and not immediately be grabbed by both arms. Jay had explained, with his customary tact and nuance.

"You're fucked, Ricky. Except for one thing."

And what might that be?

"Do you remember Dmitri, Ricky?"

"No."

"Sure you do. He wanted to buy La Cachette. I had to outbid him."

"*Dmitri?*"

"That's right. Guess what? He's still interested."

"It's not for sale."

"Well, see, Ricky. It kind of is. If you want out of there."

"*Dmitri?*"

"Yeah. He's not so bad, as these guys go. Lives in London. Buys stuff. Invests. Plays tennis with politicians. You get the idea. Plus, he's got good connections at the Kremlin."

"For fuck's sake, Jay..."

"Can I tell him it's a deal?"

"Where do I end up?"

"Moscow. Dmitri owns an apartment building. Not too central, but handy for the metro. You'll like it."

"Shit!"

"I'll take that as a *yes*. Now, do you know where St. Katherine's Dock is?"

"Yes."

"Dmitri parks his boat there. I say *boat*, it's more like a ship."

"But I can't leave the building, Jay."

"You don't have to. Just get on the roof."

"What?"

"He'll send his helicopter."

The helicopter swooped over Waterloo Bridge. Ricky looked down. To the left, Somerset House; to the right, the National Theatre — monuments from the landscape of Ricky's youth, never to be seen again. He almost hadn't seen them just now. A squally blast of late English autumn had nearly blown him off his rope ladder. He might have been symbolically impaled on a flagpole bearing the rainbow colors.

Blackfriars Bridge, Southwark Bridge, London Bridge — Ricky felt as if his once-adoptive homeland were spewing him out of its gullet. And the Tower of London: For centuries the preeminent and final residence for traitors like Ricky, until the invention of jet travel made more exotic locations accessible.

Over the Tower and down into the dock, with Dmitri smiling up in his designer polo shirt and nautical slacks. And down the rope ladder again, without mishap.

"Mr. Ponton! Welcome aboard."

"You're taking a risk, aren't you?"

"I'm making an investment. Don't worry — I'm fully hedged."

Then downstairs into Dmitri's glittering stateroom-cum-disco, as Dmitri's princely yet tawdry vessel elbows its way out into the Thames like a politically-connected gangster exiting a nightclub.

Ricky pondered the nature of Dmitri's *investment*. One big, Moscow-sized, middle finger to the Yanks? And what about those *hedges?* Loose talk in the changing rooms after tennis?

Did any of it matter? Fuck them all, he thought.

Here was what mattered: Chen Yu, dead or as good as, somewhere in the panda archipelago, her father braving the gyres of the Mozambique channel in Ricky's over-powered, under-sized surf-racer; Kerri Law on her way to Virginia, cargo-class, Ricky's tenuous deal with Krall trashed by Big Data's inability to blackmail Prince; the billionaire CEO President, now with his hands in the nation's till, turning on a dime to kill the Chinese Spring and lock in the new plutocracy; Hong Kong fully annexed and subjected, part of the new Free Republic of China, a fresh despotism just as benign as the old, decayed one, but so much more efficient on account of being run by businessmen; Big Data in ruins, never to be rebuilt, and all privacy, data, truth, and *transparency* at the mercy and discretion of Weihan, Fairmeadow and twinkle-eyed Josh; and, a final insult, Ricky's colonial mansion of a sanctuary and his personal lemurs in the greasy hands of a New Century oligarch.

What else? Well, how about Jiao? Ricky replayed her phone call.

"Mr. Ponton, this is all your fault!"

"No, it's not."

"The blood of thousands is on your hands."

"No, it isn't."

Thousands? No, no, no. But Ricky wasn't guiltless. What if it were only hundreds — could he settle for that?

No, Ricky, you can't start bargaining now. Take responsibility. You did it. And you failed.

"I need asylum."

"What?"

"They are accusing me of corruption. I must have asylum."

"What do you expect *me* to do?"

"Talk to the South Africans. Demand that —"

"Jiao, you're crazy."

"I saved you from the Americans. Did you forget already? You must help. There is no time."

Yes, okay, she had a point. She just didn't have any hope.

"Stay on the line."

Ricky opened the door to his cubby-hole and yelled for Walter — not the proper way to address a man of his age and distinction, but the deal was that Ricky stayed in his room.

Walter appeared. Ricky explained. Walter shook his head.

"The answer's no."

A pause. Some heavy breathing at the far end.

"You know what they will do."

"Look, Jiao, can't you talk your way —"

"There is a complete purge. They say old-guard reactionaries and disloyal military must be eradicated."

"Is that the way they talk? I thought they were businessmen."

"They are eliminating the competition. Will you help me or not?"

"There's nothing I can do."

A soft, muffled choking sound on the line.

"The best is the enemy of the good. I told you so. You should have listened."

The line went dead.

Dmitri's boat began to round the great curve of the river that began at Limehouse. Ahead were the towers of Canary Wharf, colored gold by the declining, late-afternoon sun. Dmitri dropped onto the over-upholstered banquette where Ricky sat. He pointed to one of the towers.

"Wealth management," he said. "If you need it, I can recommend someone. As discreet as you like."

"Thanks."

"You must have accumulated some assets, yes?"

"What?"

"This Big Data Underground. Was it not profitable?"

"Oh, I see what you mean. Yeah, of course. Big time."

"I thought so. Listen. I tell people all the time, sure, it's okay to keep your money in London. Sometimes they put on an act, okay, but they're not going to touch you. But *you*... Maybe not okay for you. So you go offshore, you understand. We keep in touch, yes?"

"Sure. You bet."

"And then maybe, somehow, one day, in Madagascar..."

"Yes. One day."

A walkie-talkie attached to Dmitri's belt crackled. It seemed that the captain needed a word with the boss.

"What? How many? Jesus fuck!"

Dmitri poked Ricky on the shoulder.

"Come."

Ricky found himself led to the rear of the boat.

"Look!"

Dmitri's mega-yacht had attracted a flotilla of followers. Some hosted camera crews, while others looked like pleasure craft with nothing better to do. But, prominent in the front rank, were two powerboats with police markings, and a further unmarked craft, the most powerful of all, which appeared to be crewed by men in black balaclavas. This latter craft repeatedly zoomed abreast of Dmitri's cruiser, making aggressive feints towards it, then backing off again.

It all looked like a low-budget Bond-movie rip-off.

"Fuck they think they are doing?" Dmitri said.

As they entered the bend at Greenwich, Ricky saw that they had tailgaters in the air, too — five helicopters. Three were painted in military colors. He guessed the other two were TV news. Ricky remembered that the Thames Flood Barrier lay around the next bend; it wasn't high tide — but would the barrier be up anyway?

Dmitri was on the phone, waiting, impatient.

330

"Who are you calling?"

"My friend."

"Which friend is that, Dmitri?"

"The one who plays tennis with that two-faced fuck."

Ricky chose to drop his line of questioning. Dmitri began an earnest conversation in Russian. The military helicopters began to edge down. To starboard, the boat full of secret policemen pulled ahead, its booted and be-gloved passengers bracing themselves against the wind. Dmitri stopped talking and put his phone down. Then he issued a command to the bridge.

"Keep going."

A not entirely confident smirk in Ricky's direction.

"Okay. Now we see."

Dmitri's boat ploughed around the bend at North Greenwich. The barrier lay ahead. Dmitri stood up and waved at the secret police boat. No response. But the flood barrier was down. Against prevailing regulations, Ricky presumed, Dmitri commanded his captain to put his foot down. A great wash of white water erupted from the stern of the boat. As Ricky and Dmitri watched, their pursuers, both by sea and by air, fell back.

Dmitri looked content, but in the manner of a cat, Ricky thought — one that had cleverly escaped some peril, but hadn't had time to lick its fur back into place. All the same, Dmitri gave Ricky a look of newfound respect.

"You are special. It appears."

"Hope I didn't put you to any particular trouble, Dmitri. Or expense."

Dmitri seemed to consider that for a moment.

"No, no, no. Not at all. It was nothing. Communication problem."

"Are we home free?"

"Of course we are free."

He went to the bar and snatched a bottle from a fridge.

"They think they are in a movie. Fucking Ealing Studios. But it ended a long time ago."

Dmitri offered Ricky a glass of chilled vodka, giving it a satirical shake as he did so. Ricky took it. So now relax, Dmitri said. Enjoy the cruise. Okay, the weather wasn't that great in the Med at this time of year, but think of the antiquity, and the great ruins of European civilization! Oh, and wave bye-bye to the Brits when we pass Gibraltar, yes?

"The Brits, eh? I think we love them, yes? Bloody jolly James Bond, ha-ha!"

"So where are we going?"

Dmitri said that his captain had already plotted their course, and the *Londongrad* — a funny name, yes? — would steam at full speed across the northern Med, and transit through the Dardanelles Strait. Not hanging about in the NATO sphere of influence, it would forge on into the Sea of Marmara, heading for Istanbul. A quick chug through the Bosporus, and they would be safely afloat on the Black Sea. Shortly thereafter, Russian navy vessels would accompany them to the port of Sevastopol, in the Russian *oblast* of Crimea.

As they sipped their vodka and Dmitri's sleek, five-star pleasure palace left the dregs of London in its wake, Ricky half-listened to Dmitri's tales of adventure on the wild frontiers of the global economy. This crazy new Sino-American Axis of Profit presented challenges, but also opportunities, in Dmitri's considered opinion.

And as Ricky Ponton slipped beyond Canvey Island and the last tender rub of England's civilizing embrace, he wondered, perhaps like that lost brigade of idiot romantic narcissists before him, whether he had done the right thing.

The answer, of course, was no. Jay had been right. Jiao had been right. Even the ditzy cat girl had been right, towards the end. Ricky should have worried more about dirty politics than truth and purity and the sacred memory of Ricky Bloody Ponton, the sainted, sentimental bludger.

He should have sacrificed Kerri.

She would have forgiven him.

CHAPTER 50

Krall's two-car garage, at the rear of his Adirondack cabin, housed his collection of election memorabilia; the biggest toolkit Teri had ever seen; and an ancient Jeep Cherokee.

"I keep a beater for the bad weather. Snow tires an' all."

Krall used the toolkit to break off the padlock from Meera's metal briefcase. Together, he and Teri examined its contents: exactly a quarter of a million dollars, all in hundreds, neatly shrink-wrapped in ten-thousand-dollar bundles. Krall shut the case and tapped it with his forefinger.

"Let me do the talkin', okay?"

"Okay."

They entered the cabin and stomped the snow from their shoes. Sandy sat by the wood stove. She looked pale, Teri thought. And she was wearing her old sweatpants again, rather than the smart clothes Megan had picked out for her.

"Hey, Sandy," Krall said. "How're you holdin' up?"

"Oh, I'm fine, Ray, thank you. I... Oh."

Sandy had zeroed in on Teri.

"Hope you don't mind me bringin' Teri up here, Sandy. Only she ain't got anywhere else to go right now. And we don't want her out on the street now, do we?"

Sandy didn't reply. Krall placed the briefcase carefully and deliberately alongside a coffee table, where Sandy could see it, and then parked himself on a rustic couch, at the end nearest to Sandy.

"Come sit with us, Teri."

Teri sat. Sandy stared at her.

"Did you take that money?"

"What?"

And which money, exactly, was Sandy talking about? A moment of panic. Teri looked at Krall.

"What money's that, Sandy?"

"They said she stole campaign funds. That's why she was fired."

"Now, where would you be hearin' stuff like that, Sandy?"

"It was on Freedom News."

"Aw, you don't wanna be payin' attention to Gunner an' those guys! She ain't done anything. Have you, Teri?"

"No."

"But she was fired."

"Yeah, but they just let her go because... Tell Sandy why, Teri."

"They didn't like my tone."

"See, Sandy? She ain't stolen anything. Poor girl's even broker than I am."

Sandy didn't seem convinced, Teri thought. Suspicion shone through her pallor.

"Okay, listen," Krall said. "I'm gonna make some coffee. Why don't you two catch up?"

He went into the kitchen. Teri heard a coffee grinder whir. Sandy was still staring at her.

"Uh, so you're feeling okay, then?"

"Yes. Why wouldn't I be?"

"Well, Ray told me... He said you had some medication, and —"

"Well, that's really my business, Teri. Isn't it?"

"Oh, sure. I didn't mean to..."

"No."

A pause. Krall rattling about in the kitchen.

"Um, I guess you know that Chen —"

Sandy's hands raised in a gesture of revulsion.

"I don't think we want to talk about her."

"No? Okay. Well, anyway, the Chinese Spring — I guess it's pretty much over."

"Are you a Communist?"

A Communist? Where was she getting this stuff? Was it the medication? No, Sandy, I'm not a Communist, I'm a total loser. I don't have a five-minute plan, let alone a fucking Five-Year Plan.

"Nope. Not now, not ever. Really."

"Sometimes you talk like one."

"I talk kind of funny. It's the tone thing again."

Another pause. Krall's espresso machine whooshing. He wouldn't be able to hear them, would he? And so Teri found herself tip-toeing into forbidden territory — the collapsing building that she'd vowed to herself to stay out of. And which, on the ride up, Krall had specifically made her promise to back off from.

"So I guess you're happy about the election?"

"Of course."

"You were a big part of that."

"It's not for me to say."

"Ray says so."

"He was the Campaign Director. The credit is his."

"Credit? Ha! He credits you. It's all down to you. Sandy Quayle putting Willard Prince in the White House."

"What do you mean, Teri? I don't understand you."

Teri sat up on the couch and leaned in towards Sandy.

"So, am I right? You never actually got to talk to Prince? In person? Face to face?"

"No, you're wrong. I did talk to him."

"When?"

That rare frown on Sandy's face again.

"Well, we talked... On Amber's bus, that's right. Ray and Barbara were there. Ask them."

"What did you talk about?"

"Oh, everything. Everything to do with the campaign. Why do you —"

"And he — Mr. Prince — talked directly with you?"

"Yes."

"What did he say?"

"He asked if I thought he was going to win."

"And you said..."

"I said yes."

"What else?"

"What else? Oh, I don't remember. Then something happened and —"

"Yeah, they shot that crazy guy."

Sandy's frown darkened. No reply. Something about the crazy guy? Stop it, Teri thought. Leave it right there. You're tormenting her. Out of the building now! Before it falls in on itself.

Krall returned with three mugs of coffee. Campaign mugs, Teri noticed — Willard Prince's rich-uncle smile on the side.

"So how're we doin' here, ladies? Are we good?"

Teri took her drink.

"Yes, we're good."

They sipped their coffee. The fire in Krall's stove flared and crackled. The heat in the cabin seemed to build. At length, Teri saw that Sandy was staring at the metal briefcase. Krall had noticed, too.

"Oh, that. Heck, I was almost forgettin'. Now, as you know, Sandy, the campaign is over, we were victorious, and I am no longer on the payroll. Bonuses were supposed to be paid at this point, but let's not get into that."

A glance in Teri's direction.

"Now, before we drove up here, I had my last meeting with Willard. And he was most generous — most generous in his praise, Sandy. Especially for you. He knows how important you were. Believe it. But, as we have surely all observed, he ain't wasting time, and he's one hell of a busy President-elect. I ain't ever seen anythin' like it."

Another glance at Teri, accompanied by a glum twist of the mouth.

"I'm gettin' off the point here. Which is this. Sandy, Mr. Prince told me he wanted to express his gratitude to you. And he gave me this here, to give to you."

A long pause, in which Sandy's frown dissipated, to be replaced by an expression of — what? Longing? Teri wasn't sure. If it was something religious then Teri was flying blind here.

"What is it?"

"I don't rightly know, Sandy. We didn't look."

What a great liar Krall was! Well, of course — he was a professional. Krall lifted the briefcase on to the coffee table and pushed it towards Sandy, positioning it just so. He wanted to sustain the pretense.

"You can open it later, if you want."

Sandy hesitated. Then she opened the case, its contents visible to her alone, as Krall intended. Teri watched Sandy's gaze flit from side to side. Is it real? Yes, it's real. Then the adding up, the calculation. How much?

"I guess it's some kind of reward?" Krall said.

"Yes," Sandy said. "It's my reward."

She closed the case. That look again — not longing, but fulfillment? Or was it grace? But that was a religious term, so Teri could only guess.

"Sandy," Krall said, "I'm gonna be spending some time up here now, and I want for you to stay as long as you like. Now, I've arranged for you to see this top guy, he's a specialist down in Syracuse, and —"

"No, thank you, Ray. You've done enough."

"You just need to see this guy, and find out whether —"

"No, Ray. I can't stay here with you. I'm ready to leave."

"Leave? And go where, Sandy? With your condition, you can't just —"

"My condition, as you call it, is my business."

"Aw, come on, Sandy. I'm tryin' to help you here." A glance at Teri. "You don't even know how much."

"You can help. Please just take me to a bus station. I'm going to get my things."

Sandy got up and climbed the stairs to the upper floor. Krall was on his feet, hands on his shiny head.

"Shit!"

"What are you going to do?"

"Do? I can't keep her prisoner. Do you have any ideas?"

"You can't let her get on a bus with a quarter of a million dollars."

"Oh, sweet Jesus."

Krall's phone blipped. He pulled it out of his jacket pocket.

"Barbara? What the hell does she want? Turn on the TV?"

Krall turned it on and flipped to FNN.

Teri saw her face fill the screen. It was the photo from her driver's license.

Flint Gunner was ecstatic: TerrorWolf had been identified! And guess what the perpetrator's real name was! Talk about chutzpah!

But Gunner seemed scandalized, too, at what TerrorWolf had turned out to be: not a tattooed, long-haired, drug-addled, bearded and extremely dangerous-looking dark-skinned male; instead, a neat, petite, short-haired and extremely harmless-looking white girl. But it all just went to show how easily terror could metastasize.

Teri pulled out her own crappy personal phone, slipped the battery back in and turned it on.

"What are you doing?"

"I need to call someone."

She dialed Meera's number from memory.

"Turn it off! They're after you!"

Meera's phone ringing. And ringing. Then a voice, but not Meera's, someone else's — low, dark, male.

"Who is this?"

"Turn it off!"

336

She switched the phone off and ripped the battery out again.

"Teri, you gotta get out of here, girl. I'm serious. You do not want to end up like Giordano."

"Why? What happened to him?"

"You don't know?"

"No!"

"You've got to go. Now."

"Is he dead?"

"Yes, Teri, he's dead. Okay, now let me think..."

And what about Meera? What would they do to Meera? She wasn't even a white girl.

But Krall had taken charge again.

"Still got your passport?"

"Yes."

"And you got a license, so I guess you can drive, right?"

"Not really."

"Well, you can learn on the run. Just go slow on the ice. Take the Jeep. Tank's full. Keys are on a hook in the kitchen."

"But where do I go?"

"We're about ninety miles from the Canadian border. Take route 812 to Ogdensburg. Cross over the bridge. Maybe disguise your face, if you can. Hope the Canucks aren't paying attention. Then it's forty miles to Ottawa. Robin Hood's still legal there, for now. Maybe they can hook you up with a lawyer."

"I don't have any money, remember?"

"Lawyers are free in Canada. Like the healthcare. Don't worry."

"I can't go to Canada!"

"Sure you can. My generation did."

But there was Sandy, at the foot of the stairs, a campaign holdall in one hand and a shopping bag in the other. Was that it? Her total net worth? Her entire asset portfolio? Sandy glanced at the TV and saw Teri's image. Then she looked at Teri for a long moment. Teri moved towards her.

"Sandy, that's complete bull —"

But Sandy was already marching for the door. Krall got in front of her.

"Please change your mind."

"I have done what was asked of me, Ray. I answered the call. Now I have received my reward. And I want to go. That is God's will, Ray. And who are you, with all your lies and deceit and your cheap tricks, to stand against it?"

Teri studied Krall's face. Here it comes again, she thought. Capitulation.

"I'll get the car. Go ahead."

Krall opened the door to the cabin and Sandy stepped out into the snow. Krall turned to Teri.

"Bring the money out."

Teri returned to the lounge and picked up Meera's metal briefcase. She lugged it outside and waited for Krall to reverse the BMW out of the garage. Sandy stood in the snowy drive with her back to Teri.

Krall stopped the car, got out and opened the front passenger door for Sandy. Sandy ignored him and opened the rear passenger-side door. Before she got in, she turned and pointed at Teri.

"She's TerrorWolf. I ought to call the police."

Then she climbed into the car with her bags and shut the door.

Krall flipped the trunk open and gestured to Teri. Teri loaded the money inside. Krall dropped the trunk lid.

"Hit the road, Teri. And don't look back."

"I'm going to tell her the truth."

"Aw, you really don't wanna do that. How's it gonna help?"

"Who cares any more?"

"Take the Jeep, okay?"

"What about you?"

"I'll be just fine. Got a lot of hikin' to do. And maybe some thinkin'."

Krall got into the driver's seat, shut the door, and put the big BMW in drive. The car began to edge down Krall's narrow, icy driveway. Teri ran after it, skidding on the ice. She caught up and rapped on Sandy's window. Sandy stared straight ahead.

"Sandy! Prince is a fake! He's a phoney! He's a liar! He stole two hundred billion..."

But Krall had hit the gas. Teri slipped and fell into a snow bank. The car bumped up on to the highway and vanished.

*

Disguise her face? Amongst Krall's memorabilia collection she'd seen a baseball hat with Prince's visage on it: You Can Trust Me. It was too big for her, but when she pushed her hair up inside and tightened the strap at the back, it had stayed on. That was her disguise.

The Jeep was a stick shift. Teri had never driven a stick shift. The driver's seat was set too low. She couldn't see over the dashboard. Failing to figure out how to raise the seat — or maybe it was broken — she sat on a folded blanket that she'd found in the back. And somehow she made it on to the highway without sliding into a snow drift.

There was no satnav. Even if there had been, she doubted that she could have operated it in her present state of panic, anger and slacker-girl meltdown. But there was a Rand McNally road atlas from 1998. She found route 812 and Ogdensburg. But she didn't know where she was. So she drove in what she hoped was a north-westerly direction until she saw a sign pointing to route 812.

Then she stopped the car.

Canada? Really?

Suppose, instead, that she drove home to mom and dad. She could explain to them in person. They'd probably already seen her face on Freedom News, but they'd believe their own daughter over Flint fucking Gunner, wouldn't they?

Folks, meet TerrorWolf, the white-girl terrorist. Looks so normal, doesn't she? All-American, even — in the style of the kids these days. Maybe you bought a coffee from her at Bean Village, and you had no idea! Do you know where your daughter is?

But then, by the time she got home...

Mrs. Wolfe, can you tell us how you and your husband feel about your daughter now?

Flint, Nigel, we are just so devastated. Words can't describe our hurt. She had every advantage...

Fuck that. Canada it was. She pulled the Jeep back on to the highway.

How long could the Robin Hood Party survive in Canada? Not long, surely. And even if Teri found one of those free lawyers, could they do much for her? Almost innocent though she was, she hardly possessed the political glamour of an international libertarian rogue like funny-looking Ricky. And look what had happened to him — exiled to freedom-loving Russia.

Would the RHP go underground? Communicating by word-of-mouth, using typewriters, publishing samizdat screeds, moving between safe-houses, living in secret basements? Would they have any use for Teri? Or would she be a liability?

And if the Mounties caught up with her, could she ask for asylum in Russia, like Ricky? Would he help?

Or she could be homeless, like Sandy. If they allowed that in Canada. After a while she would be unrecognizable.

When she reached Ogdensburg, she slowed the Jeep, keeping safely under the speed limit. She drove past the town and turned left on to the road that led to the bridge over the St Lawrence river.

Approaching the customs post on the US side, she saw a row of police cruisers parked outside. She slowed the car almost to a stop, but then crawled forward again. A single uniformed officer motioned for her to stop. She stopped. He took a long look at her, shone a flashlight into the back of the Jeep, and then waved her forward.

She crossed the bridge.

At the immigration post on the Canadian side, she was asked to remove her hat. She did so. Her passport was glanced at and returned. Again, she was waved on.

Breathing slowly and deeply, she maneuvered the Jeep carefully on to highway 416, the road to Ottawa.

About a mile down the road, she threw her hat out of the window and turned on the radio. The first thing she heard was a song by Reagan Pruett — "You Can Take My Life But You Can't Take My Love."

A couple of miles later, she began to consider what her new name might be.

CHAPTER 51

There had not been a broker immediately available at the real estate office to show Sandy the house. So she had made an appointment for two hours later, found herself a cab, and now sat on the front porch with her shopping bag full of money.

It was surprising how little a quarter of a million dollars weighed — only five or six pounds if it was all in hundreds, as Sandy's was. The bag was bulky, but Sandy was used to that, and she did not expect to have to lug it much further. She had found Mr. Prince's metal briefcase far too heavy to carry and, at the expense of a little guilt, had discarded it.

The bank was offering the house at one ninety-nine, a price far below that once paid by John and Sandra Quayle — all those years ago when money seemed like something magical and ethereal, and not a dead weight that you had to haul about with you. The real estate office had warned Sandy that the house had been empty for a while and, before that, had been rented out intermittently. It wasn't in the best shape. Was Sandy sure she wanted to see it? There were some nice alternatives in her price range, all in neighborhoods that still had, well, neighbors. No, thanks, Sandy said; she knew what she wanted.

On arrival, she'd made a circuit around the house, peeking in through all the windows that hadn't been boarded up. It looked like kind of a mess in there, but she would take great satisfaction in cleaning up.

The next thing she would do would be to mow the front yard. That would make a big difference. All the empty homes had yards grown wild. The critters would be fine; there was plenty of space elsewhere, and nobody to hunt them any more.

There were repairs to be made. And there was the garage, of course. She would have to think about that, later. If she could get the house for less than one ninety-nine, then so much the better. At the real estate office, she'd made a point of showing them the money. They'd given her some funny looks, but at least they knew she was serious.

As for Stimsonville itself, Sandy felt only disappointment. It looked just as depressed and sad as ever. And if the town had felt a new sense of pride in its great alumnus, then it had not been evident downtown. It was too early, perhaps, for gratitude. President Prince's work had only just begun. But not too soon for hope, surely?

But it was the house that mattered most to her. Dare she offer one fifty? Why not? They could only say no, and she could up her bid. The more cash she had left, the better; starting a new life, even with the help of Mr. Prince's most generous gift, would be tough. And as for the medical bills that Ray Krall had warned about — well, Sandy would buy the drugs she could afford and trust in God's mercy. Yes, it was true that she could, just about, have afforded all that high-tech treatment if she hadn't decided to buy the house back. She'd made her choice. And if it was a brave one? Well, hadn't she learned that you had to take risks to succeed? Look at Mr. Prince.

A gust of wind blew across the yard and whipped at the weeds. Sandy felt grateful for her warm, winter coat. She'd picked it up at a thrift store during a layover on the slow, three-day bus ride from upstate New York. It had cost twelve dollars. She thought of the glances she would have attracted, had she entered the lobby of the Aspire Building wearing it, and couldn't help but smile.

She had enjoyed her adventure in New York, mostly, but she knew now that she didn't belong there. And God, via Mr. Prince, had made it possible for her to return home. He had rewarded her for accepting her mission, and accomplishing it. Of course, Johnny-boy would not be coming home, and her heart ached for that. But you could only ask for so much.

Would she be lonely? To begin with, perhaps. She would have to make new friends, and look for a job. It was easier to find work if you had a proper address. And you could keep in touch with people. Yes, and Sandy could even get a computer and start emailing again!

Who could she contact?

Well, there was Megan, of course. But Megan had rented out her apartment and had moved to London with her new husband. Or Milly — except that Milly was now preparing for her job in the White House and might be too busy to want to talk to Sandy. Barbara? Sandy didn't quite have the nerve for that. And as for Teri — well, the less said about *her* the better.

Ray would certainly have responded, Sandy thought. But he had crashed that big car of his on an icy Adirondack back-road, and the newspaper said that alcohol had been involved, and by the time the ambulance arrived it was too late. And he was such a careful driver, too.

Something bobbed at the edge of her vision. She looked. A big old rabbit, sitting up and staring at her. It reminded her of Hunter Bill and all his craziness. What would he be raving about if he were here now? Oh, Sandy knew *that* for sure: The whole moon-flag thing.

We left our flag up there. You follow me?

The Chinese moon rover had driven to one of the Apollo landing sites. And it just so happened to have parked in precisely the right position to hide from all telescopic view the American flag planted there. And there was now no way of telling — short of going back up, building a bigger telescope, or interrogating the Chinese astronauts — whether or not Old Glory had been supplanted. The possibility of such a *switcheroo* would have driven poor Bill madder than he already was. And, for some reason, Freedom News wasn't making a big deal of it. Bill would have found that suspicious too, no doubt.

The wind dropped and Sandy heard the sound of an approaching car. There had been no traffic at all since her arrival at the house, so might this be the real estate broker arriving early, perhaps to check on the state of the house? No, the car that came into view had lights on its roof and a stripe down the side. It was the Sheriff.

Sandy felt a little jab of fear. But why? She was doing nothing wrong.

The Sheriff pulled up at Sandy's house and turned off his engine. But he didn't get out of the car right away. He stared at Sandy, then got on his radio. It looked like he had another officer with him.

Sandy stayed put and waited. Had the Sheriff come looking for her? Had the real estate people called him? Why would they do that?

After about five minutes, the two policemen got out of their car. The Sheriff began a slow amble up Sandy's driveway towards her, while the other officer propped himself up against the car and folded his arms.

"Hey, Sandy."

"Hey."

"Just heard you were back in town."

A pause. The Sheriff examining the house as if it might have committed a minor misdemeanor.

"This where you used to live?"

"Yes."

A judicious nod of appreciation.

"Pretty grand, I guess. Or it used to be."

"I'm going to fix it up."

"Are you, now?"

"Uh-huh."

"How're you gonna do that, Sandy?"

"Fix the windows, fix the —"

"No, I'm asking how you can afford to buy this place, Sandy."

"I've got money."

"That right?"

"Yes. I have."

A pause. The Sheriff staring pointedly at Sandy's shopping bag.

"What's in the bag?"

"The money."

"Can I see?"

"Yes, you can see."

The Sheriff summoning his junior officer. The officer pulling on latex gloves, crouching down and rooting cautiously in Sandy's shopping bag.

"How much you got there, Sandy?"

"Quarter million. Well, less the fare for —"

"Quarter million! You hear that, Charlie? That seem right?"

A nod from Charlie.

"All right, Sandy. Cut the crap. What the hell's goin' on here?"

"I'm buying my house back."

"Where'd you get the money?"

"Willard Prince gave it to me!"

The Sheriff scratching his nose and looking at Charlie. Charlie shaking his head.

"You got that from the President-elect himself?"

"Yes."

"I guess there was a formal presentation in the Rose Garden?"

Charlie suppressing a snort of laughter.

"What? No, he..."

"He what? Sent Vice President-elect Pike down to wherever the hell you're livin' and —"

"I worked on the campaign. It's my reward!"

A hard look on the Sheriff's face, but also a twist at the corner of the mouth, betraying pleasure.

"You're such a fuckin' liar, Sandy. You always were. You and your pal Bill. Get on your feet."

"No, don't talk to me like that. That's *my* money, and —"

"Sandy, we know all about how you infiltrated the campaign. We know how you went down to the office on Mellon. We know how you suckered them in. And we know where the money's from."

"No, that's wrong! I *helped* them to —"

"So you're down on your luck, or maybe you got greedy and screwed up — I mean, look at this fuckin' pretentious little mansion here. And you end up livin' in that filthy, illegal, so-called village. And you start resentin' all the rich folks — like Willard Prince and all — and you do your little song and dance down on Mellon, and they fall for it. But you're all riled up, because of us cleanin' up your fuckin' slum, so off you go and sign up with the Robin Hood folks. I'll work for you, you say, so long as the money's good. And now you're palling around with terrorists, Sandy. And that's kinda serious. Are you hearing me? Okay, Charlie."

She resisted, but found herself yanked to her feet, hands behind her back. Cold metal around her wrists. Charlie's strong hands on her collar and her elbow.

"So let's see what we got here. Shit, listen to this..."

The Sheriff reading from a handheld computer.

"Assisting a designated terrorist organization. Receiving stolen money. Unauthorized access to computer systems. Theft of a memory stick from an apartment owned by Mr. Joshua P. Merriweather. Destruction of property belonging to Fairmeadow Security. Criminal possession of computer-related material. Criminal trespass and damage to property — that's the Country Club, Sandy. Theft of a thousand dollars in campaign donations from Mr. Donald R. Spurling. Conspiring against America's allies. Don't know what that one means, but it don't sound good. Theft of a cellular telephone belonging to the Vice President-elect. The list goes on. Jesus Christ, Sandy."

A nod to Charlie, and Sandy dragged down her own driveway to the waiting patrol car.

"Hey, but look on the bright side, Sandy. Where you're goin' you get a roof over your head and the fuckin' healthcare's free. Paid for by honest chumps like us. Don't bother sayin' thanks. We don't give a shit."

As the car pulled away, Sandy leaned back and closed her eyes. This wasn't happening. God wouldn't do this to her. He couldn't. Not after what she'd done for Him.

There was endless suffering in the world. She knew that. But hadn't Sandy Quayle endured her share?

Whatever her crimes, she would atone forever if only He would help her now.

The car turned onto the state highway and headed east. Where it met the interstate, Sandy was able to glance down at the pine woods where the village had once stood.

It might never have been there.

She thought she would not to ask God for anything else.

CHAPTER 52

resident Willard Gaffney Regent Prince felt at peace, and with good
reason. Much of the world remained fucked up beyond any reasonable
hope of repair; and the Arabs, the Africans and the rest would just have
to climb out of the shit on their own. But in America, thank God, things were at
last going in the right direction.

He didn't care much for his oddly-shaped new office; but — if he had his way,
and who the hell was going to stop him? — he wouldn't be spending too much
time in it. And maybe Barbara could have it redecorated.

According the newspapers, he was to be the *CEO President*. That sounded just
fine. He liked the ring of it. CEO and Chairman. Creating a vision. Inspiring
followers. Then delegating. Wasn't that what he'd always done? Sure, but it was
time to crank down the workload. He'd earned it — he'd earned everything he'd
achieved, and nobody was going to take any of it away from him. On second
thoughts, though, maybe he'd leave the vision thing to young Josh. The kid
seemed to have an aptitude for it.

But signing Acts of Congress was man's work. He lifted his pen. Some of those
guys from the Committee had compared what he was about to do with Lincoln
signing the Emancipation Proclamation in — when was it? — 1863? Maybe they
were right. Whatever. They were all good guys, sound on the important stuff,
but they mostly thought too much. Well, except for that shit-for-brains casino
jerk. Freedom was a simple enough concept. There was no need to over-think it.

Amazingly, all those assholes in Congress seemed to get the point too,
regardless of their nominal party affiliation. In fact, there was only one *real* party
now, Josh had said — the Prince Party. In the future, as Corporate Citizens
exercised their constitutional right to free speech, their cash would be heading
in one direction only. Why waste your capital on religious *values* shit, or *rights*
for deadbeats and moochers? Maybe there really was something in Josh's bullshit
about the *marketplace for ideas*, after all.

Anyway, Congress had done its job, for once. He searched for the red
sticky-tabs that Milly, his personal secretary, had placed in the document for him,
and signed his name, in full, wherever he found one. In order for the treaty to

347

come into force, however, he remained obligated to make the tedious journey to Beijing and sign his name a few times more, alongside that of the new President of the Free Republic of China. What was the guy's name again? Never mind. It was all in a good cause.

The New Pacific Partnership. Sounded good, didn't it? International cooperation, and all that shit. *Partnership* was one of those words you were required to use sometimes. It was well understood — by young Merriweather just as much as those Weihan fucks — that it would be the survival of the fittest. Business as usual, in other words, only more so, and without any of that Big Government shit in the way. Prosperity beckoned.

A new era would begin. There would be a new dispensation and new jurisdictions to match. Deregulation, at last; a flickering hope for generations, now to come true. The fabled level playing field. No more impediments. No sand in the gears. Weihan and Fairmeadow would keep things that way, or so Josh promised. And they would use what Josh called their *network capabilities* to keep a lid on trouble-makers and prevent backsliding. See? There's your international cooperation, right there. And here's your new century — China and America, unified and dominant, government serving the Corporate Citizen, and not the other way around. Just like Josh said.

As for the New American Century Fund — well, he was sad to let it go. But he'd left it in fine shape, and Jerry Aylsham over there in London and that stuck-up kid of his — Hartley? — would make decent new owners. They'd already replaced that Giordano bastard. Fuck *him*. Hadn't he understood that the NACF was a systemically-important institution? It was always going to ride out any storm. There had been hardly any redemptions — even in the depths of the crisis — and that spoke to the esteem in which the Fund was held. Even those shitheads at the Treasury, with their TARP III diligence crap, couldn't deny the debt owed to the NACF by the American economy and the American taxpayer. Besides, they'd been replaced.

And a whole heap of garbage had been dealt with — all those whiney Chinese students with their *democracy* shit; that *Big Data dickhead*; those fucking *Robin Hood* assholes.

So the future was full of promise. It was settled. There *would* be a New Century. He put his pen down.

What next?

Milly had printed out his schedule for the day. There it was on his desk. Oh, right — how could he have forgotten? Milly had listed their names: Josh, of course; the CEOs of FNN and the London Globe; and the US chief of Weihan, whose name, like so many of them, was unpronounceable.

A glance out of the window: The weather in Washington was dreary.

But it would be fine in Florida.

It would be a great day for a game of golf.

Also by Rory Harden

Who thinks running guns to Africa should be a nice little earner? Who's accidentally acquired a soccer-mad private army of child soldiers? What happened at the Glue Factory? Who forgot to switch off the fountains? Oh, and by the way...

Why is Africa's richest country so poor?

A deceptive plot to take over the "richest country in Africa" in the name of Democracy. An ethically-challenged businessman on a voyage of self-discovery. A glimpse into the dark heart of the "New Democratic Consensus".

Also by Rory Harden

Who thinks he has an answer to the Greater Persian Question? Who's going to save a nation on the brink? What's going down in the Libyan desert? Why all the motorcycles? What's the deal with the iguanas? And, most of all...

Who is John Dolt?

Ever thought you'd make a good dictator?

Rory Harden

THE POPULIST

"Smart, funny, thrilling—and subversive."

A fortuitous encounter in the bathroom section. Menacing objects in the African sky. A secret and luxurious fortress in the Costa Rican jungle. A strike of all the really productive people. A private army on the streets. An honest man thrust into the seat of power.

About the Author

Rory Harden lives in London with his wife, Nancy, and two adopted cats, Spike and Monty. He enjoys travel, books, music and computer programming. And he plays guitar and bass – not too badly, sometimes.

www.ingramcontent.com/pod-product-compliance
Lightning Source LLC
Chambersburg PA
CBHW070909260626
47162CB00007B/2615